Check Or Treat

Aurora Steinhart

Page edge design by Painted Wings Publishing

First edition: 2025

Print ISBN 13: 9798991485562

 Formatted with Vellum

CHECK OR TREAT

AURORA STEINHART

For more updates and sneak
peeks
be sure to scan the QR code
for links to my socials!

ALSO BY AURORA STEINHART

<u>Checked and Balanced</u>

Book One in

"The Lady and The Stag"

A hockey romance experiment

where we meet Tiana and Gunnar

for the first time.

<u>Elevated Ambitions</u>

Book One in

The "Up in the Air" Series

A contemporary billionaire romance

where SHE is the billionaire.

<u>Hunted By Fate</u>

Book One in

"A Gown of Leather and Bone"

A dark, romantic fantasy ft. a succubus general and a human hunter on a mission to save their world from the terrors outside of their wards.

To the ones who found themselves in Tiana,
and the ones that wished for a Gunnar,
I hope this couple continues to heal
you the same way it is healing me.

PLAYLIST

I LISTEN TO SO MUCH DAMN MUSIC WHEN I WRITE. UNFORTUNATELY, I'M NOT ABLE TO CATALOGUE IT ALL HERE. IT WOULD JUST BE SO MANY PAGES. SO NOW I HAVE RESORTED TO QR CODES FOR SUCH THINGS.
ANYWAY.
ENJOY THIS HORRIFICALLY CHAOTIC PLAYLIST FOR CHECK OR TREAT. IT'S A MESS. JUST LIKE ME AND JUST LIKE THIS BOOK.
BUT I THINK WE KNOW BY NOW THAT AURORA DOESN'T DO ORGANIZED. IT'S ALWAYS A MESS OVER HERE AND THAT'S HOW WE LIKE IT. DON'T WE, GIRLS? 😉

PLAY BY PLAY
(PART TWO)

And here we are.

You guys know the drill by now.

If you don't, and you're new here–which you shouldn't be, this is the second book in the series, go read **Checked and Balanced**–this is a little thing I like to do here.

It's a list of all the spicy chapters for you to enjoy... or skip; depending on your preferences.

But I doubt we're here to skip any of Gunnar and his... interests. 🙂

1. Chapter One (startin off strong, let's go!)
2. Chapter Three
3. Chapter Seven
4. Chapter Nine
5. Chapter Fourteen
6. Chapter Seventeen
7. Chapter Twenty-Three
8. Chapter Twenty-Eight
9. Chapter Thirty

DISCLAIMER

SO... WE'RE BACK AGAIN.

You guys said I was a liar and said the last book had a plot.

Well, listen. While you maaaayyyy be right. I hadn't written the disclaimer to be a lie.

I had merellllyyyy not been very confident.

Still am not. But I digress.

At the time, I had just finished writing Hunted by Fate (shameless self plug. Go read it) and that book was extremely plot heavy. And I had wanted to write something sort of lowkey and chill I guess.

I mean, I really just wanted to write a bunch of smut because I'm a horny degenerate at the end of the day.

If you've seen my threads, then you know that I don't write smut because it sells. I write smut because I love writing smut. Point blank period.

Unfortunately, I am physically incapable of writing without a plot. I had actually tried with Checked and Balanced and I literally was not able to finish that book unless I added what little story was in that book. So that's why that story had a plot.

I was never going to finish it without plot.

So now that that's out of the way, I have a different disclaimer for y'all in this book.

First things first my little degens, this book is not ooky spooky kooky.

"But Aurora the cove-"

AHP BUP BUP! NO. It's a seasonal book. The fuck am I gunna do, put fucking LEAVES?! This isn't fall people, it's Hallos ween.

There's not like a haunted house situation or no like... There's nothing crazy "Halloweeny" about this book. It just happens to take place during Halloween.

OKAY? OKAY NEAT!

NEXT UP!

Tiana is an undiagnosed, low support needs autistic.

This was something I discovered half way through writing CAB. She was very particular about things, and as I mulled over it, I decided to run with it.

I am likely autistic myself. I'm undiagnosed. But a lot of Tiana's experiences in Check or Treat are things I have had to deal with in my life. Her experiences with her thought processes and fears, frustrations in this book are *my* experiences.

It may not make sense. It may sort of go against some bits of her character. But for a good majority of CAB, Tiana is masking. And masking, if you don't know, for autistic individuals is essentially having to present something to the world to seem more acceptable. More welcomed.

It's a hard thing to unlearn in everyday life. But when you get close to people, you're able to let go and be yourself. This is a learned process. Something to make you seem more socially acceptable because the you under it, is not easily accepted.

Online, when you see my videos, I am mostly unmasked.

But when you may meet me in person, I'll more than likely be masked because it's difficult personally for me to interact face-to-face with people. Just as Tiana struggles with. Unless she's doing her job.

Autism is, of course, a spectrum. And personally, I have struggled with the thought process just in writing this because autistic thought processes can be very black and white.

Therefore, it's hard for me sometimes put some of her actions into words the proper way to get my point across.

One thought is, "Oh is it wrong for me to write someone that is autistic and horny, because people don't put those two things together."

But autistic individuals are more often than not, sensory seeking.

In CAB, Tiana discovered that her sex life with Gunnar was stimulating. It drove something in her that pushed her to want him more, because of the sensory aspect of it all. Which is why she's so open to sex with him.

It's not really spelled out for you on paper in CAB, but at least, personally, that's how my mind works it out.

It's a hard balance, I feel. But I need you to keep in mind that Tiana is dealing with struggles of her own that can make her insecure.

She has never loved someone this way, and she's looking back on experiences to discover bits and pieces of herself. So she's I suppose, off in this book because she's having feelings and thoughts she didn't have in the past. And those can be jarring, scary. Not sure what to do. And so she buries herself in things because those negative emotions for autistic individuals are distressing. So you focus on the things that bring you happiness, joy because you fear the distressing things.

But she also knows the implications of some of her hyper-fixations and the frustration that comes with only having a one track mind sometimes.

Give Tiana some grace in this book, because she's dealing with things she's never experienced.

Her and Gunnar are learning these things together. And I'm very proud of them. Even if it's hard.

They always do the hard things. And that's why I love them.

Chapter Twenty-Two

Art by: Olivia a.k.a
@liverosess on
Instagram

CHAPTER ONE
GUNNAR HAYZE

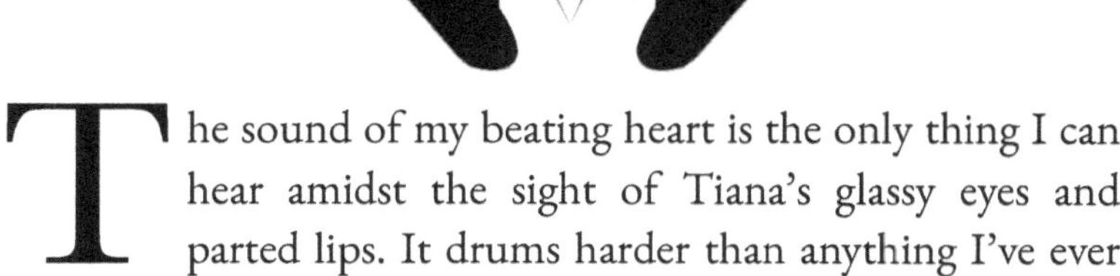

The sound of my beating heart is the only thing I can hear amidst the sight of Tiana's glassy eyes and parted lips. It drums harder than anything I've ever encountered.

More than any big game, hell, more than the fucking draft.

Because I've just asked the love of my life to marry me.

I am so wholly terrified about this, even though I know for a fact she'll say yes.

But with how long it's taken her to answer. It certainly doesn't help my nerves.

I watch her face for a long moment, getting lost in the way her eyes glimmer. The way her chest moves slowly in shocked breaths as her eyes dart around the velvet box in my hands.

Soon, her eyes come back up to mine, filled with admiration and love, and she nods furiously.

"How is that even a question?" I hear her murmur before she throws her arms around me in a crushing hug.

Her wondrous, beachy scent envelops me. Coupled with

the heat of her body, the pounding in my chest turns from fear to elation.

I wrap my arms around her, squeezing so tight I'm scared I'll crush the lass. I breathe her in deeply, enjoying the moment of her in my arms.

This woman... the one I chased like a bloodhound... the one that I swore one day was going to be my wife, is now my fiancée, and I can't... fucking believe it.

I mean, I guess I can. I worked my ass off to get here.

But, *fuck*, it's Tiana's world. Who knows how things will go when we're living on Tiana's time.

She leans back, sitting on the couch as her hands grip my shoulders. A few stray tears of happiness run down her cheeks, and her eyes search mine for a long moment. Soon, her teeth tug at her lip as her eyes flick to my lips, popping back up to my eyes before she grabs my face, pulling me in for a deep kiss.

My eyes widen in shock for only a second before they close and I sink into the kiss with her. As she deepens it, I flick the ring box closed and reach beside me to deftly search for the coffee table. When I feel the edge, I push the ring box onto it before bringing my hands back to her hips and pulling her into my lap.

Her legs straddle my hips, sitting pretty in my lap as she holds my face, kissing me slowly, deeply. And with my hands on her hips, I can feel the way they move. A pulse goes through me and straight to my cock, hardening it in mere seconds. I feel her fingers tense their grip against my face, and the energy in the room shifts.

It seems as if my sweet girl is taking the lead.

That's made even more apparent when her grind deepens against me through her pencil skirt. She's still wearing her clothes from work. Since she was so tired when we got home, all I could do was to carry her up and remove her suit jacket before laying her on me.

Soon, her skirt bunches up around her hips as she finds a rhythm in her movements against my length. A groan leaves me, my tongue slipping from between my lips to find hers.

Hers meets me in the middle, tangling together as her hips move like ocean waves. So fucking fluidly.

"Get on the couch," she pants between her kisses. It's desperate, it's urgent; it causes my brows to rise in surprise, and I nod slowly.

"Yes, ma'am," I whisper.

Wrapping my arms around her back, I push up onto my knees, moving to grip under her thighs before I come to a stand and move us both to the couch. She settles on my lap, where I lean back against the cushions so she can control me the way she wants; move me and use me the way she deserves.

She leans forward, her arms around my neck as she continues her passionate kisses, my hands taking a tight grip on her perfect ass. My hands flex, feeling the way her flesh gives under my grasp. All the while, I groan another noise of satisfaction. The combination of her grinding and just the way her ass feels makes my eyes roll. All the way back into my skull as she uses me.

"B-Baby," I groan out as my head leans back against the couch. I descend into the torture this woman inflicted on me, and become wholly blanketed by it.

My fingers tighten, trying to keep my composure with the pressure of her grind, but it's so. Fucking. *Hard.*

In more ways than one.

I lean my head up, watching as her head tosses back. She's completely lost to the way I feel under her. Her lips parted as soft moans pour out of her. It's intoxicating watching her, even if I'm harder than granite and feel like my dick is going to burst.

And as if I thought too soon, that tangle in my spine whirls tight, forcing me up that summit at breakneck speed. With the emotions from the proposal and just the way she looks so lost to her pleasure, I groan a tortured noise, my cock twitching as I threaten to paint the inside of my boxers.

"Tiana…" I grunt as I move my hands from her ass to her hips, trying to pull her up enough to relieve some of the pressure.

She merely moans in response, "Gunnar."

"No… fuck… I…" I growl in frustration as I toss my head back. "Ugh…Tiana, I'm gonna… fucking… come," I grit, trying with all my might to resist the urge.

She merely presses harder against me, working against my strength as she seeks more friction.

My eyes roll, with that pleasurable tangle squeezing my spine, my neck, and swirling around my throat to tighten harshly around it. It grips with all its might as my hips buck, my groans picking up as I come, soaking the inside of my boxers with my release.

"Fuck… Titi, please," I damn near whimper as I buck and writhe under her through my orgasm.

Her hips don't stop until she reaches behind her, her hands brushing against mine as a zipping noise fills the air.

I get a singular second of reprieve when the weight of her body leaves my lap, and I breathe through the pulsing in my cock while my body slumps against the couch. My arms droop at my sides as I glance at her, watching as she pushes her skirt off and quickly comes to tug the band of my sweatpants and boxers down.

My brow furrows as I watch her. "Tiana, what th-"

No idea what's come over her, but before I can even finish

my sentence, she rips my sweatpants and boxers completely off and throws them to the side. My cock is damp with my spend, and the cool air of her apartment breezing against it causes my balls to tighten. But as I catch sight of her, sans her skirt, lust spears through my blood. I harden in an instant, almost delirious at this point from her wants.

I feel her hands grip my shoulders, and soon the warmth of her pussy as it swallows my cock.

"Fuck!" I hiss with a jolt. I'm incredibly sensitive from her grinding *and* already having come once.

All I can muster is to grip her bare ass in my hands, squeezing with almost all of my strength as she lowers herself down on me. I try to hold her up, pulling at least some of myself out of her because it's so sensitive that I'm bucking and twitching, damn near running at the way she feels right now.

"You can take it, Mr. Hayze," she says in her silky, vixen voice. I hear it through the pleasure, and my brow contorts in confusion.

"Since..." I pause, groaning in frustration as my head presses deeper into the cushions. "Since... fucking when did you try to kill me?" I pant.

"Since you asked me to be your wife," she whispers as she leans in, gliding her flattened tongue up my neck while she pushes against my strength and shoves all of me into her.

I groan out at the same time she moans, our sounds mixing as she takes me all the way to my balls. But feeling her wrap all the way around me puts me on another plane of existence.

"Tiana, I'm begging, it's so much," I pant softly.

Her hips roll, moving up and down on me. "Beg some more," she responds breathlessly.

My hands grip for dear life on her ass, giving in to the way she bounces on my cock. Every fucking inch she takes like a god-damned champ. And while I would love to be celebrating the fact that this is going to be my wife that's taking my cock like this, I can't because I can't even fucking *think* right now.

The only thing that exists in this world currently is the way Tiana's pussy grips me.

"I need you to come for me again, Gunnar. I need you to fill me," she pants against the wetness she's licked on my throat.

"Keep this shit up and I will," I manage to grit back with a pained grin.

She's fucking killing me right now, but someone, I think, has gotten a little too bold.

I use all my strength to hold her hips in place on her way down, half of my cock still in her, and she glares down at me in shock.

I glance up at her through my lashes, my tongue sliding across my lower lip as my eyes track down her body to my lap. Soaked, and my cock is shiny with her slick. It only spurs my urge for this next bit higher.

A feral grin spreads on my lips as my eyes come back up to her face. "Do I have your consent to treat you like a whore?"

She pants in confusion, her brow furrowing, with her head tilting in question as she looks down at me.

"Because I'm about to fuck you like I don't respect you," I add.

Before she has time to think, I wrap my arms around her, dropping my hips back–as much as I can while sitting on a couch–to pull out and turn within an instant to shove her into the couch. Grabbing both of her wrists with one hand, I pin them above her head, where she writhes and grunts to get out of my grip.

I press my thighs into the underside of hers, pushing them up and out to hold her in place. My cock throbs from the loss of her tightness, and when I look down, I see how eager she is for me; drenched and plump, just waiting for my cock to *really* stretch her.

A grin pulls against my lips as I use my free hand to run through her center, letting her soak my fingers.

"Do I... have your consent..." I ask as I lean down, nipping at her throat. I press two fingers into her entrance, rubbing my thumb quickly over her clit. "To fuck you like a whore?" I finish with a pant as I glide my tongue over the small nips I left.

"Gunnar, please," she whimpers as her hips buck against my palm.

I slow my movements on her clit, pressing my fingers in and out of her, changing the speed at random intervals to drive her fucking mad.

"Use your words, baby. You played a dangerous game and lost. Now you're paying the price," I say with a light chuckle of taunt.

"Y-Yes... Make me your whore, pleasepleasepleaseplease-please," she pleads. Rather desperately, too.

I find the longer I stir her up, the more desperate she becomes, and I *love* when she's desperate.

"Ohhh," I coo against her skin. My teeth nip into her neck, moving my hand from her pussy to my cock, covering myself in her and groaning against her throat. "You're such a good listener, pretty girl, yes you are," I croon as I line myself up with her entrance. Pressing the head into her, I pump shallow strokes, feeling the way she grips all of me.

"My perfect cock sleeve," I whisper as I slowly press into her. "It's like you were made to take my thick cock, weren't you, sugar?"

Her eyes roll, her head tilting back as she pants and moans. "Gunnar," she moans.

"That's right, say *my* fucking name. I want to know whose

cock is stretching this tight fucking cunt," I grit as I begin to piston my hips in and out of her at a dizzying pace.

I have no idea why I took the lead. My cock is achingly sensitive from one orgasm and her teasing me. But she has to know who owns her perfect pussy.

With one hand still holding her hands above her head, I bring the other up to grip her cheeks together, pulling her face toward me. I latch onto her mouth, licking and kissing her as my pounds turn punishing.

Hard and deep, I throw my strokes, my eyes glancing down to see myself bulge in and out of her stomach. Slipping my fingers into a free space between the buttons of her blouse, I rip it open, baring her stomach for me to get a better view. A feral grin pulls at my lips as I press my palm into where I bulge from her stomach. She moans out, groaning a tortured noise as her body tightens, trying to process the feeling.

"Right here... You're gonna grow my baby right here, aren't you, sugar?" I ask in a low taunt as I tilt my head, watching the way her face tenses and changes from the pressure of my cock.

Her moans pitch higher, her body trembling under me as I press back with every bulge I make through my thrusts.

"I can't wait to make you a fucking mother. You're going to look so fucking beautiful carrying my kid," I pant.

My thoughts are gone with the feel of her, and I don't even know what I'm saying.

I pound harder, with her tits held in her bra bouncing against her chest as her moans turn to screams and her thighs attempt to press back against mine.

I lean up, looking down at her body, the way her tits move, and I release her hands, coming to grip tight on her hips.

Stroke after stroke I keep pulling her body on my cock, grunting with each one before my hands let go of her hips to hold on to her tits as I switch from pulling her onto me, to moving my hips.

One of my legs tripods to the floor, giving me more stability as my knee closer to the inside of the couch buries into the cushions.

"Gunnar, fuck, I'm gonna come, I'm gonna fucking come, please," she whimpers as her screams silence and all she can muster is silent gasps.

"Come for me, baby. Come all over my cock. Be a good little slut and lock my cock in place like you always do. I wanna fill that fucking womb of yours with my spend," I grunt.

My eyes lock onto her soaked pussy wrapped around me, and her screams return. She pitches into a shriek as her pussy tightens around me, holding me in place as I come. My spine crumbles as the pleasure chokes me, my groans damn near growls as I come for the second time.

Her pussy clenches in waves around me, as my hands release her tits to grip tight on her hips. I use it as the smallest bit of grounding as her hips continue to grind and milk me for everything I have.

"Jesus, Mother Mary, Joseph and the baby one," I growl as my head hangs above her. Drips of sweat fall from my forehead to land on her chest. I focus on those drips as my own orgasm is wrenched from me by the length of hers. As it slows, my chest heaves, my breaths coming in quick bursts as I glance up to grin at her.

She's merely trying to come down, so I shift my gaze to her chest. It heaves with her breaths and I lean in to kiss softly over her rapidly beating heart. It pumps hard against her ribcage, and I kiss up her sternum, her throat, to make it to her lips.

"Pretty sure I pumped you full," I whisper softly. I continue pressing soft pecks into her parted lips, my hands roaming up and down her sides as she continues to come down.

"It fucking feels like it," she pants back in response.

I give her a laugh as I look down, my cock still held inside her. My head tilts, and I slowly take a test piston into her. I pull out slowly, watching as my cum drips from her and a groan rolls through me as I see the way I've marked her.

Shit never, ever gets old.

"Your pussy looks so good with me dripping out of it, baby," I say as I kiss her again. My hand comes up to stroke her cheek, taking the smallest pecks against her lips.

"That was intense," she responds through her heavy breaths.

"Do you still want to marry me?" I ask playfully.

Tiana glances at me with a playful roll of her eyes before she slaps at my chest.

"Yes, Gunnar Hayze. I still want to marry you," she whispers with a sweet smile.

CHAPTER TWO
TIANA DAWN

"Are you sure this is a good idea?" I ask.

My voice wobbles, and my fingers damn near ache from how hard I've been gripping them. I've been pacing and wringing my hands since we got to my office.

After a long weekend with Gunnar, we are finally back in the arena, and I wish more than anything that I was currently *not* in the arena. Because over said long weekend, Gunnar somehow talked me into this thing I'm now fretting over.

Telling the team, my dad, and Charlotte that we're engaged. And apparently, the assistant coach. He's finally come back from paternity leave, and now he's here too.

I can't imagine what Russel is going to think about all this.

He's been the assistant coach alongside my dad for a while. But he knocked his wife up out of season, and she went into labor just a bit before it started, so he took several weeks off.

Russel Bloom is his name. Though the team refers to him as Stamen.

One player has a family that keeps bees, and he had informed us—once upon a time—that a stamen is the male reproductive part of a flower... so. They named him Flower Dick, apparently.

...Yeah.

Anyway.

I had agreed to this insanity, though reluctantly, because his reasoning made sense. There is no way I'm holding some sort of engagement party when this whole thing could be an email. But he wanted to see the team's reaction.

That's fair... I guess. I don't understand why men do the shit they do. I don't think I ever will.

But fine, whatever.

So now, having to face said announcement, my nerves are running through me like ice and lava. Fear, excitement. I keep looking at the large ring on my finger every so often, using it to remind myself that this is good.

The problem I have always had is that I experience very large emotions. And those very large emotions make me *inherently* off-kilter, whether they are good or bad. My body recognizes them as any kind of stress. Of course, because I'm a bit of a pessimist, the head-movies are almost always much worse than how it actually turns out to be.

Granted, expression and experiencing my emotions are two different things. But sometimes the experience of said emotions causes expression to spill over in a way I can't control.

For whatever reason, I am terrified to see what everyone will think. Maybe it's because they know I haven't had a man in so long, and now this rookie comes in to sweep me off my feet.

Some of these players I've worked with since I got to the arena years ago. I don't like the idea of them perceiving me. Especially when they technically know a different version of Gunnar than I know.

Absolutely insane that I let this man talk me into this kind of announcement so early and at the *arena* of all places.

It makes sense because Charlotte, my dad and the rest of the team will be there.

Of course it'll be sans my mother, but I imagine we'll be able to cross that bridge when we get there.

I take another deep breath, twisting and wringing my hands as I try to push away the nerves.

Everything I've done thus far has failed. All I can imagine is the thoughts of the players, or what people may say. Even if it's good, it's all attention and interaction that I don't enjoy indulging in.

Not to mention, I just don't know how to react to well-wishes.

I wish everyone could just give me a fucking thumbs up and send us on our way. That would be my ideal scenario.

Gunnar already said he was taking the lead and actually announcing it to the team with *his* words. But I still have to be there and experience the emotions of what everyone will think. I have no idea how Charlotte will react. She'll probably be happy for me, sure, *probably*. My dad will more than likely be some level of shocked... or perhaps not.

I don't even know what I'm thinking anymore.

I've lost myself in the what-ifs of it all, pacing back and forth until I slam straight into a large pine-scented body. My wide, terrified eyes look up at Gunnar.

Of course, he's been in the room the entire time, waiting for me to be ready enough to go out to the rink.

But as I meet his gaze, he gives the smallest, sweetest smile. One that somehow calms at least some of my nerves.

One of his hands comes out of his pockets to stroke a thumb over my cheek. "Sugar," he whispers.

"I'm scared," I murmur.

"I know, baby," he says softly.

"How do I make it stop?" I ask.

My mind continues to run. My thoughts scrambled in a menagerie of screaming words and sounds that I can't push away.

Gunnar's head tilts almost curiously as his brow furrows. "What do you mean?"

I take a deep breath. "The fear. The screaming in my head. How do I make it stop?"

His head tilts just a bit more, a mask of sympathy washing over his features. "Sugar... everything is going to be okay," he says softly.

"But I-"

He presses his finger to my lips, halting me.

"There are no buts. We have figured out the legality of all of this. They know we're together. I'd already asked your dad for your hand... so he knows. And I know it's scary. That this is uncharted waters for us, but everything is going to be okay." Though his voice is calm and sweet, the voice in my head is screaming for me to run, to flee, to fucking *escape*.

He steps closer to me, wrapping an arm around my back and tilting my head up with the hand he has on my cheek.

"I promise. And I always keep my promises, don't I, baby?" he asks with a small smile.

I take a deep breath, letting his cologne fill me, and I nod slowly. "Okay... Okay," I whisper in agreement.

"Thatta girl, sugar," he whispers. Leaning down, he presses a kiss to my lips as he pushes some of my hair behind my ear. "Are you ready?" he asks.

"No," I murmur against his lips.

"Too bad," he says with a small grin. His hand moves up to wrap around the back of my head and pull it toward him, placing a small kiss on my forehead before he lets me go and moves to my office door.

My nerves feel like they're going to explode through my chest, and I want to *run*. I want to escape this situation. I feel like my stomach is in knots. And I don't even know why. There is no reason for me to be as scared as I am.

But I AM!

Gunnar opens the door, ducking as he walks out before he reaches in for my hand.

I look at his calloused palm for a moment before I step forward, taking it.

His fingers wrap around mine, and he slowly pulls me from the office. As we exit, my heels begin their click-clacking as we walk on the cement floor. It feels like it pushes some of the fear away, so I focus on it, letting it ease through me as we make our way down the hall.

Gunnar leads us to the ice rink, where the rest of the team, my dad, Charlotte, Russell, the team and...

"My mom?!" I groan in a low whisper.

Yep, clear as day. She's in her pressed pantsuit, arms across her chest as she stands in the box beside the rink with Charlotte and my dad. Her face is confused, as if she doesn't exactly know why she's here.

My heart pounds *hard* in my chest, roiling the already heightened nausea, and I feel like my breathing stops completely.

"You didn't fucking tell me my mom was going to be here!" I whisper to Gunnar.

I glance up to see a smirk tugging at his lips.

"Do you really think I would have been able to get you out of that office if you had known your mom was out here? I've gotta play the game carefully, sugar. I know you better than you think," he says with a wink.

Throwing my head back in frustration, I glare at him. But he merely gives me a shrug.

"Let's get this fucking over with," I grumble as he continues leading us down the tunnel to the rink.

I take a deep breath, trying not to look anyone in the face, because I swear the moment I do, I may vomit.

When we reach the glass, the entire team is already on the ice with Russel.

A middle-aged man with short brown hair and green eyes. He's your average, run-of-the-mill looking hockey player. He's also almost always in the black and red Seattle Stags hockey warm-ups.

He pauses as he waves at me, and I give a shy wave of my own.

Gunnar whistles as we approach, and I give my mom a nervous smile without meeting her gaze.

"Funny seeing you here, Mother," I say nervously.

"It is. Your father said there was something that the team needed to tell me for whatever reason. I imagine this could have been an email, but we're here so," she sighs with a shrug.

You and me both, woman.

There has always been more tension between my mother and I. Not because of any dislike, merely because it felt like she was always harder on me than she was with Charlotte. I don't mind it, I suppose. The dynamic is just different between us. We both aren't very good at expressing things, and we aren't touchy feely. So we... interact differently than her and Charlotte do.

Granted, Charlotte and I are just completely different people in general.

As I turn my attention back to Gunnar and whatever the fuck his plan is, my dad whistles to the team, where they come to a halt on the ice. Russel barrels to the box, crashing into it and flinging his foot over to join Charlotte, my dad and my mom.

"Long time, no see, Ti," he says with a grin as he comes up to hug an arm around me.

"Yeah, good to see you," I murmur mindlessly as I lean into him.

I would love to offer a warmer greeting, but I'm three seconds from puking on his skates.

What is it that thing they say when you're in front of a big crowd? Imagine them all naked?

Yeah, no, fucking pass. I'm not doing that shit here.

I merely keep my gaze on the way the bright overhead lights shine on my heels, inhaling calculated breaths.

Gunnar takes my left hand, turning it to face the team through the glass, and holds it up for them to see.

They take a minute, but suddenly there is loud, raucous cheering, and Gunnar quickly steps in front of me.

"Bench," he murmurs, and my eyebrow quirks as I look up at the back of his head, until I register his words. Suddenly, I realize what he means as the entire team skates full tilt toward the door of the tunnel. I yelp as I jump quickly into the box with my family, falling into them as the team damn near tackles Gunnar.

They whoop and cheer, and my eyes widen before I look to my mother.

Charlotte looks like she's damn near in tears, and my mother has the kindest smile on her face.

"He proposed?" my mother asks sweetly. Her head tilts, and her eyes have a sort of pride I don't think I've seen from her since I graduated law school.

It actually gives me a little well of warmth in my chest. I nod softly, offering my hand to her.

She gently takes it in her hands and looks over it carefully.

"He did very well," she remarks as she looks up at me with a small smirk.

I feel heat creep across my cheeks as I nod. "He did," I respond.

"Congratulations, Ti," my mom says as she lets go of my hand and comes close to hug me.

My body tenses as I hug her back rigidly. I'm not exactly the most physically endearing with my family, but it's a big occasion, so I let her.

With Gunnar, it's different. I can fully give in with him.

It's just not the same with my family.

She rubs my back softly before she pulls away.

"You deserve love, Ti. I'm glad you found it," she whispers before she moves out of the way.

Her words sink in, a burn forming in my eyes. But I don't have time to really focus on it before Charlotte jumps me, wrapping her arms tightly around me as she sobs hysterically.

"I CAN'T BELIEVE YOU'RE GETTING MARRIED! I'M SO HAPPY FOR YOU! THIS IS THE BEST DAY OF MY LIFE!"

My eyes widen as I look at my mother. She merely rolls her eyes as if to say, 'You know your sister'. All I can muster is a nod in return as I pat Charlotte's back.

It's as if I'm the one calming her in this entire situation. I don't mind. It makes me feel a tad better about my reaction.

My dad comes up as Charlotte lets go, and she wipes a few tears from her face as she backs away.

"Congratulations, Tiana," he says sincerely.

"Thanks, Dad," I say nervously in return.

Russel comes up next with a gaping jaw. "Tiana, I leave for a few weeks and now you're engaged to the rookie?! What the fuck happened?!" he asks.

I laugh softly as the emotions of everything begin to ease.

"I couldn't believe it either. But he's a good rookie," I say as I look over at Gunnar.

The men ruffle his hair with their icy mitts, knocking and shoving into him in congratulations.

"Guess I'll have to keep a good eye on him," Russel says.

Looking up at Russel, I offer a small smile and a nod. "Sorry I didn't have a better greeting for you. I was nervous about." I gesture wildly around the commotion happening around Gunnar. "This," I say.

"Yeah, no, I understand. I know how you get," he says as he grips my shoulder.

I smile at him. "Thanks, Russel," I say softly.

"Congrats again, Tiana," he says before he moves back to the group of men.

Russel has always sort of known how to work around me. One of the few other people who pick up on me and my intricacies. But he's always been married, and we have never been interested in each other like that. He's like a brother to me more than anything. He can just read me really well.

Nothing more, nothing less.

Russel shoves through the group of men, whistling and calling them all back onto the ice, trying to relieve Gunnar of the cheers.

As the team moves back onto the ice, Gunnar shakes his head with an enormous smile and a chuckle. He moves toward me, shaking out his shoulders from the manhandling, and turns his attention on me.

His attention has always been like electricity. Searing hot against my skin and unmistakable.

One hundred percent effort and focus, always.

It's one of the first things I fell in love with.

His hazel eyes glow with pride and happiness as he

approaches me. Leaning down, he presses a kiss to my lips before he throws an arm over my shoulder.

"Ready to go home, baby?" he asks as he rubs my arm softly.

My brow furrows as I look up at him. "Home?"

"I told Gunnar you guys could have the day off. Your mom is going to take care of any work you have to do today," my dad says.

My mom looks up from her phone, where she was checking something, her brow furrowing. "I am?"

"Yes, Tamisha, you are," my dad grits playfully through his teeth as he nudges her in the arm.

"Oh. Right. Yes," she says with a nervous grin as she quickly hides her phone in front of her.

I look between Gunnar and my dad, wondering what kind of trick this is.

"So... we don't have to be here today?" I ask.

"Nope. Go have fun. Gunnar and I already talked about this, and we agreed it would be difficult for you to stay after all this, so you can go do whatever it is you'd like to do," my dad says.

My cheeks heat, and there is a small rush of giddiness that runs through me.

Glancing up at Gunnar, I bite my lip with a small grin, and he leans down. Hooking a finger under my chin, he tilts my head up before he presses a small kiss to my lips.

"Told you I know you well, baby," he whispers.

I roll my eyes and slap his chest.

"Welp, we're leaving. Have fun being tortured!" Gunnar calls with a wave as he leads me away from the rink.

The sound of hollering and sticks banging against the glass echoes through the tunnels as we retreat further from the rink.

I take a deep breath, relishing the fact that it's over and I did, in fact, survive. Even though I really didn't want to do any of this.

Gunnar's arm tightens around my shoulders, squeezing the other one.

"Told you it wouldn't be so bad, sweetness," he whispers, adding a small peck to the top of my head.

I roll my eyes, wrapping an arm around his back as I lean my head into his chest.

One would think that if you have a day off, you're going to want to perhaps go out and spend it with your fiancé.

No. Not I.

I want to go home and curl up on the bed or the couch, and recharge and not hear a single peep from a damn soul outside of those walls until tomorrow.

"So would you be mad at me if I just wanted to go home and do nothing for the rest of the day?" I ask with a sigh.

"Sugar, you really need to learn that I know you a lot better than you think I do," he says with a laugh.

The longer I think about how well this all went, it has me thinking about the wedding... the cake tasting; the dress buying. I get to plan *all* the things now. A venue, the guest list, and the other little bits and pieces that go into planning a wedding. The reception, even if I don't really enjoy crowds. Making a registry of things. The dresses for the bridesmaids.

Granted, it's not like I enjoy those things. I just really, really enjoy the planning of it all. The lists and the organizing.

My thoughts run, a rush of excitement flooding my veins, and I glance up at Gunnar with a nip to my lip.

"But what if I... I don't know... wanted to plan our wedding?"

Gunnar glances back down at me with a small smirk on his lips.

"You really want to get started on it that quickly? Is being my fiancée that bad?" he asks teasingly.

I halt when we reach the door to my office to grab our things, turning to face him and taking his hands in mine to smile up at him.

"I think that would be my worst nightmare," I say teasingly.

He smiles lovingly at me, letting go of one of my hands to wrap it around my jaw. Pulling himself to me, he latches his lips to mine, devouring me in a deep, passionate kiss.

"Whatever you say... Mrs. Hayze."

CHAPTER THREE
GUNNAR

I have never seen Tiana go into planning mode.

Not like this, anyway.

I could tell something was on her mind as we came back to the apartments. She had been murmuring to herself almost incoherently as she drove us home.

Which is not entirely *new*. But this time was definitely *different*. She had an unseen vigor as we walked up to the apartment, and as soon as we came in, she went straight for one of the back rooms.

Somehow, she just had a whiteboard stowed away somewhere.

Ever since we came home, she's scribbled over it and mumbled to herself for hours. It's already nighttime, and even now, she has it set up on the couch cushions. Moving back and forth along the ground on her knees, she continues going over all the plans she's made so far.

Already, she's decided she wants the reception at the glass garden, which is probably the best idea. But from there, it *ran.*

It has continued to run at a speed I wasn't sure she possessed. The only real fast thing about Tiana is the way she drives, but her energy itself isn't high, or even close to intense.

This... instance, however.

She hasn't even changed out of her work clothes. She came home and went straight to a closet and pulled this monstrosity out.

There are several circles drawn all over the board that takes up almost the entire couch. She's got columns of acronyms on one side, and there's another bit of random numbers on the other side.

Apart from really not knowing what the hell she's actually doing, it's almost fascinating to see her sort of dive into... whatever this is. Almost like watching nature play out. Not much you can do as far as interference, but a wonder to observe.

It's as if with every stroke she makes on the board, I can see the little sparks firing off in that brain of hers. It's so precise that I don't think I've seen better plays and plans from her father.

He should employ her as an assistant coach.

I've sat here watching her, leaning back on my hands with my legs stretched out in front of me, one foot flopping back and forth. My tongue has slid and twirled around my chain while I grip it in my teeth, mindlessly trying to absorb and understand this new facet of her she's showing me. When we came home, I removed my shirt, because that's just what's more comfortable for me.

I wasn't sure what she meant earlier in the office when she said there was screaming in her head. I don't have that problem. But if this somehow helps quiet some of the racket, I'm more than happy to indulge.

At least until I find her mumblings are speeding up, faster

than I've ever heard her talk, and I think it's time for her to take a break.

I stand from my spot on the floor, taking a large stretch before stuffing my hands into my pockets. As I walk toward her, I release the chain from my teeth, letting it hit my chest. She doesn't even really pay me any attention as I approach. Her words do get louder, as if she's talking to me, but with her focus, gaze and movements still stuck to the whiteboard.

"I think if we set all these people up in this area, it'll be the best way to keep everyone from fighting," she says as she keeps drawing lines and arrows.

I grip her wrist, stopping the scribbling, but she continues speaking as she gestures with her hands.

"I know how Leroy and Reynolds like to chirp at each other, so I think they need to be separated. I will be damned if any of them are chirping nonsense at our wedding."

I wrap my other hand around her cheek, pulling her head to face me. And while her gaze comes to me, it's apparent that her mind is elsewhere, as if she's chasing her thoughts within. Eventually, her gaze focuses on me, and she talks directly to me finally, as if *we* are having a conversation instead of her saying it to the air.

"And I don't know if we should have Adrian sit with the team or if he should sit with my parents and Charlotte because I think th-"

I lean in, cutting her off with a deep kiss as I wrap my hands around her jaw.

She moans softly into it, and her hands come out beside her as she kisses back.

I pull away, smiling down at her as my thumb glides against one of her cheeks.

"Sugar?" I whisper.

"What was that for?" she asks with a furrowed brow and a scrunched nose of confusion. I know she's probably upset that I cut her off, but if she keeps her mind running this long, she'll burn out.

"We don't have a date yet. And you have already made the entire guest list, planned the venue *and* what we would be eating. It's been hours. I need you to breathe. Please, babe," I tell her with a kind smile.

"But the wedding-" she says, and I shake my head to stop her.

"We have time. It'll be okay. For now, let's go rest, yeah?" I ask.

Her eyes roam over my face, thinking for a moment. I imagine trying to think of a way to get out of my demands.

Such is the way of a lawyer, I reckon.

"Tiana..." I say sternly. "Bed. Now," I add.

"The w-"

"Nope," I say quickly before I squat down in front of her.

I glance up to see her brow furrowed in question, and her eyes wild with confusion. I give a small smirk in response before I wrap my arms around her legs and come to a stand.

She makes a loud squeal as her arms scramble for something to steady her. Though, she doesn't land her target in time, and her upper body folds in to slump over my shoulder.

"Gunnar! I have things I need to do! Put me down!" she growls as she hits her fists into my back. But since she's not too strong and I've taken hits that would make an elephant cry, it does absolutely nothing to me.

Her body bobs against me as I walk us down the hall and to the bedroom, kicking the door shut behind me with a little flick of my foot.

I bring my hands up to her waist, pulling her off my

shoulder to set her down in front of me. As she steadies her footing on the floor, her arms fold across her chest, and she glares up at me in disdain.

"You messed up my thought process," she grumbles with a pout.

"You haven't even changed out of your work clothes, and you haven't eaten *all day* because you've been going nonstop."

"You said you wanted to marry me, and I started thinking about all the things that need to be done before then," she murmurs.

"Sugar. Go shower. We're getting in bed. From there you can do whatever you want, as long as it has nothing to do with the wedding," I say sternly.

Her brow furrows, and I can see a hint of mischief running behind those green eyes as she glares at me.

"Make me," she says.

Confusion tugs at my features as I look at her. "Make you?"

"You heard me, goon. Make. Me." She has a taunting sort of mock in her tone as she plants her hands on her hips, leaning toward me. Her face tightens, almost daring me to challenge this.

My brow raises as my head tilts, looking at her almost in disbelief. I have no idea what compels me to ask this. But it's almost a knee-jerk reaction.

"Are you being a brat?"

A blush crawls across her cheeks, her eyes widening for half a second before it's replaced with a glare.

"I've done some research... maybe I am. So what?" she asks with a dismissive shrug.

I look her up and down, my tongue sliding across my lip in heated curiosity.

"What are you saying?" I ask.

Part of me knows what she's asking, but the other part just wants to hear her say it.

Her offense drops... just a bit as she loosens only the smalll-llest amount.

"Maybe I want... you to..." Her voice trails off as she takes a deep breath.

I step closer to her, wrapping a soft hand around her hip as I tug her into my body. Her gaze shies away from me as she sinks a little nip into her lower lip. Bringing my other hand to her chin, I tilt her head up to look at me.

"Eyes here, sugar," I whisper.

Slowly her gaze trains on my face, and she tilts her head back, her chest pressing into me.

"Use your words, come on. What is it you're saying?" I ask.

"Maybe I want to try something... I've been interested in... I saw my chance to try it, and I'm taking it," she says. Though the last part of her statement comes with a bit more defiance.

A small grin tugs at my lips. "Will that help you get in the shower so we can sleep?" I ask.

She nods as the corner of her mouth tugs with a small smile.

"What made you do this 'research'?" I ask.

I see how her eyes want to shy away from me. And they want to *so* badly. They always do. But she enjoys trying to appeal to my likes.

"I was curious what it means for me to be so submissive to you in bed. So I did some research... and I want to explore the things I've found," she says with another dismissive shrug.

"Do you know what it means to be a brat?" I ask. My dick hardens in my sweatpants, and I take a soft grind against her, making her feel it.

She makes a small squeak as her cheeks go redder and my grin widens in response.

"I don't listen to your demands... you make me beg for it," she says softly.

My brow quirks with delight as my tongue slides across my teeth, popping off them with a soft click. I'm intrigued by the little game she wants to play. And I am more than happy to indulge in whatever gets her to come around my cock.

"You sure you wanna make that decision?" I say with a small smirk.

She says nothing, her glare stuck on me.

I suppose if I take that role in these sort of situations, she could play a brat if she wanted. But she knows what I do, and if she wants to play with a dynamic or explore something like this... I'm for it. At least it'll get her mind off of the wedding for a few moments.

"Clothes off. Shower. Now," I say sternly.

She tries to hide the small bit of excitement as she bites her lip, before she steels her gaze and tilts her head, glancing at the ceiling with a finger pressed to her chin in thought.

"Mmmm... no," she says as she crosses her arms over her chest. Her eyes slide back over to me, a glimmer of excitement in them as she waits.

"Fine," I say with a sigh and a shrug before I grab her hips. Like a sack of potatoes, I toss her over my shoulder.

She squeals, squirming and fighting against my grip as I bring her to the bathroom. I flick the door closed behind me.

I really like the amount of space in these bathrooms. Walking in, there is a long double-sink vanity along the left wall, with large mirrors above the entire piece. The toilet rests at the very end, but on the right wall is a massive jetted tub, with a glass-enclosed shower right beside it.

Inside the shower, is a small tiled ledge for propping your leg up on... or other things. Whatever you fancy.

With her still over my shoulder, I slide my hand up the back of her calves, her thighs. Though rather slowly. The backs of her legs are incredibly sensitive, and I love to tease them.

I keep moving until I reach her ass, taking a gentle squeeze of one cheek before I slide my hand around, looking for the zipper on the back of her skirt. When I find it, I drag it open, and then shift my grip so that I can lift her hips enough for me to tug at the hem. I feel the band slip past her waist, and I tug it the rest of the way off, throwing it to the floor.

It doesn't even seem as if she wears panties anymore. But a man is not complaining.

"Last chance to listen, Tiana," I say.

She says nothing, and I lay a hard swat across her bare ass with the loud pop echoing in the bathroom.

She makes a tiny squeak, obviously trying to hold it back.

I tsk as she stays her bratty little course, before I move to the large shower. Luckily, these showers are actually big enough for me. Which is more of a struggle than you'd imagine. This one has a rainfall shower-head in the middle; which has been extremely mint after game nights.

I slide one of the glass panels to the side before I lean in to turn on the shower. It sprinkles for just a second before it starts up full force. Leaning out, I grip her by her hips and pull her off my shoulder, placing her feet on the floor. Her arms cross while her eyes are stuck to me in a glare.

She's horrible at pretending to be upset about me ruining her focus, but for the sake of play, I'll let her think she's good at it.

"I've ruined too many of your blouses, so if you would like me not to ruin another one, I'd suggest uncrossing your arms."

She blinks, her eyes narrowing on me before they roll and she throws her arms to her sides.

I move forward, looking down at her with a small tilt to my lips. Her eyes merely glance up through her lashes, and I bring a hand up to tilt her chin up.

"You're going to get naked, get in the shower, and then you're going to wash your body at my command. I'm going to sit on the counter and watch you. But every time you don't listen, something happens," I tell her.

Her eyes narrow on me as one brow quirks in question. "What is this 'something'?" she asks.

"Torture, I reckon," I tell her with a shrug.

She rolls her eyes again before she brings her hands up, unbuttoning her suit jacket and shrugging it off her shoulders to hit the floor.

She throws her arms out in an annoyed 'There?' expression before they rest at her sides.

"Thatta girl, sugar," I say with a grin.

She merely glares, but boy is that excitement just twinkling in the gorgeous green pools of her eyes.

I slowly undo each button on her blouse, watching her eyes closely. They stay on me, but a heated blush fills her cheeks, and my lips tilt in a smirk.

Once I unbutton all the buttons, I press the fabric of the blouse off her shoulders, letting it fall to the ground with the suit jacket and skirt.

"Can you do my bra?" she asks timidly.

I take her by the shoulders, spinning her harshly around. Gripping the clasp in the middle of her back, I pinch it, releasing the hooks and letting it spring from around her ribcage.

Leaning down, I move her hair over her shoulder, pressing

a small kiss on her neck as I press the straps off of her shoulders. The bra falls to the ground, and I give a small slap to her ass.

Tiana sends me a glare over her shoulder before she pulls away, stepping into the warmed enclosure. With the time it's taken her to comply, the bathroom has filled with steam and the heat in this room has climbed.

I take a few steps back, leaning against the edge of the counter and crossing my arms over my chest. Dipping my chin, I flick out my tongue to secure my chain. Tilting my head back, I allow it to drape over my lower lip. My teeth grit the length, tightening the part in the middle for my tongue to play with as I watch Tiana.

She steps under the raining shower head, and I watch as some of her focus drops just enough to relish in the feeling of it.

Though... *fuck,* I may have bitten off a little more than I can chew with this punishment.

She looks so fucking *good*. Her skin glistens, with the water running down her body in these perfectly carved rivulets as it travels over her dips and curves.

However, she's too focused on wetting her hair to notice the massive bulge in my sweatpants now.

I stifle a groan, running a hand through my hair before I replace my arms across my chest. My teeth grit harder on my chain, my tongue plucking the tightened center of it. Sometimes the links give me something to focus on... though, they don't do fuckall when it comes to a naked Tiana.

Her eyes finally glance at me, and I give her a small smirk. Though it's a chore, considering how bad I wanna press her against the glass and fuck her.

"Wash your tits," I tell her with a nod toward her bottle of soap.

Her brow quirks as she reaches for her soap. As she grabs

the loofah hanging on the wall, her gaze falls away from me, and she squirts some of the soap onto it before she puts the bottle back down. She squeezes the loofah under the running shower a few times, getting it sudsy.

Soon, her eyes slide to me in taunt as she glides the soap over her arms, covering her body with those beachy smelling bubbles.

My head tilts to the side as I press off the counter to press my sweatpants down enough for them to fall. Stepping out of them, I kick them away. I'm then left in my boxers with an aching boner that would very much like to be set free.

Down, boy. It's not time yet.

But my cock never listens to me... God, *especially* with Tiana.

I catch a glimpse of her eyes widening for a fraction of a second before she steels her features and continues washing her body.

"Face me," I murmur. Though I don't realize how much more raspy my voice becomes as I admire every fucking inch of her.

She doesn't. She turns around to face the other end of the shower, propping her leg up on a ledge inside. Slowly, ever so fucking slowly—because of course I'd fall in love with a woman that likes to torture me—she rubs the loofah up and down her smooth legs. The bubbles coat every fucking part of her, and for a split second I'm jealous of those damn suds because I want to *be* them.

But, I try to stay my course and give a playful sigh with a jump of my shoulders as I lean off the counter again. I pull the band of my boxers down, freeing my cock before I grip it at the base. I'm achingly hard, pulsing and throbbing because I just want *her.*

Tiana's head finally turns, her guard lowering, as if she

can't stop herself. Her lips part on a small gasp, and her movements halt for a moment. With her torso still bent over, she pauses where she scrubs her legs.

I slap my cock against my other palm, and the weight causes a thick *thwack* to echo in the bathroom before I stroke it from root to tip with a tight grip once... twice... I toss my head back, trying to allude to it feeling much better than it does because I want her to see what she's missing.

Though nothing will ever fucking compare to her pussy, I've gotta play the game, at least a little bit.

"What are you doing?" she asks quietly.

My brow raises with a small smirk to my lips.

"If you don't listen to me, I'm gonna come all over your floor. When it *should* go in you." My hand moves fluidly, slowly, and her eyes can't help but watch. I pant and add a rough groan for good measure. "Fuck," I say in a low, deep growl.

"You wouldn't dare," she says with a snarl.

"Try me, sugar," I tell as my breaths lighten.

Her brows furrow in faux anger, and she takes her foot off the ledge to face me. She holds the sudsy loofah above her chest, letting the water from the shower run through it just enough to soak her tits and body in a downpour of bubbly rain.

"Fuck," I groan.

She's making this so fucking hard for me.

The naughty thing.

The soap runs over all of her body, through the ridges of her tight stomach, the bones of her hips... through the valleys of her cunt, right... where *I* should be.

"Touch yourself," I add as my pace speeds up on my cock.

The pleasure shifts, heightening to a point that makes it hard to concentrate on what I'm supposed to be doing.

She presses her soapy breasts against the glass. Her tight little nipples break through the collecting steam on the shower door, followed by the rest of the skin on her tits as they compress. The sight, coupled with the moist and heated air, causes a pulse of painful desire to rush through me, and my head tosses back with a thick groan. Though there is no faking this one.

But she didn't follow the rules, so I use my free hand to press my boxers down further, letting them fall before I step out of them.

My strokes against my length speed up. With my orgasm beginning to close in, my breaths come quicker.

"Last chance, Tiana. I'm gonna come," I pant.

Her eyes widen, and I finally see her break as her hand moves straight for her pussy, sliding her fingers through it.

I grin in satisfaction. Though, I really am glad she finally listened because I did not want to come on her floor.

My hand stops, a growl escaping from me as I step forward. I quickly slide the glass pane open and step in.

Threading my fingers through the hair at the nape of her neck, I tug her head back. Looking down in her eyes, I give her a grin of victory.

"Wash me," I growl tauntingly.

Her eyes widen, almost shocked for the words to come out of my mouth.

Trust me, babe, me too, but you wanted to play the game.

My cock throbs; it fucking *aches,* but I'm dragging this out. I want her needy and begging before I plunge myself into her.

She doesn't listen, with one of her hands moving to grip my cock, and I spear my free hand straight for her wrist.

"I know you heard me," I hiss.

"Gunnar... p-please," she pants.

A grin twists my lips as I look at the tortured desire in her eyes.

"Awwww... you're so needy... So desperate to be fucked," I tease with a soft pant and a breathless chuckle.

Her eyes show a hint of relief. But she doesn't realize who she's playing with.

"Wash me," I say again.

The relief leaves her eyes, and I offer a triumphant gaze of my own, my brow quirking in delight.

She squeezes the loofah, gathering more suds before she rubs it over my chest. As she does, the water collides with it, rolling down my body.

"Watch," I growl as I lean in.

I tug her head to the side, baring her neck for me to kiss and lick the water from her beach-scented skin.

Her eyes glance down, catching sight of my cock covered in the soapy water.

"See how hard it is? You could've had it, if only you listened," I whisper. "Tk tk tk..." I click with my tongue. "Naughty girl."

"Please... I need it, I need *you*, please," she whimpers softly.

I come up from her neck, looking down into her eyes as her hands drift further south.

"Tell me how bad," I rasp as I lean in to capture her lips with a kiss as I bring my free hand up to her breast, pinching and twisting one of her nipples between my fingers. She pants and groans, pressing her head back against my grip.

"So... so fucking bad, it hurts. Gunnar, please," she whispers against my lips.

I grin. "How can I deny such a needy little thing like you?"

Panting, I turn her body with the grip I have on the bundle of hair at the nape of her neck. I press her against the glass, her hands resting at either side of her head on the panes.

The heated water at my back pushes my passion higher and higher, the lust coursing through all of me as I nudge her legs open with my knee. I crouch, gripping my cock and running it through her slick core.

I release a deep groan, relishing in how fucking wet she is before I press it to her entrance. I advance slowly, letting her grip and surround me.

Her moans echo through the bathroom as I fill more and more of her. The relief is instant. Like a flood through my system of pure pleasure.

My steps falter just a bit as I descend into the feeling of her, settling and letting her breathe through the stretch. Soon, I roll my thrusts slowly in and out of her, losing myself in the heat of the water beating on my back and the feel of her pussy.

I lean down, kissing and nipping at her shoulder as I thrust into her.

"Is that mind of yours quiet now? Is the way you're stretching around my cock the only thing you can think about?" I pant against her skin.

She nods against my hold on her neck, and I tug her head back and to the side, coming up to kiss her sloppily on the lips and my pace picks up, finding a rhythm. The bathroom fills with the sound of me pounding into her, wet skin slapping against wet skin combined with her pleasured moans.

My free hand wraps around her, slipping between her legs to press into the slick wetness there. Her moans rise into a higher register as I press and stroke her clit.

"If this is what I have to do to get your mind quiet, I don't mind giving this to you," I pant.

"Fill me. I wanna feel you come, please. Please... please-pleasepleasepleaseplease," she whimpers. Light and begging, the glass doors rattle as I thrust into her, with that tangle at my spine coiling tight as I hear how tortured she is for my release.

"You want to feel me fill this pussy? Have me dripping out of you?" I ask in a whisper.

She nods, her eyes clenching shut.

And usually I'd want to see her pupils blow, her mind wipe away as she orgasms, but she needs to have a moment where her thoughts aren't there. Where her body lets go of the world around her and gives in to something that feels good.

"Come for me, lock me in that pussy," I grunt as I speed up my fingers against her clit, burying deeper and deeper into her as my orgasm closes in.

Within a few strokes, pleasure tightens around my throat, choking the life out of me as I come. With white hot stars blasting against my eyelids as they clench shut.

Tiana screams out, her orgasm barreling through her as her pussy tightens around my cock, locking me in place. My hand on her neck lets go, finding her hands against the glass. I tangle my fingers into hers, holding them tight as she rides her wave.

She takes me for everything I am every single time, and I *love* it.

"Good girl, baby, milk me, take it all," I grunt as her pussy keeps going. She whimpers and pants as her body wrings everything from her, and from me. Until finally, it finishes its waves, letting me take a few small thrusts in and out of her. I pant against her wet and steamed skin, pressing kisses into her shoulders before I rest my head against one.

I leave my cock in her, letting my hand drop to her waist to hold her hip as I slide the other hand from her clit to rest on her other hip.

Her breaths move in and out of her in a calculated heaviness as she comes down, her body somewhat limp as she leans back against me.

I drift us back under the water, dragging myself out of her before letting the rainfall hit her chest. My arms wrap tighter around her waist as I lean my head down to rest on top of hers. I soothingly rock us side to side until her head falls back against my chest.

I glance down, seeing that her eyes have closed, and her face has relaxed as sleepiness starts to pull her under.

"Sugar?" I whisper softly.

"Mm?" she murmurs.

"I'm gonna wash your hair and then we're going to get in bed, okay?"

She nods sleepily, and I look around her shower for her shampoo. When I find it, I keep one hand around her waist as I lean over to grab it. I tilt myself so she can lay back on me while I squeeze some into my hands to rub into her scalp. Her head wiggles and moves under my scrubbing, and she makes small sighs of relief as I do.

When I finish scrubbing her scalp, I move her under the water, rinsing all the shampoo out before I grab her conditioner.

Squeezing some into my hands, I run it through her curls, scrunching the ends up before I take a few clumps and twirl them around my fingers.

While I am obsessed with her hair, I always wanted to be able to take care of it if something happened to her.

Not to mention, when I was doing my little deep dive rabbit hole search, I thought about if we ever had a daughter–or a son with curly hair–and I needed to do her hair. So, there was one night I just spent researching for hours and hours. Which means I now know how to make sure her coils are always perfect.

It takes a while, since she has a lot of hair, but eventually, I rinse out the conditioner and try to press in her leave-in conditioner. I spend a good amount of time coiling the strands around my fingers.

I slowly move her to the small tiled bench inside of the shower, where she leans back against the wall with a satisfied hum. Leaning out and grabbing a towel from the rack outside the door, I pull her to a stand.

"Arms up, sugar," I whisper.

She groans as she puts her arms up, and I wrap the towel around her back, securing it under her armpits. She then grips her arms tight around her. I lean back out to reach for my sweatpants, since I know they're one hundred percent cotton, and use the fabric to squeeze the remaining water from her hair. I press her out of the shower, and lean down, wrapping an arm under her knees to cradle her so I can carry her to the bed.

As I walk out of the room, she rests her head against my chest. A satisfied, yet sleepy smile paints her face, and I give a small shake of my head in amusement as I place her in the bed.

I let her rest there while I go back to the bathroom to grab another towel and dry myself off a bit more. I pick up the clothes we left behind to throw them in the hamper before toweling off my hair to throw that in the hamper as well.

When I return, Tiana has already curled up in the bed in the fetal position, gripping the blankets over her shoulder. I see the little flap of towel hanging out from under the covers and tug it from under her, throwing it to the hamper.

All the while, my mind works over the things I saw tonight.

Wasssss letting her play the brat a good idea?

No idea, to be fair. But it helped her get out of her head.

And I've never seen her lock in on something like this. I suppose her getting us through the mock trial may have had her locked in, but I wouldn't know, considering I wasn't able to hear that much from her in that time.

But I wonder if this is a normal thing for her.

I'm still getting to know her on this level, and she's a tad different from other women I've been with in the past. And while that's part of why I love her, I have to be cognizant of her needs if the men in her past were so unwilling to learn how she worked.

All I ever want to do for Tiana is learn how she works, ever since the beginning. And if her being a brat for a few minutes helps that, I'll let her.

As I crawl into bed, I decide that I'll talk to Charlotte about it since I'm sure she knows. The thoughts continue to run as I pull Tiana into my arms. She snuggles into my chest at my touch, where her fresh beachy scent lulls me into a wonderfully calm sleep.

CHAPTER FOUR
TIANA

I remember little from last night, especially after my orgasm.

Gunnar had somehow stopped the screaming of plans in my head, so I could actually fucking relax.

Something that is *significantly* harder to do on my own.

When I get in these modes of tunnel vision, it feels as if nothing else matters outside of it. It's just circles and circles and circles of thoughts. Problems that need to be solved, things that have to get done pertaining to this one specific thing, and I can't sleep until they're solved and squared away.

It can be annoying, because there's always a voice in the back of my head that is quieter than the others. That I need to eat, to drink water, or I need to go to sleep.

But I *can't*. Food is too much of a thought sometimes; I physically can't make myself grab my water cup, or I just am not tired; therefore, sleep is not an option. Anything outside of the immediate problems I need to solve, means nothing.

The last time I got tunnel visioned like this was when I was trying to find a way for Gunnar and me to be together. I lost sleep; I lost some weight because I just wasn't eating. The problems I needed to solve were far more important.

It's not stressful, I suppose, in the moment because I'm enjoying solving the problems. It's stimulating, and I like the way my thoughts feel when I solve problems. It pushes me forward every time. But because they're so stimulating, it feels as if there is nothing that will satisfy me more in that moment than solving the problem.

Ergo, lack of sleep and food.

But I hadn't realized how fast my thoughts were running last night until Gunnar stopped me. I didn't want to stop because I was so focused, and it's *frustrating* when my thoughts are interrupted when I'm so invested in something.

He was right, though. When we came home, I had gone for hours; I didn't even realize it had turned to night when he interrupted me.

It was nice the way he turned my focus. I don't think anyone has ever attempted to stop me in the past. They usually would just... leave. They'd just come back when I wasn't focused on whatever was the thing at the time.

But with Gunnar... It's hard to think about anything else when he fills so much of me at once. Not to mention, he took the stress of washing away the day for me.

Showering is part of my routine, just part of what I do, but some days I just don't *want* to. Especially when there are things I'm consumed by. But he washed my hair. He even coiled it the right way.

I wasn't even aware that he knew how to do that.

When I wake up this morning, my hair is done. While it is still damp, I can at least do enough to it to get it ready for work. A thing that in and of itself makes getting ready for my day... so much easier, and much less stress.

Gunnar usually isn't in bed on weekday mornings. He

wakes up early to begin with, probably from his life growing up in hockey.

So he is usually getting ready himself or he's getting me coffee. Usually both, because he knows it takes longer for me to get ready than it takes him.

As I get ready, brushing my teeth and pulling on my outfit, I listen for Gunnar to come back to the apartment. I already know he's out grabbing coffee if I don't hear him elsewhere in the apartment.

We obviously have keys to each other's places at this point and just bop back and forth between the two. Though most of the time we sleep at my apartment because I have a ton more things than he does. But I'm also specific about fabrics, so I enjoy sleeping in my sheets because of the way they feel on my legs.

It usually gives Tucker breathing room, so he's not clambering over us when we wake up in the morning. That's also part of Gunnar's routine—taking Tucker out in the morning when he goes to get my coffee.

Because Gunnar has become so attuned to me and my routine, right at six, I hear the front door open.

"Sugar? It's go time, come on!" I hear him call through the apartment.

I fluff my curls one more time before I make my way to the bedroom, pulling my heels on before I meet him out in the kitchen.

Of course, he wears his hoodie and a pair of warm-up sweatpants with his backpack on his back.

My heels clack against the tile in the kitchen as I pass by him and snag my coffee.

"What's the move, sweetness?" he asks as he leans down to kiss me.

"I want the BMW today," I say with a kiss to him in return.

He grabs the keys from the counter, along with my tote, and leans in, guiding me to the door with a hand on the small of my back.

As we leave the apartment and I wait for him to lock the door, my thoughts begin to run, realizing I haven't even thought of the color scheme I want to go with for the wedding. When he turns to me and we begin walking, I lean into him, resting my head against his chest as he puts his free arm around my shoulder.

"What do you think of forest green? Do you think it would clash with the glass sculptures? I want it to be cohesive," I ask as we walk to the elevator.

"Sugar, whatever you'd like to do, I'm with," he responds.

"Noooo, I want your opinion. This isn't just my wedding, Gunnar," I groan as the elevator doors open and we step in.

Gunnar pulls his arm from around me to snag his chain from his chest, bringing it to his lips as he leans over to press the button leading us down.

My mind runs, the memories of the glass garden coming back to the forefront. I try to remember the layout of the garden, the different rooms and areas in the place, while trying to imagine the tables, the seating and any of the decorative things that would look good in that space.

But soon the strength of Gunnar's arm pulls me from my thoughts as it wraps around my back and he pulls me into his body.

"Baby," he whispers with a smile.

I look up at him with a furrowed brow but melt into him because it feels nice to feel his body against mine.

Safe. Always safe, and always grounding.

He brings a hand up to my chin as his teeth release his chain and he presses my head up toward him. His arm tightens around my back, pulling me in deeper.

"I need you to go a whole day without thinking about the wedding," he says.

"But why I need t-"

"No. No, babe. I know you want to. And I know that it's important. It *is* important. But I don't want you to burn out. You have a high-stress job, you have things on your plate, and your job is important to you as well. You worked too hard to let it go by the wayside for this."

My brow furrows in annoyance as I cross my arms over my chest, tucking my coffee into my inner elbow.

"Since when am I not allowed to do things?"

"You can do whatever the hell you want; you're a big girl. But I've never seen you get that deep into something for that long. I don't even think you ate," he says.

I glance away. Because he's right. And I *hate* that he's right. Because while it's stimulating and fun... it can be destructive if I'm not careful. And in the past, there were men who teased me for it.

Called me strange, or even anal. *High-strung.*

The memories of those words flood in, and I feel a small dip in my stomach. One of... fear?

Of course, their words didn't matter when I'd heard them. But now that I'm perceiving it this way from him.

It's scary, because those men left me for the same reason.

"Fine..." I murmur.

"You know this isn't because I don't want to marry you. I wouldn't have asked you if I didn't want to marry you," he says with a smile as he leans in to kiss me.

I feel a flutter in my chest. The one that takes some of my doubt away, especially when he kisses me like this, and I return it.

Rolling my eyes playfully, I pull away to look back up at him. "Mmmm, somehow I don't believe that," I murmur.

As the elevator dings and the doors open, we exit, making our way silently through the lobby to the elevators for the parking garage.

When we enter the second elevator for the parking garage, Gunnar's lips pull at the corners, and he pulls me back into him. He wraps a hand around my face, pulling me in to kiss me again as he grinds his hardened length against me.

Somehow, this early in the morning, he's hard as stone. Yes, usually he has morning wood. But this isn't morning wood; he's been awake for at least an hour at this point.

"Does this feel like I don't want to marry you?" he whispers against my lips.

I push out of his hands with a playful slap to his chest. "If a boner is your gauge for deciding you want to marry me, you need to rethink your decision-making skills."

"While you are entirely right, you're also entirely wrong. And that's okay! We can't always be right; it's hard being so well adjusted," he says as the elevator dings open.

His hand comes up to ruffle my hair on the top of my head as he leads the way out of the elevator, and I groan as I shove at his backpack.

Unsurprisingly, he doesn't even budge.

"Sugar, you are in fact a pipsqueak. But I think it's adorable you think you can move me," he says as he looks over his shoulder at me.

"I can move you; I just have to be naked," I say. My heels echo through the parking garage as I click-clack into a trot to get ahead of him.

I make a specific point of swinging my hips just a tad more, and I glance over my shoulder as I take the lead, only to see him staring at my ass.

"That's not fair, you know I love your ass!"

"Cry about it, goon!" I yell back with a wave over my shoulder.

Half-way through the workday, I find myself bored at my desk. There isn't much happening right now. A lot of my work is done, and there has been nothing intense happening, at least in the law world. But that always gives me a bit of a pause.

When it's too quiet, bad things are afoot.

I glance at the clock, debating whether to go out to the rink.

With not having much work, an idle mind is in fact the devil's playground.

Today, the devil reminded me of the talk Gunnar had with me this morning. Where I wasn't allowed to plan for the day.

It's fair, okay. It's a fair request. There is nothing inherently wrong with what he asked or how he asked it.

The problem is that I am perceiving it as a threat because of my past. And *that* makes me anxious. Because what if my impulsivity for these things takes precedence and I go against his rules? Will he be upset with me? Find me unbearable?

The visions of what could happen, and the idea of not having Gunnar in my life for my quirks, it causes my blood to race through me. My anxiety climbs exponentially at the idea and I decide to go see Charlotte out at the rink.

When in doubt, Charlotte will talk me out.

That has been my motto for years.

Charlotte is carefree, and to be honest, she can have more

logic than I do in some of these situations where my anxiety throws the logic away.

Go figure, right?

I wring my fingers as I get up from my desk to make my way down the back tunnels and toward the entrance of the rink. All the while, my mind swirls with the things I want to tell her and how to say it.

When I approach the box where Charlotte usually is, I take a deep breath, trying to steady the running nerves.

Charlotte doesn't get as excited when I come to the rink, since I come out here so much more because of Gunnar.

But of course with Charlotte, she just has so much energy by default.

"Tiana!" she says cheerfully, and I give her an exhausted smile in response.

Her brow furrows as she looks at me. "What's wrong?"

I let out a long sigh as I come to slump on the bench beside her.

"Gunnar won't let me work on the wedding," I grumble as I cross my arms against my chest. My fingers tap nervously against the inside of my arm as my eyes focus on the way the ice chips and shreds under the player's skates.

"And... why?" she asks softly, almost confusedly.

My eyes lock onto Gunnar as he skates past, but he hasn't noticed me. He's also extremely focused right now, as it seems my dad is going harder on them with the teams on the docket coming up.

"So when we went home yesterday, I pulled out the white-board," I murmur. Glancing over at Charlotte, I wait to gauge her reaction.

"Tiana..." Charlotte groans.

There it is.

"I know! But my head went there!" I sigh as I run my hands over my face.

"You know you have to be careful with the whiteboard!"

With Charlotte and me being twins, we've always been together. But we're not identical, which means we are so far on different ends of the spectrum. But she knows what happens when the whiteboard comes out.

When I lived with my parents in college, I stole Charlotte after she was done for the day, and while she did little as far as actually helping me study, she sat in my room with me and listened to me ramble for hours.

Usually, by the time I looked up, she was passed out on the bed, and it was nighttime. It didn't matter; she usually knew what it meant for me to bring out the whiteboard.

Which means she also knows what happens with said thing.

"I'm on his side, Ti. Sorry," she says with a small shrug.

"I don't remember asking," I murmur with a roll of my eyes as I stretch my legs out. I lean back against the wall, crossing one ankle over the other and flicking them back and forth in irritation.

"Nope. But you sure came and told me. Why? No clue, but you did. Which means you need help."

I glance at her, and she gives me another shrug. Shaking my head, I turn my attention back to the rink.

"I don't know what to do. I just want to plan the wedding because all of it is so... fun and stimulating. So many things to solve and problems to get squared away," I say with a sigh. My eyes lock onto Gunnar as he checks one of his teammates.

"Do you need help planning it?" Charlotte asks as she comes to sit beside me.

"No," I grumble.

"Right, so here's what I'll do-"

"Charlotte!" I groan as I sit up, throwing my hands out.

"Stop it. You are physically incapable of asking for help unless you're literally hanging by a pinky. So, *I'm* gonna step in because this is different, Ti. This is a wedding. A *man*. A man you're spending the rest of your life with," she chides.

I return to my previous position, though my foot moves faster now, flicking in an attempt to rid me of my annoyance.

And maybe my thoughts haven't caught up with my heart, or maybe I have some growing to do. Because this *is* different. This is the first time I have ever had a man in my life that *wanted* to spend his with me. Someone who saw something in me he couldn't be without.

The reality of that is staggering when I take a step back and look it in the eye.

Someone decided they wanted to be with me forever. That's massive, and for some reason, my brain is incapable of digesting that information.

I'm so used to men coming and going in my life, not wanting to stay or finding some reason to leave.

This is just so different, and so is the thought process that goes along with it.

I sigh, running my hands over my face as I push myself from the wall and take a deep breath.

"I'm just... not used to this, Charlotte," I murmur.

I know Charlotte will understand better than anyone how I may be feeling about this.

She has to.

She's helped me through several panic attacks through school, and she always knew what to do when things got too heavy for me. And in all honesty, I may not have friends, but I always have Charlotte.

"You know I've never done this before," I add.

"I know. And that's why you have me!" she says cheerfully.

I deadpan glance at her, and she throws her hands out, as if *she's* the prize here.

"What do I do? What if he learns more about me and marries me and then finds out I'm a nut job and divorces me?" I ask.

"I don't think that's going to happen. You fixed up his family's truck, and he chased you from the jump. I'm sure if he weren't into it, he wouldn't have asked you to marry him."

I glare at her, and she merely gives me a shrug.

The sound of the whistle blowing echoes through the arena, and all the boys halt against the ice. But Gunnar has his back to me, even if he's bent over with his stick across his knees with his back expanding in deep inhales.

Russel and my dad are going through some kind of demonstration, and all the players have their eyes glued to the both of them. I, however, keep my eyes glued to Gunnar.

But a thought creeps into my mind. Considering someone is not as scot-free as she thinks she is.

Crossing my arms over my chest, I glance at Charlotte, who is paying zero attention to me because she's focusing on whatever the hell my dad and Russel are saying.

"So are we going to talk about the fact that you didn't tell me you and Adrian were dating and that I had to find out from him?" I ask.

Her body stills, going eerily rigid before she slowly turns to me with an apologetic smile. Slowly, she puts her hands up as she slowly slides away from me on the bench, as if I'm some kind of rabid animal.

Good.

"Now, let's just..." she says with a nervous chuckle.

"No, no *'let's just'*! When were you going to tell me about this!? Why did I have to find out from him!?" I ask.

She rubs the back of her neck nervously. "Listen, Adrian didn't know what you would think, and we were sort of keeping it under wraps. He was nervous," she says.

My eyes narrow at her. Being twins means I can tell when she's not giving me the full truth.

And she *surely* is not giving me the full truth.

"Annnnd... I may have moved out to his property...?" she adds with a shy grin.

I roll my eyes. "So you have a boyfriend and don't even live where you used to live? What if I wanted to come visit you at your apartment randomly only to find you weren't there?" I ask as I gesture outwardly with my hands.

"Mom and Dad knew. But you've been so busy. It's just not something that came up. I'm sorry, Ti. You know I love you," she says as she slides closer to me. She wraps her arms around my shoulders, snuggling her face against mine.

"Mm..." I hum in annoyance as I glance away.

I don't know why she wouldn't tell me. But if my life is getting so busy that she can't feel like she can't come talk to me, I fear I may need to spend some one-on-one time with her. I am not exactly the best at verbalizing things or emotions, or telling her I appreciate her company.

But I do, and maybe I can try to do that moving forward. Considering she does actually mean a lot to me.

Either way, I push the thought to the back-burner to work out later. My eyes catch on the big goon in the middle of the rink again.

Gunnar has come to a stand, with the blade of his stick on the ice, and he leans against it with his hand on his hip as he continues watching the coaches.

When he's in his pads and gear, he looks like a monster. A

good monster, I suppose. He's just absolutely massive. As if he isn't already, but my pulse thrums in my chest at the attraction I have to him, causing my mind to wander. Visions of last night in the shower come to the forefront, but then another thought comes to mind, and I can't stop my big, stupid mouth.

"Have you and Adrian had sex?"

Though apparently I am horrific at controlling the volume of my voice because I definitely said that much louder than I needed to.

Realizing how loud my question came out, my eyes widen and I quickly snap my head to look at Charlotte. Who still has her arms wrapped around my shoulders, though her face is now off of mine as she looks to the ice.

Her eyes meet mine in a shock of green fear before we look back to the rink, and I feel the combined energy of our panic as we wait to see if anyone heard me.

However, it appears *everyone* heard me, because the entire hockey team turns around to look at us.

I catch the merest glimpse of Gunnar's confused gaze before, with the weight of a fucking sixteen-thousand pound dumbbell, I drop behind the wall.

Hoping... praying... whatever the fuck I need, that no one fusses us further. Charlotte is still frozen in her spot on the bench, and I yank her wrist to pull her down, behind the wall with me. She lets out a small squeak as she falls to the ground beside me.

"Why did you stay up there!?" I whisper.

"Why the fuck did you ask me that question *so loudly*?!" she whispers back.

"I can't control the sound sometimes!"

Charlotte groans, and soon shady darkness covers both of us, blocking out the bright arena lights.

I glance up at the intrusion, to find Adrian and Gunnar looming over, sans their helmets and their sticks.

Adrian's brow is scrunched in some sort of confusion, while Gunnar tilts his head at me in reprimand.

I sigh in annoyance as I glance between the two.

"Hallways. Now," Gunnar growls.

CHAPTER FIVE
GUNNAR

"Now... why in the hell did you ask Charlotte that question?" I ask as I look down at Tiana.

I wasn't sure I heard her at first in the rink. But as soon as I saw her dive behind the wall, I knew it was my girl.

I also wasn't really sure what to think. Tiana isn't usually this... haywire? And she's not even really all that haywire. But she is off. And that is enough to make me curious.

I've brought her out to the tunnels behind the rink–which is annoying to do in full fucking gear–and I look at her with an arched brow as I wait for her to respond.

But ever the fiery lawyer I fell in love with, she glares up at me with her arms crossed against her chest.

"I think I'm allowed to ask my sister whatever the hell I want, thank you," she says in response as she swishes her curls in defiance.

This woman is going to be my wife.

Hell fucking yeah.

Focus, Gunnar. You're supposed to be scolding her. Get your dick out of your hand, fuckass.

I shake my head of my thoughts, and I come back to focus on her. She has a hint of confusion on her face, but it's quickly replaced with her resistance.

"Yes, you are. But not in the middle of practice where everyone can hear you!" I say as I throw my hands toward the rink.

She glances away, her eyes beginning to shine with something akin to... fear? Sadness?

"I couldn't control the tone. I'm sorry," she sighs softly. Her hands tucked into her elbows shift, with her palms flattening against the outsides of her arms, and she rubs them in comfort.

A small pang runs through my heart as I watch her. Tiana is not the best with words and vocalizing her emotions properly. That much is sure. So, I've had to learn to watch the way she moves and reacts in order to really gauge how she's really feeling.

Sighing, I run a hand through my hair, and she glances up at me nervously.

"What's wrong, sugar?" I ask softly.

Her eyes bounce from the floor to my face as she thinks, with her teeth worrying the inside of her lip.

"I... can't stop thinking about the wedding. And I wanted to talk to Charlotte about what I could do."

My head tilts sympathetically as I listen to her. "Why are you so ashamed of that?" I ask.

She glances away again, her cheeks tinting pink as she does. "Sometimes... I get into these modes of hyper-focus. And it's the only thing I'm capable of doing. I can't... stop myself from stopping. All of it is so stimulating and I like the way the thoughts feel."

My brow quirks. "You can... *feel* your thoughts?" I ask.

She sighs as she nods. "I like the way it feels to solve things I am focused on. And I enjoy doing things that feel productive, even if I know in the moment they aren't. They're just fun, and I really like to plan," she responds.

"Is this a normal occurrence?"

I don't think I know how it feels to... *feel* my thoughts. Most of the time, I don't have much of any. But if it concerns Tiana, then I'm willing to try to understand this unique process she may use. Even if it may be a small detriment to her day, at least in her eyes.

Her heel scuffs back and forth against the finished cement, her eyes stuck on it as she speaks, "Not as much as it used to be. But I haven't had something like this since I had to work on the mock trial for us. But it's... frustrating because I don't know how to make it stop. And Charlotte knows how it is for me when I get into those modes."

My brow furrows as I look at her.

A strange quirk, sure. Alongside not having first-hand experience with this, I've also never been with someone who deals with these sorts of things. But I'm willing to help. And if there's any way that Charlotte knows how to help her, then I would be more than willing to talk with her.

How to go about that? No idea. But I'll find a way.

I step up to her—though awkwardly as these skates are hard to walk with on this finished cement—and she makes the smallest smile, as I imagine I look insane. Taking her chin in my hands, I tilt her head up to me and give her a smile. I run my thumbs over her cheeks as I try to give her a hint of safety in whatever tumultuous waters she may be enduring.

Her eyes show some relief, if not a bit of embarrassment, as she melts into my hands and she looks up at me.

"Sugar, don't ever be worried about your little traits and

quirks. I just want to know how to deal with them. We're still learning things about each other, and this is just another one of those things. I don't want you to throw your life to the wayside over our wedding. It'll all get done, and we'll be able to figure it all out with time. Because there *is* time. But I will allow you to have a day or two to plan and problem solve to your heart's content if that'll help ease some of it," I tell her with a smile.

Her eyes brighten, excitement flaring amidst the vibrant greens as she nods with a small nip to her lip.

Did she think her quirks were going to push me away? She should know by now I'm not going anywhere. But if the men in her past didn't understand her...

I tilt my head, looking at her. "Are you worried I'll leave you for something like this?" I ask curiously.

Her eyes glance away again as she pulls her lip between her teeth. "I don't know. I've been left in the past for less," she sighs softly.

If I could beat the asses of the men who made my sweet girl worry about shit like this...

I shake my head with a soft sigh before I lean in to kiss her. Her hands come to grip my jersey as she stands on her tip-toes to kiss me back, because I am way too tall with my skates on.

As I pull away and she rests back on her heels, I grip her cheeks again, lowering my voice to a sincerity that I'm hoping will help her.

"Sugar. I'm here. Forever. I need you to know that. I am not going anywhere. Especially not because your brain does the things it does."

She smiles at that and wraps her arms around me. At least as much as she can with my gear on. I wrap my arms around her and lean down to press a kiss to the top of her head as I rub my hands up and down her back softly in comfort.

"I'm just... kind of scared. I've honestly never been scared for a guy to leave me before. But since meeting you, I've sort of realized how... mistreated, I think I was. And I love you, so... I don't want to lose you. And it's scary to have that feeling when you've never experienced it before," she says with a soft sigh. Her arms grip tighter around me, her head pushing further into my stomach as she squeezes me. As if she really is scared I'll leave.

I'd kill them if I saw them at this point, I think.

I continue rubbing her back, rocking my hips side to side in an attempt to calm her.

"I'm sorry, baby. But I'm here. I'm not going anywhere. You'll have to attempt to get rid of me. And you couldn't even succeed the first time," I tell her with a playful grin.

She rolls her eyes as her head comes to look up at me, her neck craning all the way back to glare playfully at me.

"Get back on the ice. I'm sorry for being loud," she says with a smile.

She presses back onto her tippy toes again, and I meet her in the middle with a small kiss before she pulls away.

Tapping at the middle of my jersey, she seems a bit more at ease now as she walks past me to go back to her office.

"Just please don't ask that at the rink again! I don't know if I could handle that look from your dad one more time," I call as she walks down the hall.

She throws a wave of confirmation over her shoulder as her heels tip-tap against the floor and her hips sway as she makes her way to her door.

I watch her until she's out of sight, shaking my head with a small chuckle and a whistle to myself. And when I can't see her, I head back out to the ice.

When I get back to the rink, I hop back into some drills Russel has us doing. I really only met him a few times before he had to go on paternity leave. Bubbles is more of a strategy guy, to be fair, while Russel works our endurance and stamina to the bone. It's been a hard fucking practice, and before long, we're finally able to take a break.

The man works us like sled dogs, and I realize my stamina is fucking garbage, comparatively.

Taking my helmet off and huffing deep breaths, I toss it into the box on the ground before I throw my stick to the side. I whip my mitts off, crashing on the bench beside Banks, where Charlotte squeezes water into his mouth while he waits for a player change out.

I lean my head back against the wall, taking a little cool down as I think.

Charlotte knows everything about Tiana. She would know how to handle whatever Tiana is going through. And *I* would like to know as much about my future wife as possible.

Exhausted, I tug my chain from inside my jersey, pulling it into my mouth. I spit it out with a grimace before I snag a water bottle from the wall and spray it over myself, letting it run over my chain and hair before I bring it back to my lips.

Charlotte looks at me with a brow of confusion, while Banks merely glances over at me.

He already knows what I'm doing. Charlotte, on the other hand...

I lean over, away from the two of them, shaking out my wet hair before I sit back against the wall.

"What... was-?" she asks slowly.

"Sweat chain," I cut her off as I cross my arms back across my chest and my eyes zone out on the other players on the rink. Crossing one skate over the other, I stick my feet all the way out in front of me as my tongue slides back and forth against the chain in thought.

"Sweat chain?" I hear Charlotte murmur to Banks.

"Hayze here has himself a lil' oral fixation. Likes to chew on that chain there. When it's in his jersey, it gets sweaty, and he don't wanna suck on a sweaty chain, so he cleans it," Banks responds.

With my gaze still zoned out on the players, I press my fist to the side, and Banks bumps it before I bring my arms back over my chest.

"Thanks," I say through the chain grit between my teeth.

"No problem, brother," he responds.

"Charlotte?" I ask mindlessly. One player has a weird press in his skate, and I focus on that as I speak.

"Yesssss?" Charlotte responds in her cheery tone.

"Do you know about Tiana's..." I pause, trying to remember the word she used. "Hyper-focus? She was worried about it with the wedding planning stuff?"

Damn, how the fuck did that motherfucker get this far without knowing how to handle a stick?

"Loosen your fuckin' grip! You're not jerkin' it off, fuckass!" I chirp at Crawshack.

"Hey fuck you, Hayze!" he yells back.

A small grin rises on my lips as I shake my head and I finally connect my attention to Charlotte.

"Yeah... Ti gets sort of... sucked into things that require a lot of brain power. She's always been like that. She told me about the whiteboard," she says. Though she glances away nervously. Almost like Tiana does.

It is strange sometimes to see how similar they look. They're twins, but I can tell the difference. Personalities aside. Tiana has glasses, and she has a specific freckle right next to her lips that Charlotte doesn't have.

My brow furrows as her words make sense in my head. "The whiteboard is... a normal thing?"

"For Tiana, yeah. It's basically her best friend. I've seen her go wild on that thing for hours when she was in law school. She studied constantly because she is just a problem solver at heart, and when there's a problem, she will not stop until she figures it out. That's kind of just how she is."

I think for a moment, sliding my tongue back and forth across the taut bit of chain in my teeth as I listen to her. "She seemed really upset by the fact she gets like this," I add softly. My focus goes back to the rink as I listen to Charlotte.

"She knows what can happen to her if she's not able to stop herself from focusing. And to an extent it can distress her. But she can never really say or show you it's distressing her because she's just so focused on that one thing. She sort of just rolls with it. I mean, you know how Tiana is. She's going to do the things she's going to do, other people be damned," Charlotte says.

My foot rocks back and forth, watching the way the puck glides on the ice as my teammates pass it to one another.

"But she was worried I'd leave her over it," I respond.

"Well. Tiana doesn't exactly..." Charlotte pauses, and I glance over at her to gauge her expression. She looks as if she's trying to find the best way to explain it.

"She's never cared about someone like she cares about you. And she's never had to worry about losing someone she cares about because of her quirks. So, I think she's just trying to navigate this in the best way she can. Another problem for her to solve," Charlotte says.

My eyes bounce to the rink, focusing now on the skates that scrape into the ice.

"How do I help her?" I ask quietly.

"Tiana really does well with a change of scenery. Even if at the moment it doesn't seem like she wants to go, sometimes if you just take her out for a small trip, it'll help. Drives help also, but if she's kind of too deep in her head, she needs something more... interactive that will get her out of her head long enough to switch up her focus."

"Hm..." I think out loud. Looping the chain around my tongue, I tilt my head back against the wall, sighing softly as I look up at the massive dome above the rink.

I want to help Tiana. I always want to know *how* to help Tiana. But I don't want her to think I'm changing her. I just want her to be comfortable with her quirks. Safe in the way she is.

But if she's worried about me feeling some kind of way about her thought process, I have to skate this lake carefully. It could scare her, and that's the last thing I want to do.

"Charlotte and I are goin' to a pumpkin patch this weekend if you wanted to tag along," Banks says as he takes another swig of water.

"Does Tiana like pumpkin patches?" I ask as I tilt my head to look at Charlotte.

She nods furiously with a grin. "Oh, one hundred percent! Fall is Tiana's favorite season!"

My mind works for a moment, my skate tapping against the wall in front of me. "Do you think she'd be willing to give up her Saturday for one?"

"That's up to Tiana. With the wedding planning and it being on a weekend? Yeah, I don't know; you may have to work her into it," Charlotte says with a shrug.

And that much is true. Tiana is very rigid about her weekends. Considering she spends some time with people during the week, she always says she needs the weekend to recharge. So she's usually just a little couch potato during the weekend.

It's nice, actually. She always looks so cute snuggled up on the couch with one of her blankets and a book. Sometimes she doesn't talk for a while. She goes into these states of utter silence, but she'll ask for my company. And I enjoy it. I enjoy sharing the space with her and just appreciating her presence and company.

But, will Tiana want to go to a pumpkin patch in the fall on one of her recharge days?

I guess I'll have to find out.

CHAPTER SIX
TIANA

"On a Saturday!? Gunnar you know what Saturdays mean to me!" I groan.

First he reprimands me in the hallway, and now he wants to take my weekend? What has gotten into this man?!

I glare at him, my eyes narrowed as I cross my arms over my chest and tap my heel furiously against the carpet of my office.

"I know, sugar, but it'll be our first Halloween, and I'd love to pick a pumpkin with you," Gunnar says as he sticks out his lower lip, widening those hazel eyes of his in a pleading pout.

He came into my office after practice, just like he always does, with his piney forest scent and damp hair. But the look on his face... there was something there. Nerves perhaps.

And now I see why.

Gunnar *knows* what my weekends are to me. He is *very* aware. So why he's asking me to spend it at a field with a bunch of strangers, and noises, and smells, and THINGS!

It's beyond me, and I have it within my right mind to think he's lost *his*!

"Give me one good reason we should go," I say.

He grins a boyish smile, trying to convince me somehow.

"Welllll for one, it'd be a double date," he starts.

I throw my arms out in shock. "A double d-!"

"Let me finishhhh," he says with extra emphasis on the end as he leans in.

I raise an eyebrow, rolling my hand for him to continue before I replace my arms across my chest.

"It's with Charlotte and Adrian. They invited us. I just wanted to help you get out of your head for a little while, and I think a pumpkin patch would be fun since you love fall so much," he says with a smile.

My eyes narrow on him... *glare* at him.

He knows how to get me to do things, and I hate it because it's never against my will. He just knows how to reward me with the things I *do* like.

I toss my head back in frustration as my hands clench at my sides and I stomp my foot. Because it would be nice to do cute fall things together.

Is it wrong for me to throw a temper tantrum at my big age? YES! But I don't care. It's my recharge time!

But at the same time... I love the way the leaves look in the fall and the way the air is so crisp and fresh. And to be fair, I *do* love pumpkin patches. I just don't like them when there are things I need to do.

"Did Charlotte put you up to this?" I ask in accusation, my eyes narrowing as I lean in to poke a finger to his chest.

"To an extent, maybe. But I also think it would be good for you. The outside isn't all that bad," he says with a grin.

I roll my eyes again. "To you!" I groan as I throw my arms out.

Gunnar laughs as he wraps an arm around my back,

pulling me into him. "Sugar, outside is a necessity, and what if I can find a pumpkin that looks like a penis?"

My brow furrows and my lips lift in a grimace. I've never heard him actually say 'penis,' and it's not only jarring, it throws me off completely.

"Why did you say it like that?" I murmur as I look him up and down.

"Well, I'd say cock, but I don't wanna fuck you in the office right now," he says with a shrug.

"That's definitely a lie, but I know what you're saying," I say with a small shake of my head and a smirk.

"Oh, yeah, that's why I said *right now*. Your dad is still here, and you have a hard time keeping that pretty little mouth of yours shut. So I'd rather just fuck you at home," he says as he taps lightly on my lower lip; while a small grin rises on his.

"Are you saying you wanna fuck me when we get home?" I ask seductively as I come up to press my hands up to his chest.

"Aside from the fact that I usually do? Yes. But... there is a condition," he says with a smile, tugging me deeper into his body.

My brow furrows as I look up at him. But goddamn him, I can see that mischievous little glimmer in his eyes.

My jaw tightens, and my eyes narrow in a glare. "You little shit," I whisper through my gritted teeth.

"Hey, you're not the only one who can negotiate a deal," he says as he brings a hand up to my chin, holding it tenderly. As if that'll sweeten the deal.

And fuck him, because it always does. I love a chin-tilt moment.

I seethe, huffing deep breaths through my nose.

Because I know what he wants. But I also know what the fuck *I* want, and it sucks because I know I want *him*.

He's addicting, and it doesn't take much for me to get on my knees.

I'd fucking bark if he asked me.

"So if I don't go on this little double date, I get no sex?" I mumble.

"As much as it pains me to say no to pumping you full of my kids, that is the condition, correct," he says with a fake sigh.

"You... are...." I grit.

"Yeah, yeah, insufferable. You don't think that when I'm buried in your pussy, so is it a deal or not?" he asks.

Fucking hell, the way he talks to me. No wonder I'd bark.

Every single time he pulls out a new card to slap on the table, it sends a new and powerful jolt of lust through all of me. It also makes rejecting the deal that much harder.

"Fine. It's a deal," I say with a tilt of my head and a groan.

"Wonderful! Glad we could work this out. Now let's go home so I can fuck you to sleep," he says with a clap as he releases me. He strides past me to grab my stuff from my desk before he comes over to throw an arm around my shoulder.

We walk out of the office, stopping to lock the door before we make our way down the hall and to the exit doors.

"Horny today, are we?" I ask with a roll of my eyes as he holds me close to him.

"Sugar, I will not lie to you, I was terrified you were going to say no, because I actually am really horny today," he whispers as we walk toward the exit.

CHAPTER SEVEN

TIANA

The drive back to the apartment is calm, especially since Gunnar merely rested in the passenger seat the whole time. If what I saw today is any indication of their practice, I imagine he really is worn out.

With his silence, I have the entire ride home to myself to think. And *think* do I ever.

Especially with the words he said to me in the office.

God, the way his voice sounds when he taunts me. I can't help but become so submissive at the snap of his fingers.

In all honesty, I didn't know if he was actually capable of keeping sex from me. Or maybe I just try and call his bluff. But... the way he said how horny he was before we left the office. That's what *really* sticks out. It has visions whirling in my head.

Imagining... envisioning...

Heat floods all of me, my curiosity piquing alongside my arousal. It's not like I've never not been on the business end of his 'moods.'

But with my mind betraying me so often lately, I need...

something. I need *him* and what he can always do for me when my mind gets too loud to handle. And I have a feeling I'll dive into wedding planning when we get home... and I don't want to. I want to spend time with him. But I can't stop myself.

Fuck it.

When we get out of the car, go through the parking garage elevator to the lobby and head to the elevator for our floor, I lean in close, wrapping my arm around his back as his free arm comes around my shoulder. His fingers stretch out, wiggling for me to take, and I bring my hand up to clasp in his against my shoulder as we get in the elevator.

With the feeling of his touch, and his overall calm, the thoughts run vividly through my head, wanting so badly to know the intensity of the taunt he told me at work.

I lean my head into his body, watching as I fiddle with the fingers I hold.

"When you said you were horny... how horny did you mean?" I ask quietly as I glance at him innocently through my eyelashes.

Gunnar, as always, has his chain in his teeth, and I can see the way his jaw ticks as he grips it tighter and his eyes flick down to me in a heated glance, his lids lowering as if gauging what I need. There's a subtle movement under his chin as he slides his tongue against it in thought.

But he's silent as he presses the button for our floor; his lips tilting with a small smirk. He releases my hand, sliding it across the back of my shoulders, the nape of my neck, to wrap loosely at my throat before he glides it up to pinch my chin between his thumb and forefinger. Pressing my head up, his eyes search my face, lingering on my lips and I watch the way his tongue continues to slide along his chain through his investigations.

"Why? Are you trying to find out?" he whispers through the chain that he grits in his teeth.

Of course, he always tries to talk with it in. And because he does it so often, he's very good at holding it there when he needs to speak.

Heat crawls across my cheeks, over my chest and down my stomach. With the confined space we're held in, and the memories of what we've done in this *exact* area, a pulse is sent drumming *low* in my core.

My breath lightens, pulsing in and out of my lungs in an unsteady burst as my heart thrums in anticipation.

"Yes, please," I whisper.

His brow quirks as his lips tilt in a devilish smirk, his tongue hooking up with the chain on it to tap his upper lip before he drops it. As the chain and its pendant fall to his chest, he leans down, pressing a kiss to my lips. It's deep, claiming, slow, until the door of the elevator dings.

He pulls away, his eyes lingering on me for another moment before he reaches down for my hand and leads me out of the elevator.

With his lack of words, my pulse ratchets up higher. A teasing sort of thing he's never done before. One that has my anticipation damn near choking me.

When he opens the door to my apartment, he presses me inside against the small of my back with his free hand. Then, he flicks the door closed with his foot and drops my tote he's held in his other hand.

Quickly, he turns to me, wrapping his hands around my cheeks and bringing me in for another deep kiss. A soft groan eases between us as his grip on my face pulls me deeper into his body.

I make a small noise of relief as his attention sends a shot of pleasure through my blood. Like the first hit of a dangerous drug, I feel my entire body relaxing with the calm of knowing all of his focus is on me right now.

He presses his hips against me, and I feel his hardened length against my stomach as he does.

"Does this answer your question?" he rasps against my lips, picking up his kisses as if he needs me to even breathe.

There's a husky dominance in his voice, and I feel the energy pumping off of him. The one that's got a hint of dark possessiveness in it. The one where I know I'm about to be in a completely submissive spot and I *live* for it.

But I know what I want, and I know what game I want to play. So I throw my first card to the table in challenge.

"No," I pant as I wrap my arms up and around his neck.

I feel his lips widen in a grin against my lips, his hands roaming to my suit jacket to slowly unbutton the front before he takes my hands from his neck. He places them by my sides so he can press my jacket off my shoulders, letting it drop to the floor. Then, his hands move down my blouse, unbuttoning each button before he presses that off as well, though his touch lingers at the skin of my shoulders as he does. Not an ounce of movement is wasted as his hands slide along my body. It's always meticulous, calculated; always thought out, and I love that about him.

"Take my cock out," he pants into our kiss.

A grin tugs at the corners of my lips, leaning more into this thing I want to explore, and I nip at his lower lip, tugging softly on it. All the while, my hands roam down his sides, searching for the band of his sweatpants before I come to the front of them, cupping his hardened bulge through the fabric.

The heel of my hand presses into it, feeling the rigidity beneath, and I feel him twitch against my touch. A groan rumbles our lips.

"I said, out," he growls.

My hand moves down, leaving the bulge to cup his balls, and his hips roll; beckoning me to listen.

"Tiana," he warns again, though it's deeper and more commanding.

His hands glide down my back, with his fingers tightening against my skin as he moves, showing some level of restraint before he reaches my ass. He grips both cheeks as he moves his kisses down my jaw, licking and nipping at my throat.

Slapping my ass once, I yelp as he grips it one more time before his hands rub and search the back of my skirt for the zipper. When he finds it, he drags it down, then his hands move to the band to press the fabric off me. It slides down my thighs until it drops to my feet, and I step out of it. My heels echo through the apartment as they tap against the tiled floors. It's a minor distraction from the inferno threatening to devour me.

His hands run up and down my body, feeling and caressing me before they come up to my tits. He kneads them through my bra, swiping a thumb over a hardened nipple as he sucks at the skin on my neck.

I continue massaging his balls, trying to stay my course of resistance long enough to spur his dominance even higher.

"Last chance," he says again. But I don't listen; I merely slide my hand back to the bulge, using my fingers to rub the head of his cock through his pants.

He releases a growl of frustration as his hand comes up. Gripping the hair at the back of my neck, I freeze, glancing up at him with a mischievous gleam in my eyes as I catch my lip in my teeth. He tilts my head back, a hand latching onto my hip to control me easier as his eyes search mine.

There is a silent question swirling in the hazel, one that continues to ask if it's okay, and I try to give him a look of reassurance as I smile lovingly at him through the bite in my lip.

The hand on my hip releases, shoving my hand away from his groin before I glance down to see him press the band of his sweatpants. He moves it low enough to where his cock can spring free, letting a groan of relief go before he presses it down further. He tugs on the base of his cock, releasing his balls so the band can slip under them, pinning his pants in place before he takes a few tight strokes.

His groans are guttural, primal as he descends into the feeling of fucking himself.

My eyes stay glued to the sight, watching the way the tendons in his hands tighten and flex. Up and down, he strokes a few more times, until pre-cum beads at the tip.

"You need to learn how to listen when I tell you to do something, you understand me?" he whispers, with a breathless, rasping pant clawing out with his words.

His words are a command, one I want to give in to. But I *love* this feeling. Tempting him, challenging his dominance with a submissive tug of my own, knowing it'll result in even more pleasure.

I can't help the way my pulse hammers in my core, and the inside of my thighs heat to incomparable temperatures, feeling the slickness pooling there.

"Watch," he groans as he strokes his cock. From root to tip, he continues moving. And I want so badly to touch it, put my mouth on it, feel it *in* me.

My hands move, wanting to feel it, but he tugs at my neck again, holding me in place.

"Nah, ah, ah. No ma'am," he says with a grin.

"Please, I need it," I whimper.

"You had your chance; it's my turn now," he says.

Leaning in, he nips at my neck, groaning into the skin as his hand twists around the head of himself. The sound of his groans sends shockwaves through me. A sound so sinful, I wish I could hear it on repeat forever. He strokes himself again before his hand pauses, and he pistons his hips slowly in and out of his grip.

Oh, holy fucking shit, that is too hot for words.

"*Fuck...* it's so good," he pants against my skin.

"Please... let me taste you," I whisper.

He nips into the skin at my collarbone, licking across it. "You wanna behave now?" he whispers.

I nod desperately because the tension is suffocating. I love watching him, but fuck, I love *fucking* him more.

"Tell me you'll be a good girl, sugar," he rasps.

"I'll be your good girl. I'll do whatever you need," I plead.

He leans up from my neck, tightening his grip on my hair to pull my head farther back to look down into my eyes. They shimmer with mischief, devilish intent and a feral level of passion.

His hand grabs mine, fixing my grip to wrap it around his cock before the same hand wraps around mine from the other side. He sets the pace, moving our hands together along his length. Hot and rigid as he can be, I feel him pulse under my palm.

"We work so well together," he pants with a grin.

As our hands continue to move and he gives in to the feeling of us stroking his cock in tandem, his head tosses back, exposing the tense column of his throat. It moves under his skin, showing the way his breaths come in and out of him.

"That's it, mama. Get me nice and hard so I can feel every bit of your throat when I fuck it," he groans.

He holds our hands in place as he switches to pistoning again, merely fucking our hands. The sight is hotter than words, but the feel is like a display of the way it is for him to be inside of me.

But the need, the urgency. I need to feel it. *Him.* My pussy almost aches now at the thought.

"Please... sir, I need-" I whimper as I lean back into the grip he has on my neck.

His head tilts down to lock gazes with me, his eyes half-lidded in mindless pleasure as he grins. "Sir? I like that. That's hot. Say it again," he pants as he watches me.

"S-sir... please... I need... you... This... it's so-" I groan in frustration as I press my body closer to his. "I'm begging, p-please."

"God look at you," he says as he releases the grip he has around my hand and his cock. He grabs my jaw, with the hand on my neck moving to my hip for him to press me backward, toward the kitchen island. "Barely even touched and you're whimpering for me like the needy cumslut you are."

My back hits the edge of the counter as he corners me, and my neck cranes to look up at him.

"P-please," I say again.

He tsks, a click of his tongue as he taunts me. "'Ya know, begging looks a lot better on your knees," he whispers with a grin. His eyes glimmer, and I nod desperately, because if I get the chance to fucking taste him, I'm going to take it.

He lets my jaw go, moving his hand down to wrap loosely around my neck as he watches me sink to my knees in front of him.

I tilt my head back, my lip nipped in my teeth as I wait for his command. With his height, he is entirely dominating.

"Open," he says with a few strokes of his cock. Pre-cum drips from the tip, his hand gripping tight around his shaft. "Fuck," he growls as he tilts his head back. Only for a moment, before he looks right down at me.

My jaw drops, my tongue falling from my mouth before he taps his cock against it.

"Beautiful, naughty thing, you are. So eager to have my cock stretch out that pretty throat," he pants. His eyes lock onto the way his cock looks against my tongue.

His free hand moves to the back of my head, gripping a

handful of my hair. The small shockwaves of his tug sends pleasure skittering over my skin. With just the right amount of pain, I let him move me, control me to the rawest extent. Because *this* is what I want. A moment where my fucking thoughts don't have the chance to control me. Only *he* can.

I am at the whim of whatever he wants, and I love that I can give this to him. That I can surrender this bit of myself to him so that for a few moments, I can have peace alongside my pleasure.

He tilts my head to the side, pressing the head of his cock into my mouth as his hips shift forward. Angling it, he presses it into my cheek before he pops it out and slaps it against my tongue. His chest expands and deflates with heavy breaths as he watches me.

"Have I ever told you how beautiful you look on your fucking knees? How pretty your eyes are when you look up at me?" he says with a grin before he tsks with his tongue. "I'd make you crawl to me if it meant I'd have my cock in your throat." He slides his cock against my tongue as his other hand comes down to caress under my jaw.

My cheeks heat as I crane my head back more, opening wider for him.

I want to taste him. I want to feel the way he stretches me. My throat, my pussy, his strength behind it all.

I need it more than I need air right now.

There's a suffocating anticipation. One that compresses that spring inside of me, burning with tension, just wanting to be released. I never thought I could be this... needy for someone. Never thought I could be wanton for sex like this. But *fuck*, for Gunnar...

He presses my head forward, guiding his cock in my mouth with a tight grip at the base, his eyes watching as I take him deeper and deeper. I keep my mouth open, letting him press into my throat, as I glance up at him with obedient, wanton eyes.

My air cuts off as my tongue glides along the underside of him, wrapping my lips around him to suction his length.

His fingers make soft strokes against the underside of my chin, fingertips moving down to graze my throat as he lets out a low groan, his eyes rolling as he shudders.

His groans are guttural, deep, as he gives me all of him.

I watch the way his chest heaves as I push him further into my throat, the stretch a welcome burn.

"Fucking hell, sugar," he pants out. His hands come up, running through his hair and running over his face as he looks back down at me.

My hands come up, wrapping around the bit of him my mouth can't reach. I pull him out of my throat just enough to swirl my tongue around the head. Soon, my head bobs back and forth, my hands twisting and stroking with my movements.

His groans pick up, letting me continue for just a bit before his eyes roll and his hands grip the back of my head. He presses himself in deeper, forcing into my throat. He's so big I can never take him balls deep, but the man surely tries.

"Deep breath," he pants as he pulls out enough to let me inhale. "Tap my thighs if it's too much," he adds.

And I do, inhaling through my nose before he slowly presses back into my throat, more and more. He growls as he hits the back of my throat, wiggling my head against him. Spit runs down the corners of my mouth as my eyes water, but I keep my gaze on him.

"That's it, hold me there," he grits through his teeth. He quickly brings a hand up, grabbing his chain to sling into his mouth to bite down on before it comes back to my head.

My air depletes some, but I stay. My hands rub up and

down his thighs as my spine serpentines seductively under me, waiting to hear his command as I keep my eyes right on him.

Shallow gags pulse against my throat, and he grins with a heavy pant as he watches... admires.

"There's my good girl, take it," he growls as he tosses his head back with a groan.

He holds me there for another moment, another gag before he pulls me off. Letting me breathe, he pulls his cock completely out of my mouth. Webs of saliva attach from my lips to the head of him as he gives me a small pant of satisfaction.

"Gorgeous sight, that," he says as his slick cock twitches before me.

My teeth nip into my lip, and he pulls me up from the floor. His lips find mine, kissing me with heated passion, and a tight grip on my hips.

He's showing some level of restraint before he spins me around. Pressing hard on the center of my back, he lowers my chest to the cooled marble of the kitchen island before he leans over me. With one hand on my hip, the other comes around to grip the front of my neck, tightening my throat just enough.

His powerful chest, covered by his hoodie, presses against my back. Strong breaths course in and out of him as his cock moves through my center. I feel the way his hips navigate against my ass as he finds my entrance without the help of a guiding hand.

"God, I know your body so well that I can just..." he pauses, his hips hitching to press the head of his cock inside me.

The sensation is maddening, considering the tightened grip on my hip, and throat. I release a pleasured moan in response.

"I could find your pussy in the dark. I'd know these fucking walls *anywhere*," he pants in my ear as he punches forward. "It's like home. Like *I* was *made* to be in here," he growls.

I cry out with a sharp moan, my body tightening as he fills me. Though he didn't prep me, I am plenty wet enough, and my eyes roll at the stretch. It's like every corner of my body has been infiltrated, and it's insane in the best way.

"Ohhh... there she is. Fuck, she takes me so fucking well, huh? Stretches so perfectly around me," he pants against my neck with a teasing chuckle.

"Deeper... please... all of it. I need all of it," I moan. My hips grind back against him, trying to take more of him, but his hips move back, not letting me take more of his length.

I groan in frustration, tossing my head back. His fingers glide delicately along my throat in a tease.

"Oh, she wants all of it? What has she done to deserve all of it?" he pants as he nips and licks at my jaw. He thrusts just the head in and out of me, working me into an absolute frenzy as I wish for all of him.

"I've been such a good girl, please. I need to feel all of it," I whimper.

"I surely don't remember the good girl that didn't listen when I told her to pull out my cock... now she *begs* for it..." he pants against my skin, his tongue clicking in taunt. The graze of his breath against the wetness he laid on my jaw is a cooling comparison to the heat that seemingly devours the rest of my body.

He pulls out, using the hands on my throat and hips to spin me around to face him. The hand on my throat moves to my hip, hoisting me onto the counter. Pressing my legs open, he nudges his massive body in between them.

"'Ya know, I really love your ass, but there's just *something* about the way you look when I fuck you into submission," he says as he presses on my chest, forcing me to lay back on the counter.

I watch as he grips his cock, slapping my clit with it before running it through the wetness, his eyes locked on it in rapt attention. Pressing himself to my entrance, he forces himself in with a deep groan.

My back bows, registering the stretch, the fill. The feeling is diverted, just for a moment, as his hands come to my knees, holding me open as he rocks his hips in and out of me.

The cooled marble at my back is a welcome reprieve, but it does nothing for the pulsing in my clit as he pistons slowly in and out of me.

My moans sing through the apartment, my body tightening and writhing under him as he presses balls deep into me. My hands roam my body in ecstasy, enjoying the way my skin feels under my fingertips before they make it to my tits, pinching and rolling my nipples through the lace fabric of my bra.

He leans over, holding himself in as he releases one of my knees to grip at my jaw.

"Such a pretty girl... A fuckin' goddess wrapped around my cock. How did I get so lucky?" he asks with a grin before he kisses me. My eyes close, the pleasure climbing more as his thrusts speed up, filling me with every bit of him he can offer, and my arms come to wrap around his shoulders. I hold him close, and the rigid muscles underneath his hoodie tighten and contort under my touch as he moves. Soon, the hand on my jaw moves back to my knee, and he wraps both of them around his hips. He reaches for my hand from his shoulder to press between us.

Wetness coats my hand in an instant, all from his teasing, his punishments, and then he pushes my hand lower. Forcing me to grip the length of him as he pulls out, only pressing in enough to have my hand still wrapped around him.

He's hot, covered in my slick and hard as a fucking rock as he slides in and out of my pussy *and* my hand.

"Feel that, sugar?" he pants against my lips.

My moans claw through the apartment, my eyes rolling at the combination of everything happening all at once. I get lost in the way he slides into my hand, and the way I've made him so slippery.

"That's us. We feel so fucking good, don't we?" he groans.

"Fuck," I whimper. The sound of his voice, the teasing, the gruff sexiness of it, undoes me.

"I know. You always make such a gorgeous mess of my cock," he says. Soon he presses my hand up to my clit, and he presses his fingers between mine. His thrusts pick up, pounding into me as we strum my clit with *our* fingers.

"Gunnar, f-fuck! Fuckfuckfuck," I breathe almost in desperation at the sensation. My mind flays, and my thoughts vacate. The only fucking thing on this planet right now, is *this*. And it consumes me *whole*. Ecstasy has flooded my entire system, causing a floating feeling to accompany the way he feels inside of me.

The pleasure climbs higher, and I chase that light on the horizon as he fills me with every stroke.

"There she is. That's it. You're so fucking close, mama. Come with me. I wanna feel you choke my cock when I come," he pants.

My eyes roll, my back bowing and my head tilting back as he thrusts with reckless abandon, our fingers still stroking over my clit as I get closer and closer.

"Oh, fuck!" I scream out. Loud moans leave me, with pleasure bursting through my entire body in a torrent of scorched release as my pussy tightens around him.

"God... fuck!" he grits as he comes with me. He fills me with rigid pumps of heat, spilling into where I've choked him, and he growls as his hands plant into the counter.

"God... fucking... dammit," he growls as his back arches, his cock held balls deep as I writhe and buck through my orgasm against him.

It rolls through me over and over until it slowly dies, my chest heaving with breaths as I try to come down from the intense high of him.

"Fuck," I pant as my arm comes up to cover my face.

I move my arm enough to glance at him, giving an exhausted yet satiated smile as my tongue slides across my lower lip.

His head hangs, his back heaving with his own breaths as he glances up at me.

Clumps of damp hair lay on his brow, a smile tugging at his lips before he leans in to kiss me.

"You did so good for me, baby. So so good," he whispers as he slides a hand down my side.

He pants against my lips, moving up to press kisses into my forehead as he wraps a hand around the back of my head, stroking softly at my hair. "Your throat okay?" he whispers.

I let out a soft chuckle. "Yes, it's fine."

"Good. I'm sorry if I went too deep. When you want to play brat, I get extra dominant. Do I need to tone it down?" he asks. His head buries into the crook of my neck, placing soft kisses on my shoulder and collarbone as he continues to stroke my side.

"No, no. I like it. It's what I want," I tell him.

He rises, pressing his forehead to mine as he takes a deep breath.

"Are you sure?" he asks again.

My eyes connect with his. They're satisfied, calm, and peaceful. But with the smallest hint for concern.

I nod with a smile. "It's what I *need*, Gunnar," I whisper.

I give him a knowing look, as if he understands the underlying implications... because he always does, and I see the smile rise on his cheeks.

"Let's go shower now, yeah?" he asks with a sweet grin. His voice has softened entirely, and I can tell the dominant Gunnar has gone back in his cage.

"You're too good to me," I say with a soft kiss.

He pulls out of me, his cock softening, slick with his cum and my wetness, and he tucks it back into his boxers. A small bite of his lip accompanies the smile he makes as he watches it drip out. He lets a soft breath go before he leans in again, kissing me deep as he uses his fingers to press his cum back into me.

I let out a small squeak before he spins me on the counter, moving me sideways to press his arms under my knees and behind my back.

He picks me up, carrying me back toward the bedroom, and I lean my head against his chest, listening to his pounding heart.

"I always told you I would be, sugar," he says with a small chuckle.

CHAPTER EIGHT
TIANA

I don't enjoy the amount of noises happening here today.

And I do not know why they chose to go to the pumpkin patch this early in the season. It's at the stage where it's not entirely cool during the day. There's *some* coolness but a little heat to the day as well.

I usually enjoy pumpkin patches. But I wanted to spend my day planning the wedding. There were colors I wanted to go over, and I have to get the guest list squared away.

It doesn't help that I also have no idea when the fuck this wedding is actually happening. But I have STUFF TO DOOOO.

Walking into the pumpkin patch, there's your usual archway of fall-flavored decorations. There are kids running and screaming in excitement. Not one of my favorite noises, but I have no choice here.

There's a large area spread out with all the pumpkins they've gathered for picking. In the area across the way, there's a tractor pulling several smaller cars for the kids to ride in, and a farmer drives them around the field with parents off to the side taking pictures of them.

There's also a massive air bladder for kids to jump on, as well as a corn maze farrrrr to the back. When you get deeper into the main area, there's a sheltered space where they sell pumpkin desserts or apple doughnuts and apple cider. Some other knickknacks and whatnots rest in there to buy. And in an area of forest toward the exterior, there's a bunch of picnic tables beside the playground.

When I get to unknown places, I have to take in everything. Usually what all is here and how to go about going through all those things.

But the... sensory aspect... that's the actual concern.

All the unfamiliar smells. Farm, fried foods, apple, cinnamon, and even pumpkin.

The sounds; kids yelling, parents shouting, workers talking to other patrons.

The beam of the sun. The *brightness* of it.

However, my mind lingers on some of the decorative pieces in the area. The leaves and different bits and bobs cause my mind to roam. Slowly drifting back to the wedding and the different colors I could use for those same elements and where they could go in that big glass atrium area.

Charlotte stands beside me, scrolling through her phone. Though, she soon holds it up for us to take a selfie, and I merely glance at the screen as she gives the camera a peace sign.

She takes the picture before she brings the phone down and out of the sun, furiously tapping the screen.

I go back to observing.

I don't have time to dwell much on everything as Adrian and Gunnar walk up to Charlotte and me with small cups of apple cider.

We're all dressed perfectly for fall, I think. Charlotte is in a long coat, with a scarf and her hair in a perfectly messy bun at the top of her head, with long leather riding boots and leggings. She is also wearing a thin sweater under the jacket. Charlotte has always dressed for aesthetics, whereas I have always dressed for comfort.

I'm wearing a Seattle Stags hoodie, with a pair of black leggings and black Ugg boots. The perfect fall outfit, in my opinion.

Gunnar is also in a Seattle Stags hoodie, but he wears his with a pair of dark jeans and a pair of tan Timberlands. While Adrian is in his normal flannel, though today it's a blueish situation with tight Wrangler jeans, his Ariat cowboy boots, and a cowboy hat.

As they approach, I take sight of the four of us, realizing we're all actually spending time together in one space outside of the arena.

It's weirdly... how do I explain?

It's strange, honestly, that all of us are here together. Because I don't hang out much with Adrian outside of work. I mean, if at all. And I haven't exactly seen the dynamic between him and Charlotte. Which means that, along with somewhat trying to get the wedding out of my skull, I feel as if I need to make sure Adrian is good for her.

I also haven't really seen much of the dynamic between Gunnar and Adrian. Which I think would be interesting to see, considering their history.

All of this is a lot to take in at once, and my heart beats a nervous tune in my chest as I try to digest everything.

Gunnar wraps an arm around my back as he pulls me flush to him, handing me the cup of cider before he smiles at me.

"Gorgeous day, isn't it?" he whispers as he leans in to kiss me.

And damn it, I can't be off-kilter when he holds me like

this. His touch is always something that causes my thoughts to flee. Because it's never felt so nice to be in someone's arms before Gunnar.

So *safe.*

"It is," I murmur as I kiss back.

I hold the cup of apple cider behind his head as I wrap my arms around his neck and he grips tighter on my waist, pulling me into him.

"You ready for a good day?" he asks against my lips.

And I decide I *will* try to have one. He brought me out here to have a good day, so by DAMN I'm going to have a good day!

I nod, smiling. "Yes, we'll have a good day," I giggle.

"Thatta girl, sugar," he responds.

A heat runs through me, and I giggle again before I let go, taking a sip of my apple cider.

It's delightfully heated. With the tart sweetness of the apples and spicy warmth of cinnamon, it eases some of my apprehensions, because I really *do* love fall.

This would have been much more anticipated if I weren't so focused on the wedding, but I'm kind of glad he asked me to come. I don't like my mind being just one track sometimes, so it makes me happy that he is also trying to figure out ways to help me with my frustrations.

I gaze lovingly up at Gunnar as he looks over the four of us here. I take the moment to admire his powerful jaw, the hint of stubble on his skin and the perfectly carved cheekbones.

God, I would love to have his fucking kids. Such a beautiful man.

"Alright, Charlotte, you're with me. Banks, be good to my girl or I'll beat your ass," Gunnar says as he releases me to walk over to Charlotte.

My brow furrows as my head damn near spins at the sudden switch up.

"Wait, what the fu-" I try to say in bewilderment.

"You couldn't beat my ass if you had two brass knuckles, Hayze." Adrian cuts me off before he takes a sip of his cider.

"I've checked your ass into the boards more times than you've gotten your dick sucked," Gunnar says as he shoves at him.

"Size and strength don't equal tact. I've taken down bulls bigger than you."

"Hey, can someone tell me what the f-" I try to cut in.

"Don't need tact when you're just a goon," Gunnar says as he gives a little two-finger salute from his forehead.

"There's a reason I'm the captain. You couldn't find the puck if it had nipples on it," Adrian responds with a shrug.

Charlotte seems to be completely oblivious as she continues to take pictures of the farm.

"Hey, I'm perfectly fine with finding the puck. It's just not always my job," Gunnar says with a shrug as he shoves his hands in his jean pockets, rocking back onto his heels.

"Yeah, well, mayb-"

"CAN SOMEONE TELL ME WHAT THE FUCK IS HAPPENING!?" I yell.

The three of them look at me. Charlotte looks up from her phone, sucking in her lower lip as her eyes widen, bouncing back and forth between Gunnar and Adrian. Adrian freezes, merely watching with a small quirk to his brow. With Gunnar tilting his head, his brow furrowing in concern as he steps up to me. Only for my eyes to widen as I realize what happened.

I suck my lips into my mouth, looking up at Gunnar as he comes close. My heart seems to run with a vengeance in my chest, and I connect nervously with his eyes.

Not because of anything he would do. But because *I* lost my control.

"What do you need, sugar?" he asks quietly.

"Can someone... please tell me... *why* you are going with Charlotte? And why I am going with Adrian?" I ask.

"I'm sorry. That was my fault. I should have told you my plan," he says with a soft sigh as he brings a hand up to my cheek.

I glare at him, waiting for him to finish.

"I wanted to ask Charlotte a few questions, and I figured you could spend some one-on-one time with Adrian. It won't be long and we'll converge before we go pick our pumpkins. But I understand your frustration. I'm sorry, baby. It won't happen again," he says quietly.

I continue glaring at him before I stand on my tiptoes to kiss him, trying to show him I'm not as mad as he thinks, just thrown off more than anything. He returns the kiss before moving a hand to my back, stroking it comfortingly as he smiles down at me.

"I'm sorry, baby. I know you like to be informed, and I didn't do that. I won't do it again."

I give him a playful smile and a roll of my eyes. "Do that shit again and I don't mind withholding from *you*," I whisper in response as I press a finger into his chest.

"Yes, ma'am," he says before he gives me one last kiss and pulls away.

Taking a deep breath, I look to Adrian, who gives me a small smile and a nod.

"You ready, Miss Tiana?" he asks.

I sigh with a small nod before I start walking toward him.

Looking over my shoulder, I want to say goodbye to Gunnar, only to find him already in conversation with Charlotte.

He doesn't really look over his shoulder at me as they walk away; he seems engrossed in whatever they're talking about. And I can't help but feel a small pang of jealousy in my chest.

I shouldn't be. I know Charlotte and he would never betray me. But it's... *strange.* I don't like this feeling.

I let out a heavy sigh as I come up beside Adrian.

"What's the matter?" he asks.

Frustratedly, my head tosses back, with my Ugg boots kicking into the dirt as we walk toward a playground a few hundred feet away.

We pick an empty picnic table outside of the playground, sitting at it. Adrian sits across from me, and I sigh as I run my hands over my face.

"I don't like how that felt," I breathe in annoyance as I tug the sleeves of my hoodies over my hands. I clutch the cuffs in my palms, pressing them between my legs.

"The way what felt?" Adrian asks.

"He didn't even really say goodbye. He just took Charlotte and walked away. I honestly don't think I've ever felt that much jealousy before, and it's a really gross feeling," I groan.

"Miss Tiana, do you know why he was so eager to take Charlotte?" he asks.

I look up at him. His hands clasp in front of him on the table, with a toothpick in his teeth, wiggling it as he watches me.

"No. But I imagine you're going to tell me," I sigh.

He takes the toothpick out, pinching it between his fingers. "A few days ago, Hayze was real out of sorts with something called 'the whiteboard'. Him and Charlotte were talking about it, and he just wants to try to learn how to help whatever is ailin' you," he says with a shrug.

My brow furrows as I glance away.

The thought is sweet, because often, I don't know what I

want. Especially when it comes to confusing thoughts and emotions. So for him to step in and try to remedy some of my self-induced confusion... It causes a warm flutter to rise in my chest, crushing some of the nasty jealousy pooled there as I think about how much this man always does for me.

Time and time again, he shows me I am his world. With that realization, I sit a little easier with Adrian. I take a deep breath, blowing it out to get rid of the nasty feelings.

"He's just trying to get to know you from a different perspective. I reckon I'd do the same if I were in his position. Our ladies mean a lot to us," he says as he adds the toothpick back into his mouth.

I glance at him with a small smile, and he returns it with one of his own. Enough of my worries are quelled that I can focus on getting to know him instead of worrying about hypothetical nots.

"Is it weird dating a twin?" I ask.

"Not necessarily. You two are completely different people. Easy to tell you both apart. Charlotte is a sweetheart. And I'm sure you are too. But I don't think two people with energy like the two of them would do well together. There's a reason they say opposites attract."

I shrug. "I suppose you are kind of a male version of me."

"You barrel race and play hockey?" he asks. Though because of his tone, it doesn't sound as teasing as it should. But I imagine that's just how Adrian is.

With the fact that he may be trying to joke with me, I smile. "I didn't know you had a sense of humor, Adrian," I say.

A small smile tugs at the corner of his lips. "I've got some tucked in my sleeve for a rainy day. Don't really have much time for jokes when you've got serious responsibilities in your pack," he says.

"How does Charlotte handle that?"

"Miss Lotty has enough humor for the both of us. Says there's somethin' she loves about my severities. I reckon if she loves it, that's good enough for me," he says with a shrug.

It warms my heart to see the two of them together. I'd like to see them interact more. Just because I know how rambunctious Charlotte can get. So I think seeing someone as high-strung as Charlotte with someone so... stone-faced, like Adrian, would be funny.

I come out of my thoughts to look up at him. "When did you and Charlotte start dating?" I ask.

He seems to genuinely smile at that. And not out of kindness, but out of a real sort of happiness. As if he's thinking about her.

"A little before season started. I've always had my eye on her. But Gunnar, ya know... he told me to go for it when I brought it up."

I smile. It's interesting to know he's watched Charlotte. And he decided he was going to go for it because of Gunnar. Appears Gunnar is a little busy cupid.

It would be like that for him. He's always gone after the things he wants. It makes sense that he would direct his friend in the same way.

"Why do you like her?" I ask with a tilt of my head.

The rest of the farm sort of fades away as I put myself in this moment to learn more about the man my sister's dating. And I am curious about him in a way. Charlotte seems to adore him, and I'd like to see why.

"I like her personality. I'm a bit of a recluse myself. And I think she's good for me. She's got an air about her I quite fancy."

"She's a lot sometimes, though. How do *you* handle that?"

Adrian leans back from the table, crossing his arms over his chest.

"Miss Lotty makes the days brighter. She makes the hard practices easier. She makes my home warmer, and she keeps my belly fuller. Her 'alotness' is just the right amount," he says.

There's a small twinkle in his eyes. Even if his face doesn't show much emotion, I sure can see the emotion he has for her in his eyes.

It gives me love and admiration for them as a couple. A warmth in my chest, knowing that my sister found happiness. Because she deserves happiness. She does so much for everyone else, always being the light and cheery one. I've always loved that she kept that up. There were days I really needed it, and she always came through.

She deserves to have someone be a light for her.

"She bosses you around though, doesn't she?" I ask with a small smirk.

"I wouldn't have it any other way, Miss Dawn," he responds.

Gunnar

"Banks bein' good to you?" I ask Charlotte as I kick a leaf out of the way.

The day is cooler, so my hands are in my pockets, and I've already secured my chain in my teeth.

I felt bad about not telling Tiana about the plan. But I guess my mind was focused on learning more about her from Charlotte.

I always watch Tiana closely, trying to learn how she works, because she's sort of her own little critter. Doing whatever she wants, and everyone else has to follow the flow.

But if there is another person who knows how she works, I want to pick that brain as much as I can. Especially if they're able to be a voice that Tiana doesn't have.

"Would you believe me if I said he wasn't?" she asks.

I glance at her with a smirk. "Would you be upset if I said no?"

She punches me in the shoulder, and I grasp it with a small rub.

"Fucking ouch? You've got an arm."

"I was a defender. I have to," she says with a laugh.

I shake my head as I rub the sore spot away. "So, what do you think is important for me to know about Tiana?" I ask her.

She smiles as she looks up at the sky, letting out a sigh. She stops walking, a tensity pulling at her brow as she thinks.

"Tiana is... different, always has been. She needs things to be done the way she wants them to, or it..." She pauses as takes a deep breath of calm. "It really stresses her out. Different routes to the places she frequents unless *she* wants to take a different one. She is very specific about her food, and if she goes somewhere where she doesn't know what the meal will be, it makes her anxious."

My brow furrows as she starts walking again, though her head falls, watching the ground. Kids weave in and out around us, and I smile as we walk past.

"She may not really show her distress often. She reserves that for herself. But by the time the dam breaks, it's a little too late. So you have to be really in tune with the things she does when she's getting a little more stressed. She'll be quieter; she may pull away more. But you know she likes her space, so you have to be careful."

"Right," I murmur in response.

"She's never had a boyfriend like this. Even though you guys are engaged. It's just a bit harder for her. She had never given a shit about any of the men like this in her life. So, I imagine she may be scared. She doesn't really know how to interact with people at this level. And she sure as hell has never had a man in her space this way. And Tiana has a way of shutting down when things are changing, even if she doesn't know she's shutting down."

I feel as if this is stuff I already noticed about her, but wasn't sure if it was just a one-off situation or something that may have been happening since she met me, but I'm glad I'm getting more concrete information on her.

Tiana is a closed book; luckily for me, I'm good at opening covers. I don't mind having to work around it. That's part of the reason I love her. She protects her peace.

"When I talked to her about the whiteboard situation, she seemed really ashamed of it. And she said she was scared it would push me away."

"Mmmm. Yeah. She doesn't enjoy bringing out the whiteboard. She's been criticized for it in the past, and back then she didn't really care. But she actually came to me to tell me about it. I think she feared your reaction, that you'd think she was... strange. I don't know." She sighs as she shrugs, her arms wrapping tighter around herself. "She cares about your opinion. Which is a first for Tiana. She's literally never cared about the opinions of others. But I know she doesn't want to lose you. And she's never wanted not to lose someone before. So, I imagine her mind is all sorts of fucked up right now."

"Yeah, she, uh... she mentioned that. I told her I'm here forever, so."

"That's good. Sometimes she'll listen to words. But it's Tiana. You never know with her," Charlotte says.

I smile. "This is true," I say with a small grin as I glance at her.

"Just be patient with her. She's a fast learner, but she has a hard time processing her emotions," she says as she sends a small smile back at me.

Noted.

I nod slowly in acknowledgement.

"She loves you, a lot. That much I know for sure. So just... be kind to her. I know she's figuring things out the way she does. She just does it a little differently," Charlotte adds.

"I'll always be patient with Tiana. She deserves at least that," I respond.

Charlotte glances at me and smiles. "If I had to choose anyone on the team, it would be you. You're good for her. No one has ever taken such good care of Tiana. And I think she knows that."

My smirk tilts higher on one side. "Well, not everyone can be such a supreme specimen, so," I say with a large stretch.

"Oh my God," she playfully groans as she shoves at me again.

I laugh as I slap her hands away. "Come on, let's find the two and grab some pumpkins."

"Let's!" Charlotte giggles before she heads in the opposite direction to meet up with Tiana and Banks.

I shake my head with a laugh before I sprint after her.

CHAPTER NINE
GUNNAR

"Did you have a good chat with Banks?" I ask before I take a bite out of my caramel apple.

When we met back up with them, I didn't realize that the same place I got Tiana's apple cider also had caramel apples, and I had to get one.

Crunching on my apple, I throw an arm around Tiana's shoulder.

She glances up at me with a grimace as she watches me eat my apple. Her eyes volleying between the apple and my mouth.

"It was enlightening. I didn't know you were the one who told Adrian to go after Charlotte."

I crunch another bite out of my apple with a nod. "Oh yeah, he was really fancying the lass, and I told him to just go for it. He was nervous 'cause you know how Banks can be. He didn't know if she would like him because of how quiet he is. So he went for it, and they've just been doing stuff on the side. No biggie. Kinda sucks though, because she tapes his sticks better than anyone else's," I say with a shrug. Though the whole time I'm speaking, I have a massive chunk of apple in my mouth, while gesturing in the air with it.

She grimaces as she watches me. "Is there a reason you have to talk with your mouth full?" she asks.

"I like apples," I say with a shrug as I take another bite.

"How much longer until we go to find our pumpkin?" she asks.

"Well," I start with a mouth full of apple. I chew what little is left and swallow before I point off at the playground with my treat.

Charlotte pushes Banks on one swing, and it seems as if Charlotte is having much more fun than he is.

"Those two said they wanted to wait for the kids to clear out their pumpkins so they'd have a chance to pick the good ones. Which means we have a little time to ourselves," I say before I take another bite.

Her eyes start wandering around the area, locking on to certain areas. "When do you think we should have the wedding?" she asks.

My head tilts as I watch a couple take pictures at one of the decorative pieces in the area. "What were you thinking?" I ask in response.

She's silent for a moment and I glance at her. She leans against me, her arms folded around her. "I don't want a summer wedding... what do you think about spring?" she asks.

I think for a moment. I mean, I feel like we could get that done. I definitely know Tiana could get it planned in less time if I let her go balls to the wall with it and gave her free rein with her time. But that's just not conducive for her.

I know it's something she enjoys and wants to do, but it's also not healthy if she gets too sucked into those things.

"Spring works for me. Whatever you want to do, I'm

happy with, my love," I respond before I lean over to press a kiss to the top of her head.

Her eyes squint as the sun shines down in them, but it makes it look as if she does not want to be here.

"What's wrong?" I ask softly.

I remove my arm and come to stand in front of her, blocking the sun from her face.

"I just have so much planning to do. It's a nice day, but my mind is still stuck on what needs to be done," she says with a sigh. Though her face is... contorted in disappointment.

She seems almost... frustrated. But I don't think it's because we're here. I think it's because she wants to be enjoying this day.

I think she wants to be out of her head for this experience, and she can't pull herself out of it.

But the words Charlotte used come back to mind.

"She needs something interactive to get her out of her head long enough to switch focus."

My eyes roam across the fields and areas, trying to see what would help.

The jumping pad won't help her, too many people. I don't think she would like the tractor.

My eyes roam for a while longer until I spot the corn maze, and a grin rises on my lips.

"Come on, I have an idea," I say.

She looks up at me in confusion, and I smile down at her as I take a hold of her hand, leading her in the direction of the corn maze. But I pause, looking at my half-eaten apple and groan.

Tiana's brow furrows as she looks up at me, and I let go of her hand.

"Stay here, I'll be right back," I tell her before I press a quick kiss to her forehead.

Her brow quirks, and I take that as my cue. Sprinting to the other side of the field, I come up beside Charlotte, where she pushes banks.

"Whatcha' need, friend?" she asks with a smile.

"I'm taking Tiana to the corn maze. Can you keep my apple safe?" I ask.

Her brow furrows in question as she looks between my face and the apple.

"Uh... Sure...? I guess...?" she asks as she offers a hand to me.

"Thanks, you're a treat," I say with a smile. Gingerly, I hand her the stick, ruffling her bun before I run off back to Tiana.

She has her arms crossed against her chest, watching me with a look of utter perplexity. But I ignore it because with what I'm about to do, she's about to be a lot more confused, and I'd rather explain it all at once instead of in bits and pieces.

I take her hand as I approach, leading her to the corn maze. And luckily for me, it seems as if everyone is busy doing stuff elsewhere on the farm. No one is coming in or out of the corn maze.

I let go of her hand, stretching out my arms as I twist my shoulders back and forth to open my back.

Tiana watches me, her brow scrunched in confusion.

"What... the f-" she murmurs.

"Might wanna stretch, sugar. I'm fast," I say with a grin.

"Stretch... for... what?" she asks slowly. Her eyes dart up and down my body, trying to understand.

"I'm going to give you a ten-second head start," I say as I jump a few times, shaking my arms and legs out as I stretch my neck back and forth.

"Ten second start for what?"

"I'm going to chase you," I say with a shrug. Pulling my arm across my chest, I stretch out my shoulder. I throw my arms back and forth around my body before I bring the other arm across my chest and do the same to the other side.

"You're joking," she says incredulously.

"How many times have I actually ever joked with you?" I ask with a feral grin.

Her eyes widen, and I can almost see her heart pounding in them as she realizes I'm being completely serious.

"What do you mean 'chase me'?" she asks.

"You're going to get a ten-second head start into the maze. You have to escape me," I say as I pull my phone out of my pocket, pressing a few things on the screen before I nod to the maze.

Her brows furrow. "And what happens… if-?"

"I'm fucking you," I respond with a shrug.

"YOU WHAT?!" Her jaw drops, and she stands shell-shocked, staring at me.

"If you don't escape me, I'm going to fuck you," I state plainly.

"In the corn maze?!" she asks as she throws her hands toward the entrance of the maze.

And while her face looks shocked, I watch her eyes for a moment longer, seeing the glimmer in them.

I close the distance between us, gripping her chin in my fingers and tilting her face up to mine. Her eyes search mine, trying to decipher the words I told her. But she gets them. I know she does. The idea is easing into her as we speak, and I can see the excitement that swirls in her gaze.

"Do I have permission to fuck you in the corn maze if I catch you?" I ask in a whisper.

Her teeth catch her lower lip as she grins at me. A heated

blush crawls over her cheeks, tinting her skin pink before she nods sheepishly.

"Good," I whisper before I press a kiss to her lips.

I let her go, backing up, and she watches me for a long moment.

Looking down at my phone to make sure I've set the timer, I glance up at her with a grin. "Three... two..."

Her eyes widen in fear, her boots scratching into the dirt as she turns and bolts for the entrance of the corn maze.

Pressing the start button, the timer counts down and I wait, watching...

When the nine shows up, I stop the timer and throw my phone in my pocket before sprinting for the entrance of the maze.

Barreling through some of the first few turns, I realize there is no one here, so I pause, listening for any noises. Soon, I hear the frantic foot pounding and rustle of leaves through the twists and turns in the maze.

I didn't realize when I started this how it would make me feel. There is something inherently primal about this. The feeling of chasing the woman I'm going to fuck at the end of it... I shake my head, focusing on the sounds, and I start my sprint.

I take a left, going down one corridor to be met with a fork, and I take the right. I pause again, listening for the noises, and continue following them.

I've actually never chased someone like this. There's a rush to it, like hunting, and it pushes me faster, harder, with my breaths coming in and out of me in quick bursts. I take several turns and corridors, with the noises of scurrying getting more frantic as I imagine she hears me closing in on her.

My heart pounds fervently in my chest. A whooshing of blood in my ears as it feels like my vision tunnels. All of my focus has gone into trying to spot her. All the while, my cock has hardened to near pain with the excitement of all of this, and I feel like I get closer to her. The idea of finding her, grabbing her and bending her over...

Yeah, primal is a good word for it.

Taking two more turns, I find her. A dead end in a corridor toward the back of the maze, and when I spot her, I whistle with a feral grin.

Tiana turns to me slowly, her chest moving in heavy breaths as she spots me. Her eyes widen, a small look of fear in her eyes. I spear straight for her, and she almost tries to just go through the corn, but I'm faster and I snag her by the back of her neck.

"Gotcha," I whisper.

She makes a small yelp as she tenses in my hold, and I wrap an arm around her waist, pulling her back tight against me.

"Looks like you lost, sugar," I whisper as I lean down to nip at her jaw with a heavy pant against her skin.

Her breaths come out in quick bursts, with the small bit of skin exposed above the neck in her hoodie coated in a shiny gleam of sweat.

"Do I still have your permission to fuck you here?" I ask as I flatten my tongue along the side of her neck, dragging it up. Her sweat has mixed with her perfume and lotion, causing several distinct sensations to flood me. The one in the forefront is pure desire.

"Please... fuck, please," she whimpers feebly.

A grin rises on my lips. "I'm about to breed you like a bitch in heat, and I have zero qualms about it," I whisper as I wrap my arm around her waist, and move my hand to the band of her leggings. Slipping my hand in, I cup her pussy, dipping a finger in to find her with no panties and soaking wet.

"Horny little thing. Getting off to the big man chasing her

through the corn maze. I never thought my wife would be such a naughty freak," I pant against her skin.

"Fuck... Gunnar," she pants softly.

My fingers graze her clit, stroking it softly, trying to work her into a whimpering mess.

"Quiet here, sugar. We don't want them to hear the way you come around my cock," I whisper.

I press two fingers down further, into her, working them in and out as the heel of my palm grinds her clit.

She tries to quiet her noises with gasps and whimpers, her body tensing as she tightens her mouth shut.

"Good girl, sugar. Hold those moans for me. I promise I'll let you scream later," I whisper as I keep working her. I take a few more pumps, before pulling my fingers out of her.

She pants as she gets a moment to relax. All the while, I suck my fingers clean as the other hand unbuttons and unzips my jeans with a quickness. Pulling my cock out, I stroke it with a tight grip as I pull my other fingers from my mouth, using them to find the band of her leggings.

I yank the band of her leggings down. Her breaths are tortured, heavier now, and I know her need is at a high now.

I line myself up with her entrance, my head tilting back in pleasure as I enter her. A low, rough groan rumbles in my throat before I punch forward, filling all of her at once.

She attempts to cry out with a moan, but I quickly bring my hand to her mouth, muffling her.

"I said, quiet, Tiana. I know it's thick, but you can be quiet for me," I pant as I thrust into her.

With one hand on her mouth, I bring the other to her hip, holding her steady as I move in and out of her. I pound and thrust like a man starved, looking to pillage every bit of her pussy that she'll let me. With the grip I have of her mouth, I press her head back to look at me. Her eyes roll, coming back every so often to glimmer with hazy, mindless pleasure. Her gaze will lock on me when her eyes come back, and even through those green pools I can see how much she begs for more. I can see the plea in them, and I move faster.

"You're so fucking pretty when you're filled with my cock. So desperate, so needy, aren't you, baby?" I murmur as I get lost in the look of her eyes.

She nods against my hold as her eyes roll again, drifting away into the passion of it all as her noises muffle behind my palm. Her pussy tightens and flutters around me, and I use the hand on her hip to slip into her leggings, seeking her clit and thrumming over it quickly.

"Fuck, baby, you're close. You're so fucking close. Come for me, clamp that pussy down on my cock so I can pump that womb full of my fuckin' kids," I growl as I rub my fingers quickly over her clit, feeling her climb that summit faster and faster.

"That's it baby, it's right there, grab it. Take it, come for me," I whisper in her ear.

Her body tenses in my grasp. Her back bows against me, and I wrap my arm tighter around her, holding her to me as her pussy clenches and unclenches around my cock.

"There it is. There's my good girl. Ride it out. Take everything you need," I pant, and her hips grind back against me. Soon, she locks me in, and I can't move.

I release a gasp as her tightness causes me to come without warning. Like being hit from the side by a massive fucking defender, my orgasm crashes through me. My cock twitches in hard, full pumps, filling her with every ounce of cum I have.

I growl through the way her pussy continues its waves, milking me, and *hard.*

Fuck, the way she locks me in when I pump her full of cum is a feeling I don't think I would ever experience without her.

Holding myself in, I growl, getting lost in the feel of her orgasm as it chokes my cock. Waiting for her to loosen up, my head falls, resting on the top of hers as I pant softly. I take a few test strokes when I feel her relax, making sure it stays in her.

My hand loosens from around her mouth, sliding down her chin to hang loosely around her throat.

"Holy fuck," I pant with a chuckle. Leaning down, I pepper soft kisses against her jaw over and over, again and again.

"That was... insane," she responds.

"Fuck yeah, it was." I give another small laugh and a deep breath before I slowly pull out. Quickly pulling her pants up so none of it comes out.

I take another deep breath, regaining a hold on my surroundings before I stuff my cock into my boxers and quickly zip and button my pants. When I do, I turn her around, leaning down to press a kiss to her lips.

"We need to do that again," I say with an exhausted smile as I slide my tongue over my lip.

"Let me recover from this time first, jeez," she says playfully with a pant. She leans against me, taking soothing breaths as she recovers.

"Now we've gotta find our way out of here," I say as I look back down the corridor we came. I rub my hands over her sides, and my head leans back down against hers as I rock her from side to side.

She nods as she looks up at me with relaxed and satiated eyes.

Fuck, did that insane plan actually work? Go me.

"Pumpkins?" she asks with a grin as I admire her gaze a second longer.

My smile grows wide as I realize I may actually be helping her in the right way.

"Pumpkins," I respond. Pressing one last kiss to the top of her head, I let go of her hips, moving to grasp her hand and lead her out of the maze.

CHAPTER TEN
TIANA

I hate to say that Gunnar's trick actually worked.

After we made it out of the corn maze, my mind quieted to a point where I could focus on the farm. Gunnar and I picked out pumpkins together. Which was nice to have someone strong to pick them up. I picked a perfectly round, albeit large one because I do the same carving on my pumpkins every year. While Gunnar picked a similar-sized one, just not as perfectly round as mine.

Charlotte and I took pictures at one of the decorative pieces on the farm. Then, Gunnar and I took pictures together before we took pictures of Adrian and Charlotte.

Before we left, I grabbed another little cup of apple cider, and of course, Gunnar bought another caramel apple because he was so hungry from chasing me he devoured the one he had Charlotte hold.

Altogether, it was actually a really great day.

I loved that Gunnar took the time to try and help me get out of my head. When I get stuck in it, it gets so difficult to get out of it and then I almost shut down.

I don't know what things Gunnar learned from Charlotte. But I am glad he talked to her because it seems as if whatever information she gave him must have been right.

I don't know how to ask for help or talk about it. So it means everything to me and more that he actually is observant enough to understand me and my needs. Not to mention the initiative he takes to learn all he can about me.

Granted, it was absolutely horrifying to be chased through a corn maze by a massive man. In the moment, my heart damn near beat out of my chest and I felt like my lungs were going to explode. I could feel the pounding of his steps at the same time I heard him weave through the twists and turns.

But it was... exhilarating. I'd experienced nothing like that before.

Just to be fucked at the end of it? It was... It was *so* incredible.

When he mentioned it at first, I had no idea what to think. I mean, what *can* you think?

"Hey, I want to chase you in the corn maze and fuck you."

How the fuck do you respond to that?! So I went with it, because I've learned somehow that his methods sometimes just *work*.

I can confidently say there is nothing on God's green earth that would have lead me to the conclusion he had.

And when he counted down...

The *thrill*. Running away with the only thought on my mind was... *escape*. There's no way you can think about wedding plans or any other tasks you have to do when you feel like you have to outrun an apex predator.

But all of it just reminds me why I chose this man in the first place.

He doesn't chastise me for being in my head, or get

annoyed that I'm stuck. He just wants to help, and he wants to make it better.

That fills something in me. Something deep in my soul that makes me realize how fucking shitty the guys I dated in the past were.

Because I *do* deserve to be loved like this. And I'm glad that Gunnar gave me the chance to see it.

However, I do wish that he could chase me out of this rink right now because the owner of the team has come in to speak to all of us.

I never enjoy having to be around a bunch of people at once, and I especially don't enjoy the owner of the team.

All the hockey players have paused on the ice, leaning against their sticks, considering the man has come in *during* practice. Gunnar, specifically, since I can never keep my eyes off the brute, has his stick behind his head with his arms slung over either end. Though he sways his hips back and forth because the man can't seem to stay still. Even now, his mouth guard is caught between his teeth, and he shifts his jaw back and forth to play with it.

The rest of the admin, physical therapists and some of the other side coaches stand in the boxes. Unfortunately, that includes me.

"Long time no see, Stags! You guys have had an amazing season so far. One of the best ones in a long time," the man says.

A tall specimen, clad in a black Armani suit with shiny black Tom Ford loafers, he has an enormous beaming white smile of veneers. His hair is gelled for the gods, with not a single hair out of place. Beside him, is an almost carbon copy, except the copy is younger.

Don't really know the younger one. But I do know the older one.

Santiago Ramirez.

He bought the Stags, God I don't even know how long ago. I don't see him that often, but I correspond with him, considering some of his deals and contracts sometimes go through me after they go through my mother.

It's been a while since he's actually been to the rink. I think he may have been up at the firm for Gunnar's signing, but I didn't get to see him since I wasn't even there.

I know that my dad wanted Gunnar, but I think Santiago had to approve him.

Aside from owning The Stags, he apparently owns a large social media company? I'm not sure. He can be rude sometimes. But I suppose if you are a billionaire, sometimes that just happens.

"As you can tell, I have a new friend here with me today. This is Ricardo; he's my son. I'm sure you guys may have seen some of his movies as of late. He's a movie director, and he's looking at purchasing his own sports team at some point, so this is a 'bring your kid to work day' situation," he says as he claps the young man on the shoulders and shakes him back and forth softly before ruffling his hair.

Ahhhh yes. That makes sense. I think I remember learning about the owner's family at some point. Him and his wife run the social media company, and he has, I think, three kids? Two girls and a boy. I think one does dressage in the Olympics, and the third is sort of out of the public eye. I don't really know.

"You guys have been doing so well that I'm going to give a little gift to the community. You all are going to be doing Trunk or Treat for the kids! This gives them a chance to see some of their favorite players, and you guys get to get out of a game weekend for once," Santiago says as he claps his hands together.

The players furrow their brows as they look between themselves. But Gunnar has an air of excitement. I'm not sure why. But it's a tad endearing seeing the smile on his face.

I'm just glad I don't have to participate.

I may love fall, but I abhor Halloween. I hate Trick or Treating. Having to talk to so many strange people repeatedly for candy.

I hate costumes also, to be fair. And the energy on Halloween nights is always so suffocating. I just can't stand it.

"It'll happen in a few weeks from now, before Halloween day, on one of the Friday's you guys have a game. It was going to be an exhibition match anyway for fun, but I thought this would be a better way to give back to the people," Santiago says.

The players all clap and Santiago and Ricardo take a bow before they walk back down the carpet to exit through the tunnel.

My dad whistles, commanding some players to roll up the carpet to hand off to some of the arena maintainers.

I blow out an annoyed breath as I roll my eyes. As I wait for the rest of the admin to file out in front of me, the sound of skating starts up in the background of my thoughts before I hear a whistle.

But like a dog, I know the sound of Gunnar's whistle and I turn around to look at him. I let some people behind me go ahead of me as I look to him with a lifted-arm shrug and a furrow on my brow.

He nods for me to wait as the other players skate past him, so he has an opening, and when he finds it, he skates toward me.

There's something... so fucking sexy about the way he takes a leisurely press on the ice. No real speed to him, just moving nice and easy.

However, he purposely slams into the wall harder than

necessary, folding completely over it and my brow contorts in shock as I back up.

"The fuck is your problem?" I ask with a scrunch of my brow.

He unfolds from the wall to look down at me with a grin. "Sorry, I saw an angel and had to make sure it was real."

I roll my eyes at him with a playful smile as I cross my arms over my chest. "Make it quick, I have work to do."

"We're going to do Trunk or Treat," he says with a grin.

"I know you are. Have fun," I say with a confused expression.

Why does he think I didn't know that? Weird.

"No. *We* are," he says again. Though, this time he points to the two of us.

"What do you mean 'we'?" I ask as my brow scrunches again.

"You. Me. Trunk. Treat," he reiterates.

"Gunnar... I hate Trick or Treating. It's so many people and I have to interact and dress up. It's just not my thing," I remind him.

"So, I know you, and I know you'd say that, so I came up with a counter offer," he says.

I roll my eyes as I bring my hands to my temples, rubbing softly. "What is this counteroffer?" I ask with a sigh.

"We go get costumes. We do Trunk or Treat, and whatever you want to do on the night of Halloween is allll yours," he says with a grin and a confident nod.

My eyes narrow on him, searching his eyes. "Whatever I want?"

He nods proudly.

"Including wedding planning?" I ask skeptically.

"Especially wedding planning." His grin widens, and I'm

reminded that this man is very good at knowing what I like for rewards.

I watch him for a moment, weighing the terms, before I let out a groan.

"Fine... *Fine,* we will do this... Trunk or Treat. But I'm not talking to the people," I say.

"That's fine. I wasn't asking you to. I just want to be there with you," he says, and the way he says it tells me it really is just him wanting me to be there.

I can't say no to that. Even if I want to.

I fight the smile that tries to pull at my cheeks, and I hum playfully at him as I shake my head.

"Perfect. I gotta go do goon shit. Love you," he says as he grabs a stick behind the wall.

I roll my eyes, losing the smile contest with myself because this man just... ahhhh, this man.

He leans in to kiss me, and I kiss back before he skates off. Then, I make my way back down the tunnel to my office.

CHAPTER ELEVEN
GUNNAR

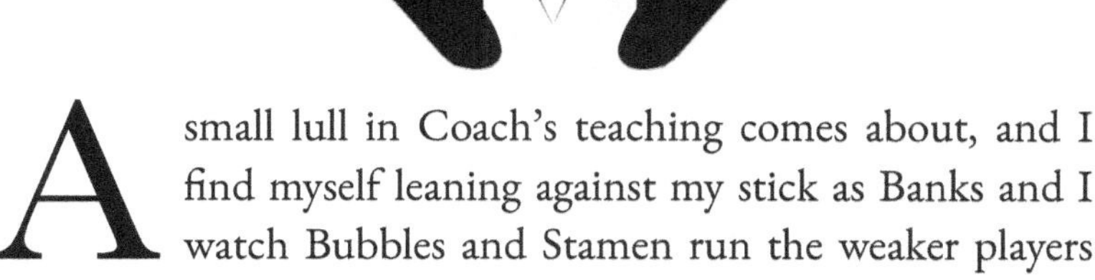

A small lull in Coach's teaching comes about, and I find myself leaning against my stick as Banks and I watch Bubbles and Stamen run the weaker players through some drills.

Pressing my mouth guard from the front of my teeth, I twist it with my tongue so I can clasp it between them. All the while, my mind gets away from me.

Whenever I have something to watch, where I can zone out, my thoughts always seem to scatter.

One of said scatterings, has been the idea of a house for Tiana and I. While she has been very focused on the wedding, I've been thinking about roots.

Stuff like that is important to me. I like knowing where we're going to lock in to the ground and build our big ol' family tree.

"Hey, I've been thinking about something recently," I murmur through my mouth guard to Banks.

"Didn't know you were capable of thought other than pussy and hockey," Banks responds. I glance over at him with a small smirk, he merely has his arms across his chest as he watches because he moved his stick behind the wall with Charlotte.

I lean up from my stick, taking a big stretch before I sling it over my shoulders. Then I hang my arms over each end.

"Well, a man has priorities. But I'm looking for land, and I know you've got some over yonder somewhere. I'm trying to find a place to... ya know. Settle down, get the land out of the way so I can build my little lady a house," I say as I twist my upper body back and forth, while my feet twist in the opposite direction on the ice. The result is a few loud pops running up my spine.

Banks glances at me as my spine pops, his eyes flicking to my back before they come up to my face. "And she makes it a home?"

I pause my stretch with a glance, and I press my mitt out for him over my stick. He bumps it with a nod before his arms fold back over his chest.

"I got land here if you wanna take a look at it," he says.

My brow furrows as I swing my stick from my shoulders to lean against as I place the blade back on the ice. "You'd sell some land to me?" I ask.

He nods. "Don't see why not. I reckon Charlotte and Miss Tiana would be more than happy to be close to one another."

"Well, it's gotta be a good distance away because Tiana needs her space. How much land you got?" I throw my stick to the side before I get on all fours on the ice, taking the time to stretch out my legs as we talk. With one leg out in front of me, I lean forward, pulling deep into my hammy.

Banks glances up, his mouth moving silently as if he's counting. "'Bout two hundred fifty acres."

"The fuck for?!" I ask as I come up from my stretch in shock.

"Got horses. Need land. Don't think I'd be able to live in a place without land," he says with a shrug.

I watch him for a moment before I go back into my stretch. "Where at?"

"Just outside Tacoma. Bit of a drive, but real worth it. I'm used to waking up early, so Charlotte and I get out here together, and she sleeps a bit on the way in."

"Charlotte lives with you?" I ask as I switch legs and stretch that one out.

He nods. "Yup. Moved out of her apartment and lives in my lil' ranch house with me. On the weekends we roam the property. My lil' filly loves her."

My brow furrows as I listen to him, and I continue my stretches.

I've had this thought since I saw Tiana with her books that I bought her. There was no house that would be perfect for her. I knew that from the jump. She's too specific.

She needs something built *just* for her. Something she can build to her heart's content. Maybe I'll look at the land, see what can be done with it and then go from there. If I really need to, maybe I'll talk to Bubbles and see if she can get some time off so she can get some of that planning out of the way that she would like to.

The problem is, she's planning the wedding as well. But... I feel like all of those things together would make her happy. Once season ends, I imagine she'll have time and she can plan as long as she wants.

Only as long as she takes a break and takes care of herself.

That much I think we can do.

I look to Banks. "You really wouldn't mind selling some land to me if I needed it?"

He nods. "Got plenty of it. I'd rather sell it to you than someone else. At least I'd be able to still use it."

"What use could you have for it other than horses?" I butterfly my legs behind me on the ice as my hands plant down, stretching out my inner thighs, moving my legs in and out.

"I like huntin'. Got a few spots picked out and if you happen to pick a place with one of my spots I'd have to work into the contract that I'm allowed to hunt on it," he says with a grin.

Those damned cogs in my brain turn, thinking about how I need to go about this.

I think I have an idea. But it'll take some finessing.

Luckily for me, and for Tiana, I can finesse basically anything.

Coming up from my stretch, I pull my feet under me on the ice before I jump out of it and come to a stand.

"I'll text you," I tell him with a soft pant and a grin before I press my glove out to him

He bumps it and gives me a terse nod.

A bit of excitement flows through me at the idea of picking out land for my little lady. Though, there is apprehension about how the fuck I need to do this without her finding out. I think I can do it. I just have to be sneaky.

I don't have time to think too much on it, because Bubbles' whistle goes off, signaling for us to come back. I bend over to pick up my stick before I grab my helmet from the wall and slam it on my head to get back to work.

Tiana

The night is blissfully cool as Gunnar and I take Tucker out to potty.

The sky is clear, with steam floating from our noses and Tucker's excited breathing as we make our way to the bench inside the fenced-in dog area.

This has become part of our routine. We come home, we get ready for the night, and then take Tucker out before we do whatever it is we decide to end our night with.

Whether that's... a nice little tryst or just a cuddle in the bed.

And I like this part of the night. It's quiet, it's a relaxing end of the day. We don't say much, we just enjoy eachother and the world around us.

I always stretch when we get outside, getting a chance to look up at the sky and see which constellations are showing their faces.

"Orion is out tonight," I murmur softly as I look over all the stars.

Gunnar's hand is a strong point of contact as he holds it above me, with my neck craning back as I spin, seeing the constellations from different angles.

He holds my hand up, holding me steady as I spin. And when I come back from the swirling gaze, my eyes come to him, where his face holds a sweet admiration. His eyes lowered in contentment, with a considering smile on his face.

Leading me to the bench, we sit and he bends over to take off Tucker's leash. He bundles it in his hand before he grasps at my cheek with the other to pull me in for a kiss.

His lips are soft, slow, sweet, taking their time before he leans back to press his forehead to mine.

"You're a beaut, Titi," he whispers softly as he strokes a thumb over my cheek.

I smile as I lean in to kiss him again, bringing my hands up to hold his face.

His free hand moves to my waist, pulling me closer to him, and I release our kiss to snuggle into him. He's always so hot, like a furnace, and it's nice on these cooler nights.

There is always a calmness to this routine. Where the dark falls around us, and the stars lie above. It feels like I'm the only person on this planet with him.

It's a strange feeling. But a good one. Because I'd never had someone make me feel like I was the only thing that mattered.

I never knew it was what I needed. With all the stress of life recently, zeroing in and out of my interests and duties, the day can get away from me.

My thoughts will run, and the world will get heavy. But there is something about... him. *This.*

Time under the stars. That makes the world feel as if... it's just us.

And I love that. I never knew this is what *this* could feel like.

"My parents want you to come to the house," he whispers. "They want to meet you formally."

Well... *That...* I did not know those words could feel like... *that...*

It feels as if ice runs through my veins. "What...?" I murmur.

I pull away from him, looking up into his eyes with a shell-shocked gaze as my heart falls *deep* into my stomach, pounding so hard it stirs bile there.

"My parents. They invited us for dinner. They want to meet you." The way he says it is so normal, and his smile. It's so... warm!?

It does *not* mimic the way my insides feel. Because in my

head, I essentially *lied* to them, *stole* their car and did things to it! And they don't even *know*!

I scoot away from him on the bench, my gaze blanking over as my breaths come quicker and my hands flap at my chest as I try to calm down. It feels like my head begins to lighten and I almost feel like I'm hyperventilating.

"What do you mean?! I-... They... I *lied* to them! I told them the Stags wanted to take the truck! They're going to hate me when they find out I *lied*! What do I do? How am I going t-"

His lips collide with mine as he tugs me back into his body, and it silences me. It stuns me enough that I end up focusing on him. He kisses me a moment longer before he pulls away and looks down into my eyes.

"Sugar... deep breath. Come on," he whispers, but there is a mild severity in his gaze.

"Gunnar, I-" I almost plead.

"No... Deep breath, let's go."

His voice is so stern that I'm not able to argue any further. My lips suck in as my eyes widen, and I nod slowly. I keep my eyes on his as I breathe in deep through my nose.

He nods as he watches me, his eyes volleying back and forth between mine while he breathes in with me.

"Out," he mouths before we blow our breaths out together.

I slowly blow the breath out, letting it quell a small bit of my racing heart as I look up at him. Though there is the smallest hint of fear that runs through my blood.

He holds my face in his hands, his eyes searching mine for a moment longer.

"My parents already know about the truck. I told them I was going to ask you to marry me, and the one I was asking fixed the truck. And I don't think they could ever hate you now. My mother especially," he whispers with a small smile.

The nerves slowly wane away. My heart rate slowly going back down as I listen to his words.

"They... they're not mad?" I say with a small, relieved breath.

"Babe, there's no way in hell that my mom would ever hate you after what you did to Pa's truck," he says. His smile widens just enough, and I'm able to give a small smile in response.

I take one final deep breath, letting it take the rest of my initial fears away.

"Okay... okay, well that's good," I whisper as I blow out the breath.

He pulls me back in for a kiss, letting go as Tucker interrupts us. Carrying a ball he found, he drops it at Gunnar's feet with heavy breathing as he waits for Gunnar to pick it up. Gunnar leans down, grabbing it and chucking it far to the other end of the field, leaving Tucker to bolt after it. He wipes his hand off on his sweats as his other arm splays over the back of the bench. I cuddle into his side, leaning my head back against his arm to stare up at the stars.

And for a moment, it's quiet. Save for the sound of Tucker running in the grass and our soft breathing. Until my thoughts get the better of me.

"Why didn't you ever tell me about your grandpa?" I ask quietly.

It's silent for another long moment, and the stars twinkling above are a focus point for me as I wait for him to respond.

"Ah... Never thought it was... something to dwell on," he says softly. His voice is slow, as if he's thinking.

I glance at him from the corner of my eye to see him staring up at the stars as well.

"But... you can tell he meant a lot to all of you. I'm

surprised you never said more about him." My hand comes up to rub his chest softly, trying to offer a comforting touch for him.

Tucker runs up to us again, and my head tilts down to watch as Gunnar leans from the bench, grabs the ball, and tosses it back down the field.

He wipes his hand off on his sweats again before he leans back.

"Pa was great. But he didn't let me sit with the sad things for too long. Game losses, or hard checks that hurt. It was hard, but he was a goon. All the Hayze boys are. He wasn't going to let any of us take disrespect, and that started with him, ya know?" he says quietly.

I get lost in his words, watching the stars as his voice weaves through my ears.

"Pa made sure we were strong. He let us cry when we needed to, and then we moved on from there. Sadness is not something to dwell on when there is so much life to live, and he made sure we all knew that. I've cried my tears for him, and now I just live with his memory," he says. As I glance at him from my stargazing, I see a small smile rise on his lips.

"How come you never told me?" I ask.

"Well, I told you about the truck, and that was enough for me. But, uh." He pauses, and I see him chew on the inside of his lip. There is sadness in his eyes. One where it looks as if the loss still hurts him, but he tries to hold on to the strength to make it appear as if it doesn't.

He shakes his head as he sniffs hard and clears his throat. "I don't uh... I don't dwell on it..." he pauses again, taking a deep breath. "He lived a good, long life. And I try to keep his memory alive in the best way that I can. I know he's somewhere up there. I hear his voice with every goal... in every celly. And that makes it better. It makes all the hard days worth it.

The bad practices. The good ones. He's up there somewhere. He's tellin' me to keep my head up, watch the puck, and check 'em where it hurts."

His eyes search the stars, as if he's trying to find the things he looks for, his teeth still nibbling on his inner lip as he watches. A small tear runs from the corner of his eye, and he sniffs once before he lets out a big sigh.

Watching him for a moment, I bring a hand up, wiping the tear away with my thumb. He glances at me with a small smirk before he looks back up at the stars.

I follow his gaze, looking up at those stars. Where part of his past lives.

I nuzzle closer into his body, resting my head into his shoulder as I wrap my arms around his waist. His arm comes from the bench to wrap around me before he leans over to press a kiss to my forehead.

"He'd love you, sugar. I have no doubt about it," he whispers as he rubs my shoulder.

"I would love him too," I respond quietly.

CHAPTER TWELVE
TIANA

Why do I let this man talk me into stuff like this?

I really have no idea.

The dick must be astronomical because the second he tempts me with it, I'm on my fucking hands and knees ready to take all of it.

Case in point, being in a costume store looking for outfits for this Trunk or Treat situation I've been talked in to.

From the second we started getting ready this morning, he was itching to get out and to this store to look for costumes. The whole time we drove here, his eyes were unfocused, clearly in his thoughts.

I personally don't understand Halloween. I'm a grown woman; if I want candy, I'll go buy it. I don't want or *need* to go door-to-door interacting with total strangers. I can see why some people do, but personally I just fucking hate it.

I *abhor* it. But if I get to have free rein of our Halloween night, fine, we can do this 'Trunk or Treat' thing.

He hasn't said a single word on his idea. As soon as we parked, he bolted from the car. He even had to do a double take and come back to the car to open my door for me, because I guess he remembered that he has his code to live by.

But the entire time he was waiting for me to get out of the car, he was shifting on his feet.

He was like a police dog wanting to get to work on a course, just riled up to the heavens.

So now he has been... *running* through this store, almost. Because his legs are so long, I have a hard time keeping up with his determined strides.

"So... what..." I ask as I follow him through the store. He is looking EVERYWHERE, for *something*.

"I think we should be a deer and a road... car... something. I don't know; we'll workshop it. But I'm definitely going to be a deer," he mumbles as he shifts and looks through every single costume in the store.

My brow furrows at the idea. As well as the... confidence...? Conviction?? In all of this planning.

He must take Halloween seriously.

"And why?" I ask.

"Well because our love was like a deer caught in headlights. I really love the Stags, you love cars, I think all of it makes sense," he says as he stands on his tip toes to reach a costume that is extremely high up on the wall.

I hate this idea.

Because it's right in an abstract sort of way. And I can't help how clever it is.

"So what am I supposed to wear if you're obviously the deer?" I ask.

"I was thinking you dressed like a road with headlights on your boobies," he says. "Ah ha!" he laughs triumphantly as he finally grabs the costume he was reaching for.

His smile is infectious as he holds up a deer costume. He is so proud of himself, and I can't help but smile back at his child-like excitement.

I look over the costume in his hands. A massive onesie situation with a large patch of white fur along the chest. It's honestly more like expensive pajamas than a costume, but whatever. If he's happy, I'm happy, I guess.

Soon, my eyes move up to his face.

"Gunnar, this is a kid's event, I can't have headlights on my tits," I say with a quirk of my brow.

Flinging the costume over his arm, he starts moving through the store again, going to the accessories.

"Right. Youuuuuu are right, sugar," he says mindlessly as his focus shifts. Next, he goes through some of the random pieces that go with the costumes.

Vampire teeth, body paint, glitter, wigs, and all sorts of other pieces.

"Can you tell me what the hell you're looking for?" I ask as I look at a random zombie costume on the wall.

Sometimes this man gets in these modes where he just doesn't speak because he is so focused on finding whatever it is he's looking for. A very common occurrence? His car keys, for some reason. The man cannot keep track of the car keys, even if I have them in a little basket on the kitchen island.

Like right now, he is so focused on whatever it is he's looking for that, I suppose I'll just help him with... whatever the fuck is happening, I really don't even know.

"I am looking for antlers. Can't be a stag without antlers," he responds mindlessly as he keeps looking through a rack of wigs.

My brow furrows with a sigh before I swing my backpack off one shoulder to dig through it, looking for my phone. When I get my phone, I pull up my shopping app, looking for a pair of nice costume antlers. Once I find some, I add them to the cart and check out.

"I bought you antlers, now what is it we're doing about this road costume situation?" I ask as I put my phone back in my backpack and sling it back over my shoulders.

He pauses over a costume, tilting his head and grabbing it from the rack before he turns around to me with a grin.

"Sugar," he whispers.

I glance at the thing in his hand.

A tight black cat costume.

My brow furrows as I look over it. "The fuck is this?" I ask.

"Can I fuck you in this?" His tone is hushed as he steps up close to me.

My head tilts as my jaw drops. "In this?" I ask as I pinch at it.

"I mean... technically you wouldn't be in it when we start, but I would like to take it off of you if that's on the table at all," he says with a grin.

My eyes narrow. "Do you think about anything other than sex and hockey?"

"So, funny you say that. Banks actually asked me the same thing the other day an-"

"Oh, so Adrian can ask you at practice but I can't ask my sister?" I ask as I throw my arms out.

"I didn't technically talk about sex. He merely said he didn't know I could think about things other than pussy and hockey," he says with a shrug.

I roll my eyes with a sigh. "Anyway. Back to my question."

"Do I think about anything other than sex and hockey? Yes...? Question mark?" he says with a nervous grin and a cautionary scrunch to half of his face.

My face slacks in stony skepticism.

"Okay, yes... I do. But mostly, my brain is just focused on

getting you pregnant and checking people," he says with a shrug.

"Getting me pregnant?" I ask as a shy tint crawls across my cheeks.

The smile on his face grows as he steps closer, closing the distance between us as he takes my chin in his hand to tilt my face up to him.

"You told me you got your IUD taken out. If I get to fill that pussy with my spend, I'm gonna take any and *every* chance I can to make that shit happen," he whispers before he kisses me softly.

My breaths lighten and my eyes merely watch his as I freeze where I am.

"I told you, I'm trying to make you a mother, baby," he adds with a small nip to my lip, tugging on it before he lets go and leans back up.

"Can I ask what the obsession is with seeing me pregnant? No judgement, merely... curiosity," I say with a nervous breath.

"I just wanna see you carrying my baby. I think you'd be so fucking sexy," he says with a grin.

I scoff with mock enthusiasm. "Am I not sexy now?" I ask.

"Oh, you're sexy in every way. But I'm tryna plant a seed, baby," he says as he lays a soft slap to my ass.

I push him away with a grimace. "Don't ever say no shit like that to me again," I mumble.

He laughs as he stumbles away. "Oooo pulled out the feisty Tiana, I like it," he says as he adjusts the jersey that's on top of his hoodie.

I roll my eyes because it's rare that I code-switch. But if I hear some dumb shit, it just slips out because hello? The audacity?

"Seed?" I ask with a grimace as I look him up and down incredulously. My arms fold against my chest as I watch him.

"Yeah, I mean, what else am I gonna say?" he asks as he hangs the costume back up and walks toward the checkout.

"I don't know. Literally any of the other things you've ever said," I say as I follow him, my eyes looking over some of the other costumes that we pass.

"That's fair, sugar," he says as he places the costumes on the counter.

The cashier rings up his costume and we leave shortly after, his hand tight in mine as we walk back out to the parking lot.

He's obviously a lot calmer now that he's gotten his little hyper-fixation thing out of the way. He damn near skips as he swings my hand between us, and I fight the smile on my cheeks as I glance at him.

Happy as a clam.

I shake my head with a small chuckle as we continue through the parking lot and to the car.

We took the BMW today, so when I go to the driver's side, Gunnar opens the door for me before he closes it and rounds the front of the vehicle to get in the passenger seat.

He throws himself in and puts the bag into the back seat before he looks at me with a relieved grin.

I give him a playful roll of my eyes as I lean over to tap his thigh softly. Turning on the car, I throw it into gear.

"So this dinner," I ask as I pull out of the parking lot.

His hand comes over to rest on my thigh as he settles into his seat.

"Tomorrow. I've already told them they need to have your steak and potatoes ready," he says with a soft sigh of calm. He throws his other hand over the back of his headrest, gripping it as he relaxes in his seat.

My heart clenches in my chest as a small smile crests my lips.

"Thanks babe," I say softly.

"Of course, sugar. I'd never take you somewhere you couldn't eat," he says as he takes my hand in his, pulling it up to kiss softly.

I'm glad that he knows my aversion to certain foods. Or at least some of my anxiety when it comes to eating with other people. I just have a thing for textures that makes it difficult for me to eat everything that someone else would. Going to other people's houses to eat is always scary because I don't know what they may eat, and I don't want to pretend to like something because I'm not the best at lying. Having to eat things I'm not comfortable with is just distressing sometimes.

I wish it weren't. But I've had to learn to live with it because that's just how it is.

My mind comes back to the actual day... My nerves climb the longer I think about having to talk to them, put on a face, *and* interact with them. I could barely do it the first time I met them. But now I have to actually communicate and seem like I'll be a good daughter-in-law.

I've never even met any of my ex-boyfriend's parents, and now I'm going to meet my father- and mother-in-law.

I can do my job in court because that's my job. There's a face I know how to interact with, a persona I know how to slip in to.

With this, it's all uncharted waters, and that terrifies me.

What if I say something wrong? Or move wrong? Wear the wrong thing?

All the what-ifs run through my head, through my heart, and settle in my stomach to whirl with fear and nausea of just plain failing at this.

"Is there anything specific I need to know about them to interact with them well?" I ask as I take a turn down a road back toward the complex.

"Nope. They're pretty even keel people. I told them you

are different when it comes to communicating, so they'll know what to expect. I just don't want you to be uncomfortable. But I promise it'll all be okay. They already really like you for the truck," he says encouragingly.

I glance at him with a sweet yet apprehensive smile.

I can't believe the lengths he always goes through to make things easier for me.

"That works for me," I say with a sigh. "But that doesn't mean that I won't be scared. You should have seen me when I had to do some of the truck stuff." I shake my head as I remember having to actually take his grandpa's truck from their property to get it fixed up.

Adrian had gone with me, and he had to do all the talking. And even though I barely said anything, I still felt like my stomach was going to eject from my throat.

But now they know I'm marrying their son and everything is going to be different when they see me now.

Absolutely horrifying, no matter how I look at it.

"Oh, yeah. Banks already told me. He said he's never seen you that frazzled," he says with a laugh.

My brow furrows as my jaw drops and I look at him. "He told you?" I ask.

"Of course. He couldn't believe how easily it got you. Honestly, I was a bit surprised. But I also kind of knew it would be one of those things for you when I found out every-thing. A toss-up, I reckon. I'd have to see it to know for sure." He shrugs.

I shake my head.

These men talk too much to *each other* and not enough to me or Charlotte.

Hell, maybe they do talk to Charlotte.

I don't know. They seem to know everything before I actu-ally do.

"Do you think they'll actually like me? The truck situation aside?" I ask nervously.

The thought seeps deeper into me. Because, sure, they could like me for the truck. But that's different from actually liking me as a person.

What if I don't seem normal to them? I don't like making eye contact, and I'll have to focus on their faces. I have to... pretend I'm being a person who enjoys communication and interaction, when in reality; I hate it.

"What time is the dinner tomorrow?" I ask in an attempt to stop the what-ifs.

"Six p.m.," he says with a yawn as he releases my thigh to put his arm over the headrest of my seat.

I nod slowly, committing that time to memory.

"Is there anything I need to wear?"

"Well clothes is a good start, I reckon. I don't really want my brothers to see your boobies," he says with a shrug.

My head tilts to deadpan a bored glare at him.

He puts his hands up in surrender. "Listen, I think that's fair. Do *you* want my brothers to see your boobies? No? Good, I thought so."

"Gunnar," I groan as we finally turn into the parking garage of our complex.

"I'm kidding, sugar. We're a family of men; we don't give a shit what you wear as long as you're comfortable. I don't even know if Brooks will be wearing a shirt."

I sigh as I park the BMW next to the Vette and the truck, turning off the engine before turning to him.

Looking down at my fingers, I pick at my cuticles, willing up the courage to speak.

"I'm nervous," I admit quietly.

I glance up at him, seeing the way his head tilts as a small frown forms on his face.

"Sugar, I promise it'll be okay. They're simple people. You think I just spawned out of the womb this way? I was raised by them, you know," he says with a playful smile, attempting to cut the tension inside of me.

A small smile pulls at the corner of my mouth as I look at him.

"I've just never done this before. And my first introduction to them wasn't exactly under normal circumstances."

"No, but it gave you a head start into their hearts," he says softly.

I watch him for a moment longer before I lean in to give him a hug. His hands wrap around my back, stroking it soothingly.

"It'll be okay, I promise," he whispers. Nuzzling deeper into my neck, he presses gentle kisses to the exposed skin of my collarbone that peeks out from under my hoodie. Not a sensual or seductive type of kissing, just a sweet and comforting type.

I take a deep breath, nodding into his shoulder before we pull apart and I bring a hand to his cheek. Stroking over the skin, I look into his eyes.

There aren't many times I enjoy eye contact. It makes me uncomfortable. But there is something about the hazel pools when he's trying to help me.

They're sure. They're steady, and most of all, they're *proud*.

And I feel like I should feel the same about myself. But it's hard.

I just want them to accept me the way he has. But all I can do is try. Because if Gunnar were in the same position, I know he would do the same.

CHAPTER THIRTEEN
GUNNAR

I feel like Tiana has taken way too long to get out of the bedroom.

She went in earlier today to get ready, and I've just been sitting on the couch watching some of the other hockey games that have gone on over the weekend.

Toronto is going absolutely fuckin' nutso this season, and we have to play them in a few weeks. To be fair, I'm scared of the Canadians. They don't play when it comes to hockey; they destroy, and as a brand new rookie on an NHL team? Yeah, I reckon I'll be shitting bricks.

Anyway, Tiana said she wanted to get ready on her own today, and she's been in there ever since. She was in shambles while she waited for her coffee, worried the edges of her fingers as she paced back and forth.

She had gone so far into her head that I don't think anything I said was going to help her.

Especially if none of my earlier words helped her at all? Yeah, there was nothing I was going to be able to do to get her out of this one.

Not even a moderate wienering.

I've learned that when she gets like this, as long as she's not outright panicking, she's trying to figure things out for herself, so I let her work through them until she's ready to come and talk to me about it. That's easy enough for her.

But now I know what her strife is. And I don't think she'll be okay until the entire ordeal is over and done with.

I can see why she's afraid. The whole parent thing is a big deal for her. But I think she'll realize it's not as bad once we're finally there.

Eventually, she finally comes out of the back bedroom. Her hair is pulled into a bun. Like a polished messy bun. It's beautiful, to be honest. Her hair is always pretty, but it's more put together in this bun she's made today.

She's decided to wear one of *her* Seattle Stags jerseys over a black hoodie. Similar to what I wear, and a smile tugs at my face at the same time happiness tugs at my heart. I got one made for her with my name on it, but it fits her better.

She also wears a pair of bell-bottom jeans, and I can't help how cute she looks in all of it.

Today, I've donned my normal hoodie and jersey combo, with a pair of jeans and Air Force Ones. Nothing too incredibly intricate, considering we're going to be carving pumpkins and I'll have to get my hands dirty.

Turning off the tv, I place the remote on the coffee table before I stand and take a huge stretch with a yawn.

As I shake off the stretch and the yawn, I shove my hands into my pockets as I approach her, looking down at her with a big smile.

"You look good, baby," I say as I lean down to kiss her.

"You don't think it's too underdressed?" she asks nervously.

"Babe, I think it would be an issue if you overdressed, to be fair. They're not dressy people, so I think you did well. It's a house full of hockey players. I reckon a hockey jersey is your best bet with them," I say with a grin.

She takes a deep breath as she nods, looking around for her little backpack before she moves to the front door to put on her Uggs.

Once she grabs her backpack, she throws it on her back and leans against the wall to tug each of her Uggs on before we leave the apartment. She holds the door open for me as I duck under the threshold and wait for her to lock it behind me. Soon, she's moving so damn fast that I find myself taking larger strides as she leads us to the elevator.

"Slow down, speed racer. Jesus," I call out to her.

She stops in her tracks, turning around slowly to look at me before she sighs in frustration.

"Sorry, I'm just... really nervous," she groans.

My lips tilt in a smirk as I come up next to her. I reach down, taking her hand into mine and bringing it up to my lips to kiss the back of it. Gripping it tight, I guide her to the elevator at an even pace so she's forced to slow down just enough.

After the two elevators, we make it to the parking garage, where she tries to get into the driver's seat of the truck.

Jumping ahead, I stop her, keeping my hand on the door to keep her from getting in.

She looks up at me with an angered brow. "The hell is that for?"

"First off, you're not driving. You almost sprinted down here because of how in your thoughts you are. Secondly, no," I say.

She narrows her eyes on me. "You're mean," she murmurs as she starts walking to the passenger side.

I follow to open the door for her before she climbs in and buckles up with a huffy cross of her arms.

I lean into the truck, my hands braced against the door frame and the top of the truck's passenger door window.

"Better knock off the attitude," I murmur softly. I give her a serious gaze, but it's only because maybe I can distract her with playing brat, seeing as how it's something she's been liking.

She glares at me. "Or what?" she murmurs.

"I'll fuck it out of you," I respond.

Her cheeks tint a bright pink and she glances away, shifting in her seat.

I bring my tone back down. "I love you, sugar," I say with a sweet grin.

"Get in the truck, please," she grumbles as she looks away.

"I know you love me too; it's alright," I say with a laugh as I close the door and move back to the driver's side. Climbing in, I start up the truck to head out to my parent's house.

"Oh my goodness, it's so nice to finally meet you!" my mother, Claire, says as she wraps her arms tightly around Tiana.

I watch as Tiana's eyes widen to saucers, like a little lemur. Her arms hesitantly come around to hug my mother back, and she tightens her grip around Tiana, rocking her back and forth.

It's like she's a long lost daughter she's finally found.

I truly can't help the warmth in my chest at the way my mother already loves her.

Soon, she pulls away, her hands gripping tight on Tiana's shoulders as she looks in her face.

"You are absolutely stunning," she says sweetly.

Tiana blushes as she gives her a soft, nervous nod. "Thank you," she says quietly.

"When Gunnar told me about the truck, I couldn't believe the girl he was marrying had done something so thoughtful and generous," my mother says as she pats the corner of her eye. It's as if she's remembering that day and trying not to let a tear escape.

"He has been such an incredible anchor in my life. He deserved it more than anything and I'm so glad that I was able to do something like that for him, and for you guys as well. It's been a gift to be able to learn about Buck and his influence on your family," Tiana says sweetly.

My mom looks to me with a knowing glint in her eyes and I nod in agreement before I place my hand on Tiana's lower back.

"Well don't just stand there! Come in, come in! I made sure you had your steak and potatoes, just like Gunnar asked. That's the least we could do after the truck," she says as she leads us into the house.

I press softly on Tiana's back, guiding her inside and to the kitchen.

My parents have always lived in this house, so I grew up here.

It's always a strange feeling coming home; a warm one, but weird nonetheless.

Walking inside, you enter the arctic entryway. Merely a small receiving room of sorts where you hang coats and take off your shoes before you go through another door, to the main area of the house. If you take the left from the entryway, there are stairs going up, the downstairs bathroom, and then stairs to go down to the finished basement. That's where my old bedroom is. Gretz, Brooks, and my parent's room is up the stairs.

But if you take the right, you get to the main area, where there's a large sunken living room dead ahead, usually we're in there specifically to watch hockey games, and then the formal-esque dining room is in a separate area to the right. Taking a left from the family room, you walk directly into an area with a dining room table that is there mostly for talks and hanging out, with the kitchen directly on the left of the table, and a separate living room to the right.

It's an extremely high ceiling here because if you look up above the wall, there's a small overlook that connects the upstairs to the downstairs. That way we can yell at each other from upstairs.

I lead Tiana back into the kitchen, where it smells of grilled steaks and buttery potatoes, with the noise of some random hockey game playing on the TV.

There's a TV in both rooms, but the family room in the front is for more serious games.

As we walk into the kitchen, my dad stands from his large armchair, walking up to us with a smile.

"Gunnar," he says gruffly before he presses his hand out.

I move my hand from Tiana's back to offer it to him, and he takes a heavy hold on it before he tugs me into him, hugging me tight and laying hard slaps on my back.

"Good to see you," he says.

My dad is a man of few words. But a good one.

"Tiana, nice to meet you," my dad says when he pulls away from me.

"Hi," Tiana says sheepishly as she gives a quick wave in hello before clasping her arms in front of her.

"Man of the HOUR!!" Brooks calls from the overlook on the top floor. Of course, he doesn't have a shirt on.

Called it.

I turn to see him leaning over the large cutout in the wall, where he waves with a big grin.

"Howdy Brookers," I say with a smile.

I glance at Tiana to see her wide-eyed, watching our family dynamic play out with a wild dart of her eyes between all of us.

"Buddyyyyyyyy! Comin' in here with a fiancée. Congrats man!" Gretz says as he comes from the stairs by the entry. He's in the middle of pulling a hockey jersey on for the college team he plays for.

"Well, ya' know. Gotta go for the shot when you see it," I say with a grin as I meet him a hard dap.

"Ain't that right, brother," he says with a laugh.

"Gretz, this is Tiana. Tiana, this is Gretz. He's a bit of a nut, but we love him," I say as I introduce Tiana.

"Hello," Tiana says with a shy smile.

"Enchanté," Gretz says as he bows and offers his hand to Tiana.

Her brow furrows as she watches him, before she glances at me in confusion.

"Just do it," I whisper through a grit in my teeth.

Tiana smiles nervously as she offers her hand, leaving Gretz to take it and press a kiss to the top of it. She watches in rapt confusion before he comes up from his bow, and she drags her hand away.

"Thank... you?" she says softly.

I shake my head with a small chuckle as I put my arm around her shoulders, guiding her to the living room.

We take a seat on the couch, where she folds one leg over the other, her hands clasped around her knee as she sits next to me.

"So, how's the pros, big man?" Gretz says as he throws himself down on the couch resting on the wall across from us.

"Ah, ya know. Checkin' benders, danglin' and cellies. You know how it goes," I say as I rub Tiana's opposite shoulder softly.

"Yeah, I saw that check you made in the first game. Absolutely fuckin' nutso for you to get yourself boxed in the first game," Gretz says with a shake of his head.

"You know what Gramps always said."

"Head up, you've got checks to cash!" my mom calls from the kitchen.

I snap finger gun point to my mom before I shrug at Gretz. "Bingo."

"First game in the pros though?" Brooks calls from above.

"That's what my dad said," Tiana grumbles with a shy grin.

The room goes eerily silent, and I look around at the three here with us to see their eyes bugging out of their skulls. My dad included.

Tiana's eyes also go wide. "Sorry, my dad is the coach for the Stags," she says nervously.

"Gunnar?" Gretz asks with a dropped jaw as his eyes land on me from where they were stuck on Tiana.

"Shit, did I leave out that little tidbit?" I ask with a cheeky grin.

Because I did. I didn't think it was imperative for them to know, to be fair. She's my fiancée. I think she stands on her own without being the coach's daughter.

"You fucked the coach's daughter?!" Brooks yells from upstairs.

"Language!!" my mom yells from the kitchen.

"Sorry! You stuffed it in the coach's daughter?!" Brooks reiterates.

My eyes roll as I bring a hand to my forehead to grip the meat between my eyebrows.

"Brooks! Do not make me come kick your ass! Have some decorum!" my mother yells again.

Wow, I honestly should have been more scared for this bunch than Tiana should be.

What absolute whackos.

"Can all of you shut the hell up? What has gotten into you guys!?" I ask with a groan.

"Brooks, Gretz, go get your asses dressed. I don't wanna see either of you without shirts," my dad grunts from his chair.

"I'm already dressed!" Gretz groans.

"Three, two..." my dad counts and Gretz scurries from the living room. Brooks dips back into the overlook, hiding himself from the rest of us.

My mom brings out a bowl of chips to place on the coffee table in front of us.

"I am so sorry for this group of ruffians," she says quietly to Tiana as she pats a hand on her knee.

"Oh, no it's okay. I've grown up in the hockey world my whole life, so that's not even the worst I've heard," Tiana says with a soft smile.

"You said your dad is the coach for the Stags?" my mom asks as she goes to sit on the couch where Gretz was sitting.

Tiana nods as she leans forward to grab a few chips, popping them in her mouth.

"For the past sixteen years, I think," she says after she swallows.

"Ohhhh... Dawn! Duh! I should have put two and two together! Oh my god," my mom says as she bumps her head with the heel of her hand.

"It's okay. I'm the lawyer, so I'm not as well known," Tiana says with a smile. Her eyes move down, fixing on her fingers as she takes a deep breath. "I'm really sorry that I wasn't more upfront when I took the truck. I really wanted to get it fixed up for Gunnar and... I know you all didn't know me, and I thought maybe if it was done in the name of the Stags it would be easier to hand it over," Tiana says nervously. She plays with a small thread she finds on her sleeve as a blush crawls over her cheeks.

"Sweetheart, no, no, no, no," my mom says as she pushes off the couch to kneel in front of her. She takes Tiana's hands in her own, and Tiana reluctantly looks up with a nervous smile.

"When Gunnar told us the girl he was marrying had fixed that truck..." she pauses with a small shake of her head. "I was so thankful to welcome in a daughter-in-law that had done such a selfless thing," my mom says softly.

Tiana's eyes water and her lower lip quivers as she nods.

"I'm sure you saw when you brought it back, but that truck is everything to this family. And I couldn't believe the amazing work they had done to it. It was the highlight of my year, since Dad died. I truly can't thank you enough."

A small tear falls down Tiana's cheek as she nods again. "Gunnar deserves it... you guys deserve it," Tiana says softly.

My mom gives her an adoring smile with a tilt of her head as she looks over Tiana's face.

"Aw, sweetie, come here, don't cry," she says as she wraps her arms around Tiana's head. She brings her in to a tight hug, and Tiana returns it. My mom rubs her back for a few moments before she pulls away, looking in Tiana's face one more time before she hugs her again.

Tiana merely takes the contact in stride, moving with the flow.

I feel at least from my perspective, she's doing so well, and I'm so proud of my girl.

"Come on. Let's go have some dinner, yeah?" my mom asks as she pulls away one last time, placing her hands on Tiana's knees.

Tiana nods with a small smile, and my mom stands, offering a hand to Tiana to help her up. Tiana takes it, pulling herself up, and my mom clutches it between them. She holds on tight to her arm as she leads Tiana to the dining room in the front.

I watch as they walk away, while a warm feeling settles in my chest. I've never had a woman make this sort of impact on my family like this. And it would be just my luck for the one I marry to be perfect for them.

I look to my dad, who gives me a small smile and a nod. Soon, we both stand and take a momentary stretch before we both turn to watch them walk away and I shove my hands in my pockets, letting the moment sink in.

"Good choice, bud," he says gruffly.

"Best choice, Pops," I say as I glance at him. He nods in approval before he claps me on the shoulder and we both move to the dining room after them.

CHAPTER FOURTEEN

TIANA

This is going much better than I expected. Aside from the insane reactions from his brothers. His family have really opened their arms to me.

I guess Gunnar was right about the entire thing. But I still worry about having to at least *appear* normal. Part of the time, I don't know what to say. I don't know what to ask, and I don't know if I'm saying enough, or asking the questions that I need to.

The more they ask questions about me, the more I feel like I'm not reciprocating properly, and some nerves creep in again.

However, we've finally sat at the table. His mother prepared a perfect steak and potato dinner and it makes my heart sing a little knowing I do have something to eat that I *enjoy* eating.

That eases the stress on that part immensely.

After his mom and I had that emotional moment, she brought me in the dining room to help finish getting things set up before the men came in.

I wasn't expecting them to welcome me this much. But it really does put into perspective how much the truck really influenced them.

After the four of us set up the table and got the food in place, Brooks and Gretz came down and we were all able to sit.

His dad still has said little of anything. But I think that's just how he is.

As we sit down, I go off of Gunnar's movements. He fills up my plate with potatoes and steak, placing it in front of me so I can dig in. All the while, the boys talk to each other. The long oval table is definitely big enough for all these massive men.

Brooks sits next to his dad on the left side of the long straight side. Gretz sits at the head of the table across from us, with the front windows at his back, while Mrs. Claire is on the right side.

Gunnar and I are at the other end of the table, with me on his right.

"When do you think I'll be able to go out for drafts?" Gretz asks as he pops a piece of his steak in his mouth.

I watch as Gunnar spoons a heaping serving of potatoes onto his plate before he grabs a steak and places it on the plate before setting it down in front of him.

"That's up to you. You don't have to go pro. You could have a normal job. But if you really want to, you've gotta work for it. I'm not gonna put in a good word for you for the fuck of it. I won't have you tarnishing the Hayze name if you can't find the fuckin' puck," he says with a small grin as he cuts into his steak.

"That's real fucked, Gun. What happened to brotherhood?" Gretz asks.

Gunnar shrugs. "Work hard and make the moves yourself. I'm not your stick handler," he says.

"Whatever. I'll get a better team than you anyway," Gretz responds.

"Sure. But I wanted the Stags. So it doesn't matter. I'm exactly where I want to be," Gunnar says with a shrug. Soon, his hand comes to grip my thigh softly under the table as he glances at me.

The feeling of his touch is always electrifying. It always has been from the very first moment I met him. This time is no different, and it causes heat to engulf my face.

"So, Tiana, what pulled you to Gunnar?" Brooks asks as he takes a sip of his soda.

My eyes widen as the attention is immediately pulled to me, the heat working down my chest as I'm put on the spot.

I look down at my plate, cutting into my steak slowly. "Well... do you want the honest answer?" I ask as I glance up.

"Always," Gretz responds with a wide grin.

"I kind of didn't have a choice because he laid it on pretty thick from the moment he saw me," I say with a small smile. I glance up every so often to gauge their expressions, their reactions, to make sure I'm saying the right things at the right times. Granted, I always speak honestly, but I've gotten in trouble for my honesty in the past.

"Ah, yeah, I reckon that tracks. Dumbass doesn't know how to quit. Never has," Brooks says with a nod.

"Language," Gunnar's mom grits as she cuts into her steak with a glare at Brooks.

He gives her a nervous grin before he goes back to his potatoes.

"He hit you with that 'angel' line? That's his go-to," Gretz asks as he points at me with his knife.

My eyes widen as I glance at Gunnar, whose face shifts into annoyance as his eyes float to the ceiling.

"He did. But I wasn't interested because, honestly, I've

never been interested in hockey players. I've been in the hockey world my whole life, and hockey players were the last ones I ever had my eye on. If at all," I say softly before I bite into the piece of steak I cut off.

"So she's not a puck bunny, eh? The fuck'd you find this lil' number, Gun? Works in the hockey world and doesn't have eyes for the benders? A gift, I reckon," Gretz says with a sly nod.

"Don't I know it," Gunnar says with a grin as he leans up from the table to give Gretz a fist bump.

"You boys," Gunnar's mom grunts as she slaps their hands across the table. "No reaching over the damn table," she grits. "If you three can't get your shit together, all of you are going outside for ten minutes. I'm serious," she says as she points at the three of them.

"Yes, Mom," they all say in unison before their heads drop back down into their meals. My brow rises in surprise as I look over them all.

Even at their big ages, she has a leash on them. And I can't help but say I love it.

"Good listeners," I murmur to her with a smile.

"Only when they need to be," she responds with a cheeky smirk and a wink before she leans back into her seat.

"When do you plan on having the wedding?" his mom asks as she bites into her steak.

"I was thinking springtime. I don't want a winter wedding; that's too soon and right in the middle of the season. It needs to be outside of season and with enough time to plan," I say with a kind smile.

But my heart beats nervously in my chest at the idea of talking about wedding planning.

If I get started, I may go on a tangent. Or I may just start speaking over everyone, with everything.

I focus on my steak, hoping and praying that his mother doesn't ask more about it, and to just focus on the things they ask about.

"Do you guys have a secure date yet?" she asks.

Fuck.

I pause, taking my time. "No... I have no idea what day. I think I'll let Gunnar choose," I say with a kind smile.

"May Fourth," he blurts.

My brow furrows as my head comes up to look at him. He's just leisurely cutting into his steak and scooping mashed potatoes onto it before stuffing it into his mouth.

As if he didn't just throw out the date that would be our anniversary out of no where.

"What?" I ask as I watch him.

He takes a moment to respond, chewing his food before he swallows. "Yeah. You know. Like May the Fourth be with you?" he says as he goes to take another bite of his potatoes.

I try to keep a straight face because this is the first I'm hearing about this from him.

But fine, *whatever.*

"Yes... May fourth...? I guess?" I say as I glare at him before returning to gaze at Mrs. Claire with a kind smile.

"Why do you work for the Stags if you're a lawyer?" Brooks asks.

I spoon a scoop of potatoes into my mouth, swallowing and taking a sip of water before I answer.

"Well. I think it makes sense. My mom owns the firm the Stags are under. My dad is the coach, and my sister is the equipment manager. They needed a new attorney for the team when the last one left, and I was just getting out of law school, so it made the most sense. And I really like my office in the arena," I say as I take a bite of my steak.

"You work in the arena?" Gretz asks.

I nod as I chew, cutting off another piece of steak. "Yeah, the first night I met Gunnar, he left the locker room to run straight for my office to meet me. At the time it was bizarre because... well... it was just strange. I'd never had someone from the team hit on me. Especially not on first meeting. But in hindsight, it's cute," I say with a reminiscent smile.

"Your sister single?" Gretz asks with a grin.

My cheeks heat, and my eyes widen in shock. "Uh... I..." I murmur.

"She's dating Banks, you filthy degenerate," Gunnar murmurs in response as he shovels more food into his mouth.

I glance between the two of them. For Gunnar, this is just a family dinner.

For me, this is fucking wild.

"Banks?! Adrian Banks!? Your sister is dating fucking Banks!?" Brooks asks with a slack jaw.

"Uh... Y-yes?" I say slowly.

"Fuckin' Captain of the Stags, 'The Stallion,' Adrian Banks?!" Gretz chimes in.

Mrs. Claire groans as she glares at the boys.

"Gunnar told him he should go for her," I say with a shrug.

"And I went for Tiana, so both of you can shut the hell up," Gunnar says with a sigh.

I don't know if Gunnar is tired of their antics. But he seems a bit more... reserved here. I imagine that's just the role of a big brother.

It goes quiet for a long moment, and my brow furrows as I look up, hoping I said nothing bad. But Gretz and Brooks give each other a small glance before they look at Gunnar.

"Please don't. Not here, you two," Gunnar groans as he drops his utensils on his plate and throws his head back. His hands rest on his thighs as he stares blankly up at the ceiling.

The two boys get up from the table, coming around like sneaky little burglars to come to either side of Gunnar.

"Gunnar and Tiana sitting in a tree. F-U-C-K-I-N-G!" the two sing in unison as they rock him back and forth between each other. I lean away as they do, giving them space to mess with him.

Gunnar's mom reaches under the table, procuring one of her slippers to chuck at Brooks, who shrieks as he ducks. Soon, she stands and lifts her foot up behind her, slides off her slipper and chucks that one at Gretz.

"Ah! Mom!" Gretz shrieks, almost like a little girl as he guards himself.

"Outside! Both of you!" she yells, and they scurry out of the dining room like tiny rats before we hear the front door open and close.

I give a wide-eyed look, watching this all go down, before my gaze roams over the four of us left at the table.

"Sorry about them. They always get like this when Gunnar comes home. They just don't know how to act," Gunnar's mom says with a smile as she sits back down in her chair.

There is a lot happening. All at once, I feel my heart rate spike at the energy of everyone in this room together.

Even if it's good energy, it's still a lot, and it becomes too much, way too fast.

My nerves grip my throat, tightening it to suffocate me, and I feel like I have to get away for just a few moments.

"It's okay, I need to use the restroom anyway," I say quietly.

"Go ahead! It's down the hall that way, first door on the right," she says kindly.

I stand quickly, nodding to them before I go down the hall. Making my way to the door she specified, I step into the bathroom and turn on the light. I close the door behind me before bracing myself against the counter, inhaling a deep breath.

So much energy, while trying to make sure I'm being a presentable, normal human to these people I'll eventually call family. I feel like my stomach is going to come out of my throat.

It's a lot of mental power to put on a face for the longest time of interaction. It's nerve-wracking. I don't know if I'm doing well enough in being myself while also being kind. I don't know if with every word I'm saying I'm making sense, or I'm just making myself look stupid.

It's a gentle balance, and a hard dance. With a large part of me still trying to understand the family dynamic.

They seem like they like me, and they're being kind to me. But are they just pretending for my sake?

I turn on the sink, letting the cool water run out before I splash my face with it, taking another deep breath to steady my nerves. Looking around, I find a stack of paper towels on the counter, and I grab one to dab my face dry with before I take deep, calming breaths.

There is truly nothing wrong happening with this entire night.

But I'm still just sort of reeling from the fact that not only am I getting married, I'm marrying a hockey player. Marrying into a family full of hockey players, and meeting them for the first time.

It's also difficult to *navigate* their dynamic. I'm not sure if I should say something or just keep my mouth shut, and the back and forth of those thoughts has my head spinning, trying to keep myself above water.

Soon, a knock comes at the bathroom door and I jump, letting out a little yelp.

"Sugar? Everything alright?" I hear Gunnar's voice from outside and I take a deep breath.

Going to the door, I pull it open and glance up at him.

Even here he holds on to the top of the door frame like he does at my apartment and I give a small roll of my eyes playfully as I open the door enough for him to come in.

He crouches, closing the door behind him and coming up to hold my face with a small smile. He searches my eyes for a long moment, as if cataloging my mood.

"Did my brothers upset you? I'm so sorry, they can be such dumbasses someti-"

I give him a reassuring smile as I bring my hand up to stop him. "They are fine. I'm not appalled or whatever you think is going on. I just hope I'm doing okay with all of it," I say nervously.

"Oh, sugar, you're doing phenomenally, I promise. It's those two who are being insane. Maybe it's because you're going to be their first sister-in-law and they truly don't know how to act. But you're doing great," he says quietly.

I smile, taking a deep breath. "Okay... good... good..." I say with a relieved sigh.

"Why'd you leave?" he asks as he runs a thumb over my cheek.

"It was just a little... overstimulating for a moment, is all. I think I was overthinking everything," I mumble softly.

"I'm sorry, sugar. I should have warned you; Gretz and Brooks can be a lot when they're together. They kind of feed off each other. A Dumb and Dumber type of situation," he says with a smile. "But I promise you aren't doing anything wrong."

I nod again, letting some worries wane away as I look into his reassuring eyes. "Thank you," I respond softly.

He smiles as he looks into my eyes. "Gimme a kiss," he says as he leans down.

I nip my lip, wrapping my arms up around his neck as his hands come to grip my hips, pulling me tight against him.

My body heats, and I let a small noise vibrate between us. His touch melts me, eases into me and lets me relax against him. He imbues a level of confidence, even when I feel like I have none.

His strength pulls me in, pressing hard against the hardened planes of his body, and I relish in the feeling of his body against mine for these few moments.

Soon, his hands drift lower, sliding down my hips to grab my ass through my jeans, and he releases a small groan. His kisses turn deeper, one of his hands coming up to my face to hook his fingers against the back of my neck, lining my jaw with his thumb to tilt my head.

My heart picks up with heat flooding through my body. With desire pulsing in the places we touch, I feel his rigid length pressing against my stomach as he kisses me deeper.

"Gunnar," I moan quietly against his lips.

"I'm sorry, sugar. I'm so fucking hot for you. I need you… *now*. I can't wait until we get home," he rasps against my lips, with the grip he has on my ass tightening as he holds back his restraint.

"Here? Now?" I ask.

"You ever heard of free use?" he asks with a grin.

My brow furrows as I pull away from him. "No…?"

"So it's this… thing… dynamic… where…" he bites his lip as he looks over me with a heated gaze. "Anytime I want to fuck you… I just do. Anytime I feel like it," he says as he nips softly at his lip.

My eyes widen, my breath hitching in my throat. "Just… whenever?" I breathe.

"If I wanna bend you over your desk after practice, I can. If I want you to suck my cock in the truck, you do…," he says with a small pant as he grinds his hips softly against me.

It's so fucking hard to deny him when he's hard. Because I

want it. I want to see it, touch it. I want to lick it and feel it. It's a marvel in the best way, and it taunts me every time.

"Anytime...? You want?" I murmur as I kiss him slowly.

The idea is... fun. Technically, we already do that.

"Does that mean... I can do it to you?" I ask as I tilt my head, kissing his lips leisurely.

His fingers tighten where they grip the back of my neck, his thumb trying not to grip harder as he moves my head. The hand on my ass roams back and forth over the cheek, stroking down my hip, and feeling my curves.

"Whatever you want, I'm yours, sugar," he pants into our slow kiss.

"Fuck..." I pant softly.

"I know," he says with a grin against my lips.

"Yes... fuck... yes, please," I pant.

He releases my neck, both hands grabbing me by my hips and picking me up to wrap my legs around his waist, his hands gripping tight on my ass.

I kiss him, grinding against his stomach as our tongues twist and dance around one another's.

"I'm gonna fuck you on this counter, but you need to be extra quiet. Can you do that for me, sugar?" he pants against my mouth.

I nod as I kiss him, grinding my rapidly heating core against him, seeking as much friction as I can.

He sets me on the counter, his hands moving from my ass, straight to the button and zipper on my jeans, and I do the same. But I'm faster. I undo all that I can, press his boxers down and let his cock free. Hard as stone, he pulses hot in my fingers as I stroke him from root to tip. I bring my other hand down, stroking over his length with both, twisting and gripping as I move.

I press the pad of my thumb to the head of his cock, letting it slide around with the pre-cum he drips, and he stops trying to undo my jeans. Pressing his hands into the counter on either side of my hips, his head hangs, his back moving in rigid breaths as he nuzzles into my neck.

He groans, kissing and licking desperately at the skin of my neck and collarbone.

"Suck it... Fuck, I need your mouth on it," he rasps against my skin.

I love the way he gets whimpery like this. It's a power unlike anything I'd ever known that I can make him melt like this.

My brow rises with a sly grin, and I push off the counter. With my movements, he stumbles back just enough to give me room to get on my knees in front of him.

I wrap my hands around his cock, stroking up and down its length as I run my tongue on the underside of its head. His hand comes to my cheek, stroking it softly as his breaths turn heavy and he watches me with a lust-hazed focus. His other hand braces against the counter, and his head tilts.

"That tongue is dangerous, Mama," he says with a low chuckle.

My eyes glance up as I grin, wrapping my lips around him before pressing him deeper into my mouth. My tongue slides along the underside as I move back and forth on him, hollowing my cheeks out as I move.

"F-Fucking hell, sugar," he grits as his head tosses back and he takes a few gasping breaths.

I slow down, coming to the head to wrap and swirl my tongue around it as I look up at him.

He tries so hard to steady his breaths as he looks down at me, his thumb moving slowly against my cheek again. "That's a good girl, keeping your eyes on me. You look so beautiful with my cock in your mouth," he whispers.

Soon, I press him back into my mouth, into my throat, and his eyes roll the deeper I press, his jaw dropping again as he moves his hands to the back of my head, gripping my skull to hold me in place as he presses in and out of my mouth.

Slowly at first, then he presses in deep, holding me there, and my eyes water from the stretch of him.

"Through your nose. Breathe for me," he grits through his teeth.

I take a deep breath through my nose before he presses in more, deeper. I feel my air cut off, shallow gags pulsing against him as his other hand wraps around my throat, squeezing.

He makes a low, tortured growl, trying to keep his noises down as he watches me.

"Good fucking girl. You know how to take my cock," he whispers with a breathless chuckle.

One more shallow gag, and his knees buckle. He retreats enough for me to breathe, and he pulls out. His cock is shiny with my saliva and twitches as he catches his breath.

"That fuckin' mouth you got on you, sugar," he pants softly as he shakes his head.

I catch my breath as I look up at him, wiping the small bit of drool from my lips.

Bending over, he pulls me up quickly, presses my pants down and turns me around. He presses hard in the middle of my back, bending me over the counter, just for me to see him in the mirror, towering above me.

I watch the way his eyes lock onto where he runs his cock through my center, swiping through my wetness before teasing my entrance. I see it in his face at the same time I feel it in my pussy. And just like always, his stretch is glorious the more he presses into me. His head tosses back as he falls deeper and deeper until he bottoms out.

He nips hard at his lip to keep himself from groaning, his

legs buckling as he holds himself balls deep in me. He waits, letting me adjust before his head rises, only to drop and look down between us. Soon, he takes a few test strokes in and out of me.

His head tilts, his strokes becoming longer as his hands grip tight on my hips.

My own head tilts back, trying with all my might to keep quiet, but this position is so fucking difficult. He feels insane when he's behind me and I'm bent over like this.

One hand leaves my hip to come and wrap around my mouth, making sure I make no noise as his thrusts pick up.

He leans over, nipping and licking at my earlobe as his soft groans work through my ears.

"Look at us," he whispers. He presses in deep, holding himself there, before his head buries into the crook of my neck and he releases a low growl of pleasure. "Look at how good you look when you're taking me, balls deep. Sexy fucking thing you are, huh baby?" he says with a heavy pant.

I look in the mirror, at the way he thrusts me forward with every hard pound. I feel his balls slap against my clit with every thrust, and my eyes roll as I feel it.

"There she is. There's my pretty girl. Lost in the feeling of my cock stretching her pussy. That's a good girl," he whispers. Kisses pepper my skin, my jaw, my cheeks, my neck. I feel him everywhere, externally and internally, and I love being devoured by it.

"I love the way you give in. I love the way you fall," he whispers against my neck.

My moans are muffled behind his palm, and I can feel the whimpers working out with them.

His hand presses hard against my mouth, tilting my head back to look up at him as he continues his thrusts.

"Eyes here, baby. Show me what I've done to you," he rasps.

My eyes flutter open, locking onto his gaze, and his thrusts pound deeper, harder, slower.

"Gorgeous fucking girl. Taking my cock like you fucking own it," he pants.

His eyes drip with passion, possession and dominance, and my body tightens at the climbing pleasure. That release that rests just over the horizon.

"Breathe, baby, breathe for me," he whispers.

I nod obediently against his hold, inhaling deeply through my nose before exhaling. His thrusts moving in time with my breaths.

Every inhale and exhale is euphoric with the way he times his thrusts. My eyes attempt to roll, attempt to escape from the pleasure of it all.

"You're doing so good for me, you're so close. You gonna come with me? Lock me in that cunt while I pump you full of me?" he pants.

My eyes water as I nod again, desperate and begging this time. His other hand leaves my hip, snaking between my legs and finding my clit.

He rubs quickly, pounding deep and working me up as he thrusts in and out.

"Fuck..." he groans as his thrusts pick up, his fingers working faster against my clit.

"Come with me, baby. I'm so fucking close. Come with me," he grunts.

And his words are that last tipping point. My screams muffle behind his palm as my eyes roll and my pussy clenches around his cock in hard waves.

He spills into me, his thrusts pausing as his hand keeps pace on my clit, wringing out every bit of my orgasm.

"Keep going, you've got more in you. Ride it out, sugar," he grits as my hips grind against his hand, against his cock, all the feelings at once as my orgasm crashes over me again and again and again.

I feel him drip out from where his cock is pressed in me, his hand slacking from my mouth to slide down and hang loosely around my neck.

My orgasm slows, waning away, and I feel his chest expand in and out against my back as he presses soft kisses into my jaw.

"Good girl, baby. You did so good for me," he whispers. He pulls his hand from my center, quickly sucking his fingers clean before he strokes softly at my hip.

He rocks our hips from side to side in calm as we slowly come down, with his head resting against my shoulder.

"So, you're good with free use? Because I'm going to take advantage of that," he asks breathlessly.

I give him an exhausted chuckle as I nod. "Yes, we can be free-use."

Slowly, he pulls his cock out, letting his cum drip from me. He groans as he leans back, watching it, before he slips his fingers into his mouth to wet them, shoving them into me to press his cum back inside.

I make a small noise before he pulls them out and slides my panties and jeans back up.

I take a deep breath, catching it before I turn around in his arms to lean back against the counter. He licks his fingers clean again before he comes to redo the buttons and zippers on my jeans.

I press his cock back into his boxers, zipping and buttoning his jeans before I give him a satiated smile.

"Honestly. I like that idea. I enjoy having sex with you... It's always been... stimulating," I say quietly.

"Yeah?" he says with a content grin as he brings a hand up to my cheek.

"It's... addictive. *You're* addictive. And it gets me out of my head; brings me into the moment and the present. And I like that. Especially when life is getting away from me," I admit softly.

"I know, sugar. That's why I do it sometimes," he says.

My head tilts as my brow furrows. "What?"

"Yeah. At the pumpkin patch. I could tell you were frustrated with yourself. And I really don't have many options as far as helping. But I do have a dick, so I decided to use that because you're always in the present with me. And well, now, I figured you were having a hard time. Aside from the fact I was just really horny," he says with a smile.

My heart swells, with my eyes burning a bit as I look at him.

Is it unconventional? Sure. Is it... strange? Yes, I would say so.

But does it work? Yeah... And did he come up with that on his own? Just from spending time with me and hearing my strifes?

Yeah... Yeah, he did.

And he reminds me repeatedly why I fell for this man, who will always do whatever he can for me. Even in the most unconventional ways.

"I figured if we were free use, I could just help you whenever you needed it and didn't have to ask beforehand. Sometimes you get out of sorts, and I feel like you just need a little reset."

I have no words. I don't know what to say. So, I do what I always do. I wrap my arms around his neck, hugging him tight.

He brings his arms around me, stroking my back as he leans down to kiss my forehead.

"Love you, sugar. Thanks for letting me fuck you in the bathroom," he whispers.

I roll my eyes playfully as I lean back, grabbing his face and looking in his eyes.

Those precious hazel eyes that always bleed with love and adoration for me.

"Love you, Mr. Hayze," I whisper.

CHAPTER FIFTEEN
TIANA

"You know, he was actually a really good kid growing up. He just had so much energy. Dad always made sure he was able to handle a stick from the moment he could walk," Mrs. Claire laughs.

Unfolding a fall-themed plastic tablecloth to place over the large dining room table, I smile at her as I listen to her talk about Gunnar.

It's nice to hear some of the stuff she's said about him. He's an interesting character to learn about. But it seems as if he's just always been the way that he is. Of course he had a dumb teenage boy phase.

Who doesn't though?

After Gunnar and me came back from the bathroom, Gretz and Brooks were back as the table, eating dinner and talking.

However, Gretz gave us a sly look before he had glanced at Brooks, and boy, the way fire swallowed my body. I was hoping with everything in me they had no idea what was actually happening in that bathroom.

I just know they did, though. If they're both anything like Gunnar, there's no way they *didn't* know.

We had finished eating dinner, and then the boys cleaned up the table as Mrs. Claire and I got the stuff ready to carve pumpkins. After she found the things she needed in one of the hall closets, we came out to the table in the kitchen. As I've gone around the table, making sure the plastic covering is in place, she's been going through her storage box of carving tools.

I *love* carving pumpkins. While I have some level of sensory issues, I really don't mind pumpkin carving.

Simply because I know what to expect from it and I don't mind getting messy from it. When I finish taping the plastic to the underside of the table, I look through some books of carving templates she has.

I usually carve the same thing every Halloween. Something that looks sort of like a moon with a cat in front of it. It's one of my favorite things to make, and I always enjoy seeing how much better I do every year.

When I find the template I'm looking for, I rip it out of the book with an excited grin. As well as a breath of relief.

I'm not really sure what I would have done if they hadn't had this template, but I fear that I would have become *much* more anxious.

I place it to the side as I wait for the boys to bring the pumpkins in from Gunnar's truck.

As I look over the template, Mrs. Claire begins talking.

"Do you have a hard time handling his energy? You seem to be much calmer than he is," she says as she looks over the tools, making sure they're clean before she places them on the table as she sifts through her little storage bin.

"Not really. Sometimes it's hard to understand the way he talks. He has a very... peculiar vocabulary," I say with a chuckle.

"Oh, yes. He actually went to college for English. He loves words. He used to read when he wasn't playing hockey," she says with a smile.

My head tilts with this new information, because I haven't seen him read *ever*.

But him loving words? Yeah, I think that makes sense, considering the way he is.

"That's interesting to know, because the only time I've seen him pick up a book is when he bought ones for me."

She looks at me with a confused tilt of her head. "He hasn't read any books?"

I shake my head. "Not really. He just buys me my own," I say with a shy smile.

"Ever the gift giver that man is. Every birthday and Christmas, he goes all out for my mom and my mother-in-law. And me, of course. He got a job as soon as he could just so he could make sure he could get us gifts," she says with a reminiscent smile.

My mind goes back to the first gift he gave me. The basket for going on our date. And the thought warms part of my soul; that's just how he is.

It's not just a thing he did for show... it's so refreshing.

Some men like to "honeypot" you. They do sweet and kind things in the beginning just to get you on their side. Then, when they feel like they don't need to put in the effort anymore, they don't.

It's so nice to know this is just part of how he is.

"Do you know why?" I ask as my mind comes back to the present.

"Well, Gretz and Brooks are a tad... feral? They all are. But he tries to make sure he does the best he can for the women in his life. My dad was the same way. So, I think he just likes to follow in his footsteps as much as he can," she says. Her smile tilts down at the corners, releasing a heavy sigh as she plants her hands on the counter.

I watch her for a moment, trying to decipher her emotions. It's hard sometimes to figure out. But the energy is always there.

The more I find out about this patriarch of theirs, the more I realize how much he really means to them.

"Do Gretz and Brooks feel the same way about him?" I ask softly.

"A bit. But Gunnar spent more time with him. He's got a bit of an addictive personality, I think. And he loved the things my dad taught him. He was... really crushed when he passed. Worst I think I'd ever seen him, to be honest." Her voice lowers, going much softer as she speaks.

My body stills, absorbing these other pieces of Gunnar and his relationship with his grandpa.

I know that the man meant a lot to Gunnar. He just seemed less able to figure out his feelings when I had directly asked him about it. Maybe he just thinks he has to be strong.

My throat tightens, my heart drumming rapidly as I listen. I personally am not one for releasing big emotions. Not until they have nowhere to go and they all come tumbling out at once.

Right now, all of my grandparents are still alive. And while I don't see them much, or have a close relationship with them, that seems to be a different story for Gunnar.

It hurts that he has to go without this massive figure in his life.

In the same breath, I am glad he can keep the light in his life. He really isn't ever sad; he tries to keep his energy high. For someone like me, who is so easily thrown off course, I feel a small sort of comfort knowing he can help if I'm in an awful place.

I just hope I'll be able to provide the same kindness when I get the chance.

I'm not touchy-feely at all. It's not my thing. The only exception is Gunnar.

But I want to offer Mrs. Claire the comfort I should have when she first saw the truck. Stepping closer to her, I place a gentle hand on her shoulder.

Mrs. Claire doesn't look up at me. She merely brings a hand up from the table, gripping mine as she takes a deep breath.

A small tear drips from her face, hitting the plastic on the table, and we spend a quiet moment together, where I sit with her and her grief.

It's high-energy. One I feel somewhat anxious navigating. But I know Gunnar would do the same for my mother or father. So, I try to give it to her.

The silence lasts for a few beats, and I watch a few more tears fall to the table, before there's the sound of raucous boys and movement from the front door.

Mrs. Claire straightens, releasing my hand. She takes a steadying breath, wiping the tears from her face quickly before she turns to me.

"Thank you," she mouths with a wink and a deep breath before she turns around to meet the boys as they walk through the arch, into the kitchen.

"What took you boys so long?" she asks. Her voice is cheery, trying not to allude to her heart breaking.

One day, I hope I can have half the strength she possesses.

Gunnar leads the three of them, with our pumpkins we picked at the pumpkin farm under each of his arms.

God, the *man*.

There is always a rush, straight through my blood, deep

into my bones when I catch sight of him. His height, broad shoulders and huge muscles... he really is a 'beaut'.

"Gretz tried to fight me and lost. And then Brooks wanted a taste. Lost. Then they tried to take me at the same time. Turns out the fuckers can't fight to save their lives," Gunnar says as he places the pumpkins on the table.

"You've got literally six inches on me and eight on Brooks," Gretz grumbles as he places his own pumpkin on the table. He crosses his arms over his chest with a pout, and I can't help the small laugh that sneaks out of me.

With all of them so close together, they all just look like younger versions of Gunnar. Basically a bunch of copies of the same guy.

"In more places than one, I reckon," Gunnar responds as he comes up to me. Grabbing the back of my head, he pulls it toward him, pressing a small kiss to my forehead before he comes behind me.

"Gunnar Lemieux Hayze!" Mrs. Claire says as she jumps up to slap him in the head.

With the vertical on this woman, I can tell she does it often.

I love that for her.

"Ouch! Mom!? The fuck was that for?!" he says with a pout.

"Stop talking about your bits at the table! And watch!" she grits through her teeth as she reaches for one of the flat, orange pumpkin scoopers from the table, whacking him in the shoulder with it. "Your!" *slap!* "Damn!" *slap!* "Mouth!" *slap!*

Gunnar lifts his shoulder, trying to guard himself as he puts his hands out. "What!? It's nothing Tiana doesn't know about," he says as he cowers behind his hood he lifts over his face. He peeks from behind the fabric to see if she's stopped, finally letting his guard down when she waggles the tool at him and he puts his hands up in surrender.

"Okay! Okay!" He rubs the spot she slapped him before he wraps his arms around my waist, hiding behind me.

"Yeah, Gunn, we don't wanna hear about your hog," Gretz responds as he looks over his pumpkin.

"I hear it's small anyway," Brooks says as he places his pumpkin down on the table.

I look over my shoulder at him with a furrowed brow. "Real smooth, using your fiancée as a human shield," I say.

"She won't hit you; I know that. You're the one making her grandchildren," he says in a cautionary tone as he watches his mom closely, as if she's going to come back to slap him.

My body tenses, my eyes widening as I gulp. My breath halts in my throat as I look around to see who all heard that.

Only to find, it looks like all of them did.

At least the brothers, that is. It seems as if Mrs. Claire has escaped into her mind.

"I'm going to be an uncle?!" Gretz says with a surprised smile.

"Eventually," Gunnar murmurs as he leans in to kiss my cheek.

I feel as if I'm going to implode from the embarrassment coursing through my fucking veins right now. What the hell is wrong with this man?

I take a deep breath, trying not to bring any attention to the fact that this man said I was going to be carrying his fucking child before we are even married.

Obviously *I* know that, but the brothers don't need to know that!

"Where's Dad?" Mrs. Claire asks as she helps Gretz go through the little book of templates for his pumpkin.

"He said he had some wood to chop for the fireplace,"

Gunnar says as he leans down one more time to press a kiss to my forehead before he pulls away.

Thank God, she didn't say anything else.

Gunnar goes over to his pumpkin, looking it over, and I grab my little template.

"Do you like carving pumpkins, Tiana?" Mrs. Claire asks.

"I do, actually. We used to do it as a family every year. I make the same pattern every year," I say with a timid smile.

"I think I'm gonna carve a dick. That should be great on the porch," Brooks says as he takes one of the pumpkin knives from the counter and begins cutting into the top of his pumpkin.

"Is it going to be bigger than yours?" Gretz asks as he saws into the top of his own pumpkin with one of the pumpkin knives.

"I think anything he makes is going to be bigger than his," Gunnar says as he goes through some of the template books, flipping through the pages mindlessly.

"Is there a reason none of you can stop talking about your penises at the table!?" Mrs. Claire groans.

"Ew Mom! You aren't allowed to say that!" Gretz says with a fake gag.

"Penis, penis, penis! It's not so fun now, is it?!" she yells as she baps Gretz in the back of the head with a pumpkin scooper.

I can't help the giggle that escapes me as she continuously puts these boys in their place.

Honestly, with the size and temperament of them all, I don't blame her.

As I cut the lid off my pumpkin and pull on its stem, I glance over at Gunnar, who has continued to look through the templates. He seems almost frustrated until he closes the book and begins cutting the lid off his pumpkin.

"You okay?" I ask softly as I lean over to him.

"Yeah, I'm good. Didn't find what I was looking for, but I have an idea," he says with a smile.

I give him a skeptical tilt of my head as I roll up my sleeves. Setting the pumpkin lid on its side, I saw off the little bits of guts still stuck to the underside. When it's detached, I slap the goo into the middle of the table, where Gretz and Brooks have put their guts.

I reach for one of the pumpkin scoops to scrape out the inside of my pumpkin when Gretz speaks again.

"Did Mom tell you what I'm going to be for Halloween?" he asks as he continues scraping pumpkin seeds and guts out of his pumpkin with a slap onto the table.

Soon, the entire room smells like raw pumpkin, and it brings back fall in full force.

A level of happy nostalgia courses through me, and I ease into this little activity with a content smile.

"No, but I imagine you're going to tell me," Gunnar mumbles as he continues making the cuts for his lid.

"Rude. First off. Second, I'm going as Wayne Gretzky," he says with a grin.

I glance up at him before I glance at Gunnar.

"Real original, *Gretz*," he murmurs as he tugs the lid off his pumpkin and scrapes at the guts on the underside with his nails.

"Hey, it doesn't take much; I already have the costume. And really, I'm just in it for the candy this year. They don't give out candy to the older kids unless we're dressed up," Gretz responds.

"I'm going to be a Dalmatian," Brooks says.

The three of us pause, looking up at Brooks, who realizes the lull and stops.

"What?" he asks as he looks at us.

"A fucking dog, Brooks?" Gunnar says with a tilt of his head.

"What? I think they're cute. My girlfriend said she was going to paint little spots on my face, and she's going to dress as Cruella," he says with a grin.

"Talk about fuckin' whipped, bud," Gunnar says with a shake of his head as he begins to scrape the guts out of his pumpkin.

"That's what I told him! But he doesn't listen to me," Gretz says.

Mrs. Claire shakes her head. "You guys, please don't make a horrific mess. I'm going to go check on your father," she says as she heads for the front of the house.

"We'll be extra careful!" Gunnar calls back.

Soon, we hear the front door close, and Gretz leans in.

"So, are you actually pregnant?" he asks.

My eyes damn near bug out of my skull as I freeze, my body tensing and my eyes stuck to the inside of my pumpkin.

"I'm trying to, but it's more than just a fuckin' pump of spend, ya' dipshit," Gunnar says.

"Oh my god???" I scoff incredulously as my shoulders drop and I look up at him.

"What? They asked!?" Gunnar says as he puts his hands up.

"What happened to gentlemen don't kiss and tell!?" I groan.

"You know about his little codebook? Ha! You still follow that thing?" Gretz asks with a shake of his head. He puts the lid back on his pumpkin before he pins the template to his pumpkin to poke the holes for his design.

"Hey, Gretz? Who's getting married?" Gunnar asks as he scoops out a big handful of pumpkin seeds.

"Hardy, har, har, fuckface. You don't need to be a gentleman to get a wife," Gretz says in response.

"My girlfriend really likes when I'm nice to her," Brooks says as he saws through the front of his pumpkin. No template, no paper, just raw-dogging the front with a dream.

Gretz and Gunnar look up at Brooks with a furrow of their brows.

"Yeah, no fuckin' shit, dumbass. You should always be nice to your girlfriend, the fuck are you talking about?" Gretz asks.

"Gretz, do you even have a girlfriend?" Gunnar asks. He places the lid back on his pumpkin when he finishes pulling all the guts out of it and looks over it with a furrowed brow.

"I don't need one. I get all the pussy I want in college," he says with a shrug.

My face contorts in a grimace as I trace my design on the outside of my pumpkin with a pencil. It's nice that it was part of their little pumpkin kit.

"Do you even *want* a girlfriend?" Gunnar asks.

"Nah. I'm tryna get to the pros. I haven't got time for a dame. But a man's gotta get his fix," Gretz says with a shrug.

As much as I would like to be surprised over the way they talk to each other... I'm not. This is just a bunch of hockey men talking how hockey men do. I've been in this world for much longer than I should be. So this is barely a drop in the bucket for what I have actually heard.

Doesn't mean it's not gross, though.

"Are you at least using a fucking condom?" Gunnar groans.

"Of course, I am! Do I look dumb to you? I don't want any kids right now," he says with a scoff.

"Can't relate. I'm trying to knock this pretty lady up any second I can," Gunnar says as he continues moving his pumpkin around on the table.

He's looking at it from all angles, and I wonder what his

plan is, as a last-ditch attempt to keep my heart from exploding from my fucking chest at these three.

"Yeah, we know. You weren't very quiet in the bathroom," Brooks says.

I feel like my chest finally implodes, and I freeze in place, glancing up at the two of them, who glance at each other with taunting grins.

"Good fucking giiiiirl," Gretz says in a stunning impression of Gunnar.

Though the impression does nothing for my nerves as my hands grip for dear life on my pumpkin tools.

"You take my cock so well," Brooks chimes in.

I pretend as if I don't hear them, because there is absolutely nothing I can do or say that will make any of this any better. Because as a lawyer, I am not going to say anything that incriminates me further. Can't stop the goon from doing that though.

So, I do what anyone should do when they're shit out of luck.

Mind their goddamn business.

"You fuckers stood outside the door, and I know you did. I heard your stupid little footsteps," Gunnar says with a groan and a shake of his head.

I glance over to see him not even the slightest bit perturbed by any of his brother's antics. If anything, he's bored with it.

There is a silent attraction in a man unbothered by someone essentially making fun of him.

Maybe just more of Gunnar being a big brother.

"What? You both were gone when we came back, and of course we had to make sure everything was good in paradise. Seems like it really is," Gretz says with a grin.

"Well at least it won't be a surprise to you dunces when we come back to tell you Tiana is carrying my kid," Gunnar says as he fixes his hand on the top of his pumpkin, holding it in place.

Regardless... I... this is *insane.* Everything else, fine, whatever.

But *this* is actually insane.

"I honestly do not know what Gunnar is talking about here," I murmur softly.

"Oh, you don't have to lie; it's fine. It's a very sex-positive household," Brooks chimes in.

"Didn't your mom just ask you to stop talking about your... bits? Is that the word she used?" I ask as I glance at them incredulously.

"Okay, so the rule is, we aren't allowed to talk about our pork and beans at the table, specifically. Everywhere else is fair game," Gretz says with a proud nod.

"Ah..." I say quietly. "Pork and beans?" I ask.

"Yeah, you know. Spaghetti and meatballs. Frank and furters. The whole jam," Brooks nods as he holds out his fist for Gretz to bump. And of course, he does.

"Is there a reason that... the normal name is insufficient?" I ask.

"It's boring," Gretz says with a shrug.

"Ah... Alright..." I say slowly.

I gulp, sawing back into my pumpkin.

Holy fuck, holy fuck, holy fuck, holy fuck. What the fuck am I marrying into?!

I don't have time to even ponder that. Because a loud smash is heard beside me. With the tools on the table rustling violently on its surface.

I yelp, jumping with a clutch at my chest as I immediately go on alert. My heart thuds, and I take heaving breaths as the scare seeps through *every fucking ounce* of my body.

Looking over, I see Gunnar with his fist shoved into the

front of his pumpkin. Jerking it back, he whips his hand out, with some of the pumpkin pieces falling off of it before he shakes the rest of the bits of pumpkin pulp off.

"What... the fuck was *that*?!" I yell as the nerves get the better of me.

My eyes volley between the gaping, ragged hole in his pumpkin and him like a rabid animal as I freeze in my spot.

"What? I couldn't figure out what to do, so I made it look like a puck went through it," he says with a satisfied shrug.

My jaw drops, my chest heaving as I look at him, then back at the pumpkin.

All at once, two more loud smashes are heard. Almost like gunshots in this small space, I jump again with each blow, only to turn and see the other two brothers pulling their fists out of their pumpkins.

"Hey hey, nice!" Gunnar says as the boys turn their pumpkins around to show each other.

"Whoop whoop! Puck-kins!" Gretz calls out.

The three of them hold their... "puck-kins" above their heads, chanting the term with excitement for a moment before they put them down to bump fists and... celebrate???

I stand, shell-shocked, my jaw agape in disbelief as I'm realizing... *this* is what I'm marrying into.

Oh. My. God.

CHAPTER SIXTEEN
TIANA

All the time, I wonder what it is about Gunnar that makes me do the things I wouldn't normally do.

Because here I am, right behind the box, watching the game again.

An entire week after my last weekend was taken from me.

Granted, we had dinner at Gunnar's parent's house last weekend, which was not something I was going to miss; I *needed* to meet them, and I wanted to make sure they weren't upset at me for the truck.

But now, here I am at a *game.* Luckily, it's a home game. But I'm still in my work clothes, which is not exactly comfy.

I should have taken the time to grab clothes before I left, but... whatever. Here we are. Already into the second period, and Gunnar is on his A-game.

"Keep pressure on 'em, they're breaking!!!" My dad yells from the box with hard claps. Russel keeps yelling with my dad as well, pacing behind the players on the bench.

He taps one player on the back, sending them in for a change out. Soon, Gunnar comes barreling to the wall, swinging his leg over to sit on the bench with the rest of the team.

His tongue forces his mouth guard off his teeth, and he shifts it enough to clasp it between them, wiggling his jaw as he leans forward on his stick. His back moves in and out with heavy breaths as he watches the game.

I try to leave him alone during games, because he gets into these modes of focus. Sort of the same thing as the costume search. And right now seems like one of them. His eyes take on an almost blank look as he absorbs everything happening on the ice.

I have to admit, it's sexy as fuck. I love that he loves his job, and I do actually love being able to see it this way. His skin and face take on this pink, sweaty look. Something a tad reminiscent of our 'activities.'

God, if only Tiana from six months ago could see me now.

I shake my head of the thought as I'm brought back to the game by Gunnar's shouting.

"Hey four-five! Fuck you! He may be the tendy, but you're the chicken shit here!" Gunnar calls out to the ice.

His gloved hand grabs at the wall as he leans in, his knee bouncing with an unreal amount of energy. He's like a dog being held back from chasing a ball.

My attention is pulled away when Charlotte leans over to tell me something.

"Hey! After the game, Gunnar wanted you to come spend the night at Adrian's place with us!" she yells over the loud crowds as the horn goes off when the Stags score a goal.

I look to the ice to see Crowder, one of our players hooting in excitement.

Waiting for the cowbells to die down, I cover my ears with my hands before they start up again and some of the noise subsides.

I shake my head in annoyance as I lean over to Charlotte. "Okay, what now?" I groan.

"Gunnar wants you both to spend the night at our place, but he wanted me to ask you!" she says again.

I roll my eyes as I pinch the middle of my eyebrows. I have no idea why these people want me to keep giving up my weekends for this shit.

The dinner doesn't count; that was something that needed to be done. And sure, the pumpkin patch was fun. But it still was not on my time. It was something I was asked to do. Not the same instance at all.

But now they want me to leave the comfort of my *own* house to come spend the night wherever the fuck Adrian lives.

"Do you have food for me? And are the sheets in the guest room not..."

"It isn't that weird silky fabric you hate, and I have plenty of your favorites; you're fine. I've got plenty of pancake mix and bacon. And I already told Adrian you want steak and potatoes," she says with a wave of her hand.

That eases at least some of my worries.

"Why does Gunnar want to spend the night there?" I ask.

"I don't know. I think Adrian told him something about horses, and he was all for it," Charlotte says with a shrug of her shoulders.

"Ugh, fine, but if we're going to do that, we have to leave now so I can pack our shit," I say.

Charlotte nods, and I lean over to tap Gunnar.

He leans back, offering me his ear without taking his eyes off the game.

"You win, goon. I'm leaving to go get our shit packed," I yell over the crowd.

"*We're* the fucking Stags, four-six! Why the fuck are you

the one wobbling?!" he yells to some other player on the ice before he leans back to me.

"Sounds good," he murmurs before he purses his lips to me in a kiss.

Of course, I have to lean all the way over to even reach him because he gave me little to none of his face.

He presses in harder when I meet his lips and flicks his eyes down to them when he pulls away.

"I'll be back to pick you up after the game. If you get in my fucking car sweaty and nasty, I'm kicking your ass," I say as I gather my things.

"10-4, big mama," he says with a nod.

I roll my eyes and look at Charlotte, nodding toward the exit.

We stand to inch through the stands, making our way to our dad.

He has his arms crossed, pacing back and forth behind the players before he taps another in.

"Head up!!!" he screams before he claps hard again.

"We're leaving. Make sure they win. I'm not trying to deal with butthurt hockey players tonight," I tell my dad when I tap him on the shoulder.

"Sure thing," he murmurs with a wave over his shoulder at us.

I continue making my way down the line, heading straight for the tunnel.

Charlotte speeds up behind me, following as fast as she can, and we walk past several big TV cameras and other people that crowd the tunnels. Medics, camera people and other arena workers.

We walk along the outskirts, trying to make it to the quieter inner portion of the arena. Soon, we make it to the back hallways, and the sharpness of the noise inside the arena has dulled to just the bass and beats of the music.

"So what's the plan? What's happening?" I ask Charlotte as I take a deep breath, leading her to my office.

The intense noises always feel like I'm being suffocated trying to make sure I don't lose my mind. So when I get the chance to breathe after overstimulation, I always fucking take it.

"I think we're going to go get your stuff at the apartments, and then we're going to come back here, pick up the boys and head out," she says.

"Fine, that's easy enough. Did you guys take your car or Adrian's truck?" I ask.

"Adrian always drives his truck for some reason. I always say my car has better gas mileage but the man likes his truck," she says with a shrug.

I roll my eyes. "Where is this place you guys live now?"

"Adrian has a big stretch of property on the outskirts of Tacoma. It's actually not far from Mom and Dad's house, but he bought a whole lotta land when he made captain," Charlotte says as I enter my office and grab some of my things. My tote and my computer and everything else. I look around to see if Gunnar left anything for me to grab, and when I see he hasn't, we make our way back out into the hallways to the exit.

When we make it outside, the sounds of the arena are now a thing of the past and I take a deep breath as the pressure of it all eases off my ears, and I can be more relaxed.

"Thank fuck. I hate that shit," I sigh with a groan.

"Why didn't you wear your headphones?" Charlotte asks as she wraps her arms tighter around herself in the cooling fall air.

"I don't know. I usually have a pair in my office, but I couldn't find them today. Gunnar wanted me out by the rink at puck drop, so I didn't have time to look for them."

As we get to my car, I unlock it and we climb in, starting it up to drive toward the apartment.

Charlotte takes a deep breath as she relaxes in the passenger seat, and the bright lights of the parking lot turn into street lights as we make our way through the city.

"So... you moved in with him... why?" I ask.

"I don't know, to be honest. I'm comfortable with him. And I really like the way we have set things up with each other. It's really... peaceful," she says.

I glance at her from the corner of my eye to see her looking out the window. Almost star-struck, thinking about her hockey player.

"Does he make you happy?" I ask quietly.

"He really does, Ti. I didn't know he felt the way he did about me when he started talking to me. Honestly, I didn't know if he had eyes for anyone. He was always so in his own little world. So, I was shocked when he actually asked to get to know me. But he's like the calm in my life, ya' know. The same way you kind of are for Gunnar. Opposites attract. You get the high-energy goon, and I get the low-key captain," she says as she leans toward me with a smile.

My lip tilts in a sideways smile as I glance from the road to her again.

"Well... as long as he treats you nicely, and he makes you happy, I guess I'm fine with him," I respond.

"I was going to date him anyway, but I appreciate the approval," she says with a chuckle as she waves her hand and turns back to the window.

I roll my eyes in amusement with a shake of my head. "Anyway... we're spending the night? Why couldn't we just come over tomorrow or something?"

"Gunnar said that he didn't wanna have to wake you up super early on a weekend and pack to have you get ready to go in the morning. He just wanted to wake up with you in the morning at our place. He told me, at least, that he wants to make sure you're getting enough sleep," Charlotte says with a shrug.

My brow raises. "Did he tell you why?"

"Aside from the mental strain of wedding planning? He said something about making sure your body is ready to carry his kids," Charlotte says with a sly smile.

"Oh, my God. He did not say that," I say with a shocked scoff.

"He did. He was telling Adrian. But he's quite adamant about getting you pregnant from what I heard," she says with a shrug.

"What the fuck happened to gentlemen don't kiss and tell?" I groan.

"Well, I guess he thinks it doesn't count because I'm your sister, and he thinks I'll help make sure you're staying healthy for it."

I pull into the parking garage, parking in my spot before I glance over at her.

She throws her hands up in surrender. "That's your mans, Ti. He wants a baby bad," she says.

"Did you know he has a breeding kink?" I ask slowly.

Her brow furrows, and she looks at me. "A... breeding kink?" she asks.

"That's what I said when he told me about it! Do you know what it is?"

"Well, yeah, I mean. It's normal, I think. Adrian has one," she says with a shrug.

"He's trying to get you pregnant too!?" I ask.

"He wants to, but it's just a kink. I'm not trying to have a kid right now," she says as we get out of the car.

I groan as I toss my head back, leading her to the elevator that takes us to the lobby.

"Why? What's wrong? Do you not want a kid?" she asks as we step in.

When we enter, I press the button for the lobby and lean back against the wall with a sigh. "I do... I mean I got my IUD taken out," I admit as I cross my arms against my chest.

"Whoa. When the fuck did you do that?!" she asks.

"It was when we were apart. It was kind of impulsive, bu-"

"I'll say," she murmurs.

"Can I finish? Is that a thing that can be done here?"

"Go ahead, go ahead. That's just wild to me," she mumbles with a shrug.

I roll my eyes. "I don't know how to describe it. I just... wanted to be the one to do that for him. I think it would be nice for us to start our family," I say with a small smile.

"That's kind of sweet. You've never been the kid type," she admits.

The elevator dings for us to enter the lobby, and we exit to make our way to the apartment elevators.

"No, I'm not. But I want to carry his... I don't know if it's just because of the way he talks to me when... ya' know. But I do. I think he would be an amazing dad," I say.

And I *really* do.

It's kind of strange to want to give a baby to the first man you've dated in... a *long* fucking time. But I feel like it's the next step for us.

I really don't know why. Or what propels me through it because at the end of the day, I know he's here whether I'm pregnant or not. That's clear.

But... It just feels right. I want to... see this little thing we created. Carry it for him, raise the baby with him. At the end of the day, I think I just want a family with *him*.

I don't think I'd want this with anyone else. I don't think anyone would be more caring of me and the baby than he would be. I'd just love to be that piece of the puzzle for him.

He already treats me like a queen. I can barely imagine how much that would increase for us to have a baby.

Not that he would treat me better simply because I gave him a child. I just have this feeling... this *warmth* in my chest when I imagine our little family.

My silence goes on for a moment longer before I feel Charlotte's hand on my shoulder. I look up to see her giving me a sweet and considerate smile.

"I think you'd be a great mom, Ti. If that's what you'd like to do, go for it. But don't let him talk you into it just because *he* wants one," she says.

"He's not. He was literally inside of me when I told him I got my IUD taken out, and he kept asking if I was sure about that. And I told him what my thought process was. He'd be here whether or not we had a baby," I say with a shrug.

"Well, that's good. He doesn't seem like the type to be like that anyway, but I just had to make sure because you never talked about being a wife. Let alone being a whole mother," she says as we exit the elevator and make our way down the hall to the apartments.

"Trust me. I'm just as shocked as you are," I murmur as I enter my apartment.

I take a quick moment to change into some comfy clothes, and then, Charlotte and I make sure I pack all the stuff Gunnar and I will need for this weekend excursion.

After I make sure I have everything I need, I get Tucker's leash on to take him out to pee.

"Alright, buddy, come on. One last pee, and then I bring you in," I tell him.

"Oh, no. You're bringing Tucker," Charlotte says.

I pause in my tracks, tilting my head as my brow furrows. "Why?"

"Well, Gunnar thinks he would have fun on the ranch. And Adrian and I got a dog recently!" Charlotte says with an excited giggle and clap of her hands.

"You guys got a dog?" I ask as I look down at Tucker.

He sits like the perfect gentleman he is, panting with excitement as he waits.

"Yes! A little corgi! Her name is Waffle, and she's the most precious little thing," Charlotte says with a day-dreamy sigh.

"A... corgi? Is Adrian okay with that?" I ask as I hand the leash out to Charlotte.

"Oh yeah, of course! He always wanted a cattle dog," Charlotte nods as she takes Tucker's leash.

I look around for some of his things. A few of his favorite chew toys, and I prepare a bag of his dog food before I try to find a small backpack to put things in. Going to Gunnar's closet, I find an empty backpack and stuff the dog supplies in it before I throw it on my back and grab the duffle bag I packed for us.

"Alright, well, I need you to take Tucker then, if that's alright. I'm going to go get in the car, and I'll meet you in front of the building," I tell Charlotte.

"Sounds good to me! Come on, buddy, let's go peepee!" Charlotte squeals as she runs out of the apartment.

Tucker trots right beside her with a wide, panting grin.

I take a few moments to go through both apartments,

making sure I missed nothing before I lock them both up and head down to the parking garage.

I quickly throw everything in the trunk, and then get in to drive to meet Charlotte at the front of the complex.

Coming around the building, I see Charlotte kneeling down, scratching and rubbing Tucker's face. He pants flurries of steam into the air as she stands when I approach.

She opens the door and lets Tucker climb over the front seats to the back, where he sits by the window, looking out as we drive back to the arena.

The drive goes by quickly and is quiet because Charlotte is on her phone looking over the Stags' social media the entire time.

I really just want to get to Charlotte's house, shower and sleep because I am exhausted. Games always take the energy out of me, and having to make this detour is draining me faster than I expected it to.

Luckily, by the time we get back, the boys are outside waiting for us.

Thank *God,* because I did not wanna go back into the arena.

I love Gunnar, and I love the team. But I do *not* love games. I don't mind watching *him,* but it is still a struggle with the sensory overload that games are. And I think Gunnar knows that.

I pull up at the exit of the stadium, letting Charlotte get out. She climbs out of my car, squealing with glee as she hops up into Adrian's arms, kissing all over his face. I actually see a ghost of a smile crest against his lips as he grabs tight at her thighs. I hear a squeak of approval from her as she buries her face into his neck and he steps off of the curb.

"See you at the ranch?" I hear Adrian ask Gunnar, and Gunnar nods before he presses a fist out for Adrian to bump.

He shifts his grip for a second to return the bump before he walks through the parking lot to his truck.

Gunnar shakes his head, letting drips of water fly from his hair before he climbs into the car. He throws his backpack in the backseat before he settles in his seat with a deep sigh. Tucker licks and nuzzles his face, and Gunnar gives a hearty laugh.

"Buddy! You made it!" he says as he ruffles Tucker's head with a bunch of hard scratches. Tucker gets more and more excited, licking over Gunnar's face before he laughs and slowly pushing him to the back.

"Alright, alright! Settle down!" he says with a laugh.

Tucker pants as he makes a few circles in the back seat, then plops down to rest with a heavy pant.

I shake my head playfully as I watch him in the rearview mirror before I look to Gunnar.

His head tilts exhaustedly in my direction with a big grin. "We won."

"Good job, babe," I say sweetly. I lean in to kiss his lips, with his hand coming up to stroke my cheek as he kisses me back, before he leans back in his seat. He expands in the seat, pressing his thighs out before resting his head against the headrest.

"I am fucking beat. That was a tough one," he says with a sigh as he runs his hand through his hair.

"Yeah?" I say as I wait for the lights of Adrian's truck to come on so I can follow him out to wherever the fuck he lives.

"Yeah, the Canadians are always tough. I mean, they grew up on that shit, so I always gotta lock in whenever we play them. It was in our barn too, so I had to make sure the pigs weren't fuckin' about," he says. He dips his chin, securing his chain in his teeth before he leans back. He lets out another heavy sigh as his tongue swirls and plays with the bit in his mouth.

Soon, Adrian pulls out of his parking spot, and I follow his truck out of the arena parking lot.

"So, Charlotte gave me some enlightening information today," I say with a slightly accusatory tone.

I see Gunnar freeze momentarily from the corner of my eye, before he gives me a slight grin. "Now, sugar... I thought-"

"You want her to help you try to get *my* body ready for having a baby?!" I ask.

"Well yes! But I also don't want you to burn out! You go all the damn time, and that's not healthy for anybody," he says as he pleads his case.

My eyes narrow on him. "So, you told her you're trying to get me pregnant?"

"I mean, it came up in conversation. Banks was wondering what we were going to do after we got married, and I said I was trying to make you a mother," he says with a shrug.

"I'm going to ask you the same thing I asked Charlotte. What the hell happened to gentlemen don't kiss and tell?!" I ask with a groan.

"Okay, so right now, only Banks and Charlotte know."

I stop him. "And your brothers," I murmur.

"Yes, and my brothers. But I only told them because they asked, and it went from there. Plus, technically, Banks will be my brother-in-law at some point, and that's cool, right?!" he says with an unconvincing smile.

I glance at him with a deadpan look, and he sighs as he grabs my hand, kissing the top of it repeatedly in apology as he glances up at me with sad puppy-dog eyes.

"I'm sorry, sugar. I shouldn't have told them. That's my bad. It's not very gentlemanly of me to do that. I just got kind of excited," he says.

My chest squeezes and I give a small smile to him. "I'm not *actually* upset. I'm more surprised than anything. I didn't think you'd tell them something like that," I say softly.

"So... I've been trying to figure out ways to help you," he starts.

"Yeah, Adrian told me," I say.

"Right. And I just wanted Charlotte to stay in the loop because she knows the most about you, since you guys are twins and all. But I figured if she knew what we were trying to do, she could help me with some things when it came to you. I only ever want to make sure you're comfortable and happy," he says quietly.

I keep my eyes on Adrian's tail lights, listening to his words as I keep following him outside of Seattle.

"I know that this whole... situation is hard for you. And that in general, you are going through a lot of changes with your space and being with someone. I can see it in your day-to-day; you're tenser, or you try to push away some things that trip you up. And I never want to change who you are. I just want to help make the hard days easier. And if we are trying to have a baby, I just don't want your body to be surprised if you accidentally run yourself into the ground with other things. You go so often, and I just want to make sure you're taking care of yourself, is all, baby." He kisses my hand in between his lengthy explanation.

It causes my chest to swell and tighten with emotion.

"So, that's your whole reason for not letting me plan the wedding?" I ask quietly.

"No sugar, not at all. I just don't want you to burn out, regardless. I had never seen you get like that, and I'm just making sure you still have energy for everyday life. Eating and sleeping are important, ya' know... for, like... living?" he says.

His lips tilt at the corners as I glance at him. He knows I'm messing with him. But that doesn't stop me from playing hard-ass.

"Next time, tell me when you're going to tell them about stuff like this. I don't want my parents to hear it from someone else if they're about to be grandparents," I tell him.

"Yes ma'am. I'm sorry, sugar. I'll be more careful next time," he murmurs as he presses another kiss into the top of my hand.

"Why is it you wanted to come spend the night out here? Charlotte said something about horses," I say as we continue on the highway, farther out of the city.

"Well, Banks does have horses, but he also has four-wheelers, and I thought that would be a fun little adventure for the weekend. Get your mind off of everything, out into nature and just hang out with no pressure for a few days. You don't have to get up super early. You don't have to worry about anything. I really just want you to have a relaxing weekend. And if you want to stay in bed all day, we can do that too. But Charlotte said you do well with a change of scenery," he says.

My eyes continue to burn, threatening tears to spill over as I listen to him.

It's always me first; it's always *my* well-being and how to improve my life. And I can't believe I'm marrying a man this thoughtful and sweet.

I feel like I don't deserve this. But I *know* I do; and it's only because of him I realize I do.

I've gone so long without proper love and care that I feel bad for myself for letting all those men walk over me.

Gunnar has allowed me to see how great I am, how much I deserve, and that I shouldn't ever take the bare minimum, not even from him.

How in the world did I get so lucky? What did I do to experience this kind of love in my life?

I never even knew love could *be* this. Where someone has your back, they have your best interests at heart. You're on their mind at the same they are on yours. A mutual feeling of respect, of love and care. Thoughts of your wellbeing... being worshipped for being you, where you were once thrown aside.

Gunnar Hayze... you beautiful man, you.

"You're an incredible man. Have I ever told you that?" I ask with a small smile as I glance at him.

"Well. An incredible man with an incredible woman. A tremendous pairing, I reckon," he responds.

My lips quirk at the sides as he grabs my hand, holding it tight with strokes over the top.

With the faint sound of his chain in his teeth, we continue our way all the way out to the outskirts of Tacoma.

CHAPTER SEVENTEEN
GUNNAR

I don't even realize when we get to Banks' ranch house, because I passed out on the way out here. And the only way I woke up was to the rough bumping of riding on gravel.

A long drive through the trees until we got behind some trees to this large, open area. There isn't a discernible driveway. More like a bunch of land where patches of grass are missing from where Banks and Charlotte park their vehicles.

At the very back of this dirt road is a single-story ranch house with a large wrap-around porch. The lights inside the house illuminate the area enough to see the porch swing that hangs under the overhang guarding the porch.

To the far right of the property, I can see a large building, and what looks like wooden fencing of a giant corral of sorts.

It was a longer drive than I expected, and the Canadians had really done a number on us with that game. I don't think we've had a harder game so far this season.

When we park, Tiana can't stop herself from jumping out of the car to look at the stars. Tucker follows her out, and she quickly takes off his leash before he barks excitedly, running around the large open area. I follow her out of the car, taking a massive stretch and a yawn as I look around the property.

Soon, more barking is heard coming from the lit house. With the hurrying legs of a little orange dog bee-lining straight for us.

Tucker turns to the noise, his ears perking up as he looks around. The little dog bolts straight for him, and they run and play around each other for a long moment before they do a little game of 'stand your ground'. Where they take turns going on alert to make sure they both are... good?

But my eyes catch on Tiana, where she looks straight out to the sky. Clear, no clouds, and bright from the moon.

That was something I hadn't even thought of.

Light pollution.

Leaning into the car, I grab my backpack, and then move to the trunk, pulling out whatever bags Tiana brought with us. Another backpack and a large duffle bag.

I situate everything on my body before I make my way over to Tiana. The stars above are so bright and clear that as I approach, I can hear Tiana mumbling to herself all the names of the stars we can see.

There are some whinnies of horses from the building to the right of the property. I reckon that's the stable.

But Tiana, she hasn't moved. She merely stands frozen, watching the sky.

I freeze in place as I watch her.

She's always looked at the stars, at the moon, every time it's out. And I love getting lost in the sight of it.

Love getting lost in the sight of *her*.

Obviously, I asked Charlotte to help me convince Tiana to come out here under the guise of just a chill weekend hangout.

When what I really wanted to do was gauge what she thought of the land.

Sure, Banks has land he could sell me. But if Tiana doesn't like it, that's not the land for us. If Tiana is as specific about her space as I know she is, she will not settle for a house on land that she's not happy with.

But, these stars, and the lack of light out here... I think that's a great start.

She continues her mumbles, but as I get closer, her voice gets louder, as if she's talking to me.

"You can see the Stairway to the Milky Way," she says in awe. "I've never seen it before..."

I come up beside her, dropping the duffle bag beside me before wrapping an arm around her shoulders as I attempt a quiet yawn.

"It's beautiful," she murmurs.

And while I usually look up at the stars, hoping that Pa is up there looking down at us, I can't help looking down at the little lady by my side.

I have never been so head over heels for anything before in my life. The way she is so deeply passionate about the things she loves, but so low-key about them, truly enjoying them in every sense of the word.

She has her moments when life gets away from her, and I have to step in to help her. And I don't mind helping her. But I love when she finds her peace. Times like now, when her mind is quiet, and she's able to just live this life she's so enamored by.

And I watch her for a while as her eyes dart and scan over the ethereal darkness before I finally whisper back, "It really is."

The next morning, a *literal* rooster wakes us up.

"*Crow caw*" like in the fucking cartoons.

Honestly, I think if I had known that, I might not have brought Tiana out here.

But Tiana doesn't budge beside me. She sleeps hard as hell, even as the rooster crows.

So with a tug at the pillow I lay on, I pull it over my head, trying to block out any of the noise from outside.

I've flipped onto my stomach, and even though I really want to hide as much of my head as I can, I have to tilt my hips because my cock is hard as stone.

I groan in annoyance as I turn my hips enough to not crush the poor little guy, before Tiana wiggles in her sleep, poking herself with it.

She exhales a sleepy moan as she backs up against it, and I groan as I realize this is just something she usually does.

Do I frequently wake Tiana up with morning sex? Yes, it gets her awake faster, I've found.

But right *now*, this is just something that seemed to 'happen', and I wasn't trying to mess up Tiana's morning with a cock inside of her!

Now I have *two* fucking cocks to worry about. The bastard *outside* that's cawing with the sunrise. And the one *inside* that's barking for Tiana.

Tiana backs up further, grinding her butt against me, and a tortured noise leaks out of me.

"Tiana," I whisper, trying to rouse her enough to make sure she knows what's happening.

"Mmmm... Gunnar," she moans softly.

"Are you okay?" I murmur.

"Cock," she sighs.

My eyes float to the top of my head in disbelief with a low groan.

Fuck. What have I done to myself?

But I'm not going to deny her. I don't think I ever could.

This is not how I wanted to wake her if I promised a fucking peaceful weekend.

I lean back, lifting the blankets to see her back arched, her ass waiting for me. I can see the bare lips of her pussy from where she lies, which only hardens me further.

"Fuck," I groan as I run a hand over my face.

Taking a deep breath and a hard grip at the base of my cock, I slap it against her ass, hoping maybe it'll wake her and she'll tell me to stop.

But she merely wiggles more.

I growl with a toss of my head.

Alright, fuck. We're doing this.

I toss the blankets off our bodies, baring her for me, and using my free hand, I part her thighs just enough to get myself to her entrance. Pressing the head in slowly, I hiss, feeling how wet she already is. My head falls back, and I release a low groan.

Insanity. This early in the morning? The sun has barely risen, and she's already drenched.

Once I get the head in her, my hands move to her hips, slowly pushing myself in.

"Goddamnit," I breathe. My eyes roll, my head hitting the pillow as it tilts back, relishing in the way she grips me. My hips move slightly on their own, wanting to go for the kill, but I restrain myself, growling as I bring my head back up to watch her cunt swallow me.

It doesn't help how fucking hard my morning wood is. She feels fucking *insane* when I'm this hard.

I hear her make small noises as I push further and further in. All the while, I'm hoping, fucking *praying* she wakes up and tells me to stop. I don't mind fucking her, of course. But I don't want her to think I poked her on purpose.

But what my baby wants, my baby gets.

Even if that's me.

"Gunnar," I hear her pant. Her breath changes from calm, rhythmic sleeping inhales and exhales to calculated, steadying breaths as she works through the pleasure of me stretching her.

"You awake, sugar?" I pant as I lean in to kiss her bare shoulder softly.

Of course, she slept naked.

It's like she planned on torturing me.

She nods, pressing herself back further to work more of me in her.

"Deeper... I need all of it," she moans in a low whisper.

A noise of disbelief works through me.

Welp, there's definitely no stopping now.

I run a hand down her side, her hip. Her skin is like silk as I caress every inch of her body, and it only causes my urgency to heighten. Feeling her fucking skin always works me into a frenzy. Working down her thigh, I reach for her knee, and drag it up, opening more of her for me.

Her head tilts back into the crook of my shoulder, baring her neck to me. As I lick and press kisses into the skin, she melts further into me, and I use it as a chance to work my arm under her body to grasp her tit. It fills my hand with a decadent weight, giving me something to hold as I thrust in and out of her. I knead and grip it in my palm before pinching softly at her nipple.

"Like that, baby?" I ask with a heavy pant as my hips slowly work the head of my cock in and out of her in shallow pumps.

"More," she moans in response.

Pulling her knee higher, I punch forward, filling her in one solid stroke. She whimpers, trying to control her noises as her body tightens.

Soon, I forget my frustrations with the morning and lock onto the way this perfect fucking woman grips me. I switch from stroking over her nipple to grasping her tit in my hand, kneading the plush flesh as my hips rock in and out of her smoothly.

Pulling all the way out before slowly working myself all the way back in, over and over.

Groaning and panting, my thoughts wipe from my skull. The only fucking thing that exists is *her* body. The way it's wrapped around my cock. Her skin and the way it feels against my bare chest. The silky, slightly damp heat of her back as it melts into my chest.

Madness. This woman and everything she is — it's madness. And I'm so *fucking* lucky to be going insane right now.

She turns her head, seeking my mouth, and I capture her with a sloppy, sensual kiss. Pressing my body tighter against her, I keep a steady rhythm, pistoning in and out of her.

"Is this what you wanted, sugar? My cock balls deep in this pussy?" I pant against her lips.

She nods, grinding back against my length before I hang her leg over my arm, reaching down to rub her clit.

My head tilts back, her pussy gripping me in torturous rolls, causing my thrusts to stop as I give in.

"I needed you. Fuck... I needed your cock so bad. I dreamed of you inside me," she pants desperately.

I love when her voice turns light and breathy. Begging and desperate, I love making her a whimpering fucking mess.

I kiss down her jaw, moving to lick and nip at her neck as I keep pace on her clit, my other hand tugging at her nipple.

"You're so fucking tight, sugar. So fucking wet, it's enough to bring a man to his fucking knees," I rasp against her neck.

I thrust harder, faster, picking up speed as my release shows its face on the horizon.

I groan, my speed picking up on her clit. "Come for me, baby. I need you to come for me. I'm so fucking close. Come with me," I murmur over and over, pounding into her with unrelenting strokes.

She bites down hard on her lip, stifling her moans and groans as much as she can before her body shudders, her whimpers leaking through the bite in her lip as she grinds through her orgasm against me.

My orgasm slams into me, choking me as my cock twitches rigid pumps of heat into her. I fill her with every ounce of myself that I can, over and over as her pussy clamps down on me, sucking me in incredible waves of ecstasy.

"That's it, baby. Keep going, wring it out, I'm right here, take it all out on my cock," I growl against her, urging her to keep coming.

Soon, I feel my spend leak from where I hold myself within her. My breath heaves in and out of my chest as I finally settle against her, taking a beat and enjoying the way her skin feels against mine.

"Jesus Christ, Tiana. I was not expecting that," I say with an exhausted chuckle. Removing my hand from her clit, I slowly let her leg down and take gentle strokes up and down her side as I press small kisses into her shoulder.

"Sorry, I felt your dick, and the dream I had was so intense that I just... I needed it," she says with a small giggle.

My brow rises as I lean in to nip at her neck. "Are you ovulating?" I ask with a grin.

"Maybe...? I don't know...? Why?" she asks as she looks back at me.

"No wonder my cock was so fucking hard this morning," I murmur against her skin.

I take another hard grind into her, feeling my cum against her walls, and she moans out as I press my chest against her shoulder. Forcing her chest into the bed, I mount her from behind.

"Remember what I said about free use?" I whisper in her ear as I take a hard thrust into her.

She bites down on the pillow, burying her face in it as her upper body tightens.

I still hadn't pulled out from where I came in her, so I move in her *so* easily.

My chest sticks slightly to her back as I lean up, caging in her thighs with my legs. I look down at her perfect ass, my cock still pressed into her pussy. I see where I've leaked out of her. The sight causes a pulse of animalistic need to rush through me.

I grab her hips, using my thumbs to press into her lower back, arching it for me. A growl of satisfaction leaves me as I press myself all the way to the hilt, her ass jiggling as I thrust into her, beginning to move in hard, claiming strokes. The headboard slams against the wall with a loud thud as I throw every bit of power I have into her.

"Perfect." *thrust* "Fucking." *thrust* "Pussy," I grunt before I pick up a rhythm, taking every bit of her for myself.

She buries her face deep into the pillow, her hips rocking back against me, taking me so *fucking* well.

Just the way she always does.

Her whimpers and pleas are muffled in the pillow, and I

grip a handful of her hair at the nape of her neck, pulling her up and propping her on all fours.

"Please, please, please, please, please," she whimpers as I throw my strokes deeper, her head tilting back as her back arches to perfection.

"God, look at you. Just fuckin' *look* at you, sugar. Such a good girl. Taking my cock, letting me pump you full of my fucking kids, just like I asked. Gorgeous little thing you are, baby," I grunt as I lean over her, wrapping my arms around her chest. I grip hard on her breasts, using them as leverage.

My hips piston in and out, a feral level of heat pulses through me. One that digs deep into whatever little dog is in my brain, forcing me to knock her up, because the only thing on my mind is getting her pregnant.

Pleasure? Out the window right now, I just wanna pump her full of my cum, make it drip out of her for fucking days.

At any other time, I would have wanted to turn her mind into mush. But right now, I don't know if maybe she is ovulating and I'm just picking up on whatever the fuck her body is putting out.

But giving in fully to a breeding kink?

Out of this fucking *world*.

I damn near growl as I come again, filling her with more of me.

"Your womb was made to carry *my* fucking kids. Made to take *my* cock, made to take *me*, weren't you, sugar? Made to be *my* cumslut, my perfect mommy, huh, baby?" I growl as I take a few more thrusts, riding out my orgasm inside her.

As my orgasm wanes, my hands release her tits, bracing against the bed as I lean against her back. Panting and gulping air, her sweaty, hot body stuck to mine as I bring my mind back to the present.

What the fuck did I just say?

I press soft kisses onto her shoulders, rubbing my hands down her sides as I press small thrusts in and out of her. She's so filled that I can feel it dripping down my balls.

I lean back from her body, looking down at where I'm still held inside her. I've made a fucking mess of her, and I feel my cock twitch as I admire it.

"Holy fuck, Gunnar. What was that?" she pants.

Her voice pulls me out of my horny trance, and I give a soft chuckle as I rub the back of my neck.

"I'm so sorry, sugar. All I could think about was getting you pregnant... I have no idea what was coming out of my mouth," I say with an exhausted sigh. "I just wanted to fill you with as much as I could."

I stroke up and down her back, my head tipping back through heavy breaths as I regain a human brain from... whatever the fuck that was. Soon, I feel my cock soften, and I grip her hips as I pull out of her.

My spend gushes out of her, and I can't help groaning as my cock twitches again, hardening more.

"Goddammit, no. We're done here," I murmur out loud to my dick.

She looks over her shoulder at me from where she's still propped on all fours, with a confused tilt of her brow. "What?"

"Sorry, not you. My... dick got hard again," I mumble as I press it down with my wrist.

Her eyes glance at my cock with a quirk of her brow before they come back up to my face. With a flick of her body, she leans forward, landing on her back on the bed.

Reaching behind her, she takes the pillow she screamed into. She settles on the bed before she hands it out to me. My brow furrows as I take it, giving her a confused look.

"Put it under my hips. You said this was part of your little fantasy, wasn't it?" she asks with a small grin.

My eyes widen as I look at the pillow, then back at her.

Oh fuck. I did say that...

"Yeah, but... you're more likely... to get pregnant...? This way?" I respond.

Her eyes roam around the room in confusion. "Yeah... That's... that's like the whole point, isn't it?"

I have no idea what I did to deserve this little lady. I must have done some saint shit in my past life because *how* in the fuck did I get so lucky?

My teeth catch my lip, nipping in glee as I hold the pillow and she lifts her butt enough for me to prop her hips up.

I shove it under her butt before I come to lie beside her, wrapping my arms around her waist as I snuggle into her side.

One of my hands comes to rub at her stomach, kissing into the skin there as I do.

"May I ask something?" she asks as she twirls a lock of my hair around a finger.

"Of course," I murmur.

"Aside from... the breeding kink aspect... why do you want me to get pregnant so bad?"

My thoughts run, my gaze stuck onto where my finger circles the skin on her stomach.

"I want to be a dad. And I want to be a good husband to my wife. And I think those things go hand in hand. At least to me. I want to watch you grow this precious little person for us. I want to see it all happen and know I had a hand in it. We also aren't getting younger. We're in our late twenties, and I don't want to wait because I don't want you to have a hard pregnancy. I want you to do whatever you want to do. Because I know pregnancy isn't going to stop you from working, and if that's what you want to do, I just want you to work to your heart's content," I say softly.

My thoughts swirl and dance in my head, envisioning all the things together.

Tiana has gone quiet, and I can almost feel her heart pounding from where I rest against her side.

I swirl my finger around her belly button, watching it.

"I want to give *you* something that no one else can. And I want *you* to be the one to give me something no one else can. I want to see what our love is capable of. I want to..." I pause, taking a deep breath as I flatten my palm against her stomach. "I want to love you in the rawest form that I can. And I want to *hold* that proof of our love. Because it's so strong... so potent. I want to *physically* see *you* grow our love. The way you'd round, the glow you'd have. At the end of it all, I just want to love *you* as much as I can. And I feel like having a little version of you will only intensify that," I say as I look up at her.

Her eyes are bright, glassy and considering as they watch me. They're intent as she listens.

"So... are we... officially in the baby-making stage of things?" she asks.

"If you want to, yes. I mean I've been coming in you, sure. But if we're actively trying, then... that's up to you, sugar," I tell her with a soft kiss to her stomach.

Her eyes volley back and forth against mine for a long moment, her finger swirling in my hair before she nods softly.

"Alright, I guess we're actively baby-making," she says before she leans up to kiss my forehead.

I can't help the grin that pulls up at my lips as I jump from the bed, leaning to the door to open it and yell into the hall, "WE'RE MAKING A BABY!!!!"

I hear one male groan in annoyance and a shriek of female excitement before I close the door, jumping back onto the bed to wrap my arms tight around Tiana and hold her close to me.

"We'reeee making a babyyy," I sing-song as I press kisses over her tummy.

I look up at her to see her rolling her eyes playfully.

"This changes basically nothing, you know," she says with a smirk.

"Yeah, I know, but now it's *actual* baby-making; you put a label on it. It's *baby-making* sex, not lovemaking," I say with a proud nod.

"Oh my God," she scoffs before she presses my head away.

I tighten my grip on her, crawling up her body to grab her head and place tons of little kisses all over her face.

She shrieks as she tries to pull away, small giggles working out as I keep kissing her. Soon, I stop and look into her eyes with a grin.

And she looks back. With a considering, warm gaze.

One that tells me she feels like she made the right decision.

CHAPTER EIGHTEEN

TIANA

Sore, I think, is a grand word for how I feel right now.

I was so tired last night that when we finally showered and got into whatever guest room Charlotte and Adrian had prepared for us; I was ready to pass out.

Maybe it was just how far away Adrian's house is from everything or not, I have no idea, but it was the best sleep I'd had in a long time.

Which is strange to say, because I rarely get good sleep outside of my bed.

But it was nice.

It was even nicer having our tryst this morning.

I wasn't expecting to have sex so easily here. But that dream had me on another level this morning. Am I ovulating? No fucking clue. I haven't had a period yet since I've had my IUD removed, so I haven't tracked anything. But when the rooster crowed outside, and I felt Gunnar hard and ready at my back, there was an *overwhelming* need for that man.

I felt like a cat in heat, just meowing incessantly for him to fuck me.

So when he climbed back on top of me after I came just to pump more into me, I *welcomed* it.

Craved it, even.

But the thought and questions that Charlotte asked me last night came to the forefront, and I felt like it was necessary to ask. As someone who never really dreamed of having kids, I wanted to see what it was like from his perspective. Someone who was so adamant about it.

Listening to his words, his explanation... I looked at it all in a different light.

Not just something that he said because it was what I may have wanted to hear. I could tell that he meant every word of what he said, and it only made *me* want it more.

He was right about our ages. I don't want to stop working just because I might get pregnant. And we *are* almost thirty.

We're in a good place financially. We work at the same place together. It's the best time for us to do this, I think.

Sure, there is the wedding to plan, but I honestly don't know how long it's going to take me to get pregnant.

But the idea of growing our love for us... The tears had burned behind my eyes, threatening to spill over. It was so deep and full of yearning, this life he had so clearly envisioned for us.

Obviously, I've never done any of this before, so I'm just going to take whatever happens if it comes. Whether I get pregnant today or next week, next month. It'll happen, if it's supposed to.

After Gunnar and I cuddled for a while, we finally go out to the kitchen, where Adrian and Charlotte are making breakfast for us. The area is filled with the smell of bacon and fluffy vanilla pancakes, with potatoes sitting to the side on another plate.

The house is a rustic homestead in the rawest sense of the word.

From what I remember of entering the house last night, you go in through the front door, into a small entry area, before you walk straight ahead, and directly to the right, there is a dining table, with the kitchen right beside it. The large bowed window faces the front of the property, right above the kitchen sink. When you turn around from the sink, the stove sits in the middle of the kitchen, with cast-iron pans hanging on chains right above it. The counter surrounds the sink, curving from the left of the sink until it leads into the large fridge.

There's a small corridor past the kitchen, where it looks as if it goes to, what I imagine, is the living room.

Our guest room is basically right beside the kitchen. But if you go to the right of our door, it's a long hallway, with a door at the end and some other doors along the walls. I imagine that's where Adrian and Charlotte sleep.

He really enjoys his roots; it seems, because this looks like it belonged to a cowboy once upon a time. It seems as if the appliances in the kitchen are the only newer things here.

Before we came out to the kitchen, I had thrown on one of my silky robes. Gunnar merely decides he's going to wear sweatpants, and as we approach the dining table, I tighten the sash around my waist, covering my body as I go to stand by the counter.

"Morning," I say with a big yawn and a stretch.

"Morniiiing," Charlotte singsongs with a mischievous, yet knowing grin.

She's wearing one of Adrian's hockey jerseys and, knowing her, there is probably nothing under it.

"Don't start, Charlotte," I groan. Because I already know what she's thinking. There's no way they didn't hear us in there. The headboard was banging against the wall! And the bed rests against the wall that faces the rest of the house! They *definitely* heard it.

Gunnar's scent surrounds me as he approaches me from behind, wrapping his arms over my shoulders as he rests his chin on my head. I bring my hands up, clasping his wrists where they lie around my chest and lean my head on his arm.

My hips move mindlessly, rocking us slowly from side to side.

"He literally yelled it at us! I'm gonna be an aunt, Ti!" Charlotte squeals as she claps furiously, jumping up and down.

"Oh my God," I groan as I tilt my head back against Gunnar's chest. "Whenever it happens. It just means we're having more sex, I don't know what to tell you," I say with a shrug.

Adrian groans in annoyance. "Do y'all think about anything other than sex?"

"Do *you* think about anything other than horses?" Gunnar chimes in.

"Horses are healthy, and they are great companions," he grunts.

"Sex is healthy," Gunnar responds with a shrug as he leans over to grab a strip of bacon from a plate of paper towels.

"Y'all sure you're ready for a baby?" he asks.

"I don't see why not. We aren't getting any younger, and with the rate I'm slamming my spend into her, I doubt she'll have much time to say otherwise," Gunnar responds.

"Oh, my God? What is wrong with you?!" I scoff as my jaw slacks. My head tilts to look up at him and he gives me a nervous smile.

"Sugar, be honest. When haven't I ever come inside of you?"

"Gunnar Lemieux?! What did your mother tell you about sex talk at the table?!?" I groan.

"We aren't at my mother's. We're at Banks', and Banks is perfectly fine with our sex-capades," Gunnar responds with a grin.

"I am?" Adrian asks as he glances at us from where he flips the pancakes.

"You had to know what was happening," Gunnar says.

Adrian grunts with a small huff.

"Don't you have a breeding kink too?" I ask with a sly grin.

Adrian pauses in his pancake making to glare at Charlotte.

"Hey, she told me that Gunnar has one! So I just thought I'd say it too. I don't know. Sisterly bonding and all that jazz," she says with a dismissive wave of her hand.

Adrian deadpan stares at her.

"Adrian. Do not start with me. I know what all of you hockey men talk about. I do not want to hear it from you," she says.

"Yes, Miss Lotty," Adrian grumbles as he goes back to flipping his pancakes. "Just try to be gentle with that bed, please. I feel like I've never heard a headboard do that."

"My condolences to your lady, because you're not trying hard enough. I've gotten harder checks from you than that. And I know you know how to move your hips, so use 'em, bud," Gunnar says as he grabs another strip of bacon. "You ever had your balls hit the clit? Absolutely terrific use of free will, I reckon."

My eyes float to the top of my head in disbelief. "What has gotten into you!? Can we not?"

"What? He's missing out," Gunnar says.

"Enough, all of you. Jesus Christ, you all have lost your damn minds. What is on the agenda for the day?" I ask, trying to get the focus back on the day instead of what everyone does with their cocks.

"Got some four-wheelers. Figured we'd go for a nice ride.

I'll be on my horse; the rest of y'all will be wheelin' and dealin'," Adrian says as he flips the pancake.

"When will that be?" I ask as Gunnar grabs another strip of bacon and puts it in front of my mouth.

I glance up at him, and he opens his maw in an "open-wide-esque" look, and I give him a playful glare before I open my mouth and let him put it in.

"Good girl, sugar," he whispers as he presses a kiss to my forehead.

"What if I weren't hungry? Hm? What then?" I ask after chewing and swallowing it.

"Don't care. You need to eat. Especially if we're going to be going out roughin' it. Food isn't an option," he says before he presses another kiss to my forehead. "Non-negotiable."

I make a small hmph in annoyance before he moves me to the wooden dining table beside the kitchen, sitting me down in the seat before pulling a chair to sit in front of me.

Gunnar leans over, resting his elbows on his knees as he dips his chin. He flicks his tongue out, capturing his chain before he flicks his head back, letting the chain rest in his mouth as he rubs softly over my knees.

"He's got two-hundred fifty acres out here," he says as his tongue swirls the chain around in his mouth.

"That's a lot of land," I murmur as I watch his tongue move the chain behind his teeth. Though his focus is on Adrian and Charlotte in the kitchen.

"Yeah, I just wanted to get out in nature. It's been a hectic few months, I think. And I would love to just get us out of that," Gunnar says through the chain, clamping it down between his teeth so he can speak.

Charlotte brings over a plate of pancakes and some syrup, with a small butter-dish.

"Since when did you become a homemaker?" I ask as I look over the pancakes.

"Since Adrian gave me a home to make," Charlotte responds as she moves back over to Adrian and wraps her arms around his neck. He's also pretty tall, so she presses onto her tiptoes to kiss him.

Warmth swells in my belly as I watch them. So does a sense of... *longing.*

Longing for what *they* have. Not jealousy. I'm happy for her, though this isn't the house I'd want. Nor is it the life.

But I see the love they have for each other. Charlotte would end up with a hockey player. I always knew that.

I don't think she would have been with anyone else. But there is no one better I would choose for her. After the conversation I had with him at the pumpkin patch, he is right.

Opposites attract. I'm more like Adrian, and Charlotte is definitely Gunnar. And we all essentially found each other.

While Gunnar and I do have a similar love, we haven't made a move like this. Where we have our own place together. Sure, we have the apartments, and we switch back and forth between them, but there is a clear separation.

I think I long for something that is *ours*. Not just his apartment, not just mine. And part of that is jarring. I've always had my space, my area, mine, mine, *mine*. But *ours*. I want *that*.

But having my own space isn't the reality anymore. It can't be if I'm going to marry him. If I'm going to have kids with him.

Tiana from months ago would probably scream. A man in her space, his clothes on her floor, or in her closet or mixed with her laundry. His food in her fridge, and his things in her house. To an extent, some of those things are still hard for me to process, but it's because my head processes it as *my* space.

She would also scream if I told her she was marrying a massive hockey player.

Either way, I think part of it would be easier for me to digest if we had a place that was ours.

And while it's scary. Absolutely horrifying having to give up that small piece of my freedom, I gain a bigger sense of... self? Of growth.

But there's too many moving pieces in our life right now to consider that.

So, for now, I'll just dream of it.

I pull away from my thoughts, looking back at Charlotte and Adrian. He's turned the stove off as he's finished the pancakes, and his hands grasp tight on Charlotte's hips, kissing her slowly as she leans in to him.

Overall, I'm happy for her. We're twins, we have always done everything together, and she was part of why I went for that position at the arena. At least I knew someone there if things got too hectic. Of course, the office to myself is a big thing. But being there with Charlotte has always been really nice. Seeing her start her life with this man, who really is perfect for her, stirs a happiness in me, watching them in their little home.

You can tell where she had put some of her influence. Where it was once inhabited by a man on his own, a woman's touch is there. In the plants on the window sills, or some of the little pieces of art she's hung in the space.

Some notes left on the fridge, or just her purse on the table.

I wonder what I would change and what I would want if we were looking for a house, before my eyes come back to Gunnar. He's already eaten half the stack of pancakes that are drenched in butter and syrup, and his cheeks are stuffed like a chipmunk as he devours them.

A small smile rises on my lips as I watch him. He's in his

own world, stuffing his face. And even if he looks insane, it's a stark and harrowing realization.

That I want *this* life. *So* badly with him.

Waking up on the weekends to make breakfast and coffee. Waking up to him in the kitchen, making pancakes with our baby against his chest and a little towel over his shoulder. Shirtless, waiting for me to wake up because he got up with the baby, letting me sleep in.

Showering together and cuddling up on our couch. In *our* living room. In a home for *us.*

I get lost in the sight of him devouring the pancakes until he looks up at me with a furrowed brow.

"Did you want some?" he asks through a mouth full of pancake.

My smile widens as I bring a thumb up to wipe away a drip of syrup from the corner of his mouth, sucking it clean before I glance down at the pancakes. Then back up at him, where he tilts his head curiously at me.

"I'll have some," I say softly.

Gunnar wasn't lying about this land situation.

After breakfast, we all get dressed.

Nothing insane, of course. But Gunnar put on a hoodie and stuck his jersey on over it with some jeans.

I decide to wear some jeans and a hoodie as well. But I borrow a pair of cowboy boots that Charlotte has.

I can't help but admit how tactical they are for this sort of thing.

The three of us stand around, with Tucker and Charlotte's dog, Waffle, tugging at a rope they found.

Adrian leads a big black Quarter horse out of the stable, clicking as he leads it to the paddock. He ties him up so he can tack the horse up, only for us to hear another whinny from inside.

"Is that the 'filly'?" I ask as I look into the wide-open stable door that Adrian walks through. I can't really see the horse making the noise, but I see the small areas they're kept in as he grabs his tack.

"Yeah, back there, that's Priscilla. She's too young to ride. But this here is Chauncey. Best horse I've ever owned. Had to bring him up when I left the homestead and finally made my place here," Adrian says as he brings out the saddle setup, throwing it over Chauncey's back.

Tucker and Waffle run around us, barking and chasing each other with barks of excitement.

"What made you guys get a dog?" I ask as I watch them run off into the field.

Adrian takes the moment to glare at Charlotte before she gives me a wide smile.

"We wanted a dog. But Adrian said that it had to be a cattle dog. He wanted an Australian Cattle Dog. Or a border collie. But I insisted on a Corgi," Charlotte says as Waffle runs up to her, barking excitedly.

"A 'compromise' is what she called it," Adrian murmurs with a shake of his head as he secures the girth strap around Chauncey before he retreats into the stable.

"A fair one!" Charlotte calls after him.

I raise a brow, and watch as Waffle comes up to me, dropping a dirtied, brown tennis ball at my feet.

She's an orange little thing, with bright eyes. Not an ounce of thought behind them, but she's cute as all get out. She tries to wag her tail, but she doesn't really have one, which causes her butt to wiggle furiously as she waits for me to throw the ball.

I watch her for a moment, being afraid to pick up the ball merely because I'm not a fan of dog spit, until Gunnar steps next to me. He bends over, teetering on one leg to scoop it up. Soon, Tucker comes to join Waffle. The two of them bark in unison before Gunnar absolutely lobs it all the way across the farm, where the two of them bolt straight for it.

I smile as I look up at him. "Thank you," I whisper.

"Of course, sugar," he whispers before he leans in. Grabbing the back of my head with his clean hand, he pulls it toward him to press a kiss to my forehead.

Adrian returns from the stables with his reins and a bridle situation, removing the lead and halter from Chauncey and hanging them over the paddock fence before he pulls the bridle over the horse's head, securing the bit into place.

"She is a real good girl, though, that dog. Listens well, fast as sin, always ready when I go out for a ride. She keeps pace right beside Chauncey, and always gets extra jerky at the end," Adrian says as he places his foot in the stirrup, swinging his other leg over and settling in the saddle.

Adrian clicks, causing Chauncey to move in a slow walk, past the paddock. Waffle seemingly appears out of nowhere, barking excitedly beside him. It seems as if she knows what's about to happen.

Soon, my attention returns to Adrian, and I watch as he shifts into a form I've never seen.

He always looks comfortable on the ice, like he belongs there. But there is something about him on the horse that makes it seem like this is where he feels the *most* comfortable.

I know he enjoys hockey; loves it, I'm sure. But I don't think he loves hockey as much as he loves this right here.

"Lotty!" Adrian calls out to Charlotte as he pulls Chauncey to a halt.

Charlotte runs up with a grin, and Adrian nods to an area behind the stables.

"Give them two the Can-Am and Polaris," he says. Chauncey shifts in place as he waits.

"Can do!" she calls to him.

Charlotte has also taken on this… 'country girl' look. She wears a button-up flannel, a pair of jeans, cowgirl boots, with a cowboy hat.

She has truly assimilated into this man's life. Part of it is… interesting. The other part is just happiness for her.

Charlotte runs off behind the stables, and I take the chance to look over the land here.

It's actually really nice. A lot of trees, but some have been mowed down to make space for the buildings that Adrian has set up here.

The stable, a garage, the paddock for turnout, and just some extra room for messing around in. You can see where he's set up a fire pit outside of the house. And with the bright sun of the day and clear skies, you can see all the way out to Mount Rainier.

I find myself more thankful to be out here right now. I've not even thought about the wedding. I've just been enjoying the day and the slowing down of it all.

I don't think I've been able to be in the moment without sex in a while. My mind is just constantly working toward the next thing, the projects, the thoughts. But this weekend has been really nice so far.

With all the things in my life happening at once, it's a whirlwind of massive changes. And I think if I were doing this with anyone else, I'd be in a worse place mentally.

But it's with Gunnar... and the only thing I fear is how to fit all the planning into life.

Eventually, the sound of a loud engine roars from behind the stables, and Charlotte comes out with one quad, standing as she parks a big blue beast beside Gunnar before she runs back. In a few more moments, she brings back a red quad. One more time she runs, and she comes out on a pink quad. My brow furrows, with a tilt of my head as I look over it.

"Yours?" I call over the roaring engines with a smirk as I clap my hands over my ears.

"He got it for me when I moved out here since I can't ride Priscilla," she calls back.

Gunnar's hand appears in front of me, with a small plastic pack in the middle of it. My head tilts as I look down at it, my brow furrowing before I look up at him in confusion.

"For your ears!" he yells over the engines, gesturing to his ears.

Looking back down at the little pack, I realize it's a pair of in-ear protectors.

Goddamn it, this man.

A grin pulls at my lips and my cheeks as I grab them, quickly opening the plastic pouch and stuffing the waste into my pockets before I twist the little tips of the squishy buds. I shove them in my ears, exhaling a breath of relief when the noise doesn't absolutely scrape at my eardrums like a knife on a plate.

Looking up at him, I grin as I get up on my tippy toes to press a kiss to his cheek. But of course, because he's so tall, he has to bend down just enough for me to reach him. His hand wraps around my back as he pulls me to his side, pressing a kiss to my forehead before Charlotte comes back to us with ATV helmets.

She holds them out to us, and we put them on, but I fiddle with the neck strap for a minute before I groan.

Gunnar is already working on his. His head tilted as he messes with the strap and gets it secured.

He looks down at me with a smile through the helmet, and I deadpan glare at him as I point to my neck. Gunnar shakes his head as his eyes crinkle in a playful smile. He tugs the open face of the helmet, pulling me toward him before he uses it to tilt my head back so he can secure the strap.

I really hate to admit how hot it was for him to man-handle me like that. It's incredibly reminiscent of the way he handles me in bed, and I get a little jolt of pleasure rushing through my blood at the thought.

But I hold still as he gets the strap in place, and he tilts my head back down, slapping down on the top.

"OW!" I groan as I shove him.

He guards himself with his shoulder with a grin as he stumbles toward the large blue ATV.

Charlotte had run back into the stable, and when I turn my attention back on her, she's sans her cowboy hat. Now, she has a bright pink helmet on her head. Her head tilts as she configures her own chin strap and climbs on her ATV.

I climb onto the red ATV, while Gunnar climbs onto the blue one. Mostly because it's so much bigger and the perfect size for him. Looking over the controls, I see the stop, the throttle and the start, making sure I acquaint myself with all the pieces.

My dad used to take us ATVing on little family getaways in the woods during the summer and when he wasn't coaching for the season, so I know my way around an ATV. One of the best ways to ride, in my opinion.

Chauncey moves forward between the vehicles, getting in front of us. Turning around, Adrian places a hand on the back of the saddle to look over all of us, and he nods at Charlotte. Waffle appears to know what's happening because she goes insane with barks. Tucker merely barks because everyone else seems excited.

She revs once, and he nods again before a loud whistle is sent into the air, and Chauncey fucking *bolts*. Tucker and Waffle take off beside him like bats out of hell as he moves to a tamped-down area of grass to the north, leading into a dense thicket. It's just kitty-corner from where the main gravel road is.

My brows furrow, and Charlotte races after him on her ATV.

I look to Gunnar, who sits on the ATV with his hands on his thighs before he looks to me and shrugs.

He revs once before he speeds to Charlotte, and I follow suit.

We keep in line, with enough space behind one another so we can move to our speed-racing content.

The area of tamped down grass moves through the trees, and we are led deeper into the forest. As we move further, the roads and tamped areas narrow as Chauncey and Adrian lead us, which causes us to move slower, as it gets harder to navigate. But we make do.

The sound of these engines, roaring one behind the other, through the trees and rocky climbs... is *exhilarating*.

We race through the trees, looping and turning, riding for a while. Maybe a mile or two before we make a slow climb up a ridge. It's not incredibly steep, but at the top of the ridge is a flat space of land, guarded by trees on either side of the flat area, but enough for us to park all of our ATVs.

Chauncey goes to the far end of the flat space, and Charlotte parks next to him, Gunnar beside her, and I come up beside Gunnar.

I can see why Adrian brought us to this space. On the other side of the ridge is a shredded hill face, which leads into a massive field, and in the middle is a small lake. It's nestled in this area of trees. An open field of long green grass is on the right of the lake, extending out with nothing. To the left of the lake is more field, but on the other side, beyond the lake and the field, is a wall of trees.

Looking over it, my jaw gapes. It's so secluded. So incredibly peaceful...

It's... *beautiful.*

CHAPTER NINETEEN
GUNNAR

I don't think I could have asked for a better day.

The sky is clear, bright. The weather is perfect, not too hot, not too cold; the perfect temperature.

I also am not sure if Banks is just able to read Tiana and me as a couple from the few things I've told him, but he brings us to an area quite a ways away from his main tiny ranch house. And it's... incredible.

As I sit out looking over the ridge, Charlotte looks over at Tiana, with me leaning back so they can communicate. At least the best they over the engines and distance.

It's really just a bunch of nods and gestures.

Tucker and Waffle are growing crazy beside Charlotte, and soon Charlotte pats the space in front of her and Waffle jumps up into the seat with her. Her long body stretches up as she places her front paws on the ATV handles. With barks of excitement going off every so often.

My head volleys between the two of them, until Charlotte nods down to the field and Tiana nods in response.

Charlotte revs her engine before she makes the small climb down the hill's face, a slow decline down into the field, and Tiana follows, with Tucker following close behind her. I watch, my heart pounding in my chest with glee, as they park their quads beside the lake and cut off the engines.

Tiana can't help herself when she removes her helmet and places it on the seat. She runs to the edge of the lake, looking into the water, and I sit back on my ATV for a minute, just watching her. Charlotte does the same, coming up beside Tiana. Charlotte points at a few things around the area and I can see the animated way that Charlotte talks to her. Waffle and Tucker take off for the trees together, disappearing into the forest to explore.

Soon, I cut off my ATV, and without the engine roaring; it makes this small area a heavenly sort of quiet as the sounds of the birds and everything else becomes clearer.

With Charlotte's ATV no longer between Banks and me, he shifts Chauncey closer. I lean my elbows against the handles of the ATV, watching the sisters for a long moment.

Soon, he releases Chauncey's reins, letting him nibble on some of the grass as he leans against the saddle horn, one arm across it and the other on his hip.

"Charlotte helped me pick it out," Banks says. But my eyes are glued to the way the sisters hold hands and run into the woods after the dogs.

"I think she did a great job," I murmur with a small smile. "What's the turnaround time for building out here?" I ask.

"Depends. Gotta find loggers to clear out the trees. I know some people and I can get that squared away when we sign the contract. How many acres you want?"

I look to him as the girls disappear into the trees, thinking. "How much do you think would be good for us?"

"Well, y'all definitely don't need as much as we do. But

you're welcome to traverse the property. You just can't do nothin' with the stuff I own. All the acreage I give ya' would be yours to do whatever with," he says with a shrug.

"I want a big house for her," I whisper as I look back over the space. "I need to have a detached garage and a good platform for cars. That's important to her," I add quietly.

"I reckon ten to twenty would be perfect for y'all. I don't imagine you'd get horses. And even if ya did, I got a stable and plans to expand, so if you really wanted 'em, they're welcome in my barn," he says.

I nod mindlessly as I listen to him, the sight of the soft breeze rippling over the lake causes sprinkles of light to reflect off of it. Almost magical to see, I reckon. The tall grasses sway with the breeze and you can hear the way it moves through the leaves in the trees.

"You're looking at about a year as far as building a home. Maybe less if you find a good builder. But I imagine y'all got leases you can't get rid of. So I reckon you're runnin' on good time," he adds.

I nod as I listen, with my vision removing the trees, thinking about how the front of the house would look, the size. The vision of my truck, the cars sitting in front of the detached garage. A small gazebo by the lake for her to read in.

All of it is *too* real. And while we plan the wedding and get ready for a baby, the house can be in the planning stages, giving us something to look forward to while they get all the foundation things squared away.

Depending on when the baby is born, I imagine we'd move in a little after their first birthday. With all the wedding planning and everything else, I think that's perfect as far as timing goes.

But at the same time... that's a lot of planning and pressure on Tiana.

"Do you think it'd be a bad idea to get married, have a baby and build a house all at once?" I ask.

Banks hums, staying silent for a long moment.

"You want the honest answer?" he finally asks.

I glance to him with a nod.

"Yeah. That's a lot of weight on you and your little lady. You're not even counting the seventy games we got for the next few months, and all her work," he says.

I grumble a huff as my attention turns back to the lake, because I knew he'd say that.

"I have to knock one of those things off the list," I murmur.

"Well, let me offer a solution, if I may," he responds.

My brow quirks and I glance at him again.

"What do you think would be more important to Miss Tiana? The house, or the wedding?"

I look back out over the land. The lake, and the grasses.

Tiana would love this space more than she would look forward to having to be around a bunch of people for a big event.

I think she enjoys the planning of the wedding, because she likes the rush of it.

But I don't think she'd enjoy the day itself. That's not saying she doesn't want to marry me. I just know Tiana, and Tiana doesn't do a lot of people.

"I think she would rather have the house," I say.

"Right. And you said Miss Tiana has a passion for plannin', yeah?"

I nod.

"Well. Have the wedding at a later date... Have a courthouse marriage, focus on the baby stuff, and when you tell her about the land, offer the idea to her. See what she'll choose," he says.

The idea works through my head. Not only do I get to offer both pieces of the pie to her, she can choose which one she wants to eat.

"You're a fuckin' genius, bud," I murmur with a small grin. "You think she'll like it?"

Looking over at Banks, he stares out at the property before nodding. "I don't think there is any land better than this for your little lady," he says.

I nod in response. "I reckon you may be right."

"I usually am, Hayze. It's why I'm the captain."

I glance at him to see his eyes glancing at me with a small smirk on his face.

Pressing my fist over to him, he leans down to bump it as we look over the ridge for just a little while longer.

After the sisters came back, we delved a little deeper into the property, past the tree line, bounding around and looking at the land.

I would look over at Tiana every so often to see her standing on her ATV, a rush of excitement gracing her eyes as we zipped and zoomed through the trees, until eventually we came back to the ranch house.

We put the four-wheelers back in the little covered area behind the stables before coming back out to the paddock. Charlotte and Banks stay behind at the stables to get some choring done, while Tiana seems a bit more tired, so I walk her up to the porch to sit on the swing. The dogs beat us to the porch and have cuddled up with one another right outside the front door, snoozing peacefully.

It's actually kind of cute how close they've gotten in the time we've been here.

Leading her up the porch steps, I sit down first on the long wooden swing, holding it steady for her to climb on. She sits next to me, nuzzling into my side as she takes a deep exhale.

Soon, her legs come up onto the swing, where she shifts herself to lay her head on my lap. Her knees bend up, meeting in the middle before she tilts them toward the back of the swing, resting them there. She looks up at me with a tired smile, a look of ease gracing her features as her eyes slowly close.

Leaning my head back against the swing, I twirl one of her curls around my finger as I use my heels to slowly press the swing back and forth.

"Did you have fun, Mama?" I ask quietly. I tilt my head to the side so I can look at her face.

God, the beauty of this woman.

I'm the luckiest fucking man on this planet.

She nods as a smile pulls at her lips. "This is a pleasant space they've got out here," she says with a yawn.

"Yeah, I wanted to see what they were working with, considering they live out here together now," I respond as I watch the curl that wraps around my finger.

"I really never thought I'd see Charlotte becoming a cowgirl. But I guess anything is possible," she says with a small chuckle.

Her head turns against my lap, facing the rest of the land. "It's a beautiful day too."

I keep my eyes on her. Mostly because there isn't anything on this land that would be more beautiful than her. Releasing the curl, I bring my arm under her chin, across her chest to stroke a thumb over her cheek.

"It is," I respond softly.

"Do you think we could get some ATVs? We could keep

them here and just come use them every once in a while if Adrian will let us. I think that would be a cool weekend activity," she says.

A smile pulls at my lips. "Whatever you want, sugar. You can have whatever you want," I whisper.

"I think it'd be nice to live out here. But I think it's just because I like Adrian's land. I don't know if I want to go through the trouble of finding this sort of thing somewhere else. It's too much work," she says with a small shrug. Her hands come up to her chest, where she picks at the skin around her nails mindlessly.

My heart pounds harder because she's merely confirming all the things I wondered. And it only makes my urge to buy this land that much stronger.

"You'd like to live out in something like this?" I ask, trying to contain the excitement in my tone.

"Yeah, it's nice out here. Quiet, peaceful. Away from everything. And the stars!" she says with joy as she throws her arms out, as if gesturing to the sky. "The stars at night are incredible!" She lets a soft sigh go, dreamily looking out to the land.

"Well. Maybe I'll see what I can find," I say.

"Don't worry too much about it. We'll get it figured out eventually. We have the wedding and baby stuff to consider. Whenever the hell this baby thing happens," she says. But her voice turns soft as she says the last bit.

"Are you worried I won't be able to perform?" I tease as I boop her nose.

Her lips tilt up in a smirk. "I don't doubt that in the slightest. I've just had an IUD for a long time. A hormonal one. I don't know how all of that works with getting pregnant. That's why I said, whatever happens, happens. Plus, apparently, it's harder to get pregnant than what the TV says," she says with a shrug.

But her eyes turn sad, and she sighs.

"What's wrong, sugar?" I ask as I stroke her chin, urging her to look toward me.

Her head turns, but her eyes shy away from me.

"Sugar, eyes here," I say with a click of my tongue.

Reluctantly, her eyes slide to me, looking at me for a moment before she looks away.

"I just don't want you to love me any less if I can't get pregnant..." she mumbles.

A frown forms on my lips as my head tilts. A drop rocks through my stomach, and I wonder if I've been putting too much pressure on *her* to perform.

Goddamnit, Gunnar. You and your fucking goon brain.

"What makes you think I would love you any less for that, sugar?" I ask.

"We're just so excited... it's something I worry about," she says with a sigh.

My face softens, and I lean down to kiss her. Though because she's in my lap, I have to bring my knees up with her head to kiss her, and she gives me a sideways smile as I do.

"Whether you get pregnant tomorrow. Next year. Ten years from now, or not at all, I'll always love you, and I'll always be here. Never worry about that," I say softly.

She glances at me as she turns her whole body on the swing, lying on her side, toward the front of the porch as she brings her hands up to rest under her head.

"But it's something we really want," she murmurs.

"It is. And, yeah, it would suck if we couldn't have kids. But it would never, ever make me love you less. And it will *never* be your fault. I'm not with you because I want a baby. I want a baby *because* I love *you*. I told you, I'm here for as long as you'll have me. Always."

I see a soft smile pull at her lips.

"What do you think we'd have?" she asks softly.

My smile widens as I continue stroking her hair, leaning my head back against the swing as I start moving the swing back and forth again.

"I'm not sure. I just want a mini-you. I think a little girl would be cute," I say softly.

And soon the visions come to life as I look out at the sky.

Tiana, asleep on the couch, with a tiny one on her chest as she sleeps. Her hair a mess and disheveled, her boob out for the baby to suckle on in her sleep.

I see the way I'd wait for them to finish before I took the baby, fixed up Tiana and put a blanket over her so she could relax a bit more and I take over.

Sure, *making* a baby is fun.

But there's nothing I think can compare to seeing us create a family. A small team of hockey players.

Along with her tote as she comes out of the office, she'd have her diaper bag, the car seat and the rest of her things. And I can't wait to run to her office at the end of the day to grab them. Because honestly, I imagine Tiana would just bring the baby to work with her. I don't see her trying to leave it with anyone. She strikes me as the type to be too involved in all the bits and pieces.

But who knows, it's all up in the air right now.

Either way.

I'm so... excited for the future.

Whether there's a baby or not. Whether there's a home or not.

We could live in a box under a bridge. And I'd wake up every day, thankful for this woman who is weathering the storm beside me.

I'm excited for us. For her. For all of this.

And soon I come back to the present, looking down at

Tiana, whose eyes have closed, and she makes a soft snoring noise.

I rock the swing softly, and decide to stay in this moment with her. This one right here where it's just us, the porch swing and the sky above.

CHAPTER TWENTY

TIANA

After I woke up from my brief nap on Gunnar's lap, we went and hung out with Adrian and Charlotte. Who were out in the paddock doing turn out with Chauncey.

Charlotte was riding him, while Adrian led him around the paddock on a lead. Even if she wasn't technically riding him on her own, she was having the time of her life.

I honestly never thought I'd see Charlotte in love with a cowboy. Hockey player? Yeah absolutely.

A cowboy? Kinda crazy.

But Adrian was raised doing this stuff, I imagine he would feel weird never doing it again. I really don't think he could ever play only hockey. I truly think he'd go stir crazy, so I suppose this entire setup he has out here is perfect for him.

After Adrian and Charlotte put Chauncey back in the stables, we went inside, and Charlotte made us lunch. They were having some kind of normal meat sandwiches. But I'm not the biggest fan of those, so Charlotte made me a peanut butter and jelly. After that, we hung out in the dining room, talking for a long time before my social battery drained and I needed a real nap.

Charlotte had said we were going to have a bonfire tonight, and I honestly wanted to have enough energy for that, so I asked Gunnar if we could go lay down for a while.

He obliged, and we could go lie in the guest bedroom for a while just resting.

So now here we are, resting quietly in the guest room. I've slowly woken up, even if I'd merely lain here with my eyes closed, enjoying the peace and the quiet.

The noise outside the window across the bed is nothing but... soothing. The wind chimes that Adrian has hanging on the front porch ring in the soft breeze and echo through the house. There are random whinnies and neighs that come from the stable beside the house.

It's perfect for a rest. Naps in general are just a part of my life. Sleepiness has always been something I've struggled with. It doesn't matter how much sleep I could get at night; I am always tired. Especially after big events or having to be around people. After large events where I need to interact, I am always so exhausted. I take a few days to recuperate afterwards.

Sometimes it's annoying. Other times, it's a good excuse to be on my own.

Also, I didn't even realize how bad the light and noise pollution was in Seattle, because I'm just so used to it. But being out here has shown me how much peace I may have been missing.

I'd even take the rooster crowing over the beeps and honks outside of my window in the mornings.

It's perfect. I haven't thought about the wedding once since we've been out here. And being able to have your mind silenced... all the constant yelling of things that need to get done, the things you need to do.

You need to eat; you need to drink water. You have to do this tomorrow... over and over and over and *over...!*

It is... life-changing to experience a peace like this.

And it becomes even more apparent when I open my eyes, staying still so as not to wake the massive goon that lies against my stomach. His arms are wrapped around my waist, with a leg thrown over my legs, locking me into his body. He's buried his face in my side, holding me close from where he was pressing kisses into my belly before our nap.

Night has crept in during our slumber, and the window across from the bed, high on the wall, shows how quickly dusk has fallen.

But it's so quiet in the house. I wonder if maybe Charlotte and Adrian are napping elsewhere too. But knowing Adrian? Probably not.

I lay there for a while, stroking Gunnar's hair softly as I think about my excursion with Charlotte this morning.

She led me through the woods, and all at once it felt like we were little girls again. Nostalgia I didn't know I missed.

We ran through the forest, chasing one another, before we came across a little brook that we jumped over, and *kept running*.

She led me all around that area before we sat on a random stump from a downed tree to take a breather, and we sat there, enjoying the sounds of the running water and the birds in the trees.

We really didn't say much to each other, because I was honestly loving that little corner of the earth.

In my eyes, it was perfect. If I could build a little cabin to come out here on weekends, I definitely would. But right now, my mind is focused on the wedding and baby making. On top of all the other duties I have with my job.

I can do them all; I have no problem with that. But I think

taking on another enormous responsibility would be a bit of a hassle. So maybe for now we'll just come visit Charlotte and Adrian more often.

Plus, Tucker has seemed to enjoy this land. Especially with what appears to be his new girlfriend.

I've never really seen Tucker interact with other dogs, but they have warmed up easily to one another. I've seen them curled up, resting, or just always spending their time together.

For a high-energy dog like Tucker, this is the best thing we could do for him. Tons of land and another furry friend to hang out with.

But there was no feeling like walking back to the small lake to see Gunnar and Adrian standing on the ridge, looking over the property.

A big-ass man on a four-wheeler, and another big-ass man on a horse.

There was a sense of... pride perhaps, that I had? For these two men who just always want to do the best for Charlotte and me. That would do anything and go to any lengths for our happiness.

And I remember riding back up that ridge on my four-wheeler, pausing when I reached him. I remember the somewhat daydreamy look Gunnar had as I put my helmet back on. It was so full of thought... his mind has been elsewhere, I could tell.

The whole day, I have to admit, has been nice. So... so fucking nice.

It's a life I can see myself living.

Soon, a sleepy groan pulls me from my daydream, as Gunnar's massive leg moves higher up and he pulls me tighter against him. When we came back inside, he took his sweatpants off and just rested on me in his boxers. I followed suit and now I'm just relaxing on the bed in my bra and undies.

The skin to skin has been very nice.

Soon, he adjusts his head, moving it to press kisses into my belly sleepily.

However, a thick, hot... *pressure* hardens against my leg, and I give a sly smirk as I continue stroking his hair.

"I'm sorry," he murmurs groggily.

"I don't think you can help it," I respond with a small chuckle. It causes his head to bounce a bit as I do.

"I can't, but that doesn't mean I won't apologize for my lack of control with you," he murmurs.

As I continue stroking his hair, he presses more kisses into my belly. "Still want to go out to the bonfire?"

"Yeah, I think that'd be nice. Did they get stuff for s'mores?" I ask.

"Sugar... do you think I would be out here roughin' it without the promise of s'mores?" he murmurs.

I can't see his face, so it's funny to hear his gruff, rambunctious self without his expressions.

"I don't know. You were brought here by horses."

"Half-truth. I was plied with chocolaty marshmallow goodness as well," he says with a nod against my stomach.

I laugh with a roll of my eyes, and he turns his head against my belly, looking up at me with sleepy eyes and a soft smile.

"That was a really good nap. I think you may be onto something with mid-days, sugar," he says as his eyes slowly blink closed.

He seems to go in and out of sleep as he rests against me.

"I love a nap," I say quietly. Brushing a few bits of hair off his brow, I push his hair back softly, admiring his gorgeously sculpted face.

"I love a nap with *you*. I think that's the difference," he responds. His eyes are closed, and it seems as if he doesn't even want to get up.

With a grin, I try to push his head away so he can start waking up, but he merely holds me tighter, smothering my stomach in little kisses.

However, he moves so fast against my stomach that his scruff tickles my skin, and I giggle uncontrollably as I try to force myself out of his hold.

"Mine!" he growls as I continue attempting to shove him off.

"It's time for s'mores, you horny degenerate!" I yell through a laugh.

"Fuck, you're right," he says as he stops and immediately springs from the bed.

I shake my head as I catch my breath from his tickle torture and the violent whiplash of his movements, turning my attention to his body as I watch him get dressed.

He is just... so perfectly sculpted. He has the right amount of body hair. None across his pecs, but some down the center of his abs. I watch the way his biceps flex and contort as he pulls his shirt on.

But I also see the veins under his skin... the ones that lead under the band of his boxers. The same ones that strain to keep his hardened cock in check. I nip down on my lower lip, admiring the way he bulges against the fabric.

I take a deep breath before I take a second to fan myself.

I get to sit on it. This is a spectacular life.

He looks at me in confusion, noticing my change in breathing, and I respond with a nod to his groin.

His eyes follow my line of sight, and he presses his cock down with his wrist, adjusting his boxers with a shake of his leg.

"Quit teasin' me. You just called me a horny degen, what'd you expect?" he says as he pulls on a pair of sweatpants.

I throw a pillow at him, and unfortunately, I chose the

wrong method of retaliation, because the man has reflexes like a puma.

Gunnar catches it, whirling in his spot to release it with a vicious lob when he gets back around. Straight into my face. The impact is so strong it knocks me back into the bed with a hefty 'oof'.

I lay there for a minute in annoyance, releasing a loud groan.

"I'm not sorry, sugar. You have a few more months where I can be mean to you before I can't anymore."

I pull the pillow away to see him grinning deviously at me as he tugs a shirt on.

"And why won't you be able to?" I ask as I throw the pillow behind my head to lie on.

"You'll be too busy growing my kid. Gotta take care of my precious cargo," he says with a shrug.

I scoff incredulously. "So who is the precious cargo? Me or the baby?"

"Both of you, silly goose." He grins at me, and I can't help but see the boyish charm in his features.

His words also ring a little deeper into me. A flush of heat running through me.

"Why must you say it that way?" I groan playfully.

"Why? You don't like it?" he says with a precautionary frown.

"Not at all. Quite the opposite, in fact," I say with a seductive glance and a small nip at my lip. My eyes volley between his face and the bulge in his sweatpants. For whatever reason, it *still* has not gone down.

His eyes heat as he comes close, crawling onto the bed. I watch the hunger fill his eyes, his gaze intent on claiming as he slowly climbs over me, forcing my back into the bed as he hovers over me. All the while, his chain dangles from his neck.

It swings, and the pendant taps me on the chin. Once... twice... before I capture the stag with my teeth, grinning at him.

Since I haven't gotten up to change, I'm still just in a bra and underwear.

"So let me get this straight... you're saying it turns you on when I tell you you're going to be making my kid?" he says low and husky. His eyes volley between my lips and my eyes, the heat of his lust climbing between us in an instant.

I tug at the pendant in my teeth, bringing him closer to my face before I press my head up. Releasing the pendant, I capture his lips with a kiss, throwing my arms around his shoulders to bring his body into mine.

His grin widens against my lips, the pressure increasing while he runs his free hand down my side. The other has him propped above me, keeping his weight from my body. He stops at my hip, gripping the curve tight in restraint.

"Tell me what you want," he murmurs. It's full of want, need and pure desire.

The heat between us is set ablaze in an instant. My own need for him spears through me and straight to my core as my heart speeds up and my breath quickens.

"Y-you," I whisper.

"Yeah? You want *me*, sugar?" he asks in a deep and gruff rasp.

I nod, and his hand grips tighter on my hip before he shoves it hard enough to flip me onto my stomach.

My chest heaves, my head spins and my breath pulses in and out of me in anticipation as his body settles on my legs. His massive thighs cage mine in, holding me hostage just like he did this morning. His rough hands run down my back, over the crest of my ass, sending jolts of pleasure skittering all over my skin. It puckers my flesh and causes hairs to rise all over my body.

"So perfect," he groans as he grips my ass cheeks.

But soon, a hard sting slaps across my ass.

Not a sexy one either.

One that hurts like *hell.*

I yelp, jumping from the slap. "Gunnar!"

Quickly, he jumps off, heading for the door with his hand on the knob.

"Get ready, sweetness. The s'mores await," he says as he opens the door and walks out.

That BASTARD!

I groan in frustration, waiting for the lust to subside before I can get up and get ready.

Once the initial pulse of heat wanes away, I push myself from the bed, looking around for my clothes I tossed away.

Even if we're sitting by a fire, I still decide I need a hoodie. Because, duh, the skeeters are biting!

I throw on a pair of sweatpants as well, before pulling my mess of hair into a wild bun at the top of my head. I pull a few stray strands out to frame my face and head out into the hall.

I go down the hall to the dining room and the kitchen, seeing if I can spot anyone. But the lights in the house are all off.

The only thing I can make out is the soft orange glow of the fire through the kitchen window.

I walk to the front door, opening it to step out onto the porch. Gunnar has already seated himself by the fire, his elbows on his knees as he turns a marshmallow on a stick over the flames.

He's in a camping chair, but Charlotte and Adrian have a double-seater situation, and she's cuddled into him as she presses her hands out to the fire.

I pull my sleeves over my hands as I make my way down the porch to meet them. As I come up behind Gunnar, I put my hands on either side of his head and pull it back. He looks up at me, his lips widening in a grin, and I return it before I lean down to press a kiss to his forehead. He brings a hand up to stroke my cheek once before I push his head back up and take a seat in the camping chair beside him.

"'Bout time you showed up," he says with a grin.

"Had to cool down after someone was a dick," I say with a grin as I settle in my seat. Throwing one leg over the other, I lean back, stuffing my hands into my lap.

The fire is pleasant because it is cooler tonight.

"I pumped you full this morning, sugar. I gotta recoup my boys. Can't send in swimmers I don't have," he says with a shrug before he bites into his blackened marshmallow.

"Gunnar, that was still on fire," I say as I look between the marshmallow and his face now smeared with melted white fluff.

"I know it was," he says through a mouthful of marshmallow.

I roll my eyes playfully as I turn my gaze back to the fire.

"Can we... refrain from baby-making talk around the fire?" Adrian grumbles.

"You're just mad your girl won't let you put a baby in her," Gunnar says with a shrug before he shoves the rest of his marshmallow in his mouth.

"Don't act like you wouldn't be the same if your girl didn't let you," Adrian responds as he leans over beside him for some graham crackers. He hands them to Charlotte, having her hold them as he reaches down to grab chocolate. He places the chocolate square on his graham cracker before he sticks a marshmallow on his stick and turns it over the fire.

"I would! But that's the difference between you and me. *I'm* allowed to, and! I can admit when I'd be upset," Gunnar says as he points a brand new, burned marshmallow at Adrian.

Adrian glares at him for a long moment as he turns his marshmallow on the fire before he looks over at me.

"So, Tiana, are you glad to be back in the arena?" Adrian asks as he pulls his marshmallow from the fire. He holds it out for Charlotte, who claps the two pieces together before she pulls the marshmallow from the stick and takes a bite. She hums happily as she wiggles in her seat.

"I am. I didn't enjoy being back at my parents, and I definitely hated being at the firm," I say as I watch the fire.

"I reckoned so. I know you love your lil' cave," Adrian responds.

I nod as I gaze at the flames, before I look up at Adrian and Charlotte.

She's finished her treat and leans against Adrian's shoulder, her arms wrapping around his arm as she snuggles into him.

It's interesting how close they seem to be. Like an old married couple of sorts.

"How do you like living out here, Charlotte?" Gunnar asks as he gets up to steal some chocolate and graham crackers from Adrian before he comes back to sit down in his chair. He shoves another marshmallow on his stick before he roasts it over the fire.

"I was hesitant at first, just because it is so far from the arena. But I spent a few nights out here, and I really loved how quiet it gets. Adrian took some time at some point to put a large boundary around his acreage, so I actually feel safe here. Plus, I enjoy taking care of the horses on the weekends. It's fun. It kind of reminds me of waking up early for hockey games," Charlotte says as she nuzzles into Adrian, looking up at him with bright eyes.

"Do you think you guys are going to stay here?" Gunnar turns his marshmallow over the fire a little longer before he brings it to his lap, pressing the marshmallow between the chocolate and graham cracker.

He leans over, opening his mouth to me, and I roll my eyes with a playful smile as I open my mouth in response.

He presses it into my lips for me to take a bite, smiling as I do. I chew my bite before he leans in to kiss me. When he leans back in his chair, he shoves the rest of the s'more into his mouth.

"I reckon so. I'll be with the Stags for a long while, and the Dawn's place is just over yonder. 'Bout thirty minutes away. We're closer to their house than we are to the arena," Adrian responds.

"You don't wanna go back down to... where are you from?" Gunnar asks.

"Montana. Not fuckall for miles and I like it that way," Adrian says with a nod.

"Montana, right. You don't wanna go back?"

"Who knows what'll happen fifty years from now. That'll be up to Miss Lotty here," he says as he wraps an arm around her shoulder to kiss her forehead.

She smiles up at him, bringing a hand up to boop his nose, and he purses his lips for her to kiss them.

She brings her hand to his cheek, bringing his face closer to kiss him before she giggles.

A smile tugs at my own lips before I lean back, looking up at the stars.

I was so hesitant to come out here. Mostly because I keep having my weekends absconded, and even next weekend, we have Trunk or Treat.

But I have thoroughly enjoyed the time out here. Part of me never wants to leave. It's so far from everything.

When I moved out to the city from my parent's house, it

was merely because it's closer to the arena and the apartment complex is nice.

But now that I'm with Gunnar, and we're working toward our future, it's different. It feels different.

I wouldn't mind being out here.

And that thought seeps deeper into me as I lock onto the stars above, naming the constellations in my head and enjoying the way the heat from the fire hits my legs.

CHAPTER TWENTY-ONE
GUNNAR

Tiana fell asleep at the fire. And it had been one of the cutest things ever.

You could tell she had been looking at the stars by the way her head was tilted back. It seemed like her gaze was stuck on space as she seemed to be more quiet than usual.

When I realized she was asleep, I had picked her up and taken her to the bedroom. I took off her clothes and left her in just her bra and undies before I put her under the sheets and came back to the fire.

The three of us that were left awake talked for a while. Mostly about what they've been up to and some of the other plans they're working on, going forward.

Charlotte let me in on some things that Tiana had told her as far as wedding planning, and that was when Banks explained the question I planned on asking Tiana.

Charlotte thought it was a great idea, but I still tried to absorb as much of the information as I possibly could. Just incase Tiana chose the wedding, so I would know exactly what we were doing.

If she does pick the wedding, I still want to do some research and look for a wedding planner. There's no way she can do all of it herself.

As much as she wants to, I will let her make her decisions as far as what she wants, but I'm not letting her take over all the bits and pieces it takes to plan a wedding.

Between baby-making and work, she'll run herself into the ground and that's the last thing I want for her.

I tell myself that I need to talk to Mrs. Tamisha. Since I'm definitely going to use her for counsel when it comes to figuring out the contract for land.

I'm going to buy it. That much is sure, and if Tiana doesn't like it, then I can just give the land back to Banks and he can keep the money I give him.

Eventually, the fire dies, and the three of us go back inside. The two lovebirds bid me good night, and I quietly move into our bedroom.

Trying to make as little noise as possible, I remove my clothes, throwing them into a pile on the floor before I cuddle up behind Tiana.

I'm not really tired. Not with the thoughts running through my skull. I slowly wrap my arms around her, pulling her close to my chest as I rub a hand over her soft-skinned belly. We both smell of campfire smoke. Her hair is heavy with the scent of it, and I nuzzle my face into it, letting the heat of her body relax me.

I would love to sleep right now. But I can't. Not with all the thoughts going on in my head.

The vision of our house, of our wedding, of the things coming up, of more hockey, baby-making. All of it. It swirls through my head; dances a wonderful little jig, making me imagine how life will be with her.

Watching her make decisions, seeing her take life by the horns and being every bit of the woman I know she is.

Overall… I'm just excited that I get to be with this woman forever.

No matter how the events of the future play out, whether we get married first, or the baby comes first or the house.

At the end of the day, I get to do it all with her.

And while I'm excited, I do worry about Tiana. Especially with the warnings Charlotte gave me.

A lot is about to happen, and I think I can handle it just fine. I just don't know how Tiana will take it.

Regardless, I'll be there to pull her out of the deep end when things go awry.

Eventually, my thoughts whirl and spin so much, that they push me *deep* into sleep.

The next morning, I wake up to find Tiana snuggled into my chest when the rooster crows again. She hides her face in my chest as the sun shines on us from the window on the other side of the room.

It's a small room, the door merely sits to the right of the bed. There is a small closet in the wall to the left of the bed, with some room to move around it, and a window high up on the wall directly across from the bed. And on the wall beside the window, is a wardrobe. There's enough room for all of our clothes to be in a mess all over the floor.

My eyes blink open and I look down at her, wrapping my arm tighter around her and kissing her forehead.

"Ready to get home, sugar?" I whisper softly as I rub soft circles into her back.

"Mmmmmm," she groans in response.

"I know, baby. But we gotta get back home, and you can rest for as long as you'd like," I tell her.

"I don't want to mooooooove," she groans again.

"I'll get our stuff ready and in the car and I'll let you know when you can come out, okay?"

She nods against me before she turns over. Burying her face in the pillows, she wraps the blankets tightly around her to hide herself from the world.

I press a kiss on her shoulder before I get up. Moving slowly from the bed, I climb out before I lean over to grab my hoodie and sweatpants from last night to pull them on. Then, I go around the room, picking up our discarded clothes and putting them in the duffle bag.

I take one last sweep of the room, making sure I don't forget anything before taking it out to the car. The sky is grey, with clouds far down in the sky and a sprinkle of rain.

It's a vast comparison from the past few days, but it is Washington.

Tucker and Waffle are curled up together on the porch, relaxing together, so when I come back to the front door, they perk up and follow me inside.

Charlotte and Banks are busy in the kitchen, where they have cooked breakfast, making the entire house smell like eggs and bacon. He has his arms around her waist, kissing at her neck as the bacon grease pops and spits in the cast iron.

"Morning," I say as I come to sit at the dining room table. Tucker and Waffle crowd the two at the stove, sitting ever so nicely for a chance at some of the goods.

Banks presses another kiss to the crook of her neck before he reaches over to the paper plate that rests by the stove. He grabs two pieces of bacon, turning to Waffle as he holds it up.

"Sit pretty," he says, and Waffle sits up on her butt, panting with what I swear looks like a little doggy smile. He tosses her the bacon and she gobbles it up in an instant.

He turns to Tucker, who is already sitting, and he merely tosses it to him. Tucker also destroys the piece of meat before he licks at the floor.

Walking past Tucker, he pulls a chair out from the table, facing it toward me before he sits down.

"Y'all 'bout to head out soon?" he asks.

"Yeah, in a little bit. Tiana's not ready to wake up yet, so I figured I'd come out here. Talk about a few things before I hit the road," I say.

I lean back in the wooden chair with a deep breath, dipping my chin to grab my chain in my teeth so my tongue can slide across it as I think.

I fold my arms over my chest as my gaze dips, zoning out on the floor as my leg bounces with nervous energy.

"What's on your mind, big hoss?" Banks asks.

"I think I want that bit of land. The one around the lake," I whisper, just in case Tiana can hear us.

"How much?"

I keep my gaze steady on the floor, thinking. "Give me fifteen acres. I think that's more than enough for what we wanna do with it. But I want the lake. And the forest beyond it," I say through the chain.

I glance up at Banks, whose eyes are locked on me as I think.

With his gaze still locked on me as he speaks, "Lotty. What's your weigh-in?"

Charlotte turns to us, tilting her head as she moves her attention from the eggs and bacon. "What's happening?"

Banks nods his head toward us, signaling for her to come over, and she turns off the stove for the time being. She wipes her hands off on a towel beside the stove before she comes to sit in Banks' lap.

Charlotte wraps her arms around his neck, smiling. "What's up?"

Banks holds her hips as he nods at me. "Tell her what you told me," he says.

Charlotte turns in his lap, facing me, and leaning forward to listen. I lean in so she can hear the low tone.

"I'm asking Adrian for fifteen acres of land. Including the small lake and the forest beyond it to buy for Tiana," I say quietly.

Her eyes widen and she bites her lip in glee. "I think that is a wonderful idea," she whispers. "What are you going to do with it?"

"I wanna build her a home on it. A detached garage for the cars. A gazebo for her to read in by the lake." My voice trails off as I tell her. Because the visions become vivid once again. Zooming through my head at Mach speed and causing a smile to rise on my face.

But I come back to the present, looking at Charlotte.

"Absolutely. I'll talk to my mom about it so you guys can draw up a contract," she says.

"Thanks Charlotte, you're the best," I tell her quietly.

She nods before she gets up to finish making breakfast, and I smile at Banks.

"I have an idea. I'll come back out here, and we'll draw up boundary lines," I say softly.

"And what of Miss Tiana? You reckon you'll be able to get out here without her knowing?" he asks as he leans back in his chair, widening his legs before he crosses his arms against his chest.

"I have an idea for that. But I'll need your lady," I say as I nod toward Charlotte.

She's made a plate of eggs for each of the dogs, and they greedily slop up their plates as she cleans up the kitchen.

Banks nods. "You know you're allowed to peruse any part of the property, right?" he asks.

"I mean, if you'd like me to. But I think we have to have boundary lines for the contract," I remind him.

"Correct. But let me know. We have Trunk or Treat next week, and I doubt you'll have time next weekend to do it. We'll plan for the week after."

"Gives me time to reach out to my attorney. See what needs to be done beforehand," I respond.

"I'll have to figure out how to get the contract past Tiana. She's my attorney," Banks says.

"Fuck, you're right..." I say as I lean back in my seat. "Give me these few weeks... I can come up with a way to make this all work," I tell him with a wave of my hand.

Banks throws his hands up in surrender with a small nod.

"Thanks again, man. I appreciate it," I say as I drop my chain from my teeth and stand. I take a wide stretch, shaking the tension from my muscles from where I was sitting.

"Pleasure's mine, bud," he says as he stands with me.

He puts his hand out for a shake, and I smile before I open my arms in a hug.

Banks lets a heavy sigh go before he brings me in for a hug, where we lay hard pats on each other's backs.

"We'll be in touch," I whisper before I pull away.

"We work together," he says.

"Shut up, it's just part of the thing," I say.

He shakes his head, and I snag a strip of bacon from the paper plate before I go grab Tiana.

Even by the time I'm ready to leave, Tiana is passed out. So, I carry her out to the car and stuff her in the passenger seat. Tucker was honestly somewhat reluctant to say goodbye to what I imagine is his girlfriend now, but he gets in the back of Tiana's BMW and curls into a ball with sad eyes as he looks up at the window.

I say goodbye one last time to Charlotte and Banks before I get in the car and drive us home.

By the time we finally arrive at the apartment a little over an hour later, Tiana is finally waking up. Even if she is extremely groggy.

"Are we home?" she groans.

"Yes, sugar," I whisper.

She makes another noise, but it's muffled from her hood being pulled over her head. It's tied tight, allowing only a little bit of her face to show.

I give a soft chuckle as I lean over the center console. Grasping the back of her head, I pull it toward me to kiss her forehead through the fabric. After I release her, I get out of the car, and Tucker runs from the back to follow me.

I round the vehicle to open her door, and she tilts her head back to see me through the hole in her hoodie.

I can't see much, but it does seem as if she's glaring at me.

Or she could just be sleepy and mad that she had to wake up.

I quickly move to the back of her vehicle, opening the trunk to grab the backpacks and duffle bag, coming back around to see her still leaned into her seat.

When I give a click of my tongue, she looks up at me in annoyance, and I give her a grin before I nod for her to get out. She throws her head back, groaning as she moves like sap to get out.

One leg, then the other, almost robotically, as she stands from the vehicle and stretches wide before she wraps her arms around herself.

"Tired?" I ask softly.

She makes a groaning noise as she leans into me. I shake my head playfully before I wrap my arm around her shoulder, leading her to the elevator for the lobby. Silently, we make our way through the complex, Tucker trotting happily at our side.

When we get to our floor, we walk down the hall, and I stop at my apartment to let Tucker have a bit of time to himself. Whereas Tiana keeps walking to her apartment.

I drop the bags there before I refill Tucker's food and water bowls. Then, I make sure he has his toys and give him some good rubs. Before leaving my apartment to go to Tiana's.

When I get in, she's curled up on the couch in the fetal position, and already, she has a blanket tugged around herself.

I quietly close the front door behind and come to kneel in front of her on the couch.

I tilt my head as I watch her, smiling as I bring a hand up to stroke her shoulder.

"What do you want today, sugar?" I whisper.

"Nothing. Only sleep," she grumbles.

I chuckle before I press a kiss to her covered forehead. "As you wish," I respond.

I stand, quietly moving back to the front door and to my apartment to start unpacking the duffle bag, sorting the stuff that needs to be washed since it either smells like outside or smoke, then go and start the laundry while she sleeps.

I decide to let her have the apartment to herself. Quiet and dark just like she likes it on these weekends. It helps it's rainy today. A perfect day to sleep away.

In the meantime, I get to work on the one thing I haven't been able to stop thinking about.

The land. The house.

I have to make sure I have at least some things out of the way so when I show it to her I have answers to her questions. Because Lord knows she'll have them.

Ever the curious critter my little lady is.

Unveiling it to her is where I have my own questions.

Will she love it? Will she hate it? Will she call me crazy? I don't know what to expect from her.

I know she likes the land, but will she appreciate my buying it without her input? I don't know. I guess we'll have to see.

I do have a pretty solid feeling about it. Plus, if I get Charlotte involved, it makes it that much easier for me.

Once I get the laundry started and I've taken a shower, I pull out my laptop and prop myself up on the couch. I swing my legs onto the coffee table and start looking up loggers and cement workers. I need to have reputable people pour a foundation and loggers to remove trees.

I can't plan anything, of course, because I don't even know if I'll be able to keep the land. But I need to have numbers in case Tiana asks.

After a long while, I start looking at builders, floor plans, house fronts, room styles.

I get sucked into my research for what feels like *hours*.

I have to admit, this planning stuff is great. I'm so proud of myself for all the thought I'm giving my little lady.

She deserves it, to be fair.

But now, maybe I understand the way Tiana gets so sucked into things like the wedding. Because for the rest of the day that Tiana sleeps, I do nothing but house research.

Tiana's weekends usually go like that. If she has too much social interaction, she just gets so tired. She sleeps her Sundays away. But she also wakes up crazy early every single day, so it makes sense.

As I research, I send all the links I have to Banks to see if he approves and what he thinks. Granted, he's not much of a texter, but at least I have something to bring up with him on Monday.

"Head... up! Damn you!" Bubbles' damn near chucks a stray puck at Leroy as he runs Coach's blood pressure through the fucking roof. "The fuck is your problem!? Halfway through the season and I have to put a fuckin' neck brace on you to keep your head up! This is elementary shit, Leroy!"

Bubbles' is *big* mad today.

I'm not sure why. But he and Stamen took some of the other players aside again, so Banks and I are just hanging out on the bench. Which gives me a chance to talk to him about the stuff I found and read over the weekend.

"You and Miss Tiana ready for Trunk or Treat this weekend?" Banks asks as Charlotte squirts some water into his mouth.

"I am. I don't know how much Tiana is. She said she's not a fan of Halloween," I say with a shrug.

"Tracks. As kids, we used to trick or treat, but after a time, she just stopped. Said it was too much energy," Charlotte responds as she places a separate water bottle up on the wall.

"Well. I told her we could do whatever she wanted us to do on Halloween as a compromise."

"That'll do it," Charlotte says with a smile.

My brows jump and I shrug. "I just wanted to share the experience with her, is all. And if she is extra sleepy that weekend, then I'll let her have that time."

"How was she when you guys came back from our place?" Charlotte asks.

"Tired. I don't think she woke until later that night, and it was only to shower and get a small meal and to get back in bed."

"Makes sense," Charlotte murmurs as she crosses her arms over her chest with a nod as she looks out to the other players doing some stick drills.

"Pretty nice being the best players on the team, eh?" I ask Banks with a grin.

"Don't know what's gotten into those fucks, but they deserve the work," Banks mumbles.

"I spent the whole day yesterday looking at loggers and concrete people," I say as I cross my arms over my chest. I tug my chain from inside my gear, pulling it over my jersey before I bring it up to my lips to slide my tongue against it.

"Goddammit," I growl as I reach for a water bottle from the ledge.

I squirt myself with the water, letting it run over my head, my jersey and down my chain. Leaning away from the two, I shake my hair out and give a sigh before I pull my chain into my teeth, clamping down on it to run my tongue along it.

"Find anything?" Banks asks.

"I sent you the links. Figured you looked at em," I say through my chain.

"Fuck, my apologies, big hoss. We got busy this weekend," Banks says.

"All good. Figured you guys were out chorin'. Plus, I know you're not a big texter. More to have for now than anything," I say. Leaning back against the wall, I press my feet out in front of me, crossing one over the other as I look out at the rink. My arms cross and my foot waves back and forth as I wait.

Banks reaches into his pocket, pulling out his phone and scrolling through it for a bit. "Ah yeah, I know these folks," he murmurs.

"Good," I say as I lock my gaze onto the pucks moving on the ice with some of the other players. "How are you going to get the contract through Tiana?" I ask.

"Solid question. Got no idea. May have to reach out to Mrs. Tamisha, see what can be done, and if I can bypass Miss Tiana entirely," Banks murmurs as he continues scrolling through his phone.

"Well, next weekend, not this one, cause Trunk or Treat. Imma have to steal both of you. Charlotte, are you busy the weekend after Trunk or Treat?" I ask as I look back at Charlotte.

She's sitting up on the higher portion of the wall behind Adrian, her feet kicking back and forth as she watches the ice.

"Nope. Adrian and I got chorin', but we're free after that," she says.

"I'll need you. I have a plan for that day, and I've already ordered the things for it. It'll keep her occupied for far too long, I think, actually," I murmur.

"Whatever you need, I got ya, buddy," she says with a thumbs up.

I shake my head, with a small chuckle and a smile.

"How long do you think it would take for them to clear out some of that space and lay a foundation?" I ask.

"That's all dependent on what you want to remove, and what you want to do with the wood," Banks says with a shrug.

"Fuck," I say through my chain as my foot rocks on the blade of my skate.

"It'll be fine. You got time, and you guys got other priorities. You're startin' to go full Miss Tiana with this," Adrian says.

A grin rises on my face. "I sorta did yesterday. I could understand why she dives so deep into wedding planning because I just did research all day long while she slept."

"Just square away your priorities. And we'll be here to help each other through it, no worries," Banks says with a ghost of a smile as he presses out his mitt for me.

I glance at him with a small smile before I bump his mitt with mine.

"Banks! Hayze! Get your asses back in here!" Bubbles yells from the ice.

Banks and I grin at each other before we stand and press our helmets back on. We grab our sticks, jump over the wall and back onto the ice.

CHAPTER TWENTY-TWO
TIANA

Ahhh... Trunk or Treat...

So many people. *So* many noises. The energy is *dreadfully* high and it makes my heart stutter in my chest. I don't like dressing up, I don't enjoy people, and I *especially* don't enjoy *this many* people.

Which means this entire night makes my blood feel like it has bugs in it.

But I'm here for Gunnar. He wanted me to be here, so, by *dammit*, I'm going to fucking be here for my big goon.

With Gunnar's idea of a deer caught in headlights, I had no idea how to make that work, considering I couldn't have massive lights on my tits. This is a kids' event.

So, I had to get creative.

I was able to make a headband that looks like headlights. They really are just spare Mickey Mouse ears that I put lights on.

While the rest of the costume is a tight black dress. Of course, it's nothing scandalous. But I was able to paint yellow lines along the front of it with fabric paint, so it looks like road lines.

All in all, it's actually really cute, and part of me is impressed with this idea.

More-so that I could think of something to make it work. Gunnar had an easy costume. Of course, I had the one that needed to be part of the pun. But it turned out well, and I'm happy about that.

It doesn't make me enjoy the event that is 'Trick or Treating' any more than before, however.

We had to come in hours ago to set up, and for the past thirty minutes the families have been lining up at the first car, waiting to go through the line.

All the while, Gunnar sits on the tailgate of his truck, his feet kicking back and forth as he shakes something in his hand before he tilts his head back and drops whatever it is into his mouth.

I look at him in confusion as I lean against the tailgate. I can't even see what it is because, for whatever reason, he brought it in a brown paper bag.

"What is that?" I ask.

He chews whatever it is for a minute before he grins and reaches into the bag to pull some of it out. When he grabs a handful, he presses his hand out to me and opens it.

In his palm, is a *fuck-ton* of candy corn.

"Candy corn? Seriously?" I ask.

"Why? What's wrong with candy corn?" he asks before he leans his head back to throw them in his mouth.

"Is it too late to call off the wedding?" I groan as I pinch the bridge of my nose.

"Whoa, whoa. Are you saying you don't fuck with candy corn!? Tiana Dawn!?" he scoffs in faux incredulity.

"And you do!? It's nothing but colored plastic." I turn to

him, placing my hands on my hips before I gesture to the paper bag.

"If that's the case, this is the best plastic I'll ever eat," he says with another grin and a shrug before he reaches for more of it.

"Why is it in a paper bag?" I ask.

"Why not?"

"Oh my god," I sigh as I pinch the center of my eyebrows again.

It's interesting to be fake arguing with a mammoth of a man who is dressed as a fucking deer.

Funny, but definitely a moment of self-awareness.

I did Gunnar's makeup before we came out here, which was a thing in and of itself because I had never done deer makeup before, so I had to look it up. The whole bottom of his nose and upper lip is painted black, and his face is covered in little white dots. There's also some other face makeup to give him a more deer-like appearance.

I actually did a pretty good job. But still. The guy is a fucking monster, and he's dressed as a deer, which means his antlers add a solid eight to nine inches to the top of his head.

It makes him appear *much* taller than he actually is.

I turn my attention to the parking lot, watching as the families move through each of the cars. With each car the first family moves through, my blood runs through me faster.

Humans. Communicating. Interacting. With humans.

I feel vastly out of place with this entire idea, and I cling desperately to the hope that none of the kids or parents will give two shits about me. It's all about the hockey players, so let it be about them.

Deciding to shift focus in an attempt to bring down my nerves, I look over to the car beside us.

Or rather, truck.

Adrian and Charlotte have parked next to us. Which is all fine and dandy, but for their 'trunk', they built some sort of ranch-like situation. They even have Waffle in the bed, in a little costume of a cow. She barks as the families come closer, but luckily she can't escape because they've tied her up to a hook in the truck bed. She still has room to move freely, but she can't go herding the kids if she wanted.

Charlotte and Adrian, however, are dressed as a cowboy and cowgirl. Which I definitely think is cheating, because that's just them on a normal weekend.

The distraction does little for my nerves, and my arms cross against my chest as I move in my little space I've made for myself. All the while, I worry the inside of my lip as I watch the excited kids move closer and closer to our truck.

Gunnar's voice breaks through my moment of panic. "You excited, sugar?"

I turn to look at him, and he gives me a reassuring grin before he grabs another handful of candy corn to throw into his mouth.

"Absolutely not," I murmur as my eyes glance back to the line.

"Ya' know. Pa was the one who had always taken us Trick or Treating. My parents always wanted to stay back and hand out candy to the kids, so Pa got to take us house to house. We had all kinds of costumes growing up. But more often than not, I dressed up as Wayne Gretzky, because well," he says with a reminiscent smile.

And with that realization, I sigh. Seeing how much all of this means to him, I loosen up. Taking a deep breath, I shake the nerves out of my arms as they unfold from my chest.

I turn to him, trying to give him a smile before I grab his cheeks, bringing his head to my lips to press a kiss on his forehead.

As I pull away, I gaze into Gunnar's eyes. There really is a sort of childlike wonder he's getting out of this, and soon my smile feels as if it warms against my cheeks.

"I'm glad you get so much excitement out of all of this," I say softly before I give him a soft peck on the lips and release his face.

"I really do. I also love kids. I remember what it was like to see some of my favorite teams play when I was growing up. If I ever had the chance to meet my favorite players, it felt like my chest was going to explode. So I'm glad that I get to give kids that feeling now. Even if they may not know me, or they do and they're excited to see me. I'm happy that I can have that sort of impact on them," he says as he looks out to the line.

My smile tilts at the corner, and I make sure we have all our candy in place as the kids slowly work their way down the line.

I do still worry about... having to look normal. Act like a human for a long while with a bunch of strangers.

I can't help my fingers when they begin to pick nervously at one another. I think of anything I may need to say, trying to say the right things when I need to.

And though I'm not as worried as I was before, Gunnar seems to notice my energy, regardless.

"Hey, look at me, sugar," he says softly.

I connect with his gaze, giving him a smile.

"I'm sorry. I don't normally do crowds like this," I respond softly.

"I know. I'm really happy you're here with me, though. If it gets to be too much, you can go lay in the back of the truck until we're done, okay?" he says quietly.

Our small moment is interrupted as the first kids come up.

"Gunnar Hayze! It's Gunnar Hayze!" one of them says.

They can't be older than ten, dressed as... *shit?* They're dressed as *Gunnar*. Or at least wearing his jersey.

Three kids dressed in jerseys with "33" and "HAYZE" on the back.

My heart squeezes with a small sense of pride as a smile tugs at my cheeks.

"Hey bud! Good to see you!" he says as he drops some candy in their bags. "You guys getting some good candy so far?" he asks.

"Yeah! I got to see Crowder and Leroy too! You guys have been on fire this year!" one of the other boys says.

"Well, you guys know how it goes," Gunnar returns with an enormous smile.

"Can we get a picture with you?!" another boy asks.

"Absolutely! Tiana?"

I'm pulled out of the observation upon hearing my name, snapping to attention as one boy holds out his phone to me.

I take it with a nod before I open the camera. Soon, the boys all crowd Gunnar in front of his tailgate, and he kneels enough to be on their level.

Even though he looks absolutely insane in a deer costume amidst a group of boys in hockey jerseys, they all hold up a single finger, and huge smiles. But Gunnar has the biggest one of them all.

Even still, he's not looking at the camera, but at the person behind it.

Me.

I can't help the smile that tugs at my lips when I see him. I take a few pictures before I offer the phone back to its owner.

The boy takes it, a shimmering happiness in his eyes as he clutches it to his chest. "Thank you so much!" he says before they all take off to the next vehicle.

"Happy Halloween!" Gunnar calls after them.

I come back to sit on the tailgate, my heart a little warmer as the next family comes up.

This time, it's a husband, a wife, and a baby girl dressed as a little fawn.

"AHHHH! TIANA! LOOK!" Gunnar yells.

The little one seems mildly confused as she waddles up to us in her tiny shoes. She must be new to walking because the father is leaning over, holding her hand as she makes her awkward little steps.

My hands come over my chest as I take a small gasp. "It's a little stag!" I say softly.

Gunnar crouches down to not seem so imposing, and she cranes her head back to look at him with enormous eyes of wonder.

"Hey there. You're a cute little deer, aren't ya?" he says softly.

The dad picks up the baby, and Gunnar stands with them.

"Great game last Friday, man. Insane checks! You're like a bulldozer out there!" the dad says as he reaches his free hand out to Gunnar to shake it.

"Favorite thing about the game, bud," Gunnar says with a laugh and a rough grip and shake of the Dad's hand. "You guys having fun tonight?" he asks as he turns around to his truck to grab handfuls of candy to put into the bag the mom holds.

"Oh, absolutely! I'll never pass up a chance to meet my favorite team," the dad says with a massive grin.

"Ain't that the truth, brother," Gunnar says with a laugh as he claps the man on the shoulder.

"Can we get a picture?" the dad asks.

"I'd be mad if you didn't!" Gunnar jokes.

The two laugh before Gunnar wraps his arm around the dad's shoulders, holding up a finger as the mom steps back to take a picture of the two. I take a step away from the truck so that I'm not in the picture.

And while I am backing away merely because this is his moment, something else comes into view.

A wider perspective on this man's life. The life where there's a group of people out there, that tune into every game to watch The Stags play a game they enjoy.

To watch Adrian, or Leroy, or Crowder... or Gunnar.

Sure, I had some of that perspective when Gunnar and I had that dinner. But it was a small instance. One that wasn't as big as this. One where for the next several hours, they talk about some things Gunnar has done, or they praise him for his work on the ice.

There is an entire group of people who tune in *just* to watch him.

That's... an interesting thing to imagine. A parallel reality I hadn't considered. One that exists in time with my own.

Where they praise him for his job, his career. And I praise him for the man he is off the ice.

It's almost a double life. Even if I'm in both of them.

It has me looking at him differently.

In a way that shows just how important he is, on and off the ice. And I can't help the beam of pride that flows through me. In the way he plays, the way he carries himself and because in all facets, he really is an incredible man.

I get lost in the sight of him for the rest of the night, interacting with his fans. Young, old, teens, adults, babies. *All* of them come out to see the Stags and Gunnar.

I watch the way these kids meet him with so much excitement, just for him to reciprocate that energy in return. There was not a single person he didn't give maximum energy to. Even as the night crept in, with the darkness swallowing the parking lot. Even as the last kid came through the line.

He kept that energy until the very end.

He took a breath only when the last kid left and he could

turn to me with the biggest smile of accomplishment on his face.

When he closes the tailgate, he takes a deep breath, grinning at me as he leans against it. "You have fun, sugar?" he asks with an exhausted smile.

My smile mimics his, and I really am glad that I came with him. That I got to see this side of things.

I may not enjoy Halloween or Trick or Treating.

But I did enjoy the fact that I got to see an entire night of people recognizing my big goon for the amazing man he is.

I smile up at him, admiring the tired yet satisfied boyish grin on his face.

"I did," I say softly.

He brings a hand up to my face, cupping my cheek and leaning down to press a soft kiss to my lips before he pulls away, pressing another kiss to my forehead. He leans over the tailgate, throwing his upper body into the bed with a loud clang, and I laugh at his ridiculousness.

"I'm beat," he murmurs softly.

I shake my head with a small smirk. "I'm gonna go say goodbye to Charlotte real quick," I say as I walk toward Adrian and Charlotte's truck.

"Alright. Make it quick; we still have to let out Tucker," he says.

Adrian is rounding a rope over his hand to throw into the back of his truck, and when I approach, Charlotte squeals.

"Hi Ti! Did you have fun?" she asks as she meets me in the middle.

"I did, actually. More so just observing, but I had fun," I say.

"That's awesome! I know you don't really like these things, but I'm glad you enjoyed it," she says with a grin.

"Are you guys going back to the ranch house?" I ask.

"Yeah, we've got a lot of chorin' to do tomorrow morning. Adrian likes to wake up before the rooster, so we gotta get home and get to bed," she says as she looks over at Adrian.

Adrian gives me a soft tip of his cowboy hat and the ghost of a satisfied smile.

"Alright, well, drive safely, you two," I say.

"You too, Ti!" Charlotte giggles as she wraps her arms tight around me in a hug, and I hug her back. She holds that hug for a moment as she tilts back and forth, squeezing me tighter before she lets go.

As I come back to Gunnar's truck, he's already inside, sitting in the driver's seat, and I go around the side to climb into the passenger seat. I crash into the seat, slumping as I finally take off my headlight ears. I turned the lights off hours ago and have merely turned them on and off for people to see them when they ask.

"Man, did you see the little baby dressed as a deer? How cute was that?" Gunnar asks when I relax in my seat.

"It was really cute," I say with a soft sigh.

And I think back to how he looked in that moment. The way he crouched to say hi to this little girl he didn't even know. The grin on his face and how excited he was to see this tiny deer.

It'd be nice to have a tiny deer of our own. I didn't realize how gentle he was with kids.

And soon a vision forms.

A baby girl. Curly hair, just like mine, and bright eyes. Even if I don't like games, I'll always take her to see her daddy play. We'd have a set of headphones on, and she'd be dressed in a little jersey watching him from the stands.

I see the smile he'd have on his face as he blows a kiss out to us. She'd wave out to him, not knowing he's a famous hockey player, because in her eyes, he's just her daddy and that's all she sees.

I can see why he wants this so badly.

I *need* that life with him. I need to see more of those moments from him. And the moments he'd have with our little one.

I need to have that family and love he talks about.

The vision slowly fades away, and my gaze focuses, coming back on Gunnar as he scrolls through his phone. His chain is in his teeth as he goes through some notifications he missed during the time at the arena.

Soon, he glances up at me with a smile, still wearing his deer makeup. Granted, he took his antlers off, so now he just looks like a doe.

"You're a beaut', Gunnar," I whisper.

"Aww, thanks, sugar, you are too," he says with a grin.

But I don't think he realizes how much I mean that in this moment. He seems blissfully unaware of the love I have for him. Right now, that's okay with me.

I'm glad I get to have this love with him. *For* him.

Reaching up to his cheeks, I cup them, pulling him toward me to press kisses to his lips. I hear the click of the lock sound on his phone, and soon his hand comes to grip tight at my hip.

I kiss him a little longer, letting the love I feel flow through every movement I make against his lips. His other hand comes up, wrapping loosely around the bottom of my neck. Then, he shifts his grip, his thumb softly rubbing into the hollow of my throat as he moves with my kisses.

"I can't wait to make you a daddy," I whisper into our kiss.

"Mmm, sugar, you're playing a dangerous game," he murmurs back.

"I'm serious," I respond.

He presses a last kiss to my lips before he pulls away. He

looks at me with a softly furrowed brow and a tilt of his head. All the while, his thumb continues to move slowly on the hollow of my throat.

"What do you mean?" he asks softly.

My thumbs rub against his cheeks as I look into his perfect hazel eyes.

There is still so much I have yet to say to him. So many things I struggle with. Eye contact, verbalizing the way I feel, talking about my emotions and my feelings.

But slowly, I'm finding comfort in the things I once feared.

Gazing into his eyes, for one. This brings me love, care, safety.

My heart fills as I relish the feeling of his gaze.

"I think I'm finally seeing the things you're seeing. This future you keep talking about and why you're so adamant. It's different to see it happen in front of you," I say quietly.

"What have you seen?" he asks. His gaze searches mine, his grip shifting slowly for his thumb to run up and down the pulse point in my neck.

My gaze dips to his lips for only a moment before it slides back up to his eyes.

"You. The little one. You have a little towel on your shoulder, and you're shirtless. You have the baby in just a diaper in your arms. You're making us breakfast, and I've walked in on you murmuring something to them. I see..." I pause, letting the vision play again through my head. "Me, the baby, we're at a game. We're wearing Stags jerseys with your name on the back. We have our headphones on." A smile rises on my lips, one that pulls at my eyes, letting me sink into the idea of this future with him.

"She'd reach out at the ice when you wave to us," I say.

"She?" I hear him ask.

The vision falls away, and I come back to the present, only to see him smiling at me with a teasing grin.

A soft blush runs across my cheeks. "Yes... In my little fantasies, it's a girl."

"Does she have your curls?" he asks softly.

I nod. "She does," I whisper.

His smile widens, and his eyes dip to where his thumb continues to rub against the side of my neck.

"I've seen... you. You're asleep on the couch. But your boob is out cause the baby is eating. And when they finish, I take them off, and cover you with a blanket so that you sleep easier," he whispers.

His hand moves from my neck, coming to coil one of my curls around his finger. "I've seen your big belly, and me putting kisses on it. Rubbing it, holding it, holding you," he whispers. "I've seen the nights where I'm wrapped around you, making sure you're safe while you're sleeping. Pressing kisses to your shoulders and making sure you're relaxed."

His vision plays through my head and I give a playful smirk as I think about it.

"I need it," I say softly.

"I've needed it since the moment I saw you, Tiana," he responds with a grin.

"Since the moment you saw me?" I tease.

"Well. Maybe not the baby stuff. But I knew I wanted a life with you. Life just happens to be everything when it comes to you," he says.

Heat floods my body. It pours through my face, all the way up to my ears, and I lean in to kiss him again.

I have no words for this man. There's just too much love for him right now, so I show it to him the best way I can.

His hand threads through the hair at the nape of my neck, gripping a handful of it and tilting my head to kiss me deeper, the hand on my hip gripping tighter as he attempts to pull me closer to him.

Holding his face in my hands, I kiss back. Deeper, slower. I never want moments like this with him to end. I wish I could stay in these little pockets of space with him.

Soon, he drags his hand from my hair to hang around my neck again. His eyes are so full of adoration as he gazes at me.

"I love you, Tiana Dawn," he whispers softly.

And I can feel it; the way my own eyes shine with adoration for him.

"I love you, Gunnar Hayze."

CHAPTER TWENTY-THREE
GUNNAR

The weekend with Tiana was one of complete bliss. She was tired the day after Trunk or Treat, so we spent almost the entire day in bed going in and out of sleep.

In those times, when I found she was completely dead to the world, I'd pop back over to my apartment, slowly putting together the little gift I had bought her.

It arrived earlier in the week, and I had to find a way to hide it from her. Which is difficult because my "little" gift was not so little. The only place I could hide it was in my trophy room.

She never goes in there.

Monday comes quickly, and she's back to her business-girl self, while I'm here in the rink thinking of my next steps. Of course, I bought her the gift for a reason. Hopefully, today I can get some of the more minute details worked out with Banks so that I can put that gift to good use.

Tiana said she had a lot to get done this week, which is perfect for me, because I *also* have some stuff I need to work through.

Stamen and Bubbles have us doing puck drills, so Banks and I are teamed up. We move the puck through the cones set up for us before he slaps it to me and I race through the cones myself. Over and over, trying to get our times down.

After so long, the group of us are breathing heavily and ready for some water.

"Go take a break, ya degens!" Bubbles calls to the team.

Taking my helmet off, I take deep breaths before I leisurely slide over to the wall. I toss my stick over the side for it to clatter onto the ground in front of the bench before I lean over the wall, looking for a squeeze bottle of water.

When I find one, I grab it and spray it over my face and mouth before swallowing. I take the chance to tug my chain out of my jersey and clean it off before looping it over my tongue.

Banks races toward me, skidding to a stop to spray me with slush. I watch him with a deadpan look as he changes to a trot over to me, his skates pricking into the ice as he makes it to the wall. He leans against it, snatching the bottle from my hand to spray some water into his mouth.

"You still need to borrow my little lady this weekend?" he asks after swallowing. He presses himself up onto the edge of the wall, watching as everyone else fucks around on the ice. Some stretching, some just playing with their sticks and a puck.

I lean against the wall, turning my skates so that I don't slide away. My arms cross against my chest as I watch my other teammates.

"Yeaaah, I'll need her. I got all the shit I need. Just gotta rock the play, see what happens," I murmur as my eyes chase the puck on the ice. I slide my tongue against my chain, watching as I think of my plan again.

"How do you need this to go down?" he asks.

"You're going to bring Charlotte out to the complex, I'm

gonna give Tiana her gift, let her get settled, then I'll come out and you'll take me to the ranch. We gotta draw up some more boundary lines. I asked my lawyer to meet us out at your property to log the things he needs to," I say.

And I'm sincerely hoping I know Tiana well enough that my plan will work. She likes to ask questions.

Such is the way of the lawyer.

But if I rock this play the way it needs to be played, she won't ask questions, and I can get this land squared away to surprise her with it.

Slapshot during sudden death type of win. If it all goes according to plan.

But this is all... a massive *'but.'*

"Big 10-4, boss man," he says with a nod.

Speaking of the plan, I look around for the other missing chess piece, trying to figure out where she is. Only to find her nowhere.

"Where's your girl at?" I ask.

"I don't know. She does her own thing at this hour," Banks shrugs before he pats me hard on the back and grabs his stick from behind the wall to skate back onto the ice.

I spend the whole practice running over my plan for this weekend, hoping with everything in me I orchestrated everything just right. There's a level of excitement... but also nervousness. I know that Tiana will appreciate the land. But I don't feel the greatest about not talking to her about it first.

Once practice ends, I take my shower and mosey my way

down the hall to meet Tiana. As I open the door to her office, I see that she is *heavily* focused on her computer.

"Ready to go home, sugar?" I ask as I press my hands into my pockets, watching her.

I do love the way she gets sucked into things. You can see it in her eyes, the way her gears are turning, just like the vehicles she likes to watch. Mach speed, even if externally it's not entirely present in her energy.

Maybe I'm just attuned to her... and I like that.

She takes a moment longer to respond, and I merely watch her until she does.

"Yes... just give me... one..." Her voice trails off as her eyes bounce around the screen, her fingers moving to the keyboard to type something every so often.

"Everything okay?" I ask quietly. My brow furrows as I realize this may differ from the other times I've seen her lock in to something.

"Yeah, sorry. My mom gave me this case that she had to hand off last minute. She has some other stuff to work on. The deadline is sometime next week," she murmurs. Her eyes continue to bop around the screen for a little longer before she lets out a heavy sigh.

My heart patters a little nervously as I weigh her words and what they may mean.

Fuck, is my plan the reason she may be working more here? Did her mom pass a case off to Tiana so she could deal with the contract for Banks and me?

I don't have time to mull it over as Tiana's voice breaks through my small moment of panic.

"Okay. I think I'm done for the day," she breathes with a sigh of relief as she clicks around her screen. Her eyes move between her desktop computer and her laptop as she shuts them down.

Soon, the sound of her desktop rings through the room, and she stands to place things in her tote, but her eyes and mind are elsewhere as she puts her stuff away. Her mouth moves, with small noises leaving it as she thinks. It's like the wedding planning with the whiteboard.

She crosses her arms against her chest before she brings a hand up to her mouth. Worrying the edge of her fingers, she moves slowly from behind her desk, as if on autopilot. I take a hesitant step forward, keeping my eyes on her as I grab her bag. Then, she walks toward the door, leading me out and waiting for me to exit before she locks it.

I watch as she moves down the hall. Utterly silent, she leads us toward the exit doors of the arena. I keep up with her steps mostly because my stride is much longer than hers.

"Sugar, hey," I murmur, trying to get her attention.

"Hm?" she responds as she keeps walking.

Putting my arm around her shoulders, I tug her into my body. I slow down our pace, trying to wrangle her mind back to the present. But sometimes when she gets so sucked in, it can be difficult.

"Hey, come back, babe," I say again.

She halts in her steps, pulling her lost gaze up to mine.

"Sorry... sorry. It was just a curveball thrown into my day. My mind kind of... went, I'm sorry," she murmurs as she shakes her head. Almost as if she's trying to get the case out.

I turn to her, bringing my arm from her shoulder to grip her chin in my fingers. Giving her a soft smile, I tilt her head up.

"No, don't be sorry. I just wanted to make sure you're okay," I respond.

Her gaze focuses on me, and I see the way she slowly comes back to this time here with us. She gives me a small smile.

"I'm good, sorry. Sometimes when she throws these cases at

me, it catches me off guard. I'll leave it here. I'm tired anyway; I need a nap," she says as she blows out a deep breath.

A thought comes to mind. My tried and true little technique that seems to help her leave her stresses behind.

I press closer to her body, letting go of her chin to grip her hip. A blush rises on her cheeks, and she melts into me as I lean down to press soft kisses to her neck.

"Pretty girl," I croon softly.

I love being able to take her day away from her. I've learned in my time with her that her mind seems to be her worst enemy. With a lot of things.

There is always something going on in that head of hers, and I love that she's given me the power to bring her peace. That I can quiet those loud thoughts that make her feel too much at once.

She lets out a soft exhale of relief as my arm snakes around her back, and she bows against it. I kiss and lick her neck, with the scent of her body encasing me in her heat. In an instant, my cock hardens, and I grind it against her with a low groan.

"Do I need to take it all away? Do you need the quiet?" I whisper.

"Please," she whispers in response.

That's all it takes for me to scoop her up in my arms in a cradle hold and damn near sprint out to the Vette.

Which I am *wholeheartedly* glad we took today.

It's not very gentlemanly the way I toss her into the passenger seat with all of our stuff and shut the door.

Not sure what possesses me next, but the car is in my way, and I'm wearing sweatpants, so I slide against the hood of the car to get to the driver's side door and throw myself in.

I find Tiana putting our stuff on the floor at her feet, and I throw the car into drive to speed our asses to the complex.

The entire time I'm driving, Tiana leans over the center

console, kissing and licking my neck as her hand rubs my cock through my sweatpants. It's absolute torture the way she grips me through the fabric, grinding the heel of her hand against the rigidity.

"Titi, fuck..." I groan as my head leans against the headrest. I keep my eyes on the road, thank God, but it feels *so* fucking good.

It's hard to concentrate on driving with her hand on me, but I try to make my way to the apartment as fast as I can. Somehow I make it to the fucking complex without painting the inside of my boxers. When I do, I park quickly, leaving all of our stuff in the Vette while I come to the passenger side to open her door and kneel to hoist her up into my arms.

She wraps her arms around my neck with a soft giggle as her legs go to my waist, and she kisses at my neck as I move us to the elevator.

When it opens and I get us in, I beat rapidly on the button, trying to get it to move as fast as it can. As the elevator moves, I wrap my hand around her jaw, moving her from my neck so I can latch onto her lips. My tongue dips into her mouth, wrapping around her tongue as I move my lips over hers.

"Fucking hell, Tiana," I pant as I kiss her.

Her hips grind against me, seeking friction, and I move my hands to her ass. I grip and help her move before the elevator opens.

"Keep going, baby, get that pussy wet for me," I pant.

When we get to the lobby, I book it to the apartment elevator, letting her work herself up as we ride the next one. I press her against the mirror, kissing and licking her mouth before the door opens and I get us to her apartment. All I can think about is her fucking pussy wrapped around me. I wanna bury my cock in her and lose my mind.

I take us straight to the bedroom, closing the door behind

me before I take her to the bed. Setting her down on it, I catch sight of her eyes, shrouded in a hazy lust. Her lips are puffy and swollen from our kissing, and her chest moves in soft breaths.

I always love having the chance to admire my sugar.

"You're so fucking beautiful," I growl as I lean down again, pressing kisses into her lips slowly. One of my hands wraps around her throat, creeping down the front of her body, unbuttoning each of the buttons on her jacket before pressing the panels open.

I tug at the sleeves of her suit jacket, and she pulls her arms from them so she can wrap them around my shoulders, tugging me closer.

I comply, leaning into her body and grinding my cock against her as my hand snakes down her body, down her skirt to bunch it up around her hips. Her skin sends fire through my blood as I feel it. So fucking soft, and so touchable, every *single* time.

"You drive me fucking insane, Tiana," I rasp as I press my fingers into her pussy.

A gasp leaves her as my fingers stroke against her clit, and already, she's so fucking wet.

My hand reluctantly releases the soft grip I have on her neck to reach for the band of my sweatpants, pressing them and my boxers down. As they fall, I pull my feet from the legs and kick them both away. With my cock free, I grip it, stroking myself up and down as I lean back down to kiss her. All the while, I swirl my fingers around her clit, working her up.

"I'm so sorry, sugar. I don't have time for these buttons," I murmur as I let go of my cock to slide my hand under her shirt. I turn it, leveling it between the buttons before I yank up, popping all the buttons off to open it. Soon, I'm able to get her shirt off, leaving her generous tits on display for me in that lacy little bra of hers.

I tug her skirt off her, throwing it to the side, and then, I have her body spread out before me.

Leaning up, I take in the sight of her. Legs spread, her cunt shiny with her wetness and my cock hard as a fucking rock.

Goddamn it, this woman is going to be my fucking wife.

I'm the luckiest man alive.

A groan runs through me as I wrap my hand around my dick, stroking as I look down at her, my thoughts working.

Do I want to taste her? Do I want her to taste me?

A grin rises on my face as I lean down to kiss her. Her hands come to wrap around my face, pulling me in deeper and kissing me back with just as much fervor.

"I need to taste you, baby," I rasp into her lips.

"Please... I wanna feel your tongue," she pants in response.

My kisses leave her lips to kiss down her jaw, down her neck. More and more, I kiss down her entire body before I'm on my knees before her. My hands run up and down the insides of her thighs as I press them open, holding them against the bed.

Looking down at me, she leans on her elbows, watching me with anticipation, and a grin rises on my face.

"You like watching me eat this pussy?" I ask. I lean down, keeping my eyes on her as my tongue falls from my mouth, dipping into her seam.

Her warm taste coats my tongue, and my brow quirks as I try to keep my gaze on her. With wide eyes, her lips part on a small gasp, her eyes trying to focus on me as she slowly nods.

"So... so fucking much," she whispers.

I move down farther, seeking her clit with my tongue, and when I find it, I press into it, flicking up and down.

Her eyes roll, her head falling as she breathes out a moan.

"Fuck," she whimpers.

"Eyes here, Mama. Watch," I say against her pussy.

Her head reluctantly pulls up, her gaze finding mine, and I dip my tongue deeper, flattening it against her cunt.

"Gunnar... Gunnar, fuck," she moans as she gives in, her hips writhing against my face.

But I keep my eyes on her, licking and sucking every bit of slickness from her. I flick more against her clit before I let go of one of her legs to press my fingers into her.

Her mouth parts and her eyes can't leave me now, not with the way I work her pussy.

"Good fucking girl, baby. Watch me. Watch the way I feast on you," I pant against her.

Her hand comes up, cradling the back of my head, pulling me in deeper, her moans growing louder as I work her closer to the edge. Her eyes will roll, or they'll try to escape, but they always come back to me, darting around my face, from my eyes to my mouth and back again.

"That's it. Control me," I add as I speed up my fingers. My tongue moving faster against her clit.

"Fuck... fuckfuckfuck," she whimpers as she climbs more... and more. I feel her tighten, flutter. I see the way her stomach tightens, with her head tossing back.

"Come for me. You're right there, sugar. Come for me, take it, grab it," I pant as my fingers speeds up, my thumb replacing my tongue for the moment I'm speaking before I use my tongue again.

She falls to the bed, her back bowing as she screams out and her hands come to grip at my hair, tugging me in deeper.

I release her other thigh, letting her come around my fingers and my tongue, using the now free hand to grip my cock. I stroke fast, groaning into her as I live in the pleasure with her.

As her orgasm keeps moving, I stand, pressing my arms under her legs and hoisting her up against me. I latch onto her mouth, still covered in her slick, and kiss her deeply. My mouth moving in time with hers as I position her above my cock, moving her to tease her spasming entrance with the head.

Soon, her hand comes between us, seeking my cock. When she finds it, she grips me just the way I like, stroking before she holds it steady for me to press her down onto me.

A groan escapes me, a tortured one. Since she's still somewhat coming, I have to force myself in. But fuck me sideways, upside down and from the front it's so fucking good.

"Tight... so... so fucking tight," I grit as I work more of myself into her.

Her hand lets go of my cock to come up and grip my shoulders, with her gaze coming to mine.

"So fucking... big," she returns with a pleasured grin.

I let out a small, tortured chuckle

As I work into her, I growl, feeling her cover me, and my eyes lock onto hers as she takes me. Our mouths part together on a breath we share, fire pulsing between us as she sinks deeper onto me.

"There she is. Keep going, take all of me," I pant as I push more and more of myself into her.

"Fuck... you fill me so... so fucking well. I love the way you make me stretch," she pants as her head leans back.

My knees wobble from the light breathiness of her words, and from the hard practice day, but also from the fucking way her pussy makes me weak in the knees.

I turn around, sitting us on the bed, and she anchors her feet against the edge, her hands gripping tighter on my shoulders as she grinds and moves herself up and down on my cock.

My hands grip for purchase on her ass, feeling the way her hips move and take charge of me.

"Thatta girl, show me who this cock fucking belongs to," I grit as I lay a soft slap to one of her ass cheeks.

"Fuck, it's mine. It's all fucking mine," she moans in a light desperation as she bounces up and down on me, her head thrown back as she loses herself.

"Fuck yes it is, pretty girl. All fucking yours," I pant as I watch her.

Her tits bounce in her bra, her face relaxed and lost to ecstasy. But most importantly, every one of her fucking thoughts is gone. All that's left is the way my cock fills her.

She keeps going, moving and toying with me just the way she wants before I wrap my arms around her back and roll her onto the bed.

Hovering above her with my cock still held inside, she looks up at me in mild confusion, trying to get a grip on the fast movements.

The pendant on my chain dangles in her face, and she gives me a sly grin before she nips at it, holding the stag between her teeth with a grin.

My hips move without thought, looking to pillage every corner of her. I move slow, deep, feeling every bit of her.

"Being in you is like coming home, Mama. It's the best fucking end to my day," I pant as I lean down to kiss and bite into her neck.

Her hips move under me, swirling and working me deeper with every thrust, before I reach up to pull the cloth of her bra down. Leaning down, I suck one of her hard peaked nipples into my mouth, lathing my tongue against it.

Her hands move to my hair, gripping and tugging as my thrusts turn into rolls, moving in sensually slow strokes.

"I can't wait to make you a fucking mother. Can't wait to watch you fucking swell. Pump you full of my fucking spend just to make you grow and fuck that tight, pregnant cunt," I pant against her tit.

"Please... I want it all," she groans in response.

I press a hand down to her lower stomach, feeling myself press back against it when I bury each stroke deeper and deeper. "I won't be able to fuck you this deep when you're pregnant, so enjoy it now, sugar," I murmur against her tit.

"Fuck... I am, " she pants.

"Good," I say before I lean back up. I grip tight under her knees, holding her open and watching her pussy wrap around me with every thrust I take in and out of her.

"Gorgeous fucking pussy. Takes my cock so." *thrust* "Fucking." *thrust* "Well." I slam every inch all the way into her, making her tits bounce and her pussy swallow me with every single one.

Her hand slips between her legs, rubbing her clit as I pick up pace, finding a rhythm.

I watch as she writhes under me, one of her hands tugging at her nipple, with the other on her clit, and her head tossed in ecstasy. Soon, her pussy tightens again, the rush of giving her a second orgasm making me reach that peak just as fast.

"There's my good girl, coming for me again. Lock me in that fucking cunt, take all of me," I grit as I keep pounding into her.

My pleasure climbs the longer I watch her, her fingers rub against my cock as I thrust in and out of her, and she strokes her clit.

Her moans pitch, her back bowing, until all at once she shatters. And I shatter with her, my orgasm blasting me from the side as my cock pumps rigid bursts of heat into her.

"Fuck!" I groan as my thrusts halt abruptly when her pussy clamps down, locking me in place. It moves in waves against my cock, milking me dry just like she does every time. I feel myself coming repeatedly, filling her with all of me as she holds me in place.

I growl, leaning down to wrap a hand around her throat and kiss her through the orgasm.

"Naughty fucking thing, you are, Tiana Dawn," I growl with a grin as her pussy continues to spasm.

Her waves slow, and I move against the slickness of me and her combined. My breaths beat in and out of me as I feel her loosen more and I can move just a bit inside of her. My hand loosens, and I press soft kisses into her jaw and chin.

"Is there a reason you're able to do that every time?" I pant with a chuckle as I move down further to press a kiss to the center of her chest.

"Kegels," she pants.

I shake my head with a small chuckle as I look up at her. She has her arm over her eyes as she catches her breath.

I spend a few more moments pressed against her, letting my cock keep my cum in her just a little longer. Every fucking time I fill her, it comes out, so I decide to keep myself in jusssssst a bit longer.

"How do you feel?" I whisper as I continue pressing soothing kisses into the center of her chest. My hands graze her sides, helping her come down easy.

I love these moments after sex with her. They're some of the most calming times together. Aside from when we take Tucker out at night for the bathroom.

But even though most of the time I do this it's because I want to take her thoughts away, I love being inside her. I love touching her skin, I love smelling her. I love spending this time with her.

There is a level of safety in the feeling of her skin against mine. There is... peace, with her.

I may not experience the thoughts or feelings that she experiences. And I may not understand some of the things she goes through, but she brings me calm. Like her touch at the end of the day sets everything right in the world.

I've never really had a connection with a woman like this. Most are superficially interested in things. They don't really seem to care about a deeper connection. To be fair, Tiana is really the only one that I wanted to dive deeper into. But this woman... *fuck,* this woman.

I love what she does for my everyday. I love the familiarity in her. I love that I know what to expect when it comes to her.

Sure, there will be more for me to learn.

But I can't wait to learn it.

Slowly, I lean up, taking her leg from one side of me and slowly moving it around me. Her face is quizzical as she watches me and I give her a small grin as I turn her on her side on the bed.

All of this, I imagine is very bizarre for her, especially since I'm still inside of her, but I try to take my time. Even when I lay down behind her, pressing my hips under her, as if she's sitting in my lap on our sides, and I wrap my arm around her waist, snuggling into her.

"What... was that?" she asks.

"I always drip out of you when I pull out. I wanted to try and keep myself in," I whisper as I press kisses to her shoulder.

"Aren't you soft?" she asks as she looks back at me.

"Sugar, you act like you've never seen my cock soft," I whisper as I rub my hand over my stomach.

"It shouldn't be that big when you're soft," she murmurs.

I laugh as I nip at her trap. "I'm a show-er, not a grower. Granted, it still grows a bit. But I'm a show-er too, part of the game," I breathe into her neck.

"Is that why it's always big? Even when it's soft?"

"Sure is."

She pauses for a moment, her breath coming in slowly as she quiets.

"Does anyone else...?" she breathes.

"The showers? Yes. It's always been a... thing," I say with a small chuckle.

"So they know how big your dick is?"

"Well, technically we know how big everyone's dick is. But mine is the biggest," I say.

"Oh my god," she sighs.

"What? Do I look like the guy who would hide my dick?"

"No, you don't. But I had to ask anyway," she says.

I give another laugh before I cuddle closer, wrapping her body with my own.

It's silent for a bit, my hand rubbing softly at her stomach as we listen to each other's breathing, before her voice breaks the silence.

"Is there a way I can get you to stop destroying my shirts?" she asks softly.

"Sorry. I'll buy you some more," I laugh.

CHAPTER TWENTY-FOUR
TIANA

The rest of the week, I spend stressing out over this *stupid* fucking case that my mom gave me.

So unexpected, *so* stupid.

A divorce contract that has become incredibly messy as the two of them argue over custody and property.

I've had to communicate with the wife's lawyer constantly, who is not exactly the sharpest tool in the box. And the whole thing is just a big fucking mess.

The whole thing stresses me out because it popped up on me out of nowhere, and so any amount of brainpower I've had during the week is used on that.

But because of the stress of it all, I've been begging for Gunnar, every single day. It takes me out of the day and helps my mind be silent just long enough for the stress to not eat me whole. It has helped immensely, and I wonder if there is something wrong with me if I'm solving my problems with sex...

I decide there isn't anything wrong with me, because I'd be a fool not to fuck this man whenever I wanted.

Plus, we're making a baby.

Fuck it, he's free game, regardless.

Either way, when this weekend comes, and I finally have a chance to do whatever it is the fuck I want to do, I *relish* in it.

Gunnar spent the entire time pleasing every whim I had. I wanted him more than words, and I needed to be relaxed for the weekend, so when I sleep that Friday, I sleep like a fucking baby.

Saturday morning, I sleep in. But when I wake up, Gunnar isn't even in the bed.

Weekdays, that's pretty expected of him. But on weekends, he usually spends wrapped around me until I wake up. He moves at my speed on the weekends, and I love it so... so, so, *so,* much.

I stretch wide, taking a massive yawn, and looking around the room to see if maybe he's somewhere in here.

He isn't.

So, I crawl from the bed, going to the bathroom to brush my teeth and wash my face before I come out to the living room.

However, the entire area is... an *absolute* clusterfuck.

"What... is this?" I ask as I look over the mess that has been made of my living room. There are times where Gunnar makes a mess of my space, and I spend a good majority of time cleaning and explaining how I like my space.

Usually he complies.

This shit, however...

"Sugar! You're awake!" Gunnar says as he steps back from an absolutely enormous white board.

It's so big that it's on a stand, with fucking *wheels.*

My brow quirks as I look between him and the whiteboard. "Yes... I am awake, what is this?" I ask slowly.

It has a little metal tray at the bottom to hold a bunch of

new dry erase markers, with some small magnets to go on the board as well.

"So, I have planned a perfect day for you," he says as he comes around to wrap his arms around my shoulders.

I look up at him in confusion. "Gunnar, please I have had my weekends stripped from me for the past three weeks, I can-"

"Ah pa pa, hold on," he says as he brings a finger to my mouth. "You aren't going anywhere. Charlotte is coming over, I bought you this board, because I have some errands I need to run today for Bubbles'. And you have unfettered access to wedding planning."

My heart almost stops in my chest, and I peak out behind him to look at the massive whiteboard again, before looking back at him. My jaw gapes, slowly tilting into a smile.

"All... all day? I can plan the wedding... as long as I want today?" I murmur softly.

"All day. I've arranged for some food to be delivered to you at specific intervals, and Charlotte is given strict instruction for you to at least take a bite or two in between your mania. But you are allowed to do whatever it is you want until I come home. But I'll be gone most of the day, so, go crazy," he says.

I didn't hear anything else he said because all I register is the fact I can plan the wedding *all* fucking day.

I get to spend my brain power on stuff that I want to spend it on, and no one will stop me...

It's literally my dream weekend.

Guilt. Free. Planning.

"I... love you so fucking much," I say as I wrap my arms around his neck, my eyes looking back and forth between his in disbelief.

"I love you too, sugar," he responds as his arms move to grip my hips. He tugs me close to him before he leans down to kiss me.

Soon, a knock comes to the door, and Gunnar lingers there against my lips for a few more moments before he moves to open it.

"Ahhh! Tiana! Are you ready!?" Charlotte squeals as she comes inside.

My hands clap over my ears at the shrieking this loud in the morning, and she shrinks back.

"Ah...! Sorry!" she whispers. "Are you ready?" she adds with an apologetic grimace.

"Yes, I'm ready. Sorry, I just woke up," I sigh.

"Did Gunnar already tell you what's going down?" she asks as she comes deeper into the apartment.

"He did, and I love it. I haven't had a peaceful weekend in a long while," I respond with a smile.

"What, the ranch house wasn't peaceful?" Charlotte asks as she nudges into my shoulder.

"It was fun, but I definitely wouldn't say peaceful," I respond.

"That's fair," Charlotte sighs with a smile. She throws her arm around my shoulder and hugs me in close.

Gunnar comes up to me, his backpack on his back that he grabbed while Charlotte and I were talking.

"I'll be back in a bit, sweetness," he says softly as he wraps a hand around my cheek. He leans down to give me a soft kiss before he leans up to press a kiss to my forehead.

"Eat something, please," he murmurs before he pulls away.

I roll my eyes playfully, and shove gently into his chest with a smile and he gives me a wide grin as he walks to the front door.

As he leaves, I watch, and he turns around at the open door with one more blown kiss before he closes the door softly behind him.

"So! What do we do first?" Charlotte asks as she jumps onto the couch.

She gets on her knees, facing the back of it, looking over the whiteboard as her feet kick behind her.

A smile rises on my face as I look at her and then back to the door.

Gods... this man... I am so fucking in love with him.

I grin as I turn to go to look at all the brand new markers, and a new eraser. I also have so much more space compared to the whiteboard I had.

I can't believe he did this for me.

I suppose I should believe it. He's always accepted me in every way, shape or form.

This gift should come as no surprise for me.

But it does anyway.

CHAPTER TWENTY-FIVE
GUNNAR

It takes me a good minute to get out to the ranch house, and when I arrive, Banks is already outside. The man is always chorin', so it comes as no surprise that he's mucking out the stables as he waits for me. Waffle follows him back and forth, trotting with her short little legs like she has not a single care in the world.

While our original plan was for Charlotte to be dropped off by Banks, and for him to drive me back in, we changed it for us to drive ourselves. It made more sense for her to drive out and me drive in than for Banks to be doing all that moving with his big ass truck.

I get it, he's a farm boy. But there is no way that's good for his gas mileage.

But whatever, not my pigs, not my farm.

As I come up the gravel road, I see him moving soiled hay into some wheelbarrows outside of the stables, and a black Suburban parked next to Banks' truck. Because, along with my lawyer, I called someone else in to help us.

And she is right on time.

I hear Waffle's barks as she races up to the truck. It seems as if she's looking for Tucker, and part of my heart aches a bit that I didn't bring him out here.

Mrs. Tamisha stands outside of her vehicle, leaning against it as she scrolls through some things on her phone. I can see where Tiana gets her casual looks from because she's just in some jeans and a Seattle Stags hoodie. Along with some sunglasses.

As I park my truck, her head rises, and she looks at me. I give her an excited wave as I cut the engine and climb out.

"Suds! How goes it?" I call out to her. Waffle jumps and barks at me, so I crouch down, scratching her head, before she turns over on her belly, and I scratch that.

"I'm so sorry, girl. I don't have Tuck with me today. I'll bring him next time, I promise," I tell her softly.

I finish scratching her belly, and she flips over, running back off to follow Banks again.

She throws her phone into the pocket on the front of her hoodie and presses her glasses up onto her head before she folds her arms against her chest.

"Gunnar," she says in greeting. A ghost of a smile pulls at her lips. But if I know her, I reckon she won't let me know she's happy to see me.

"You know why I asked you to come out here today?" I ask.

"Well, according to Charlotte, and some words said to me from Adrian, I'm here on the topic of... land?" she asks in confirmation.

I open my arms, and she looks me up and down incredulously before she slowly comes in for a hug. I squeeze her tight, rocking her back and forth before she pushes out of my arms.

"Aww, you don't want to hug your new son-in-law?" I tease with a grin.

"For one, you two aren't married yet. Two, it has nothing

to do with you, I'm just not touchy-feely," she says with a flick of her hand as she looks out at Banks. He's still going in and out of the stables with his wheelbarrow.

"Noted, Suds," I say with a small salute.

She looks at me with boredom before I lean back against my truck, folding my arms against my chest.

"So, Banks offered to sell me some land. And I offered to buy it. Because I want to build a house for Tiana."

Her brow furrows as she looks at me, her gaze narrowing as her head tilts. She observes me for a long moment before she speaks.

"And why not just buy Tiana a house?" she asks.

"Tiana is too specific to look for a house. She needs something built just for her. And I think she would enjoy being close to Charlotte. The stars are really pretty out here at night, too," I say as I look out over the land again before smiling at her.

She's silent for another long moment, her eyes moving up and down along my body in observation before her attention is pulled away to the crunching gravel coming from behind me.

It alerts us to the last person we were waiting for. More barks come from Waffle as the vehicle approaches, and she runs to greet the new person.

I turn around to see a small coupe coming to park next to the rest of our vehicles. Soon, a short, stocky man in a suit comes out of the car to come up to us.

"Mrs. Dawn, Mr. Hayze," he says nervously as he tugs a briefcase spewing with papers alongside him. Waffle jumps and barks at him, and he yelps as he holds his briefcase close to his chest, guarding it as Waffle inspects him.

A loud whistle is heard from the stables, and Waffle retreats over to Banks.

"Philip, good to see you," Mrs. Tamisha says.

"It's a bizarre thing to be out here on a Saturday, but Mr. Hayze promised it would be a fun excursion," Philip says as he comes to stand beside us. I'm pretty sure he's from Great Britain because he has a rather posh accent.

Kinda cool for Tiana to give me someone with an accent.

He doesn't seem thrilled with me when I try to mimic it. But it's fun to try.

"I imagine you'll learn quickly that Mr. Hayze is a very smooth talker," Mrs. Tamisha says with a sigh.

"Oh, Suds, you flatter me," I say as I press a hand over my chest.

"Anyway, tell your attorney what he's here for," she says as she gestures a hand out to him.

I turn to Philip, whose eyebrow rises as he waits for me to explain.

He looks somewhat scared to be here. But he'll be fine.

I reckon, at least.

"Right, so, I'm buying land for my lady. Unfortunately, my lady is the seller's attorney, so I had to steal her mom to get his portion of the contract squared away," I explain.

But Philip merely looks at me with a slack-jawed, wide-eyed look.

I look between him and Mrs. Tamisha, who shrugs.

"...Repeat...? Please?" Philip asks.

I look to Mrs. Tamisha before she gestures at Philip again.

"My attorney before was Tiana Dawn. Who is now my fiancée. She picked you to fill in for her so that she and I could be together, correct?" I reiterate.

"Yes, precisely," Philip says with a nod.

"Okay. So. Mrs. Tamisha is going to be my mother-in-law at some point, and she is Tiana Dawn's mother. But Tiana Dawn is Adrian Banks' attorney."

"....Okay..." he says.

"And I, me, Gunnar Hayze, am buying this land for Tiana Dawn, as a surprise. So Mrs. Tamisha is representing Adrian Banks, so that I can have a littttle bit of leeway when it comes to presenting the land to Tiana Dawn, my soon-to-be wife," I say slowly.

"Right... so I'm representing you. Mrs. Tamisha is representing Adrian Banks," Philip says.

"Yes, perfect," I say with a deep breath.

"My apologies, the logistics got a bit... skewed there for a moment," he says with a sigh.

"Right, well," I say as I run a hand through my hair.

Banks soon comes to join us, with Waffle following close. Throwing his dirty gloves to the ground beside us, he dusts his hands off.

"Hayze, Mrs. Dawn, Mr... what's your name?" he asks as he gets to Philip.

"Philip, Mr. Banks, pleasure to meet you," Philip says as Banks shakes his hand.

Philip hisses from Banks' grip, who pulls his hand away with a flick of pain.

Banks doesn't pay it any mind.

"Right, anyway, who here can ride an ATV?" he asks.

I raise my hand, Mrs. Tamisha raises her hand, but Philip does not.

"You okay with horses?" Banks asks.

"I... they're fine animals, yes?" Philip says.

He seems to get more confused the longer he's here. But I reckon he'll figure it all out soon enough.

"Good enough for me. Everyone follow," Banks says before he turns back to the stables.

Chauncey is tied up and tacked up outside of the stable, waiting to be ridden, but Banks goes around the back of the stable. Waffle hot on his heels at every turn.

A moment later and the sound of an ATV roars to life. He drives it around to the front of the stable before he runs back around to grab another one.

He then walks into the stable, pulling out some motocross helmets for Mrs. Tamisha and me, while he hands a riding helmet to Philip.

Mrs. Tamisha and I take a moment to put on our helmets and get on our ATVs, before I look back at Banks.

He's pulled a bucket from the stable, flipping it over for Philip, who awkwardly climbs onto the back of Chauncey.

"I don't know how to ride this thing!" I hear Philip yell over the sound of the ATV's. Waffle is more than excited to get moving. She runs and barks like a tiny bat out of hell as Banks moves.

But Banks merely responds, "Don't worry about it!"

He puts his foot in the stirrup, swinging a leg over to place himself in front of Philip. His confusion turns to fear, even as he places his briefcase between him and Banks. Banks reaches back for Philip's hands and wraps them around his waist to hold him steady.

Banks looks at me, nodding before a high-pitched whistle sounds through the air, and with it, comes Philip's screams as Chauncey bolts through the property, straight into the woods. Waffle keeps speed right behind Chauncey and the three of them disappear.

I rev my engine, waiting for Mrs. Tamisha to take the lead before I follow behind.

Tiana and her mother must be more alike than I imagined because this woman has an iron grip on the throttle and hauls ass directly behind Chauncey, Banks, Philip, and Waffle.

I follow, and we bound our way through the trails in the woods, heading directly for that strip of land with the lake.

After a few minutes, we've ridden our way all the way

through the woods, and we come up to the ridge that looks down on the lake.

But Banks keeps moving with Philip, down the ridge, moving around the lake and pointing at certain bits of land. Waffle is at his every move. Down the hill, through the tall grasses. And it makes me smile.

I know he would have wanted something like a Border Collie. But I think he really likes this little dog. It surely seems as if she likes him.

I watch them for a while, and soon, Banks reaches into his pocket, pulling a map out and pointing at it before handing it to Philip. He lays it out against Banks' back, seemingly marking it as Banks moves around the area, and soon disappears into the woods.

I turn off the engine for my ATV, and soon Mrs. Tamisha does the same, removing her helmet and swishing her straightened hair out as she places it in front of her on the ATV.

"So this is it, huh?" she asks as she looks around.

I keep my helmet on, but I nod. "Yep," I say with a smile to myself.

"What made you choose this spot?" she asks as she continues looking around.

"I like the lake. I'd like to put a gazebo by it for her to read at. And I want to build a house somewhere in those woods. I haven't really had the chance to *really* look in there. But Tiana did, and she loved it. That's really all that matters to me," I say as I lean over the handles of the ATV, pointing to some spots mentioned.

"It's a beautiful spot," she murmurs in response.

"Yeah. She loved the stars out here. And I know it's far from the arena, but I know she'll be happier to be close to Charlotte," I respond.

It's silent for a long moment, and I look over at her to see her looking at me, with... pride? I'm not sure. It's the same sort of contemplative look she gave me at the ranch house.

But I smile back. "What?"

"You take real good care of her," she says softly.

"I always promised her I would. One of the first things I said to that girl," I say with a smile.

"Thank you, you know," she responds quietly.

My head tilts, confused about why she's thanking me.

"I didn't think Tiana would ever find love. It was never on her list of things to do with her life. Men weren't..." she pauses as she looks out to the land. "They weren't a big thing for her. But as a mother, you don't want your kids to be alone..." Another pause and she sighs softly. "One day we won't be here, you know? She may have Charlotte, but what if something happened to Charlotte? Who would be there for Tiana?" Tamisha asks quietly.

Her gaze drifts down to the lake, and I listen to whatever wisdom she may store in my pack for a rainy day.

"Tiana was always... vastly different from Charlotte growing up. Even if they're twins, their differences were apparent. Tiana never talked as much as Charlotte did. And while Charlotte wanted to play sports, Tiana wanted books. She read, or she was always in the library. She didn't have as many friends, and she was happy that way. But it was hard watching her grow up so lonely, even if she was happy with it. I thought that when she grew up and found more of herself, she would find more people to surround herself with," Mrs. Tamisha continues.

I cross my arms against my chest, looking out to the land as I listen to her. My fingers find the string on my hoodie, fiddling with it as she continues to speak.

"As she got older, she still didn't have many friends. She had some boyfriends. But they never lasted long. She said they were annoying... not worth it. She would say they were..." she pauses with a small chuckle. "I think 'bums' was the word she used. Needy, clingy. She just really wasn't into dating. And I was just coming around to the idea that she might just never have a husband or someone to call her own. If that's what she wanted, I would support her no matter what," she says.

Tiana doesn't talk much about her childhood. Or much of her past. But it all makes sense when her mom talks about it.

"But she struggled, you know. With her routines, with eating, with her space and her rigidity. She would have these... break downs sometimes, when life was overwhelming for her. And she would get over them, but there would be a period of panic for her. Weeks at a time where she said it felt like her world was crumbling. It was... distressing to see. The time she spent by herself. She's never been good at talking about her feelings. Not until it was too late and she couldn't hold them in anymore," Mrs. Tamisha takes a heavy sigh, and I glance over to see her arms crossing her chest.

She's silent for a moment, a small tear escaping and glistening in the sun as it runs down her face.

"I wanted, at the very least, someone who would always be there for her when things were difficult. She deserves that. She deserves someone who can care for her. But because I didn't know if she would have someone, I was always harder on her. Because if she would never have someone of her own, I had to make sure she was strong enough to care for herself... I would never send my kids into this world without knowing if they could handle themselves," she pauses, taking a deep breath as her head drops and she shakes it. She sniffles once, blowing out a steadying breath before her head comes back up and she uses the sleeve of her hoodie to wipe another small tear away.

I hear her move, and I move my body enough on my quad to face her.

She looks toward me, but her eyes don't meet mine. They pin to my ATV as something to focus on.

"So to know that, when me and Richard are gone, Tiana and Charlotte will be well taken care of, by two men that would move the sun and the moon at the right times every day to make their world go around, that means everything to me. To Richard as well," she says with a small smile. Her eyes slowly come up to meet mine, and she gives me a grateful smile.

My lips thin, holding back the way her words feel to listen to. I didn't expect this thing I want to do for Tiana to come with this sort of admission. But it's nice.

It explains why her mom has always been rougher when it comes to Tiana. I imagine someone as rigid as Tiana can come off a type of way to people. Charlotte is looser, more carefree. She probably didn't have as many struggles as Tiana did.

But... I love that about Tiana. I love that she can handle herself. I love that she is able to care for herself. She doesn't rely on me to take care of her, but she *allows* me to. And that's... safety. That's all I've ever wanted for her was safety. And to know that I gave her enough confidence in me to allow her that peace...

I tilt my head, giving Mrs. Tamisha a small smile. Even if she can't see it in my helmet, I try to portray it enough in my eyes for her to see it.

"They deserve to have their moon hung every night," I respond softly.

"They surely do, Gunnar," she says.

It takes a bit of time for Philip and Banks to come back from their excursion, and by the time they do, it's late afternoon, with the sun trying to set over the horizon.

Eventually, we come back to Banks' ranch house, where he quickly untacks Chauncey and lets him and Priscilla out for turnout, while the rest of us go inside to sit at the dining room table.

Philip presses the map out on the dining room table, where a large red area is confined on the map. Then, he takes his seat at the table, pulling out his laptop and typing furiously.

I brush a hand over my damp, sweaty hair, taking a deep breath as I look over the map. I go over the lines, making sure at the very least, the lake and the forest are inside the boundary.

Luckily for me, it's the perfect scrap of land.

When we returned, Mrs. Tamisha went into her vehicle to grab her work bag and then brought it inside to pull out her laptop, getting some things ready while we waited for Banks.

Soon, Banks comes in, kicking off his cowboy boots by the door before he comes to sit at the table across from me. Waffle trots at his side, jumping up into his lap and leaning against the table.

He scratches her head softly as he looks over the map.

"So, the boundary looks about to your liking?" he asks.

"Yeah, I think that's doable. What's the situation with water and electricity?" I ask as I continue looking at the map.

"Well water. And, uh, electricity we can get squared away pretty easy," he says.

"And the road into here?" I try to spot where the main gravel road to his place is, and the main road in and out of this area that takes us back to Seattle.

"We'll square that away when the time comes. I could just take Lotty and Chauncey out. Kinda run a preliminary tamp down road in the area for the meantime. You'll need to come back out and tell me where you want it, and over the next number of weeks we'll go tamp it out," he says.

I nod as I listen. "Good... alright. For now, just lead it to the lake. I'll figure out specifics later when things get squared away," I say.

"10-4, bulldozer," Banks responds.

"Alright, so Adrian, since I'm your representation here, what are your stipulations with this land?" Tamisha asks as she continues her typing.

"Fifteen acres. Stated right here on this map. With allowance for him to build only on them fifteen acres. But he's allowed anywhere on the property," Banks says as he leans against the back of his chair, tapping the table with his hand as his other hand pats Waffles' butt.

"Gunnar?" Mrs. Tamisha asks as she continues typing.

"Sounds good to me," I respond with a smile and a nod. I tug my chain out of my hoodie, pulling it into my mouth before I interlace my fingers on top of the table and press my chest against the edge, watching everyone.

"Price?" Mrs. Tamisha asks.

"Does there have to be one?" Banks asks in a bored tone.

"Well, it is a contract," she murmurs.

"Gimme a grand and we'll be straight," Banks says with a shrug.

I grit my teeth on my chain, holding it in place for me to speak. "A grand? That's it?" I ask.

"There ain't much of a price you can put on family," he says.

I roll my eyes with a groan. "Can I give you like... Ten? Fifteen? A thousand per acre?"

"No need," he says. He nods to Mrs. Tamisha. "A grand," he says again.

I groan because I didn't want him to give me land this

cheap. I just wanted nice land, I would have paid anything for it.

"If you want, you can contribute fourteen grand to upgrade my stable," he says with another shrug.

I nod with a grin. "Deal," I say eagerly.

Mrs. Tamisha sighs as she types more into her computer.

"So you want... the price of the land... to be one thousand dollars. And then fourteen thousand... for... the stables?" Mrs. Tamisha asks incredulously.

"That's correct, Mrs. Dawn," Banks confirms.

She looks at me, and I nod.

"Yes, absolutely."

She sighs as she rolls her eyes. "Alright," she says with a shrug.

"Do I need to have Miss Tiana sign this or look over it at all?" Banks asks.

"Nope. I'm the lead attorney, I can trump her if it's something I find to be within your best interest. And I don't believe Tiana would have an issue with this. So all the paper work can be done today," she says.

I look at her in shock. "Just like that?" I ask.

"Yep. Philip? You got all that on your end?" Mrs. Tamisha asks.

"Yes ma'am," he murmurs as his eyes dart around the screen.

"Perfect, we can get these printed and signed sometime this week. Both of you will need to come to the firm for signing, but all the legal jargon or other can be done and typed up today," Tamisha says.

"That's... amazing. Thank you guys so much for all your help on this. I can't wait to show it to Tiana," I say softly.

My heart pounds, a rush of excitement flooding through me.

I just... bought land for my lady. Holy fuck, I hope she loves it. I know she seemed like she loved it when she was here. But buying it for her is a whole new beast entirely.

Tiana isn't the biggest fan of change, and my not telling her about this could set her off.

I'll set some money aside for more books, just as a precaution.

But I think... I have a good feeling about it all. My mind runs, thinking about the building process. Getting to let Tiana plan to her heart's content.

I'm so excited for us... for this. God, I'm just happy I get to live this life with her.

Soon, Banks' voice breaks through my internal celly.

"When are you going to show it to Tiana?" Banks asks.

I shake my head of the visions, smiling as I look at him. "I have a few tricks up my sleeves yet, cowboy," I say with a click and a wink.

CHAPTER TWENTY-SIX
GUNNAR

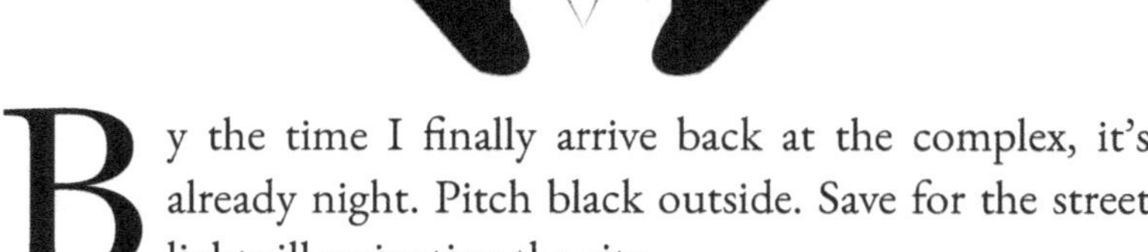

By the time I finally arrive back at the complex, it's already night. Pitch black outside. Save for the street lights illuminating the city.

I go to my apartment first, being quick to let Tucker out and hide some documents before I quietly make my way to Tiana's apartment.

When I walk in, all the lights are dimmed, and it's far too quiet for what I assume would be two rambunctious sisters.

Charlotte is in the kitchen, cleaning some dishes, and tidying up. While the whiteboard is completely covered in symbols and acronyms with different colors of lines. I'm not sure if she was moving her original plans from her last whiteboard to this one, or if she just made a new plan entirely. Either way, she used it the way she wanted to, and that makes me happy.

As I slowly shut the door behind me with a click, I try to see if I can spot Tiana. But she's no where to be found. Charlotte smiles and waves at me as I come in and drop my backpack by the door.

"Where's Tiana?" I whisper.

"She wasn't feeling very good a little while ago, so she went to the bedroom to lie down, and she's been there ever since," Charlotte whispers back.

"You made sure she ate right?" I ask.

"Yeah, she ate most of what you had delivered. But she said she started her period," Charlotte says.

"Ahhh gotcha. Well, I got it from here. Thanks Charlotte," I say quietly.

"Ah, it's no problem," she says with a smile as she packs away some of her stuff to head for the door.

"Drive safe, okay? Make sure you text Tiana when you get home," I whisper, and I put my arms out for a hug. She returns it with a side tilt and a nod before she quietly creeps out of the apartment, closing the door behind her.

I take a moment to check out all the things Tiana planned on her whiteboard. But it seems as if this woman thinks in code, because I cannot make out anything on this board aside from the line of dates along one edge.

Some dates have lines drawn across the board to acronyms, along with more acronyms, random times, and more dates.

A lot of this looks like she copied it from the other white-board, but with some other changes as well. I'm just glad she got to have this time she so desperately wanted.

I feel bad it was taken from her by her period, but hope-fully it's not hurting her too badly.

I shake my head with a small chuckle at the whiteboard before I move back to the bedroom. As I slowly open the door, I see a big mound under the comforter, with small up and down movements from Tiana's breathing. I make sure to be as quiet as I can when I shower, then come to crawl in bed behind her.

Snuggling close, I wrap my arm around her waist, pressing kisses into her bare shoulder.

"Gunnar," she sighs.

"What's up, sugar?" I whisper as I rub a hand over her stomach.

"I started my period," she responds.

My brow furrows as I relax against her. "Okay...? And...?"

"That means I'm not pregnant," she murmurs.

"Yes, I understand that."

"That means whatever we did... didn't work," she says with a sigh as she turns around in my arms.

Her green eyes glimmer with a watery teariness, and I bring a hand up to her cheek to stroke it.

"Babe, that just means we get to have more sex. What's wrong with that?" I whisper with a smile.

Her brow furrows a bit in question. "You aren't upset that what we did didn't work?"

"You've had an IUD for a bit. If anything, I would honestly be more surprised if you got pregnant right away. But I'd be proud of my boys, though, for being such splendid swimmers," I say with a cheeky grin and a proud nod.

She gives me a small smile as she rolls her eyes. "This is also one of my first periods since having my IUD removed, and I am in... so much pain," she says with a sigh.

A small frown tugs at my lips. My hand rubbing small circles into her back. "I'm sorry. Did you at least have fun planning?"

She smiles, her eyes drifting off as she thinks. "I did. I found the bakery for the cake, so we can do the taste testings. I looked at places that I want to try dresses on at, and some dresses that I want," she says with a daydreamy look.

I know that this whole thing can cause some issues for her

mentally. But when she gets the chance to indulge, it does seem to make her really happy.

Part of me is mad at myself for having to stop her. It's something she enjoys. But I also have to make sure she's caring for herself. That's important too.

My thumb continues to move over her cheek, and I give a small smile as I watch her face. "This process means a lot to you, doesn't it?" I whisper.

Her eyes drift away, a sigh leaving her. "I just... love to plan. I love the mental energy that goes into something like this, and seeing all of my thoughts come to life..." her voice trails off. "Are you upset that I'm not involving you more?" she murmurs as her eyes come back to mine.

"No, sugar. Not when it's something you'd rather do on your own. I'd rather you take the reins and do what you'd like than for me to get in the way for the sake of being there."

Her face softens, her teeth catching her lip as she wraps her hands around my face, pulling me in for soft, sweet pecks against my lips.

"I love you," she murmurs between her kisses.

I continue rubbing her back, kissing her back. All the while, her mother's words come back to my head. The ones where she praised me just for being a good man for her daughter. Where now, no matter what, Tiana won't be alone.

She's spent most her time and her life alone, and she found peace in that.

But she also found peace in *me*, and in my company. And I think that means more to me than anything will.

This woman, who would rather be happy in her own company, enjoys mine. Somehow, I give her something that she wasn't expecting to find. And there is a sense of pride in that. So I suppose I can see why Mrs. Tamisha said what she said.

I think if I were in the same position, watching my kid be

so dead set on going through their high-stress life on their own, I would want them to find someone to weather their storms with.

To me, it wasn't ever about that. I just love being with her. I love her tenacity, her drive.

Her presence has given me a sense of structure, where before it was chaos. Not a bad chaos, just one that had no rigidity.

I never craved structure, to be fair. But with Tiana, there is comfort in where she finds hers. And while she has opened her eyes to some things with me, I've also opened my eyes to the way she lives her life.

I don't think I would want this sort of routine and structure on my own. But I'll do it with Tiana every single day if it'll bring her peace.

Anything to give this woman the life she deserves. I would do... anything for Tiana Dawn.

And I'd do it for the rest of my life.

I always will.

"I love you too, sugar," I whisper back. I grip the back of her head, bringing it to my lips to place a soft kiss on her forehead.

She preens into my kiss, a smile melting her lips as she absorbs my affection.

Soon, she snuggles into my chest, folding her hands up under her chin and cuddling deeper into me. I wrap my arms tighter around her, stroking her lower back until I hear her breathing even out and soft noises of sleep sounding off in the small space between us.

I lay there awake, for just a little while longer, enjoying the peace and quiet we share together.

CHAPTER TWENTY-SEVEN
TIANA

Going into work on a Monday in the middle of experiencing your first period in a *long* time, is something I wouldn't wish on my worst enemy.

Even though I spent all of Saturday and Sunday in bed, I was in absolute agony. I haven't had a period in ages, and when it finally came, holy fuck... it... surely came.

I don't remember my cramps ever being that bad, even when I first started getting my period.

I spent the entire weekend in the fetal position. Even in the shower! I curled up on the floor and let the water beat down on me like some sort of feral street dog in the rain.

By the time today came around, I had to be dragged out of bed.

Gunnar was at my bedside with some ibuprofen and water, and he at least helped pull me up and out of bed. I didn't want to get up at all. But I had to get to work on this damn case my mom gave me.

Did the ibuprofen work?

I don't know; I guess it sort of did. I'm at my desk working, but I want to die, if I'm being completely honest.

I need to get pregnant. And quick, because I don't want to do this next month. It's making me miss my IUD something fierce.

Which is another thing I spent the weekend upset about.

I'm not pregnant. I really shouldn't be this upset. Getting pregnant is not a cut and dry situation and it's our first maybe few weeks trying.

But... I am disappointed. Even if Gunnar isn't. And while his acceptance of it all helped my sadness, I just...

I don't know. I want to experience that life we dream of.

I decide it's silly to be so sad so soon, so to distract myself from the pain, I focus on the case my mom gave me. I'll have to go down to the courthouse sometime this week to represent my client in their proceedings. Which is another thing I don't want to think about right now.

Do I want to do that? Not really. This has gotten so messy, and divorce trials can always be a place of high energy and tension.

It's suffocating more often than not. Not to mention, I'm not really completely personable with these clients. They're my mom's so I don't know them the same way I know the Stag players.

When I'm working with the players, it's much less stress because I'm on normal terms with all of them. I also know how they respond to most things.

I don't know *shit* about this person.

I take a sip from my water cup, swirling the ice around as I stare at the screen, hoping that this trial isn't an absolute nightmare. That maybe, by the grace of fucking Thor himself, that they'll figure out some of their shit and not bring it into the courtroom on Wednesday.

I already told Gunnar I was staying home from the game this weekend. Especially since I want to try to figure out what we're going to do for Halloween.

Thinking about it has been one of the few things to really give me an ounce of excitement. Well, along with just spending time with Gunnar on a day-to-day basis.

I get to choose whatever it is we want to do.

One thing I definitely had on the list was that I wanted to make some pumpkin bread, because I love it, and I think baking with Gunnar would be interesting. We cook dinner together sometimes, but it's mostly me because the second he steps into the kitchen I absolutely lose it. There is too much control I like to have in the kitchen, and some of his movements are just too wrong for what I expect. So I kick him out, nine times out of ten.

I fear he may not be able to cook as much as I thought he would be able to. But that's fine.

However, baking, with instructions, that's something that should be easy to navigate.

There is another thing I had planned. I bought something special just for it. I have never done anything like it before, and I know Gunnar will like it. But part of me is nervous because what if it doesn't look the way I expect it?

A knock on the door frame pulls me from my thoughts, and I shake my head clear as I look at the time on my computer.

Noon.

My head rises to see Gunnar. A massive smile graces his lips as he crouches to enter my office.

"Hey sweetness, you doin' okay?" he asks. His hair is damp, but not his normal shower dampness. More like sweat damp.

A small smile tugs at the corner of my mouth as I look up at him. "I'm... ehnnnn," I say with a sigh.

"Banks and I are going to get some lunch, do you want me to bring you anything back?" he asks as he lingers in front of my desk. He's in a pair of Seattle Stags warmups. Usually the same thing that Russel wears. Which Gunnar rarely wears, which tells me he's not done for the day.

He doesn't come in here often during the day, not since we started dating. He doesn't want to bother me too terribly much if I'm working.

I think he knows that if I want to see him, I will come find him.

I find it to be sort of sweet. Before, he tried to come find me whenever he could, when he was trying to get me to go on a date with him.

But I like that he gives me the choice to decide.

My focus comes back to him, registering his question.

"No, I just want cookies," I groan.

"Sugar for my sugar, copy that Big Mama," he says with a salute.

I give a confused, yet playful eye roll. I'm marrying the man and yet some of the things he says, and the way he says them, is still a mystery to me.

"Since when do you and Adrian go to get lunch?" I ask curiously.

"He needs to go grab something and he asked me to go with him. So I figured with your poor state, I'd grab something for you while I was out," he says with a shrug.

I sigh again, tipping my head back. "Alright well, if you come back here without cookies, I will be very upset," I say with a grin I try to fight.

I want to allude to feeling worse than I do, merely so he can baby me. But it's so hard to do in his presence. He just makes me so happy.

"I would never do such a thing," he responds with a grin.

He steps closer to my desk, holding a hand out for me.

My heart melts into a pool of love in my chest as I stand, coming around to grasp his hand softly.

He closes the distance between us as he pulls me into him. He smells like sweaty ice man, which isn't as horrible as you think it would be.

I think if it was any other man, it would. But there's something about Gunnar's smell.

Maybe it's part of my little primal code because I love every way he smells.

I look up at him with a contented smile, and instead of his rough and fast movements, he slows, making sure to be gentle with me as he brings a hand up to my cheek. He leans down, pressing a soft kiss to my lips as he presses a coil of hair behind my ear.

"You look beautiful today, sugar," he whispers.

I press a small kiss to his lips in return before leaning back. "I do not feel beautiful," I say with a shy, playful smile. Heat fills over my nose and my cheeks at his compliment, either way though.

"Those two things are not mutually exclusive. I'm sure that bender from last week didn't feel beautiful when I checked him. But boy howdy, it looked beautiful," he says quietly.

"You were playing. How do you know it looked beautiful?" I ask with a furrow of my brow.

"I watched the highlight reel."

"Oh my god. Please get out of my office and get me cookies," I say before I press another kiss to his lips.

"Roger that, sugar tits," he says as he pulls away.

"So we've added tits to the moniker?" I ask with a quirk of my brow as I go to sit in my office chair.

"Well, they're sweet, and I love sucking on them," he says with a shrug.

I bring my hands over my face, running them over it with a sigh. "Gunnar Lemieux Hayze," I groan.

"Damn, fine, I'm going," he says as he holds his hands up and heads for the door. "I still love you!" he says as he walks out, blowing a kiss back to me.

I roll my eyes with a small smirk. "Love you more!"

Even with his teasing, his antics always seem to make me feel a bit better. There's just something about his energy that has me able to get out of my head into whatever moment I'm in with him. It's well needed. And much appreciated.

And with his antics, I feel just good enough to go through the rest of the day working on this stupid case.

I don't get to see Gunnar again until the end of the work day, when he's showered and enters my office with the smell of his piney cologne.

When he enters, he has a white box for me, wrapped in a little red bow.

I smile as I stand, packing up my stuff. I actually got quite a bit done today, which has me leaving the office feeling a lot more accomplished than when I came in. But knowing that I get to go home and cuddle up in bed with Gunnar for the rest of the night is something that gives me way more excitement than anything else.

"You didn't have to get me something crazy. I just wanted some chocolate chip cookies," I say with a smile as I shove my laptop into my tote.

Gunnar comes deeper into my office, waiting until I finish

packing my things before he leans over my desk to press a kiss to my lips.

As he does, he presses the box toward me, and I take it as he grabs the handle of my tote.

"I'm sorry that I couldn't bring it after lunch. Banks' plans ran late, and when we came back, we had to suit up quick," he whispers against my lips before he pulls away.

I come around my desk to lead him out, waiting for him to exit before I lock the door and come to walk beside him.

"It's okay. I was actually really focused on work," I say with a sigh of relief.

"Well, good. I'm glad you weren't wallowing in your pain all day," he says with a soft nod as he throws his free arm around my shoulders.

I smile as we continue walking through the halls, heading to our vehicle. As we do, I untie the little bow on the cookies, letting it unravel before I hold it and open it up to find a stack of chocolate chip cookies.

My heart sings and I resist the urge to squeal as I look at the treat.

We took the Vette today, just because out of all the cars, it's the smoothest.

I pull one of the cookies out of the box, taking a bite and chewing as we continue through the halls. "What would you do if I were pregnant with twins?" I ask curiously as I swallow.

Fuck, these cookies are damn good.

Twins, however, are something I think about often. Since Charlotte and I are twins, it worries me because it's usually up to the mother if twins are formed.

"Double the fun," he says with a shrug.

"Gunnar," I groan.

He leans down to take a bite of my cookie from my hand.

"I kid, sugar. I know it'll be hard on you. But I wouldn't mind," he says as he chews.

I look up at him with a quirk of my brow as we finally exit the building, heading for the Vette.

"What if I have two boys?" I ask as I finish the cookie in my hand, reaching for another one and taking a bite.

"That'd be rad. Two lil' goons? A dream come true. You'd do that for me?" he asks as he grins down at me.

I swallow my bite and look up at him with a bored expression. "With the size of you, your brothers and your dad? No, I think I would actually panic," I respond.

"That... sugar... is a fair conclusion. But on the other hand... two goons," he says, his eyes on the cookie in my hand as he opens the passenger door for me.

I roll my eyes as I look at him and climb in.

"Three goons," I say, deadpan.

He leans down, pretending to go in for a kiss, and I lean in, but he veers off course to take a bite of my cookie.

"Ah yes. Can't forget Tucker. Good thinking," he says with a mouth full of cookie as he closes the door.

I groan as I watch him go to the other side, opening the door to lean in and place my tote in the back before he removes his backpack and throws to the back with it. He climbs in, starting the Vette before he smiles at me.

I give him a bored glare as I look at him. His eyes glance down at the cookie in my hand before he quickly dives toward my hand for another bite.

This time I'm prepared and yank my arm around, and he bites at my elbow.

"Gunnar!" I groan as I reach for my elbow, rubbing it softly.

"Shit, sorry, sugar. I just wanted more of the cookie," he

mumbles as he grabs my elbow and brings it up to press a bunch of kisses to it with an apologetic smile.

I glare at him before I relinquish the cookie in my hand to him, and he gives me one last kiss on the elbow before he bites the cookie softly and leans back up. His hand grasps what's left of it as he takes a bite, and then he pulls out of the parking lot.

I take out another cookie, holding it close as I glare at him. Taking another bite, I chew.

"My question," I murmur after I swallow my bite and take another.

He takes a bite of his cookie. "I'm kidding. Of course, it would be horrifying. Two babies at the same time? Yeah, I want us to be parents, but I also have had little experience with babies. I think one would be fine," he says through cookie as he makes it down the streets to the complex.

I watch the world go by outside, and soon I feel the strong squeeze of his hand on my thigh. I look over to see he's finished his cookie.

"Mmmm..." I murmur.

His thumb rubs softly over my thigh, and I'm silent for a good bit of the drive home, watching the street. There is a lot about to happen soon... the wedding, the baby, whenever that happens. Life, in general... there's a lot and we have no plan, no direction. Part of that makes my nerves climb. I wonder if I'll be able to plan it in the right way for things to go the way I want them to.

It's dumb, I think. To have such rigid expectations for my life. But I try to do as much as I can to mitigate the feeling of panic. If I plan as much as I can, at least I controlled the variables that I could. I can handle the things out of my control. But what if there was something I could plan, and I didn't? That would mean that the failure of that thing would be my fault.

Overall, life is about to be a lot, and I'm on deadlines... fictitious ones currently, but deadlines nonetheless.

I haven't done what I need to... and it's giving. Me. Stress.

"What's on your mind, sugar?" he asks.

I finish my cookie and close the box, crossing my arms across the top of it as I lean my head back against the seat.

"I think we need to re-prioritize things," I murmur.

He's silent for a long moment. "What do you mean?" he asks quietly.

"Well... if we're trying to have a baby, how do we plan that and the wedding at the same time? That's a lot all at once," I say softly.

His thumb movement changes. It goes from moving back and forth to tapping, almost in thought.

"What if we put the wedding on hold?"

I look to him in confusion. "Why would we do that?"

His eyes glance at me before they go back to the road, and there's a rush of giddiness pulling at his lips.

"I'll make you a deal," he says with a grin.

I roll my eyes. "Oh lord. What now?" I sigh.

"So yes, you like to plan things. And while I know you also want to get the wedding out of the way, we could always have a wedding later. We can get married legally, just to have that squared away. We focus on having a baby after legally getting married, and then when they're old enough, they can be the ring bearer or the flower girl. That'd be cute, wouldn't it?" he says.

My mind imagines this little idea he has.

The thing is, I want the baby part to come first. We're both almost thirty. I don't want to be pregnant in my thirties. I just feel like it'd be so hard to handle physically. I wasted a good portion of my younger twenties in college and working, setting up my future.

I've done that part. I've laid the groundwork, and he's right; we can always have a big, extravagant wedding later. And it gives me more time to plan something massive.

Some would find it crazy to rush into having a baby with someone you haven't been with long. I would probably call them crazy myself.

But I want this life with Gunnar. I want that family.

I glance at him, to see him glancing back at me.

"Who taught you how to bargain with me?" I ask as I cross my arms over my chest.

"Doesn't take much if you know what you like. I know how you think, sugar. It's not my fault you fell for a guy that reads you like a book," he says with a shrug.

And with that, I remember why I fell in love with him.

He's always supported me. My thoughts, my ways. He's always worked with the way *I* work.

And even now, he tries to find a way for me to have my cake and a way to eat it too. A way that works out with minimal stress.

It's nice... having a second brain. Someone that anticipates my thoughts, the way I'll react, and a way to articulate ideas and plans when things get to be too much.

I uncross my arms, placing my hand on his. "You're so good to me, you know that?" I say softly as I lean against the center console. I run a hand up and down his bicep and I see pink tint his cheeks as he glances at where my hands touches.

A smile tilts against his lips, while his eyes turn considering, thoughtful, and he nods. "I always said I would be, sweetness." But his voice isn't playful. It's sweet, soft.

"We can do your plan. But I'm going to need at least one time where I plan something on my terms," I say with a smile.

"Halloween," he says with a grin.

"I have an idea for that," I respond with a smirk.

CHAPTER TWENTY-EIGHT
GUNNAR

The past week and a half have been *mostly* normal.

It's been pretty difficult trying to keep myself from telling Tiana about the land. Because I so badly would love to. But I've already planned for that.

After Tiana's period ended, she started feeling better, and she went from dying to jumping my bones any chance she could. Granted, that's easy to do, considering I usually want to jump her too.

But ever since she got her period, she's been... adamant on the baby-making aspect. Especially since I offered the wedding idea to come later.

A man is not complaining, but I also don't want her to get down or discouraged if it doesn't happen as fast. I told her I will always be here, and maybe it's partially my fault on obsessing over the idea so much. But Tiana also is the type to not accept 'failure.'

And while I would never see the lack of a pregnancy as failure, I know she may take it a different way. I have to reassure her that she'll never be a failure in my eyes.

All these thoughts go through my head as I make Tiana's coffee this morning. They actually canceled our Halloween game this weekend, so she took her sweet time waking up on this beautiful Saturday.

I let her sleep because on the weekends, I usually wake up before her, and I'll take Tucker out to do his business. Then, I'll come back to Tiana's apartment to cuddle her before she wakes up.

We have been using both of the apartments for whatever we need, but honestly we mostly sleep in hers. She's very particular about her sheets, because she says she doesn't like the way mine feel. But I think she also she really likes sleeping in her bed.

I don't mind. I enjoy being in her space. But I give her more of it this morning, since the past few weeks have been a lot on her.

After I make her coffee, I go to sit down on the couch, watching a random movie on one of the streaming apps as I play with my chain in my teeth. Until eventually, she comes out of the back bedroom, yawning and scratching the back of her head before she tightens the sash of her robe around her waist.

"I made you coffee, sugar," I say from the couch.

She gives me a sleepy smile as her hands come up to curl under her chin in excitement, her feet tippy-tapping against the floor as she makes her way to the kitchen to grab her tumbler full of coffee.

She presses the little sip hatch back and takes a gulp, moaning in happiness as she comes to the couch.

I press my arm up to lie against the back of the couch, and she nuzzles into my side, holding her hands around the cup.

"How'd you sleep?" I ask as I lean over to press a kiss to the top of her head.

"Not bad, actually," she says as she takes another sip of her coffee.

"Do you know what you have planned for today?" I ask as I bring my arm down to rub her opposite shoulder slowly.

"I dooooo, actually!" she says with a small giggle.

My brow furrows and I look down at her. "What was that giggle?"

"I just have ideas," she says with a shrug.

"Alright, I trust you," I return with a smile.

"That's it? You're not going to press me?" she asks as she looks up at me.

"Nope. No need to. Whatever it is, must be terrific," I say with a small grin.

"You don't even want to know SOME of it?" she groans as she sits up from where she's pressed herself into me.

She crosses her legs as she turns on the couch, looking at me. And I can't help the glance I take as her robe opens up and her pussy is on display in some of the gorgeous panties she wears.

I steel my features before I look back up at her face. But her eyes have narrowed, and I realize it won't be easy to get any small facial ticks past her.

"Can't help yourself, can you?" she asks with a small smirk.

"When it comes to you? Never," I say as my grin widens. I fold my arms across my chest, gritting my teeth harder on the chain to slide my tongue against it in a last-ditch attempt to keep my dick from hardening any further.

But she notices that as well, her eyes flicking down to my sweatpants where a bulge has formed.

I press my thighs further apart, shifting my hips and trying to expand myself as much as I can. Which doesn't necessarily help me by any means. If anything, it presses my hardened dick further against my sweatpants.

The chain against my tongue provides some level of distraction as my head leans back against the couch and I tilt it in her direction with a teasing smirk.

However, now that I've been caught, my eyes flick down to her pussy again, my cock hardening even more. My leg jumps up and down to get rid of some of the energy coursing through me.

"How about we play a game?" she asks with a grin.

My brow arches as I admire her. "Is this part of your plan?" I ask.

"It wasn't. But I've had to learn to be a bit more spontaneous with you," she says with a shrug. "It's called 'Down Boy'," she says as she leans back against the armrest.

My eyes narrow as my teeth tighten on the chain, sliding my tongue back and forth against it from where it pulls taut in the middle.

"Go on," I say with a nod.

"I'm going to do things... and you can't do anything... until I let you," she says as her legs open in front of me.

My eyes widen, and the jumping in my leg stops. My throat works in a gulp, and her eyes catch it, flicking down to my neck before they come back to meet my eyes.

"This is mean, Tiana," I murmur.

My cock throbs the harder it gets, and I blow out a soft breath as I run a hand through my hair.

"But fine, you think I can't listen? Do your worst," I say. I'm calling her bluff, and whether I fucked up on that part, we'll see.

I turn, leaning my back against the armrest of the couch, facing her. My leg closer to the inside of the couch bends, and I tuck my foot under the leg that plants to the floor.

Though the floor leg bounces again as the anticipation ramps up more and more.

Her eyebrow quirks, and she moves her cup to the coffee table, setting it down slowly before she leans back against the couch. She slowly presses one panel of her robe open, just enough, and I see the space where her breasts meet. Two soft mounds pressed perfectly together, glistening with whatever lotion she rubbed on herself this morning.

Fucking. Hell.

Already, I know this is going to be... absolute... torture for me.

My teeth tighten on the chain, watching her move, and I attempt with every ounce of my composure to hold on to my stony features.

From the panels she presses open, her hands slide up her body, coming to knead and grip her tits through the thin material of her robe. She completely avoids her nipples, and in response, they tighten, hardening to small peaks that show through the fabric. Soon, her thumb flicks over them, and she lets out a soft breath of pleasure.

I gulp again, my foot bouncing again to keep myself from moving toward her.

But my eyes wander, roaming up and down her body. The way the fabric of her robe drapes over her perfectly sculpted body. I can just see the seam of her pussy through her panties.

Her hand switches from rubbing to pinching her nipple as the other releases her tit to slide down her body. Slowly, seductively, her delicate fingers run over the dampening material covering her.

"Every time you move before I say, I take a step back," she says as she presses softly into the space. A soft moan leaks out of her, her head slowly falling back as she does.

"This... is so mean," I whisper through the chain, my eyes bouncing from her pussy to the hand on her tit to the soft relaxation of her features as she gives in to herself.

How I wish I could be the one making her wet like that.

"You decided not to ask about my plans; this is your punishment," she says with a shrug and a soft pant as her head tilts forward to connect her gaze with mine.

No, please not the eyes, baby. My weakness.

"Please, I wanna know them all, Tiana, let me touch you," I plead gently.

"Ah... ah ah..." she says as her hand rides up her body, away from her cunt.

I groan in frustration as my head tosses back.

"Can I touch myself?" I ask as I stare up at the ceiling.

"Nope," she says.

"Fuck," I groan.

My cock feels like stone in my pants, and I have half a mind to fucking bust already.

"No coming either," she pants.

"What?!" I say as my head shoots up to look at her.

"You can't come. I need it," she says with a feral grin.

"Where the fuck did all this dominance come from?" I ask as I watch her hand move back down her body, pressing back into the material.

"Since you asked to put a baby in me, Gunnar Hayze," she says as she presses against it again.

A moan leaves her, and the lips of her pussy part behind the material. She's wet enough that they slide apart with ease. And soon, my hands come up to tug at my hair as I watch, my teeth tightening on my chain as I anchor my tongue to the taut bit.

I cross my arms against my chest, breathing through the chain as my teeth grit and my jumping leg moves faster. The foot secured in the pit of my knee wiggles back and forth, waiting for the go.

This really is just like a fucking dog not allowed to go after a treat. This is so fucking torturous. I wanna be in her, Goddammit.

Soon, the hand kneading her breast peels open the panel hiding it. She reveals her tit, her nipple hard as she pinches it. Her chest heaves between her breaths and moans, and the movement causes her breasts to sway just the right way.

I feel like my cock is going to split in fucking half. I'm hard as a fucking diamond, and I have no idea how to remedy it without touching her.

"Tiana," I damn near whimper.

I watch as her brow arches, and her finger hooks into the fabric to pull her panties to the side, baring her cunt for me.

She's slick as she slides her fingers through, covering them as she presses deeper to stroke her clit. Her moans grow louder, her fingers swirling in just the right way for her to make those noises that I so desperately wish I was the cause of.

Her fingers dip deeper, coating them in her slick before she removes them. With her tits bare, she leans forward, getting on her knees to grip my shoulder with one hand before she offers me her fingers covered in her.

"Open," she pants softly, her eyes focused on me.

My brow quirks and my mouth opens slowly, with the chain releasing from my tongue so that it falls against my bare chest.

Slowly, she presses her fingers into my mouth, her hand on my shoulder snaking around it to thread her fingers through my hair and cradle the back of my head.

I take whatever the fuck I can get from her. I snatch her wrist, pressing her fingers in deeper, glancing up at her as I lick and suck the taste from her. My eyes roll, her slick coating my tongue in that taste I'll always know is her.

"My good boy," she whispers with a grin.

A jolt of pleasure runs through my blood, straight to my cock, and I groan at the way it feels.

No one has ever called me that before. But holy fuck, I damn near came from the way she says it.

"Fuck," I whimper against her fingers as I look up at her.

She slides her fingers from my lips, grinning as she presses a kiss to them before she leans back against the couch.

Her eyes flick to the hardened mound in my sweats, nipping at her lip.

"Take your cock out," she says as she nods down to it.

I breathe a soft breath of composure, my hands going to the band of my sweatpants to pull the band down, releasing my cock.

With how hard and throbbing I am, the cool air of her apartment is a welcome fucking feeling. But I dare not touch it because it wasn't part of her rule, and I need her to fuck me at this point.

I also have to admit... I enjoy being her toy. It's fun. I didn't know this was something I enjoyed.

Learn something new with this woman every day.

She stands from the couch, tugging one end of the sash around her waist. The tension releases enough for the knot at her belly to unravel and the panels of the robe open.

Soon, her full body is on display for me. Her perky, bare tits. Her pussy in that scrap of fabric she calls underwear, darkened and damp with her wetness.

Fucking hell... need... need... now. Now.

My cock twitches hard as another jolt of lust pulses through all of me. The tension is unbearable. I bring a hand up to bite hard at my knuckle as my leg continues to jump. Soon, my other arm comes across my chest, tucking under the elbow of the hand held to my mouth.

The visions race through my skull, my cock in pain at this point.

"Sugar... please..." I say through the bite I have of my knuckle.

She shrugs the robe from her shoulders, letting it pool below her in a silent fall of fabric.

Soon, her fingers hook into her panties at her hips, pulling them down enough for them to land with the robe, and she steps out of them.

When she moves to get back on the couch, she turns around, getting on all fours as she rests her head against the armrest. Her head tilts to look at me, a devilish grin pulling her lips taut.

My eyes widen, watching with rapt curiosity as her hand appears between her legs from under her. Ass up, head down, her eyes on me, she runs her fingers through her wet cunt.

Soaking. Fucking. Wet... Right there in front of me...

Right. Fucking. There.

I want to bury my face in her, shove my cock in her, but she hasn't given me the go... and holy fuck, do I want to fuck-ing *go*.

She moans as her fingers part her core, opening her for me.

My head tosses back, a groan leaving me as I run my hands through my hair, tugging hard when I reach my scalp.

"You want it?" I hear her ask softly.

"I don't think I've ever wanted anything more in my life, sugar," I rasp as I bring my head back up to watch her.

"Go get it," she says.

My eyes widen, my heart thudding in my chest as I move. Leaning forward, I grip her hips, tugging her straight back into my mouth. Her pussy collides with my lips, and like a man starved I lap at her entire seam, using my tongue to part her and reach her clit, sliding in deeper. I move up and down, pressing my tongue into her to move back down and suck at her clit again.

Her moans ring through the room, sending every fucking echo straight back to my cock.

But all I want is her fucking taste. I need her in my blood at this point. I continue to lap and lick at her, sucking all the wetness from her cunt. My hand fists my cock, pumping to relieve the pressure, my eyes rolling at the combination. My pants and groans vibrate into her, causing her to moan and pant more.

"Gunnar...! Gunnar, fuck!" she whimpers as she buries her head back into the armrest. Her hips move and wriggle, but I grip hard on the one hip I have, keeping her in place for me to continue licking her.

God, I fucking love tasting her. I love making her moan like this. Fucking incredible.

I take one last lick before I press up to my knees. Gripping my cock, I slap it against her clit, leaning over her as my grip tightens even more on her hip. I slide it back and forth through her wetness, stopping when I reach her entrance. Slowly, *so* fucking slowly, I press the head into her. A feral groan crawls from my throat as my head tosses back.

I pause when I get the head into her, letting just that small bit of her ease through my blood.

"God fucking damnit, Tiana," I growl.

I resist the urge to shove every bit into her, and by fuck, it is so fucking hard to do that. Her hips swirl against me, wrapping my cock in the most mind-numbing sensation. I let go of the base of my cock to grab her hips with both hands, holding her in place to keep her from pressing more of me into her. Because I know my girl, and she'll rock back if she gets the chance.

My hands tighten on her hips, my nails digging into her flesh, and I take a few deep breaths to steady myself.

I lean over her, one of my hands gliding up her body to wrap around her throat as I press my chest against her back. I make sure to keep my hips pressed back so I don't give her more than she asked for.

"Tell me what you want, sugar," I rasp. Because I'm already this far into the game. I need her words. I need her control now.

"Fuck me," she pants.

"How?" I pant, taking the smallest test stroke into her. If it was up to me, I'm fucking her senseless. But I like this little game. I like being on her leash, and I want her to tug at it, just enough. Make me her fucking animal.

"Deep," she moans out.

I punch forward, shoving all of myself into her, and we moan out in unison as my hand tightens around her throat, my head dropping to rest on her back as she settles around my length. Her pulse thrums against my fingers, and I press just a little more, giving her a small rush as I grind my hips against her ass, feeling all of her before I pull out just enough to punch back in.

"Speak. Please. Tell me what you need. Tell me what I am, please," I pant. It's desperate, damn near a whimper. The pleasure feels like my brain is melting, delirium consuming my skull as I beg her for instruction.

"Such a good fucking boy, aren't you?" she moans.

"Yes... fucking hell, I'm your good boy. I love filling your pussy, baby. I was made to fill it. I'm only here to get you pregnant... fuck," I whimper. And by fuck is it ever. I don't think I've ever been so desperately submissive in my life.

But I love it. I love the way she makes me cower under her, even if I'm on top.

Fuck... I've always loved a woman that can lead.

Her hand comes up around the back of my head, stroking through the end of my flow, pulling me deeper into her shoulder as my arms wrap around her waist. My hips piston quickly, fucking deep into her like a horny bull trying to pump her full of my cum.

"You feel so fucking good, fuck, fuck," she moans out.

"Mine, it's my fucking pussy. I own it. It's only fucking *me* that drips out of it," I growl. My thoughts are gone, merely responding because she's got my brain in her hands right now.

My hand creeps between her legs, rubbing at her clit, while my head buries into her back as I grunt and pant with every thrust. The pleasure snakes around my spine, climbing more and more as my thrusts pick up.

"Fuck, I'm gonna fill this tight cunt. I'm gonna pump you full of me," I whimper. I've never had a woman make me a mess this way, and I feel like I need more of it.

"Come for me. I wanna feel you come, show me how good you are," she moans.

And with those few words, I do. She undoes what little restraint I have left, and I spill into her, groaning as my thrusts slow. Her cunt tightens, her moans filling the living room as she grinds back against me, riding herself through her orgasm. Her pussy locks me in place at the end of my climax, working me in waves and taking it all from me.

"God... fucking... dammit," I grunt as I wait for her to finish. Her hips continue moving, her pussy spasming, and I keep working at her clit.

"More, you have more in you, keep going, wring it out," I grit as her moans continue flowing, the lock she has on me rippling against my length in mind-numbing pleasure.

Soon, her orgasm slows, her twitches fading away as her body slumps under me. Her back expands against me as she gulps breaths. I relax against her back, pressing kisses into her skin. Though they're more for me than her because I'm reeling from the absolute insanity she put me through.

But it was... *incredible* insanity.

"That was mind-blowing," I pant softly. "Where did you learn how to do that?" I ask as I press my hands into the couch. I press up from her body, removing most of my weight from her to lean back. My head falls back as I catch my breath, and I feel myself soften before I look down and pull myself out of her.

"Christ," I groan. Every time I spill out of her, it feels like I'm seeing it for the first time. It gets me every fucking time.

"Research," she says. But her voice is muffled from where she lays her head on the armrest of the couch.

I lay a soft slap on her ass, and she groans back.

"Did you like it?" she murmurs.

"I loved it. We need to do that again sometime," I say as I stuff my dick back in my sweats and lean back on the opposite armrest.

I throw my hands behind my head, leaning back through the satisfaction pumping through my veins.

She slowly gets up, reaching for her undies on the floor before she runs to the bedroom. A few minutes later, she comes back in a new pair, her arms covering her breasts as she scoops up her robe from the floor and shrugs it back on.

I watch every one of her movements. Mostly in shock that my sweet little brat could do something like that to me.

I feel like I wanna kneel at her fucking feet and kiss them. My fucking Queen, if I've ever had one.

I do, technically. But, fuck, I wanna treat her like one.

She ties the tie before she lets out a relieved sigh and crashes into my lap, relaxing against my body. I extend my leg, letting her lay between them and I bring my hands from behind my head to massage at her shoulders. Her head tilts, laying deeper into me, and it gives me a clear path to lick and kiss at it.

"So, what *did* you have in mind for today if that wasn't part of your plan?" I ask.

Her head tilts enough for her to look at me, and she gives me a wide grin.

I can only gulp in response.

CHAPTER TWENTY-NINE
TIANA

"Gunnar, you have three seconds to listen before I kick you out of this damn kitchen," I growl as I turn to him with a bored look.

He's been shadowboxing at my side, jumping from foot to foot as he makes fake punching noises. He doesn't even seem to hear me as I empty the pumpkin puree into the bowl of melted butter, scraping out the can before I toss the can in the trash and set the bowl aside to crack the eggs.

"Sorry, I'm just really hyped from that thing we did earlier," he says as he jumps around me.

It was earlier. Considering we lay on the couch for a long while after we relaxed, before I decided on the actual plan I had for today. At least the day plan.

The night plan I've been thinking about, and some of my nerves run a little higher at the thought, but I push it away to focus on the pumpkin bread.

"I'm never taking the lead again," I groan.

"No! Please, I'll be good, I promise," he says as he wraps his arms around my waist, tucking his head into my shoulder to press small kisses to my neck.

My brow quirks at the same time one edge of my lips does. "You really liked it that much?" I ask with a grin.

"Maybe not the teasing; that sucked. But the rest? Yes," he says with a soft nod against my skin.

I roll my eyes as I crack egg after egg into the melted butter and pumpkin puree mixture.

"Did you start the oven?" I ask as I finish cracking the last egg. Then, I toss the empty shell into the trash.

"Sure did, Big Mama," he says.

"Did you butter the muffin tins?"

"Already done."

I smile with a small scoff as I mix all the wet ingredients together before I pour the dry mix in.

"So, why pumpkin bread?" he asks as he rocks his hips. He brings mine with him, swaying us both from side to side as I mix everything together.

I don't mind making a homemade pumpkin bread recipe. But I like this boxed one; it's one of my favorites, so I usually make this during the fall.

"It's one of the few things I really like to eat. I don't really like pumpkin spice lattes an-"

Gunnar turns me around in his arms, looking down at me in confusion. "Say that again?"

My brow furrows as I look at him. "I don't... really like pumpkin spice... lattes?"

"Right, see, and here I am thinking I misheard you. Now... why don't you like them?" he asks.

My eyes glance away. "I've never really had it, to be fair," I say nervously. "Why? Do you like them?"

"I mean. It's not my preferred drink, but I figured with as much coffee you drink and the urgency of this pumpkin bread you would have loved pumpkin spice coffee," he says with a shrug.

"I had pumpkin bread as a kid and liked it. But it's all different," I respond.

His head tilts, his eyes considering as he smiles and leans in to press a kiss to my forehead. "Gotcha... noted," he says softly before he turns me back around.

I smile at his strange ways before I continue mixing the pumpkin bread batter.

I also don't really enjoy other 'pumpkin-y' things. But this... this is one of my favorite things about fall, aside from the cooling weather and Christmas coming.

Which reminds me...

"What do you want to do for Christmas?" I ask.

"I guess that really depends on what the families are doing," he says as he sways us again.

My mind works, trying to figure out all the things I need to do before Christmas.

"I am actually glad we moved the wedding out," I say softly.

"Yeah? How come?" he asks.

I pull the muffin tin closer, pouring some of the batter into the cups.

"When things aren't so urgent, and I feel like it's something the world can take over for me, there's a lot less strain on myself and my thoughts," I murmur, focusing on the way the batter ripples into each cup as I speak.

"Why does it have to be so urgent?" he asks, pressing small kisses into my neck as he continues to sway our hips.

"It doesn't have to be. That's just the way it feels in my head. All gas, no brakes type of situation where all I can do is focus on what I want," I say with a small sigh.

It irritates me. The way I can't stop a lot of the things that will capture my attention. That's how law school was; that's how I got through it.

I enjoy law and problem-solving. It helps with my day job.

But when the things I get interested in steer me away from my life and the things that need to be done, it's frustrating.

There are times I may want to stop, where there is a small voice in my head that tells me there are other things that need to be done. But I'm not done with the current thought, and I need to finish it before I move on to the next thing.

It's always been a gift and a curse, being able to be so focused on something. But there have been far too many times where it's gotten out of hand, where I needed to be pulled out of it.

And while in the moment, I may not enjoy when Gunnar pulls me out of those intense thinking sessions–because it's hard to shift my focus–I am glad he does.

I'm really not able to do it much myself otherwise.

As I finish scraping the last of the batter out of the bowl, I place it to the side, tapping the trays on the counter as I wait for the oven to beep so we can put them in.

I turn around in his arms, wrapping my arms around his neck and smiling up at him.

"I appreciate all the things you do for me, you know?" I say softly.

He smiles back down at me and leans in to press a kiss to my forehead. "I enjoy doing these things for you," he says.

As always... curiosity courses through me. I feel like I should know. But with the number of times I was thrown away in the past, I wonder what makes him so... fueled to be there for me?

"But why? Why do you enjoy these things? Most people would find it annoying to care for another grown adult," I ask sheepishly.

His head tilts as he brings a hand up to one of my curls. His eyes lock onto it, and I glance from the corner of my eye to see him wrap it around his finger.

"It's part of my job as your partner. Because that's what we are, at the end. Husband, wife, boyfriend, girlfriend. A partner, in life and in love," he says. His hips move again, rocking us as he brings a hand up to pull my head to his chest. I bring my arms down, wrapping them around his back tightly.

I lean into him, hearing the strong beat of his heart as he rests his head on top of mine.

"You made it clear from the beginning who you were. And I have no issues if there are things you need more help with. It's why I'm here. I love to help, and I love to be here for you. If you need help with things that are harder for you in your everyday, I will do them all, every day. At the same time, in the same way, exactly the way you need just so you sleep a little easier at night, sugar," he says softly.

Burning wraps around my eyes as I listen.

How can there be no second thought with all of this? He doesn't question it; he doesn't think it's strange. He embraces it, *me.*

"I've never had someone love me like this before," I murmur.

"I know, baby," he responds softly as he strokes a hand over my hair.

That hurts. Not towards him. But toward myself. Instead of hating love and men, I should have realized sooner that I deserved this love. I know my worth; I know who I am.

I should have known years ago that I was worthy of *this.*

But I'd never cared much for things that didn't concern me. In my eyes, if the men didn't want to be in my life, then *they* weren't worth caring about.

I think I just never considered my worth in it all.

"You've never questioned the way I live. And you've never been... put off by how I am," I murmur.

"Well, you're a human. You have your likes and dislikes, just like anyone else. You deserve to protect those boundaries, and you deserve to have someone that respects them," he says.

I feel my chest squeeze, a soft sigh leaving me.

"But why me?" I ask.

"Well, at first, it was attraction. I thought you were gorgeous. Obviously, I still do. But I wanted to know you. I wanted to know why you were so guarded and held your cards so close. It drew me in, the mystery of it all," he says.

I lose myself in that first day in the locker room, when he couldn't stop staring at me, and a small smile rises on my lips at the memory.

"Talking to you... the challenge of it all, it just made me want to work harder. Now I was chasing this mysterious angel, the one with her walls stacked to the sky, and a fire that warmed the castle hidden behind them. And the harder I chased, the more I knew about you."

My heart beats faster, the way he spins words so perfectly... I bite down on my lip, trying to hold back the tears.

He continues, "This woman who was so... herself. She took care of herself, and she guarded that. Few people guard their space that way. So to the T with your life, not letting anyone tell her otherwise. The way you observed things around you, enjoyed the things you loved, all because you loved them. Not for show or to brag, but because you just love those things. Too many people nowadays try to fit in, to go with the crowd. You're just you... every single day of your life."

Tears have slid down his skin as they stream down my face, and my eyes lock onto where they move over his muscles. My teeth have tightened to near pain against my lip as I try with all my might not to sniffle.

His swaying has been calming, even if my insides are on fire as I see myself through his eyes.

"I love you so much, Tiana," he says softly.

I pull away, smiling up at him, even with the tears in my eyes.

His brow furrows, a small twitch, as his head tilts.

He brings his hand from around my head to wipe away some tears from my cheeks.

"I never knew what love could feel like before I met you," I admit, my hands gripping his hips tight as I look up at him.

I feel like I've never had the chance to really tell him how I feel. I should have much, much sooner. But it's hard for me to verbalize these feelings, these thoughts. They're already a storm to work through, no matter how happy they make me.

But I want to try, because he deserves to know how much I love him back.

"I thought... relationships were useless... I didn't know what a man was supposed to do for his woman. And... I think that's why I fell. You never made me question what was supposed to happen. You just made it happen," I say softly.

His eyes search mine as I speak, but I glance away, my hands coming up to my chest as I pick at my cuticles nervously.

I take a deep breath, willing myself to continue.

"Every day, you made easier. And I was so confused, I'd never had a man... do anything like this. I didn't know what to think of it. But every day you proved I was more than a conquest. You wanted me in ways I couldn't understand, and slowly you showed me how to understand those things." My voice catches in my throat, the tears running more as my voice cracks.

"A man who..." I pause, taking a deep breath. "Who cared so much about the people in his life. Preserved their influence, always kept a smile on his face, even through the dark times.

Who worked so fucking hard every single day of his life and made none of it look hard. Strong, willing," I say. My eyes come up to meet his, and they shine with love as they connect with mine. They're considering and intent as he listens.

"I didn't think I would ever be loved the way you love me, Gunnar. I never thought I would find pieces of myself that were missing because of you. I never knew a man could be so selfless, so thoughtful, so kind. Funny, if not irritating at times," I say the last bit with a small broken chuckle as I sniffle. "I never thought I'd ever feel this way about another human... but it's one of the greatest things I've been able to experience."

His hazel eyes sparkle, a tune of pride singing in the glimmer. And I smile in return. He wraps a hand around my head, bringing it to his lips to press a kiss to my forehead. He lingers there, pressing more little pecks against it as he rocks us.

"Good girl, sugar. That's a good girl," he whispers softly. "I'm so proud of you."

Out of context... I imagine that's strange for anyone to hear.

But because he knows me so well... understands me even more, and the whole point of my tears... the reason I can't believe I've fallen in love... because he knows how hard this is for me, verbalizing these feelings properly, I smile at him, taking his words to heart.

"I love you, Gunnar Hayze," I murmur softly.

"I love you most, Tiana Dawn."

The pumpkin bread came out exquisitely. We waited for them to cool and then covered the ones we wanted to eat with icing. Of course, Gunnar had to make a joke about it. But it was fun, and so far it's been the perfect Halloween for me.

We sat down in the living room with our pumpkin bread muffins and watched some of my favorite fall movies. Coraline and A Nightmare Before Christmas, before too long I wanted to go rest in the bedroom with Gunnar.

Sure, watching a movie is sharing space, but there is something about sitting in the dark, pressed against him, listening to him breathe.

It's been amazing. A day where nobody needed us, where no one dragged me from my cave to do this thing or the next. And not once did he complain. He was excited to lie in bed with me, to rest in the calm, dark room until we eventually fell asleep.

And now, here I lay against him, my eyes blinking open, locking onto the bedroom window, seeing where the sun is in the sky to note how low it is, what time of day it might be.

It's pitch black, which means I have one last thing on the plan. A calmed breath passes through me, and I snuggle into Gunnar's arm, where he's tightened it around me. His head leans over, pressing a kiss to my forehead as he holds me.

It seems he has woken up as well, and as I loop my leg over his body, I nip happily at my lip. His cock is hard under his boxers, standing at attention for me, and I pretend as if I don't notice as I snuggle into him.

I press soft kisses into the side of his chest, my fingers tracing the outline of his deer antlers on his chest. All the while, the hand around me rubs soft circles in my back as he lays there with his eyes closed.

"How do you stay so... calm when your dick is that hard?" I ask quietly.

"Very... very... very... carefully," he says with a grin. "And I've had a dick my whole life, so I'm also just used to it," he adds.

I find that asking questions sometimes helps the nerves of me starting things like this. So I keep going, even if they seem nonsensical.

"Do you still masturbate?" I ask.

"I really don't need to. You satisfy any craving I have," he says with a shrug.

My cheeks heat at that.

"How often did you before you met me?"

"I'm a pretty horny guy. So... it was pretty often. When you're playing an adrenaline-inducing game every day, where you're constantly competing, your testosterone gets pretty high," he responds.

Interesting.

"You know. I know it's Halloween, and I said I didn't want to dress up, but there was one more thing I wanted to do," I say softly.

I look up to see one of his eyes peek open to look down at me. "Oh?" he asks with low excitement.

I nod. "Stay here. I'll be right back," I say.

I take one last kiss of his chest before I stand, sauntering off to my closet and closing the door behind me.

CHAPTER THIRTY

TIANA

I take a deep breath, hoping with everything in me this looks good for him. I quickly showered, cleaning off the day before I squeezed myself into this black... lingerie thing.

I ordered it for his cat woman idea. I just wanted to appeal to one of his ideas.

Long fishnet stockings cover my feet, with a lace band encircling my thighs. Attached to the lace band are little clips that lead up to the black lace garter belt that cinches in around my waist. With it, I paired a lace thong. With a slit in the middle so he doesn't have to remove them, considering how much he loves when I wear them. The bra I wear is perfectly see-through and matches the rest of the ensemble.

I tug on a pair of heels I bought specifically for this. Tall, black, damn near stripper heels. And since I teased him earlier, I was going to leave myself to his mercy.

There are so many changes going on. The idea of the wedding changing, my focus shifting from that to preparing for a baby.

The world feels heavier... even if I'm able to push it away sometimes, it creeps in. It weighs on my shoulders and it makes me think of the future. And sometimes I need so badly for him to take that weight from me. I want him to make me beg. Fuck me the way he did after he asked me to marry him.

Being able to control him earlier was fun, but something about the way he leaves me at the mercy of him... makes everything right.

A tall mirror sits against the wall in my closet, and I roam my gaze over myself again. I take in the way the lace looks wrapped around my body. I fluff my hair just a tad more before I take a deep breath and open the closet door. Gunnar lies on the bed, his arms behind his head as he opens his eyes to look at me.

I nip at my lip, lingering with the light of the closet at my back before I call into the room, "Alexa, dim the lights."

There's a beep noise in response before the lamps in my room illuminate, covering the room in a blood red hue.

Gunnar pushes himself up against the bed, his eyes wide and his lips parted as he takes me in. I glance down to his groin, where his dick is so hard it can't even be considered a bulge. He's pitched an entire tent.

"Christ," I hear him murmur as his eyes roam over me.

I flick the light switch off for the closet, taking slow, precise steps toward him in my heels. He pushes to the edge of the bed, placing his feet on the floor as I approach.

His eyes twinkle, looking over me like I'm some sort of goddess. They roam up and down my body in awe as he grips my hips.

Opening his knees for me, I stand in the middle of them, propping the toe of my platform against the floor as I place my arms around his neck.

"Sugar," he says as his eyes linger in a few places. My pussy, my tits. My face.

I nip my lip, curling some of his hair around my finger.

"I need you..." I whisper as I lean in to kiss his lips.

"I'll give it. Whatever you need," he murmurs into our kiss, almost desperately.

"Take the world away from me," I whisper.

His hands tighten on my hips, gripping into the bones before he stands and spins, throwing me onto the bed. My heels clack against one another as I land on the bed, my head coming to rest on the pillows. He pulls his sweatpants off, fisting his cock and stroking himself as he looks over me laid out on the bed.

He releases his cock, and I watch as he crawls to me on the bed. Soon, he's above me, his hand pressing into my lower stomach before it slides up the middle of my body, through the valley of my tits to tighten around my neck. His chain swings, the pendant hitting my chin as he hovers over me. With one hand pinned into the mattress, he looks at my face, over my body before it comes back to my eyes.

"Do you have any idea what you do to me, Tiana?" he rasps. It's as if he controls himself in this moment, as if the instance from earlier skewed the idea of who controls the dynamic right now.

"I have an inkling," I choke against the tightness at my throat. My eyes flick to his cock. So fucking hard, it twitches, moving slowly against the twitch since I know it's heavy.

"What do you need? Tell me," he growls.

"Fuck me like a whore," I beg.

His brow arches, a wicked grin rising across his lips. "You know I respect you, right?"

I nod, though feebly. "I want to let everything go right now. I need that," I say.

The way his body presses and hovers above mine, the way he hasn't touched me too much in this outfit. My temperature rises, the tension rising in me the longer he waits.

He leans down, his grip shifting on my throat to grip my chin, tilting my head to the side as he drags his tongue along my neck. "My perfect little cumslut... coming out to play. I haven't seen her in a while," he says, low and teasing.

His other hand slides down my body, pressing into my pulsing core, slick with my anticipation. His head rises to look down at where he discovers an opening in the panties.

"Filthy thing, you are. You know how much I love seeing this cunt in panties... what a good girl," he says as he leans down again, nipping at my collarbone as his fingers slide through my core. He just barely grazes my clit, my hips grinding the smallest bit to urge him closer.

"Always so needy, aren't we? Can't wait for my cock... tk, tk, tk," he says with a click of his tongue. "My desperate girl... she wants to be stretched and filled, doesn't she?"

"Fuck... yes... so bad, please," I whimper.

I groan in frustration, my head tossing back as he lazily slides his fingers against my clit. The pressure just enough to turn me on, get me going but not enough to sink into.

"Please..." I whimper.

"Shhh, I'm taking my time. Call it... repayment," he says with a wicked grin. He swirls the lightest touch into my clit, making me writhe in frustration.

"Gunnar," I groan.

"You made me come so hard I felt like my slate was wiped clean. I have more than enough stamina to tease you... make you a whimpering, begging mess who damn near cries to have my cock in her... and that's what *I* want. I want you to fucking *beg* for it, Tiana," he says.

He moves his fingers down, slipping into me, three at once.

I groan at the pressure, at the light press of his thumb against my clit with it. He doesn't have the smallest fingers, but they come in handy.

His mouth moves down, encompassing my nipple through the light material of the bra. My moans turn to pants, my breaths coming quick as the tension keeps rising. His fingers move in and out, torturously slow, and I want more, I *need* more. I need *him*.

"Gunnar... fuck, please, harder," I pant into the air.

His upper half rises, looking down into my eyes as his fingers keep their pace on my core.

Soon, his chin dips, his tongue flicking out to grab his chain and loop it around his tongue. He wraps his hand around his cock, stroking it with a hearty groan before he pulls his other hand from my center, rubbing my slick over him, both hands coming to stroke himself one over the other as he looks down at me. He moves to the side of me, his cock mere inches from my face.

He grips my head, pressing his hips forward. He moves his hand to the back of my head, grabbing a handful of my hair at the nape and tilting my head back as he leans down.

"You want this cock?" he asks with a soft pant and a feral grin.

I nod desperately, my eyes begging as I look up at him. "Please," I whimper.

"Open," he says.

My jaw drops open, my tongue falling out and my eyes trained on his face as he grips his cock at the base, slapping my tongue with it.

"My perfect slut. You're always so pretty when you beg for it," he says as he presses the head into my lips at the same time he moves my head forward.

I let him fill my mouth, my tongue resting over my bottom

teeth as he presses further and further into my throat. His teeth tighten on his chain, a groan leaving him as he tosses his head back.

I watch the way his muscles tighten at his stomach, his chest. They bulge at his biceps and forearms as he tightens his grip at the back of my head.

He moves his hips, in and out of my mouth, forcing a bit more of himself into my throat with every press in.

"Thatta girl. Swallowing my cock like the filthy thing you are," he grits through his chain.

He presses further, his cock expanding my throat as I take as much of him as I can.

His grip shifts, letting go of my hair to come and squeeze my throat.

"I can feel my fucking cock right here... when I squeeze," he groans, tightening his grip on my throat, and his head tosses back, his hips bucking the barest amount. "I can feel myself," he pants as his head comes back down to look at me.

Tears drip from the corners of my eyes, drool leaking from the corner of my lips before he pulls his cock out. He pants as his hold on my throat loosens.

His tongue slides across his lower lip as he grabs the heel of my platform, moving my leg up so he can get under and back in between my legs. I press the leg down, letting my knees open wide. The platform on my heels pins into the bed on either side of his knees, and he lingers there, looking over my body as his hand pumps over his cock that's slippery with my saliva.

"God help me, you're such a fucking vision," he pants softly. He runs his cock through my center, pressing into my clit and toying with it, making my legs quiver before he presses the head into me. Even just the head of him is such a welcome stretch. I never knew how good thick cock could be until I met this man.

He releases his cock to reach back, gripping my ankles and bringing them onto his shoulders. His hands roam down my legs, down the stockings, his fingertips gripping into them as they move.

With his cock at my entrance, he takes the shallowest strokes, teasing me. I know how it feels to have all of him. And I want that more than anything right now. I want to feel him everywhere, all at once *right now.*

He leans down, taking my legs with him and pressing them so far back that my knees are by my ears.

He takes shallow presses, his lips meeting mine as he slowly works in further and further.

I whimper and moan against his lips, with my feet locking behind his head, causing my heels to clack against one another.

"My good fucking girl. You bend so well to take my cock. You know how deep I can go like this?" he growls as he looks down between us. Slowly, he moves deeper with each long stroke.

He groans, his head dropping entirely as he soaks me in.

"You feel so good, Gunnar... more, please... please, please, please," I pant desperately.

His head rises, a grin forming on his lips between his heavy breathing. "You know what this call this position, right?" he murmurs as he leans in to kiss me.

I shake my head, unable to answer from the way he fills me on every downward stroke.

"They call it the mating press... because that's exactly what I intend to do to you," he says with a growl.

My eyes roll, my hips writhing against his, accepting every bit of him.

"This womb was fucking made for *me.* Fucking made to carry every bit of me. Grow *my* fucking kids, carry *my* fucking babies," he pants as his thrusts speed up, his depth insane with the way he's folded me in half.

My moans grow louder, my back bowing, taking every inch he throws into me over and over, again and again.

His head turns, laying kisses on the inside of my calves, nipping against the fabric there.

Every thrust he takes is deep, mind-blowing, throwing me deep into the realms of pleasure. I lose track of where I am, my eyes rolling, my breaths heaving in and out of me as my heart pounds in my chest.

"F-f-f-," I try to say. But I don't think he's ever been this deep before... which is saying a lot.

"Awww, what's the matter, sugar? Cat got your tongue?" he whispers with a tilt of his head and a teasing grin as he keeps pace. "Too good to speak?" he tsks. "That's too bad... I'd love to hear you tell me how fucking deep I am right now," he pants as he presses his lips to mine.

His hips rock in and out of me, my back bowing, trying to make sense of the feeling. I've never been fucking bent in half like this and there's a level of dominance here I am happy to be at the submissive end of.

He grips tight on my chin, bringing my head back to face his.

"Eyes on me, sugar. Open, where's that mind gone?" he asks.

My eyes flutter open, locking with his gaze in a hazel sea of desire.

"There's my girl. Not a thought behind those pretty eyes," he says as he nips at my lip, tugging at it.

"Gunnar... F-fuck," I whimper desperately through the pleasure.

"What is it, sugar? Use your words," he whispers against my lips.

"You're so... fuck..." I groan, my eyes rolling, my body writhing under his.

"Words, baby. I'm right here, focus," he says softly. His hand loosens on my chin, coming to cup my cheek. He leans back enough to get my feet from around his neck, moving my legs to rest on his hips.

"S-so... deep... s-so fucking good," I murmur in response. My pleasure climbs with the change in position, his pubic bone pressing into my clit and making me climb higher and higher. My breaths lighten, the orgasm creeping into my grasp.

He leans in, wrapping his arms around my head as he buries himself into me.

"That's a good girl. You're gonna come for me, aren't you? I can feel it, give it to me," he whispers against my lips, his thrusts rhythmic, smooth. In and out and in and out over and over pushing me to that summit more and more... until I break.

It hits me from the side, a scream wrenching from my throat as my back bows, pressing my body tight against where he holds himself against me. His hips move faster, riding me through my orgasm.

"There she is. Give it all to me." I hear his voice over the waves of pleasure crashing over me. My pussy tightening and moving in waves all along his length. He moves in and out until I clamp down, locking him in, and he presses as far in as he can. I groan and writhe, feeling him spill into me.

He fills me with everything, a groan bringing me further through my orgasm as my hips grind and move under him.

"That's... it... sugar... fuck," he grits as I lock him in. His head drops, his groans deep and guttural as he waits for me to finish.

Slowly, I come down. My chest heaves, and he rests his whole body on mine as his hips hold his cock inside of me.

I throw my arms around his shoulders, holding him to me as I let the weight of his body settle on me. The pressure of it is exquisite, and I let a soft chuckle go as I run my hands through his hair. It's warm and damp from his efforts, and I press small kisses onto his forehead. I run my nails up and down his back slowly, enjoying the way his skin feels stuck to mine.

My body slowly relaxes, and I feel Gunnar nuzzle deeper against my tits as he rests there.

I move my head to the side, looking at his face.

He's... absolutely passed out.

His lips are just barely parted, and he breathes steadily.

I roll my eyes with a quiet chuckle as I lay there under him, enjoying the press of his damp skin, the weight of his body and the way it feels to hold this massive man.

Even though I barely did anything, I still put his ass to sleep.

And I realize this is one of the best Halloweens I've ever had.

CHAPTER THIRTY-ONE
GUNNAR

The morning is clear... bright. Exactly how I need it to be.

Over the past week, Tiana has dropped any ideas of the wedding for now. Honestly, from the drop of focus, she's been sleeping so much more, and it appears like she is able to focus more on work and eat better.

I've been thinking a lot about what Mrs. Tamisha had said to me that day we made the contracts.

There was a reason she said those things. And while I have always tried to be cognizant of Tiana and her needs. There is more to her that I need to learn. I feel as if there are more of her intricacies I still have yet to see.

But that's okay. It's all I have ever wanted to do for her.

I enjoy watching her; I like to catalogue the things she does in my head. Her reactions, the way she may take certain things, or the way she just lives.

What originally started as wanting to get to know this gorgeous woman became so much more.

It became giving her the love and care she so desperately

deserved. While I have always been that way, there is more mindfulness that comes with the way she lives, knowing she may be a little different.

I want to be a part of her care that picks up on things about her that others didn't. I want to find all the pieces of herself she lost, and bring them back to her to work through.

I just want to be that strength her mom wanted her to have.

I have to be that for her, because no one else ever was in the past.

Even now, I watch as she presses the helmet on her head for our ATV ride out to the lake, and a smile pulls at my cheeks. She's in her head, in her thoughts, and I can see the way they run. I have no idea what that little mind of hers is working over now. But she's always thinking. I don't think there is a time when her mind isn't running.

It's either taking in the world around her, the people in her vicinity, work. It doesn't matter. I can't ever stop that. That's one thing I've learned. She just will always have a mind that moves that way. All I can do is make sure it doesn't hurt her.

As long as they aren't harming her, it'll be okay.

Banks and Charlotte are grooming Chauncey today, since obviously we've come back out here for a weekend at the ranch house.

While Tiana is merely thinking it's to get away, I have other plans in mind. But I wanted to do it without Banks and Charlotte.

Everything is in place, so I told her I wanted to take her for a ride. She agreed, and now we're suiting up.

I've already pulled on my helmet and hopped onto the ATV.

Tiana climbs on behind me, holding tight around my waist, and we wave to Charlotte and Banks before I take off.

Once again, my heart rate climbs. I honestly don't know what she'll think about buying land for us. Sure, I knew she would say yes to asking her to marry me. It was still nerve-wracking.

I know she likes this bit of land, and I know she loves it out here. But Tiana is a woman who takes charge.

So, the entire way out to the ridge, I feel my body tighten. My nerves climb, and I feel my breaths coming in and out of me quicker.

I move through some of the more tamped-down areas of land, making my way out to the lake.

It's about a mile and a half away from the ranch house. I think more than enough ways away for it to still be our space, but be close enough to Charlotte.

Especially when we have a baby, I know she'll love to have Charlotte nearby.

Eventually, we reach the ridge that overlooks the lake, and I cut the engine of the ATV off. Tucker stayed back at the ranch house because he would much rather be with Waffle.

I take a deep breath, removing my helmet as Tiana jumps off the ATV. She removes her helmet, waving out her hair.

She has taken to straightening it when we come out here because she knows she'll usually have to wear a helmet, and she says it's more of a nuisance when she has to cram her hair into it.

I watch her for a moment as a warm smile pulls across her lips. A smile that looks like longing as she gazes over the land. The small pond sparkles with the rays of the sun as a soft breeze runs over it, rippling the surface.

I take a few more seconds, steeling myself, and stand to climb off the ATV. With slow, calculated movements, I place the helmet on the seat of the ATV beside hers.

I come to stand next to her, wrapping an arm around her shoulder.

She leans into me, her arms wrapping around my middle as she continues to look over the land.

"Sugar…" I breathe, and she looks up at me with a small tilt of her head. "You really like it out here, don't you?" I ask.

She nods. "It's gorgeous. I wish we could come out to this lake at night, though. I would love to hear the sounds of the little creatures in the forest while we look out at the stars," she says as she gazes back over it.

I take another deep breath, and I reach into my back pocket.

I look at the folded contract for a moment before I hand it out to her.

Tiana looks down at the folded paper in my hand, leaning away and looking up at me with a furrow of her brow.

"What is this?" she asks as she hesitantly takes it.

"Open it," I whisper as it slips from my fingers.

Her brow arches, and she takes a small step back to face me. I tuck my hands into my pockets as I turn to her. She unfolds it slowly, and I watch as her eyes scan over the page, her lips parting. Soon, her brow tenses as her eyes move faster across the page.

"What… what is this?" she asks again as she looks out at the land before she looks up at me.

"It's ours," I say with a smile.

"What is ours? What are you saying?" she asks again. Quieter, as if she's slowly putting the pieces together.

"This land. I bought fifteen acres of this land for us," I tell her.

Her jaw drops, with her eyes moving back down to the paper before she looks back to the land, then back at the paper, then finally up at me. Her gaze turns watery, tears pooling in her eyes as she looks at me.

"You... you bought...? This? The lake? This part?" she asks.

I nod. "The lake and the fifteen acres surrounding it."

"Why... why would you do that?" she murmurs softly.

Her lip quivers until she brings it between her teeth, and she pulls the paper to her chest, holding it above her heart.

"I want us to build our house here. I talked to Banks about it. We got the contract squared away, and we have some people in place to get the trees out and the foundation put in. That is, once you figure out where you want to put the house," I say softly.

"A house? We're building a house here?" she whispers.

I nod again. "If you would like to," I tell her.

I step up to her, wrapping a hand around her cheek.

Her eyes are locked on me, in disbelief, in shock. But there is a small glimmer of excitement in them as she looks at me.

"What do you think, sugar? Do you like it?" I ask.

Her eyes move back over the land before they come back to me, smiling as a small tear escapes her eyes.

And then she fucking *runs*.

Straight off the ridge, across the field, and into the forest.

"Fuck."

WHAT'S NEXT FOR AURORA?
UPCOMING PROJECTS

December 2025: ***Merry Checkmas;*** *a Christmas-inspired continuation of Gunnar and Tiana's story*

Late January/Early February 2026: ***Checked and With Child;*** *fourth installment of Gunnar and Tiana's story where we go through their pregnancy together*

Spring 2026: **AGOLAB 2:** *the second installment in "A Gown of Leather and Bone" dark romantic fantasy series*

Late Fall 2026: **Sweet Dreams-Book One in the Twilight Lexicon Series;** *a separate fantasy series adjacent to the series, "A Gown of Leather and Bone"*

ACKNOWLEDGEMENTS

Woooooow hey guys check that shit out!

You made it to the end of the book! Helllll yeah! I'm so proud of you!

Check or Treat honestly was not a thought when I started writing Checked and Balanced last December.

To be honest, I was going to do interconnected stand-alones, but my mind kept getting fudged up with the idea of everything.

I'm not entirely sure when I decided this series was just going to focus on Tiana and Gunnar. There were times before I started working on it again where I really just wanted to keep following them.

How these seasonal sequels came about?? I'm honestly not entirely sure.

But here we are!

Happy Halloween if you're finishing this on Halloween, or Happy Fall if you're starting this in the fall.

First of all, I gotta thank the readers. I can never be anything without you guys. Every post, page read, word of mouth thing you all do for me, it's the only way I'm able to keep writing and bringing you guys stories.

I also thank you so much for falling in love with this couple. They both are parts of me. Gunnar and Tiana are both just pieces of me. And I'm so thankful to create a couple, and a world that you can relate to, and find solace in.

These two mean so much to me, and I feel like with more and more of their story I will slowly heal parts of myself with the what could have beens.

Secondly, I have to thank Ana. Not only did she make graphics for me for Checked and Balanced, she's just an amazing friend. She's always there when I need her, and she's always making sure I'm okay. Funny enough, she actually referenced my first book in her first book, and I thought it was the sweetest thing ever! So go check out some of her books! She writes small-town, cowboy romance, and she's a horny degen just like me! ***Author A.M. Fernandez***

Third, AAron. I always gotta thank AAron, because she does soooo much damn reading for me. She knows me; she knows how I write; she knows how I work, and she is always there for me whenever I need her. She will scream about my books from the fucking rooftops every single time, and this is actually her third book of mine she's been mentioned in! She took a chance on me when I was just a literal nobody indie author, and she's been with me ever since. I owe her a great deal of love and thanks for all she does!

Fourth, Amanda! She is also another indie author that I am so thankful for! She makes some of the coolest ARC boxes I've ever seen! She goes all out everytime. She made waxmelts for her ARC boxes and they smell so fucking good! I was stressing out the day before release of Checked and Balanced because I really needed to make graphics, but I didn't want to. Mind you, I hadn't even said anything to her, she just popped up in my DMs with some graphics made for me. And I can not tell you how much weight was lifted off of my fucking shoulders. She gave me a chance to fucking breathe where I felt like I was suffocating. I am so so so so so thankful for her friendship and for her as a person because she is also just so incredibly sweet. She writes billionaire mafia romance, so go check her out as well! ***Author Amanda Zuelo!***

Fifth, I wanna thank Beth at Wings and Words for helping me out with ARCs! The international readers I have met because of her have been so invaluable, and she has also created such a kind and interactive community of readers that I can rely on! I love popping in on her lives and listening to her voice because she has such a sweet British accent and I just love hearing her talk and interacting with readers when I get the chance to! Thank you so so much Beth! You are an absolute gem!

Sixth, to Olivia! She was the first person to make character art for Tiana and Gunnar simply because she loved them. Her kindness is everything and more to me and I enjoy her energy, her character. She reached out and offered to do a collab and I am so thankful I did because I not only gained an artist, I gained a wonderful friend that brings so much light and energy into my life. To this day, I still have not found a better version of Gunnar, and I always struggle finding good representations of my MMCs. She also helped me with the halloween costume for Tiana because I had an idea written, but I had no idea how to make it work. When she was doing the drawings for them, she had made this dress, which was so much better and aesthetically pleasing than the idea I had. But she captured our crazy goon, PERFECTLY! I am so excited for our partnership and so thankful for our friendship!

Seventh, to Jasmine! So, if you guys don't know Jasmine, she is such a sweet little soul. And she has a little corgi, who I am absolutely in love with, named Waffle. (See where I'm going with this?) Well!!! Jasmine loved Tucker, and while real-life Waffle is a boy, I wanted to give Tucker a girlfriend. And thus, girl Waffle was born. There are some people in my books, or entities that are inspired by real booktok people I have met.

And I am so thankful she let me use Waffle for this book. She is so funny to talk to as well. She also happens to be one of the first people to finish my ARCs whenever they come out, and I love her for that. She's quick on the draw and has such amazing lore! EVERYONE SAY THANK YOU JASMINE FOR GIVING US FEMALE WAFFLE!

You guys are the absolute best, and I'm so so thankful for all of you here. Thank you for enjoying Gunnar and Tiana. Thank you for being here for me, and thank you for making all of my dreams come true.

I hope to see you guys in the next book, and I can't wait.

Your Four Favorite Raccoons in a Trench Coat,
Aurora Steinhart

ABOUT THE AUTHOR

While Aurora is merely an alias, the face behind the name has enjoyed writing and reading for as long as she can remember.

An army wife and a lifelong Alaskan, she has spent her life baking, cooking, and reading. Her lifelong passions.

Being an army wife means keeping busy with hobbies, which has resulted in a menagerie of different pastimes.

She has tried her hand at drawing, makeup, reading, weightlifting, CrossFit, cross-stitch, diamond art, video games, content creation (TikTok, YouTube, Twitch), and now being an author. Her motivation changing day by day as she gets struck by whatever idea sucked her in.

When she's not writing, she's spending time with her husband, 2 kids, 3 cats, and 2 dogs.

instagram.com/author.aurorasteinhart

threads.com/@author.aurorasteinhart

tiktok.com/@author_aurora_steinhart